LILITU

BOOK II: BLOODY CALEB

JONATHAN FORTIN

Crystal Lake Publishing
Where Stories Come Alive!

www.crystallakepub.com

WELCOME
TO ANOTHER

CRYSTAL LAKE PUBLISHING
CREATION

Join today at www.crystallakepub.com & www.patreon.com/CLP

A NOTE ON READING ORDER

*L*ILITU: *BLOODY CALEB* CAN be read before any other *Lilitu* book. While it is technically the second volume in the series, it is set before the events of the first volume, *Lilitu: The Memoirs of Succubus*. *Memoirs* and *Caleb* both tell their own complete stories, and neither book spoils the events of the other. The same is true for *Saintkiller: A Lilitu Novella*. As a result, readers can start with whichever story interests them more.

It is recommended that readers complete *Memoirs*, *Bloody Caleb* and *Saintkiller* before moving on to the third proper volume in the series, wherein characters from all prior *Lilitu* stories converge.

CONTENT WARNING

*L*ILITU IS A DARK series intended only for adults. It contains explicit violent and sexual content, sexual violence (including implied sexual assault), profanity, depictions of suicide or other forms of self-harm, and characters with misogynistic or otherwise problematic views that in no way reflect the opinions of the author or publisher. Reader discretion is advised.

For readers concerned about certain triggers in particular, a detailed list of content warnings is available on my website: www.jonathanfortin.com.

PART I

WRITTEN ON THE FLOOR

Chapter One

The Immortalist Club

Wꜰhen my old friend Remy told me he'd joined a cult, I had two questions: whether he was safe, and whether there were orgies. When Remy answered "yes" to both, I asked how I could join.

The two of us were sitting in a dingy Whitechapel pub, the kind you didn't want to leave too late unless you fancied getting murdered. Remy looked completely out of place with his sleek golden curls and clean, doughy cheeks, like an overgrown cherub trying to commingle with rats. Still, he had an air of confidence about him, like he was convinced he was already immortal, even though that honor was supposedly reserved for members at a much higher level than he. His soft features scrunched up tight, like he was assessing whether I was adequate for a club of this nature. "It's not that you can't," he said finally. "I'm just not sure you'd like it."

"Why not?" I asked, forcing myself to sit up straight. I wasn't a gentleman like Remy, but I liked to pretend I was sometimes. Occasionally, I could even be convincing. Right then, though, I was fresh off the hour of fiddling I'd done for the pennies and free drinks, and was so drenched with sweat that my hair stuck to my head. I probably stank like the devil.

Remy Halligan—Remigius to his parents, Rem to his old boys, and Remy to everyone close enough to know his discomfort with both appellations—kept his smile broad. But there was a cool, curious distance in his eyes as he assessed my responses. "They're very...reverent. Even sex is sacred to them. It's ritualistic. More of a way to see God than to experience pleasure. Caleb, you are many things, but reverent is not one of them."

I scowled. "I can be reverent sometimes." He was entirely correct, of course. "Anyway, you haven't seen me in years. Maybe I've gotten better at faking it."

Remy's eyes held a queer, powerful light—some baffling mixture of hope, pride and power. "It's a good way to meet people," he admitted. "There are a lot of very wealthy men in the Immortalist Club. Come to think of it, they're having a little soiree tomorrow night. If you really wanted to give it a stab, maybe you could come play your violin a little. Hell, if someone there likes it enough, you might even find a patron willing to fund your efforts."

Hope blossomed in my chest like a corpse flower: beautiful, fetid, and fleeting. I'd always felt that I was put on this Earth to fill it with the most beautiful music imaginable, and every moment I spent cleaning shoes or brushing leaves off the street was a moment wasted. Even then, with my hands still sore from the hours of fiddling, I'd have played till dawn for a patron.

This was October 1862 if I remember correctly, ten years since the fire that had claimed my father and the violin shop in which we'd lived. Ten years since I'd last seen Remy, too.

Since then, London had chewed me up and spit me out, but somehow my cheery-faced old friend hadn't changed one bit. I felt, not for the first time, a pang of envy for how easy the rich must have had it, and it was hard not to hate him just a little bit. Still, all those old memories came flooding back: sitting on the roof together, legs dangling while we miffed about our lives; the time we'd stolen a bottle of fancy booze from my father's bedside table; and of course, his absolutely *awful* violin playing. Remy hadn't really begged his father to keep bringing him to my shop because he thought he could be a musician, had he?

We left the pub in a jolly mood. At the time, I didn't question why my old friend, a proper gentleman, had been lurking in such a miserable corner of Whitechapel. I simply assumed he'd been in the area, needed a drink, and saw me playing. It was good to reunite with him after so many years. Indeed, less than an hour after our rendezvous, it felt like we'd never lost touch at all. We walked together through the foggy London night, the gas lamps steadily going out, distant hooves echoing through the air.

"I looked for you, you know," he said. "When I found out. Even left you a message at a few local pubs. Why did you never call on me?"

I looked away, the smile on my lips flickering like the gas lamps. How could I possibly explain? Remy would never have understood what had been going through my mind: the terror, the confusion, the absolute certainty that I was alone. The events surrounding the fire had transported me into a wretched new world in which Remy did not belong. My old friend lacked the spine for it. Even now, his face was clean and bright beside my grime, eyes swimming with the innocence of a privileged child.

"My father might have been willing to provide for you," he went on. "Back when you were twelve, I mean. Just enough to get you back on your feet. He greatly admired your father's work."

"Well, he never greatly admired me," I said stiffly. "Our connection was the shop, Remy. That was the only reason your father tolerated you and I cutting about."

Remy let out that familiar sigh. "I suppose you're right. But one day, that money will be mine and I'll be able to spend it how I please. Hell, maybe I could be your patron once dear old dad kicks the bucket." He stopped. My face must have betrayed the implosion in my chest, for he hastily added, "Sorry, I know it's a dreadful thing to joke about. I was just worried. How have you even been getting by?"

Sober, I might have danced around it, but intoxicated as I was, it all came tumbling out. "However I can. Music, street sweeping, staying at the coffin houses."

"The shelters?" Remy gaped at me, appalled. "This is no way to live, my friend, no way at all. You must come with me to the club. In fact, I insist on it."

A sour pit filled my stomach. The idea of accepting my old friend's hospitality seemed embarrassing, even though I needed it. I wondered if Remy imagined me like the very worst street buskers: the out-of-tune choirs, the children slamming pot lids without rhythm, the Whitechapel vagrant with a cheap clarinet blaring like Bedlam while his monkey demanded coin. This late at night, there were no such crowds, and our only company in these streets were fallen bodies that might have been drunks and might have been corpses. I was too far gone to tell the difference.

I realized, rather abruptly, that the darkness seemed to have swallowed us. It was as though we had walked into a tunnel, yet I could not recall ever entering its mouth. The fog was black, and the hairs on the back of my neck stood up from primal worry, but Remy strolled on, shoulders back, posture straight, and if I didn't want to be left in the darkness, I had to follow. I had to hope that wherever he led me, it would offer light.

"They really promise immortality?" I asked, tension rising in my throat. Ten years ago, I would have laughed, but that had been a different world.

"They don't promise anything to anyone," said Remy. "Not everyone reaches that level. Indeed, I haven't reached it myself. But a select few are chosen for that, yes."

"What makes you so sure?"

He tilted his head, the wraith of a smile on his lips. "What if I told you there's proof? That I've witnessed things that last year I'd have never believed?"

Memories tickled the back of my mind: the orange glow of candles reflected on shiny leathery membrane; my nose itching with tainted perfume; the delicious promise of that which should not be. I shook my head, reminding myself that I had imagined it all.

"And where does this immortality come from?" I asked. I wanted him to give me a straight answer, something easy to doubt. Something that would help me push the memories back down. Snake oil, perhaps, or a book that convinced the vulnerable.

Remy huffed, his breath clouding before him in the cool night air like a tiny ghost. "In all honesty, I don't know. Technically, I'm not even supposed to tell you about the immortality thing. Or the orgies, for that matter. Suffice to say, I've had an awakening, and I'd like you to have that awakening, too."

I could have sworn that something was lurking in the darkness, waiting for me to lag behind. And even as we emerged from that black fog into the gaslit road of Horseferry Shelter, even as we said our goodbyes and I went inside to ostensible safety, the sensation of some lurking danger remained.

Inside was row after row of lidless coffins, almost all occupied. I paid my fourpence and found an empty one to lie in, my violin case snug beneath my arm. The leather blanket had the frail stink of whoever had lain there that morning, so I tried not to breathe. This wasn't what my father would have wanted for me, but his death had left me with little more than my fiddle and my cunning.

Next to me, fast asleep, was a failed businessman I'd spoken to before. Harold, I think? His snores rumbled through the room like some great beast, joining with the clanking steam pipes and the drunken mutters and quiet sobs to make a bleak symphony. Across the way were the crowded Twopenny benches for sitting but not sleeping. Monitors roamed on either side of them, shining their lanterns to make sure nobody was cradling their head or nodding off. As the dark figures shifted, croaked, and converged into twitching inhuman silhouettes, it occurred to me that I could have been surrounded by monsters or ghosts without ever sensing the difference.

I closed my eyes and tried not to think of my father's dying face; of the overwhelming terror I had felt. But the memories came anyway, brought on by the promise of the unexplainable.

There was something vicious in the heart of this city; some ravenous cancer that devoured all that was good. And as much as I wanted to believe otherwise, it had infected me, and made me part of it. Now, I yearned to feast upon everything this cancer had to offer. Yes, I would go to the Immortalist Club, and I would do whatever I could to impress them.

———◆———

By now, you may be wondering why I've written this account in my blood.

First, I have no ink or paper, but my teeth are now sharp enough to pierce my fingertips. And this room is a canvas, is it not?

Second, I find that writing my story is a potent distraction from my current circumstances. It gives me something to focus on, even if they end up scrubbing this room clean once they find out what I'm doing.

Third, I don't want to forget my name. I don't want to forget who I am. And I don't want to forget what I've done.

As of this writing, there is no way to know for sure how long I'll be in this cell. It could be decades. Centuries. Even thousands of years. More than enough time to lose myself.

And if I somehow perish, perhaps these bloody scrawls can tell a story for this cell's next inhabitant. May my blood permanently stain these walls, living on in this wretched place.

Even if I'm the only one who ever reads it.

CHAPTER TWO

FIRE

THERE WAS, OF COURSE, a great deal I hadn't told
Remy. In my defense, I'd spent the last decade convincing myself that the memories weren't real. But as I lay
down that night, confronted with the idea that the universe
might be vaster than I wanted to admit, the dubious recol-
lections tickled my mind: ceaseless, agonizing, and clearer
than ever before.

It happened one night ten years prior. I'd been twelve
at the time, and plagued with a restlessness that rendered
me unable to sleep. This night in particular, my agitation
was such that I left my bed and snuck into my father's
study to procure something to read. I knew I'd get the
belt if he found me, but I felt I was old enough to read
when I pleased. Mother had always encouraged me to read
before the gout took her, but only ever the bible. Tonight,
I wanted something new. Something adventurous. Maybe
I'd even pick up one of Father's dirty books, the ones with
the pictures. I'd get an extra heavy beating if he found me
with those.

I risked lighting a candle to read the spines, so I wouldn't
accidentally return to bed with a dull history text. But only

moments later, while I was searching the shelves beside Father's antique cabinet, footsteps cut through the silence. I quickly blew out the candle, only to see light stretching from the bottom of the door.

Blood pounding with terror, I opened the cabinet and crept inside, closing each door until only a tiny slit was open. The candle remained in my hand, smoke clawing up into my nostrils as the library door creaked open. What awful timing I'd had!

Through my tiny slit of vision, I watched Father enter the study with a tiny cage in his hand. A rabbit quivered within, its little red eyes wide with terror. Father seemed distracted, his furrowed brow casting a dark shadow on his face as he set the cage down. His beard was no less furrowed, the hairs curling down in dark gray spirals, his spectacles tight against the bridge of his nose.

I brought my face close to the cabinet doors, but it didn't make it any easier to understand what Father was doing. He seemed to be moving in a circle around the room, his finger pressed to the floor. His other hand held a needle, a bead of fresh blood on its tip.

Father drew two circles: one around himself, the other around the rabbit's cage.

Well, now, that couldn't be right. Father was a man of God. And circles of blood weren't very godly, were they? I blinked, certain I was imagining it, but there they were, two scarlet circles on the wooden floorboards. Each was large enough for three men to fit inside.

"Yes..." said Father, his embarrassing Prussian accent sounding especially thick. "This time, it will work. I'm sure of it."

I almost opened the doors then and there to demand he explain himself, but what would I get for that? Nothing but pain. Fear kept me in place, and curiosity kept me from looking away.

Father had once told me that noble boys like Remy didn't get whipped. They had boys who got whipped *for* them. I wondered what it would be like, having someone else punished in your place. Did the noble boys ever feel guilty? *That's why you'll never be wealthy,* a voice in my mind seemed to tell me. *That's why you'd sooner be a whipping boy yourself.*

Father opened the little cage and pulled out the rabbit, holding it carefully to ensure it couldn't wriggle free. He closed his eyes as if in meditation or prayer.

Then he snapped the rabbit's neck.

My hand traveled to my mouth, masking my silent scream as Father dropped the dead rabbit into the second circle. Then he crouched down into the first circle, crossed his legs, and closed his eyes once more. I watched Father in confused horror. Whatever he was up to, it seemed like something I was not meant to witness, but I could not show myself without incurring his wrath.

For a moment, nothing happened. Then Father yelped, hand traveling to his mouth, blood leaking down from his lips. He opened his mouth wide and licked crimson gums. Half his teeth were missing, and his eyes were bulging so furiously, I half expected them to pop out too. Horror spread through me, and I had to fight to keep the scream from escaping my throat.

There were no teeth on the floor, even after Father spat out a wad of blood. His teeth had not fallen, and there was no indication that he'd swallowed them. They'd simply vanished.

Then I noticed movement where the rabbit carcass lay. It wasn't twitching or squirming or doing anything to suggest it remained alive. No, the creature was sinking into the floorboards, as one might sink into the sea. And in its place...

I froze, unwilling to believe what I was seeing. Something was floating up through the floor: a long, slender arm, reaching out as if from a pit. Long claws dug into the wood. Then a second arm reached up, hooking into the floor before pulling up the rest of the body. The floorboards did not rupture; it was as though this creature was rising from some invisible doorway. Slowly, more and more of her body emerged until, at last, she was fully there before me: something that seemed very much like a woman, and very much like nothing of the sort.

She was crouched on the ground like a cat ready to pounce, her sinuous limbs stretching as she rose to her feet. Two great, bat-like wings stretched out to the limit of the circle and pressed against the air itself, as if caressing walls I could not see. A spade-tipped tail twitched irritably behind her. This woman was not from this world.

But as she ascended to her full height, I found her other attributes were no less distracting. Her long, sleek black hair fell down a violin-shaped back. Her bare breasts hung, round and pendulous, and her posterior was no less impressive. I was mesmerized, but I also felt an incredible sense of embarrassment.

Father gasped. "Can it be? Have I truly done it?" His voice was slurred from his missing teeth.

The woman shifted, head rotating as she checked her surroundings, and for just a moment, her face turned toward me, golden cat-like eyes instantly making contact, her smile flirtatious and encouraging. It was a mere second before she returned her gaze to my father, but it was still enough to make my heart pound. It was as though she'd said to me, *I know you're there, little boy. Come out. Come to me. I'm here for your pleasure, not his. He may have summoned me, but you're the one I truly want.*

"Speak, creature!" Father stammered. "Are—are you lilitu? Are you a succubus?"

"Mm, I am." The winged woman cracked her neck back and forth with a quiet moan of satisfaction, then reached out to touch the boundary of her circle, gracefully dragging a fingernail down what seemed to be an invisible barrier. Her every movement made my heart pound faster. I desperately wanted to tear open the cabinet doors and leap into the circle, where she could rip off my clothes, my skin, anything, if only it meant I could feel her embrace. Anything would be worth that pleasure.

"And you know what I've brought you here to do?" Father was wide-eyed, barely able to speak.

"I know why men summon me." Her melodic voice tingled with amusement. "But I can't imagine why a handsome man like you would ever need to."

Father's eyes crinkled from the compliment, but they were moist at the corners, and when his lips opened to smile, it was made all the more miserable from his missing teeth. "I didn't, until a few years ago. But my wife... gout took her. I have been very lonely ever since."

The mention of my mother shook me from the reverie, and I realized what Father had summoned this creature to do. My discomfort overtook my lust, and I wanted nothing more than to flee from that room before I witnessed anything else. But how could I? If I opened the cabinet, Father would see.

"You have crosses in this room," said the woman, bemused. "And yet you've summoned me. Some Christian you are."

"I have read of the beauty of succubi," Father whispered. "The tales say you are far more beguiling than any mortal woman. And I must say, you certainly live up to the reputation. I know that God may strike me down for summoning you tonight, but I have longed for the embrace of one such as yourself for far too long. I cannot bear it any longer."

A smile peeled through the succubus's face. "Then come. Enter my circle. Take me, as you've dreamed of doing."

I averted my eyes, but it was terrible enough hearing Father's belt buckle clatter to the floor. Oh, how I wished at that moment that I'd remained in bed and never come to this dreadful room. The succubus began squealing in delight. Father grunted and gasped, then began to scream, over and over. They were not screams of pleasure, but rather terrible pain. Reluctant though I was to see, I forced myself to stare through the crack again, and witnessed the demon pinning my father to the floor. Their pelvises were locked together, her body rocking atop him, her sharp fingers clawing bloody trenches into his chest. She grinned, her wings flapping excitedly, her breasts thrusting out with each buck. But beneath her, Father's eyes were wide, the veins in his neck and temple pulsating.

"Yes!" urged the succubus. "Yes, fill me with your seed!"

Father let out an agonized moan. Then his head fell back and tilted sideways, jaw hanging limp, staring at the cabinet—at *me*—with strangely empty eyes. His body was not moving at all.

An ache spread through me as I stared, waiting for him to move again, but he did not. It made no sense. He couldn't be dead. He couldn't be!

"P-Papa?" I whimpered, unable to help myself. I pushed open the cabinet doors and ran out—but stopped at the scarlet circle on the floor, sensing that nothing good could come from crossing the boundary.

The succubus let out a satisfied grunt as she detached herself from his pelvis. His cock flapped uselessly onto his belly. "Papa!" I howled again, my face suddenly hot and moist. But still my father did not move. The succubus slithered across his body, licking the bloody wounds she'd left on his chest. Then she turned her gaze upon me.

"Won't you come into the circle?" she whispered, tilting her head as she stuck her rump out provocatively, still standing atop my father's corpse. "I still want you, boy. I wanted you the moment I smelled you."

"No!" I screamed. "Get away! Go back to where you came from!"

"Fine," she said, wriggling as if to taunt me. "I'll be seeing your papa very soon, boy. Maybe even tonight."

"I'll kill you!" And I truly meant it. If I'd had a sword or an axe, I'd have charged right in there and cut her to bits. But all I had was Father's candle, and before I could think things through I was already throwing it into the circle...where its flames erupted upon the wooden floorboards.

The succubus let out an amused snort and sank back down into the floor. When she'd disappeared completely, the bloody ring around her faded away as well.

The fire, however, remained. It claimed Father's corpse and spread from there, crossing beyond the circle's former borders.

I wanted to hold my father. I wanted to bring him back. But I also knew that if I did not flee, I would join him in death, and I was too much of a coward for that.

So I grabbed my violin and fled, letting the fire claim our home, my father's shop, and all the lovely violins he'd spent so many hours creating.

In the years that followed, I convinced myself that it had all been a bad dream. That I had merely awoken to the fire, witnessed my father burn, and fled. Even now, some part of me wonders whether the clarity with which I write this is a sign that my mind has embellished it; my imagination filling the gaps to find meaning in a random tragedy.

And yet, ever since, the phantom of the succubus has remained: an indelible mark on my mind, reminding me always of how powerless I am.

CHAPTER THREE

THE DEMONSTRATION

"DO YOU FANCY YOURSELF a lady-killer, Mr. Schwartzenfeld?"

Bertha watched me apply my makeup, her drawn-on brows raised high. We were sharing the coffin house's only mirror, both of us getting ready for our respective roles of the evening. I'd returned for bread and coffee after a long day of street sweeping. Harold was watching me from his coffin as well, tall and bulky, face so scrunched you'd have thought he'd drank curdled milk.

"One always applies makeup before going on stage," I said as I lined my eyes. "And what is a job if not one big show, where we take the roles of automatons?"

"Boy-killer, then," said Bertha. Harold's face became all the more sour, and he made the sign of the cross against his chest. I tensed. I'd always been on the runtish side, and large men like Harold delighted in pushing me around. More than once, men of his kind had accused me of being a mandrake to justify beating me senseless.

"It's only a bit of makeup," I grumbled. "Look, I've got a very important audition tonight, and I want to look presentable." Indeed, more than presentable; I wanted to look *dashing*. I'd been doing this for years before performances, and by now I knew how to apply my makeup in such a way that I looked more masculine, accentuating my already-prominent cheekbones. I brushed a curl of flaxen hair out of my eyes and added, "A hundred years ago, it was perfectly normal for wealthy gentlemen to wear wigs, high heels, and makeup far gaudier than this."

Harold scoffed. "If you're such a gentleman, Mr. Schwartzenfeld, then why are you here? You're just another dog trying to get as many licks as he can."

In all fairness, "Caleb" does mean "dog," but I've always felt more cat-like than anything. I'm easily startled, am an unrepentant biter, and I would far rather do as I please than take orders from others. And yet like a dog I have always ultimately done what I was told, because I have never had any other choice. So it is that the cat of my nature has always bitterly given way to the dog of my circumstance.

"I'll give you this, Mr. Schwartzenfeld," Bertha whispered, drawing close. "For a shrimp, you do know how to make yourself a looker. What do you say to a little fun before your audition? Some extra pep in your step from a five-shilling bargain?"

My eyes flashed to her reflection in the mirror and, for just a moment, I thought the succubus was standing beside me, winking with golden eyes. But it was only Bertha: orange curls, full lips, and the sort of bosom men wrote poems about.

I exhaled quietly, surprised by my own jumpiness. It had been some time since I'd thought about the succubus, but running into Remy and hearing about the cult's supposed powers had brought her clawing back to the forefront of my mind. As always, I reminded myself that I'd imagined the whole thing; that it had merely been a fire that had claimed my father's life, just as Remy's cult was merely a gathering of rich old parasites, ripe for fleecing.

"Perhaps another time," I said, fixing my tie.

"How about a bargain for me, then, aye?" asked Harold, leering at the cut of Bertha's bodice.

"Aye, a five-shilling bargain for the handsome business-man," said Bertha, winking at him as well.

Harold grinned. "I ain't got any shillings, honey. S'why I'm here. But I bet you wouldn't even charge me after I was done with you. It would be a far better experience than with him. Look. That's no man, no red-blooded one anyway."

My jaw tightened. Even after all my work, in the glass I saw a face that was more pretty than handsome, more thin than robust. I'd always felt like there was something wrong with me, and Harold's words were yet another reminder. I envied him for being what I could not: tall, masculine, simple. Even his career prospects were better than mine. I was all the worst things a man could be: poor, powerless, and weak.

I made a hasty retreat before my anger got the best of me. The last thing I needed was to show up to the Immortalist Club with black eyes and a bloody nose. But even this made me feel like a coward.

Beneath the pale sky, the streets of London were a cease-less scream: hawkers, priests, drunks, brothel girls, all of them clawing for your attention, all of them wanting some-thing from you. There was enough stink, mud, and filth that it could have been a swamp. This city made you more animal than human, reducing you to your hunger and your pain and the addictions you picked up to numb it all away.

My limbs ached from my long day, and it was hard to not feel all the weaker for it. I speculate that I seemed shorter than I actually was, for I was used to keeping my head low. This was both because the world had beaten me down enough to make my thoughts heavy, and because I was accustomed to traveling roads covered in shit: horse, dog, and human. The carriages that passed me didn't need to watch out for that, but I did.

But maybe all that would change soon enough. After all, I was on my way to an event that could shift the course of my life, transforming me into a new man entirely.

A large bone-white building waited at the address Remy had provided, a staircase leading up to its bright red door. When I knocked, it opened to the face of a tall man with gaunt cheeks and tangled white hair that resembled a ball of cobwebs. His faded grey eyes rolled over me, taking me in, and even when his face twisted into a crude smile, it fell short of meeting them. "Welcome, sir! Welcome! A good day to you. What brings you to our door?"

I hesitated. "Is this the home of the Immortalist Club?"

The man looked me over, his smile still not meeting his eyes. "The Esteemed Order of the Immortalists, yes! You have been invited, then, sir?" The doorman swept his arm in a grand gesture to the hallway beyond. "Do come in, for tonight is a night for new members, oh yes! Fresh meat! Aye, we welcome it."

"Quit scaring him, Leroy," said a voice behind me. I turned to see Remy, a sheepish grin on his face, like the bastard enjoyed making me jump.

The doorman stretched the door fully open. "Why of course, Mr. Halligan. Friend of yours, is he?"

"Yes. Now, if you please..."

Remy led me inside past the strange man. The hallway was dimly lit, its walls as bone-white as the exterior and so smooth that I half wondered if they really *were* bone. Another red door waited at the end of the hall, but this one Remy opened on his own, revealing a great torchlit chamber containing a vast stage. The chamber echoed with the droning of unseen women, forming a tingling melody that seemed to crawl under my skin. There were many other people here, some wearing fine suits, others ragged like myself. I'd been afraid that I would stand out, but we all looked out of place here. The room was bloody *opulent*: a dome ceiling, a balcony encircling above us, torches hanging on the pillars. There was not a single window, nor any mirrors, nor any panes of glass at all. Hooded figures in Venetian masks watched us from the balcony above.

An enormous painting hung high on the wall behind the stage. It showed a goat-headed man making love to three women, his tongue flicking one's nipple as he inserted his fingers into another's rear. The third woman was impaled on his upsettingly large cock. All three women were writhing in ecstasy, one caressing the goat man's hairy legs, while another stroked his long horns. They were tangled within a dark grove, the trees around them forming a shadowy canopy of branches that might as well have been a colossal black spiderweb.

The goat did not look at the women he was touching. Instead, he stared right back at me. Even as I followed Remy around the room, I found myself glancing back at the painting, and those wide, horizontal pupils were always boring into me like blades. It was like what people said about the Mona Bloody Lisa.

"Is it really safe here?" I whispered.

Remy laughed. "Come off it, Caleb. If it was dangerous, I wouldn't have brought you. Half these old gents are just here to get away from their wives. Hell, Scotland Yard's commissioner is here every week. Now shush," he added, lowering his voice. "The demonstration is about to begin."

"The demonstration?" I repeated.

Remy looked at me like I was a fool. "*Proof*, Caleb."

The crowd murmured as a figure emerged onto the stage. She appeared to be a nun, but the trim of her habit was red instead of white. There was a dramatic, tantalizing beauty about her; a darkness around her eyes that I would have sworn went beyond makeup. Her thick red lips opened wide to address the room.

"Welcome, all, to the Immortalist Club. I am Mother Pursha. You have all been brought here not just by your friends and relatives, but by providence. You are here to witness miracles." Just as with the goat, I always felt like her eyes were on me, no matter which direction her head turned.

I stood rigid, paralyzed by anxiety's venom and the song of the unseen choir. There was no way these supposed miracles were real, but this place gave me gooseflesh, as though my body already had all the proof it needed.

"You may not be sure what to believe just yet," Pursha went on, "but each of you were brought here for a reason. Drawn here, so that you could become a part of something wonderful. Would I be wrong in thinking each of you have always felt, deep down, that your life wasn't supposed to be this way? That you were meant for something greater?"

My throat closed as surely as if she'd squeezed it. I'd always wondered what I'd have become, had the fire not rendered me a penniless street orphan. Everyone in the crowd around me had the same desperate sheen in their eyes. Had they, too, been robbed of greater futures?

"The Immortalist Club is a club for the elite," Pursha continued. "A place where the most deserving of society share the greatest secrets of the universe. Even the secret of eternal life. You have all been chosen to join our ranks and experience the glory of what our society offers."

The crowd murmured in excitement. So many ragged coats and dirty palms... *these* were those deemed the most deserving of society? It wasn't that I judged my fellow poor (even though, deep down, I *had* always seen myself as better than them); it was that I couldn't imagine England's aristocracy seeing the souls beneath our mud. There was no way that we had all been truly chosen by some ineffable party.

It was obvious what had happened. The club's members had been given instruction to find friends of theirs who had wanted more from life; who were angry they hadn't risen higher; who were so desperate and vulnerable that they would grasp whatever hand was offered. Remy, who was currently watching me with a smile, had surely found me specifically for that purpose. But if that was true, how the hell had he known where I'd been?

The painted eyes of the goat continued to bore into me, golden and promising, as if those uncanny pupils held endless galaxies within them.

"But how can you believe such claims?" asked Pursha. "How can you be assured we are not charlatans? My new friends, my fellow seekers of the truth... allow me to show you."

She drifted backwards until the darkness swallowed her whole. Three other figures emerged in her place, all of them wearing Venetian masks and scarlet robes. The one in the center removed his robe, letting it pool onto the stage, revealing a muscular male body—the sort I'd always been frustrated I didn't have myself. He was completely naked save for his mask and leather undergarments. The fire reflected against his bare skin, which was oiled for effect.

I gathered the two other figures were women, and waited eagerly for them to disrobe as well. Instead, they pulled knives out from under their scarlet robes, and each plunged them into the man's back.

The audience shuddered, but the masked strongman did not. Even as blood trickled down his back, he flexed his arms. Well, that wasn't all that impressive on its own; there were plenty of strongmen who could keep standing after such wounds. But then he raised his palms, and the women thrust knives through them as well. The crowd let out another huff of concern, but the acolyte did not react to his wounds. Slowly, he began dancing to the droning choir, moving those pierced hands around in slow arcs, his blood dripping onto the fallen robe.

Whatever doubt remained was shredded as the scarlet nuns stabbed a third set of knives into his neck: one into the front, another into the side. Yet even as blood spurted from his jugular, the strongman kept dancing. My jaw dropped. This was no mortal man. This was a Greek god, Apollo himself.

Our Apollo danced on, moving faster than ever. The nuns sashayed their hips on either side of him, slow and hypnotic, to the rhythm of drums I only just noticed had been there all along. It had to be fake. It *had* to be. But try as I might, I could not think of how it could be possible.

Especially as Apollo and his acolytes began levitating into the air. Higher and higher they floated, slow and graceful enough for us to know this was no trick. No strings gleamed in the torchlight. There were no rafters for anyone to hide in, either; merely the dome above us all.

Belief crawled into my mind like a scarab. Despite the bloodshed and my fear, the moment also felt...sublime. We were witnessing some divine impossibility; something that could not be considered anything but a miracle. And it all happened under the watchful eyes of the goat—no, I realized, the *satyr*—who might as well have been hovering above us all in the flesh, making love to his nymphs in his dark grove.

Yet it also brought to mind the last impossible thing I'd witnessed: the succubus, rising from the floor to consume my father's life. For so long, I'd wanted to deny it, but how could I after this? My body felt warm, that fire blazing all around me even now. It should have made me want to flee, but instead I was all the more compelled to stay, and uncover this place's secrets. To be a part of the miracle unfolding before me. To no longer be a helpless witness in a closet, but a powerful figure in my own right. I yearned to remove my violin from its case and join the moment, adding another layer of music to the dance, but I did not dare.

The scarlet nuns diverged from Apollo in mid-air, floating toward us rather than up and away. Their fingers were still wet with Apollo's blood, and as one reached a man closest to the stage, she touched his forehead, leaving a red spot. The man smiled, a dazed expression in his eyes. The other nun touched the forehead of the woman beside him, marking her as well.

I stared, transfixed and oddly hungry, as the nuns continued to mark each person in the audience with the blood, one by one, until at last it was my turn. A nun floated inches above me, her robe and habit rippling like hair underwater, her long, bone-thin wrist reaching out with a single finger extended. As it prodded my forehead, sticky and wet and oh so red, my heart thundered with both excitement and horror. I had been marked, perhaps claimed in some way, but I wanted it. I wanted more.

Above, Apollo continued to dance passionately in mid-air, red rivers descending down his golden chest, hypnotizing us with his uncanniness as the mark melted down our foreheads and into our eyes, until all the world was stardust in the satyr's gaze.

— ◆ —

The moments that followed are a blur to me now, and I expect they were a blur to me then, too: each of us being led to a colossal book on an altar, pricking our fingers to leave a drop of blood on its pages, dripping a bit more into a basin beside it, and wading naked into an enormous bath, where we washed away our filth. The performance had left us all in a collective trance, as if the sight itself had been an opiate.

At some point, Remy must have taken me aside and drawn me away from the others, because I ended up standing in the corner of a new room. Masked men and women were clustering about, drinking and chatting. I was wearing a white tunic, surprisingly smooth against my skin. I did not remember putting it on, and only vaguely remembered removing my old clothes to enter the bath. A few others in white tunics were here as well, but most were masked gentlemen (and a few ladies) wearing the attire of those who could afford anything they wanted. Established members, no doubt. Their masks were strange, papier-mâché parodies of human features, covering everything above the nose.

This room also had an unsettling painting of its own: countless hands reaching up from an endless red sea, grasping nothing. At that moment, it did not shock me like the other painting had. I was too disoriented, realizing only now how murky the past hour (or hours?) had been. How had I ended up here?

A masked man handed me a glass of red wine. "Enjoy it while you can." Remy, I realized from the voice and mouth. He sniffed his own glass before taking a sip.

I tipped the glass to my lips, letting the smallest amount of the complex, sour taste taint my tongue. It was the first taste of wine I'd ever had, and it was good enough that I felt like someone here would shout at me for drinking it. It didn't help when Remy began pointing out figures in the crowd, all of them important enough that I could be arrested for trying to speak with them.

"That man's a duke," he said, jerking his chin in the direction of a man in white and gold. "And over there is Richard Mayne, head of the Metropolitan Police."

"How far up does this go?" I whispered, before turning to see Mother Pursha standing before me.

"Welcome, Caleb," she said, beaming. "Remigius tells us you have musical talent?"

I almost choked on my wine, thinking of the stage performance. How the hell was I supposed to follow that? "Remy is very kind," I said, smiling wanly.

"Oh, don't be so humble, Caleb!" said Remy, nudging me with his elbow. "Go on. Give her a demonstration."

"I'd be happy to," I began, only to realize, to my horror, that I'd somehow misplaced my violin. Had I left it with my clothes? I looked frantically around, fully prepared to mumble out my apologies.

Then, as if on cue, a masked figure in a waiter's uniform strolled over and carefully handed me a violin case. Pursha and Remy both smiled as he left. Confused and unsettled, I opened the case to find a violin resting within. It was clean, polished, beautiful...nothing like the ratty old one I'd been playing for the past decade.

"I thought you might like a new one," Remy whispered. "Don't worry, I made sure it's tuned well."

A lump filled my throat. My old violin had been crafted by my father, and was all I had left of him. This new violin was undeniably a superior specimen, free of the scars that had marked it. And yet...

"What became of my old one?" I whispered.

"Oh, no need to worry about that, old friend," said Remy, putting his hand on my shoulder. "It's all taken care of. This is a gift for you, from me. Not just for tonight, but for the rest of your days. Go on, give it a go."

Pursha was still hovering there expectantly, red lips stretched wide. How would it look for me to refuse such a kind gift? Remy might be offended, Pursha might think me foul, and I might very well lose not just my violin, but any chance of rising through the club's ranks.

I put my glass on a table and removed the new violin from its case. It still felt like I'd wandered into a room where I wasn't welcome, even if no one but this strange nun had noticed me.

"I'm sure everyone here would be delighted for a little background music," she said as she grasped my hand, her touch ice cold. "Come, now. I shall watch from the balcony. An audience just for you."

She slowly ran a bony thumb against my knuckles, her gaze fixed on me. The stink of spoiled fruit filled my nostrils. Perfume? Then she pulled away with a wink, sending jolts of confusion through my body. I'd never been a particularly religious man, but it was my understanding that nuns didn't generally wink at men, or grab their hands for that matter.

Regardless, I cleared my throat and readied the instrument. I'd played for crowds plenty of times. There was no need to be so nervous. But this time, bringing bow to string felt like walking into some great fiery crucible. I had to impress tonight. No Blue Danube or Irish jig. Better to go for something more challenging. Something that demonstrated my skill.

I decided to play Niccolò Paganini's *Caprice No. 24*. It was one of the most difficult pieces ever written for solo violin, and I'd yet to perform it to complete perfection. But I'd come close, and any mistakes I made would likely be muffled by all the chatter. I shook my head, breathed in, and began.

Here's the thing about performing: as terrified as I felt in the moments leading up to it, once bow met string, everything else melted away. There was only the performance. There was only what I had to do. I let the world fade and became one with my violin. It was not merely an instrument of my hand, but an extension of my soul.

Some songs, you must lose yourself in and submit to, but *Caprice No. 24* requires domination. The violinist must wrestle it into submission, carefully and rapidly shifting from one interval to the next: the fast scales, the arpeggios, the quick string crossing. It's a wicked song, the bane of countless violinists eager for respect, a test that even the best are doomed to fail. But it was also written in A minor, and frankly *sounds* wicked.

Even as people turned to look and the room became silent save for my strings, I didn't let it distract me from the song—not at first. Not until my eyes drifted up to the balcony and saw Pursha sitting alone, watching me with a smirk. Her hand slid slowly down her thigh, fingers dancing like she was playing piano, until it was between her legs. She hiked up her skirt, not once breaking eye contact.

My fingers slipped. The slightest fumble, but I kept pace, continuing, recovering. I doubt anyone in the audience even noticed. I played on, keeping my eyes low lest I make another mistake. But inevitably, curiosity got the better of me, and my gaze drifted back up to the balcony. Pursha had brushed aside her undergarments and slipped her fingers into her cunt. Even from here, I could see it glistening, dewdrops leaking onto the floor as she thrust her fingers deep. She bit her lower lip, smiling, back arched in pleasure.

Once again, I tore my eyes away, unwilling to make another mistake. I squeezed them shut, letting the song's urgent pace mirror my frustration. I *was* the violin. There was nothing in the world but my violin. I fiddled on and on, pouring my soul into the shiny new instrument, and somehow, I knew Pursha was matching my rhythm. In my mind's eye, she was plucking her cunt as I plucked the strings: watching me, biting her lip, gushing onto those cold, bony hands, with all the pleasure of the demon that had taken my father's life. They looked nothing alike, and yet...and yet...

Silence. I'd reached the end of the song. I opened my eyes and let out a deep breath, only now realizing how long I'd been holding it.

Those who had been listening clapped politely, but did not erupt. I spread my arms and bowed deeply, thankful for what attention I could get. Pursha had left the balcony. The hairs on my arms stood on end, not aroused so much as anxious.

"What a wonderful performance." She was suddenly smiling, beside me, as though she'd never even left. "Remigius was right to bring you. I'm sure many in the crowd agree."

My head spun, torn between ambition and fear. For years, I'd been telling myself my father's death had been from a fire and that the demon had been my imagination. Why call that into question now, when I was on the precipice of finally being discovered? I was here to make a name for myself, was I not? So, I bowed and fixed Pursha with a smile, burying my nervousness, my questions, my fears. "I am honored to hear it."

She chuckled. "You could have a place here, Caleb. You may be a mere Fledgling now, but once you have achieved the rank of Prominent, you too can be granted the gift of immortality."

"Fledgling?" I repeated. I wanted to ask Remy, but he'd disappeared into the sea of masks.

"The first rank. Remigius is currently the second rank, Collector. Responsible for attracting new members." Pursha continued to beam, her expression static throughout the entire exchange, not once breaking eye contact, nor speaking of what she'd done on the balcony. "Who knows? If you impress the right members, you may find yourself not far behind."

The masked gentlemen around us had resumed their conversations, their gnarled hands often grasping canes, my performance seemingly already forgotten. Had they achieved their wealth before joining the Immortalist Club, or attained it as a result of their membership? I had to think it was the former; that those with wealth were prioritized. These were men rich enough, old enough, and desperate enough to pay untold amounts if they thought it would grant them just a few more years on this Earth.

"Are there...fees?" I asked.

"Merely a small amount of blood for each meeting. And we do expect members to come each week."

I knew better than to ask what the blood was for, or what might happen if I missed a meeting. This was a dangerous place, full of dangerous people. But where in London was it not so? I thought of the coffin house, the perpetual emptiness of my purse, and the long, cold, hunger-filled nights when I didn't manage to scrape enough together. How long would it be before I got knifed in my sleep?

If I listened to my doubts, it would mean giving up my dreams. If I was to escape my poverty, I had to do whatever Pursha and her kin asked. It was a matter of survival for me as surely as it was for these wealthy old men. But I would need to fight infinitely harder to rise to their level.

"Excuse me, Mr. Schwartzenfeld? May I have a moment of her time?"

A masked woman had approached me. Her arm was linked with that of a tall man, his shoulders pulled back and chest thrust out in some baffling defensive posture. Remy stood in the direction they'd come from, smiling.

I couldn't help but be amused that the woman was speaking to me as if I were a gentleman. "Certainly," I said, playing the part.

Pursha finally turned away to look at the newcomers, and a strange relief flooded me. "I take it you enjoyed Mr. Schwartzenfeld's performance?" she asked.

"Very much so," said the woman. "And I have a proposition for him."

"This is highly irregular, Clara…" the man with her grunted. He sported a slick ice-blond combover, his jaw raised so high it was like his neck had been cracked.

"I feel that it would be highly beneficial to me," said Clara. "And Remy has vouched for him." She looked me over. "Do you always play that well, Mr. Schwartzenfeld? Can you be relied on?"

"I do and I can, my lady," I said, bowing my head. Masked though she was, I could tell that she was beautiful from her slender wrists, her delicate-looking skin, and her youthful, musical voice. Her golden hair was held up in a bun, but on each side of her head hung a single, wispy curl. To have such a woman look upon me left me wishing that I were the masked one, for I feared I might flush at any moment.

"Then we have a proposal for you," said Clara. "I would like you to come and stay with us in our home, so that we can call on you to play for us during mealtimes or when we have guests over. We can offer you a generous stipend if you agree. Isn't that right, Thomas?"

Thomas let out a frustrated sigh. "I suppose if you insist on this ridiculous idea, it would be better for it to be a fellow member. But he will stay downstairs with the other servants."

"Naturally," said Clara. "What do you say, Mr. Schwartzenfeld?"

It was an offer beyond my wildest dreams. It would also, I was sure, entrench me further into this strange order.

But there was another reason that compelled me to agree: Clara herself. I had not even seen her face, but I found myself smitten. Her voice, her demeanor, what I could see of her figure... she seemed utterly feminine, gentle, and refined in a way the street women were simply not. I'd encountered such women as a boy when they came to my father's shop, but I'd been young then. Now I was a man, and Clara was the first woman of her class to speak to me with even a modicum of respect. I was utterly curious to see her with her mask off. What lovely rose of a face waited beneath? Perhaps she wanted more than just my music. Perhaps she wished for me to be close to her, easy access. Pursha had taken interest in me tonight, so why not Clara, too?

I smiled, bowing my head even lower. "My lady, I would be delighted."

"Wonderful." Clara smiled, taking her husband's arm. "Don't go anywhere. We will collect you later tonight."

They disappeared back into the crowd.

"Do you know who that couple was?" asked Pursha.

I shook my head, still trembling from it all; still swooning inside from Lady Clara's beauty.

"That was Thomas and Clara Rife," said Pursha. "Thomas is one of the wealthiest landowners in England, and he's rising rapidly through our ranks. These are very important people, Mr. Schwartzenfeld. The sort who are so financially endowed, they could destroy a man on a whim, or make him one of the most celebrated artists of our time. If you play your cards right, this could be your chance to get into the history books."

My throat became even drier at this. With a quaking hand, I reached for another drink. There were so many things I'd ruined in life, but I could not afford to ruin this.

CHAPTER FOUR

THE HOUSE OF RIFE

Thomas and Clara Rife took me home like a dog from the street. Their manor was outside of London, the sole building standing erect in a barren field. Squawking on its high, distant roof were the black silhouettes of birds, so thin that if I didn't know better, I'd have thought them to be skeletons.

As soon as I walked in, a dark shroud seemed to fall upon me, as though the beautiful furniture and lavish wallpaper only existed to hide a rancid heart. The cobwebs had been brushed away, the dust meticulously cleaned, and yet the sadness that radiated from the place was suffocating from the moment I entered. It was impossible to discern where exactly this sadness came from; only that it was breathing through the walls, leaking out from the cracks in the floorboards, and spreading across the ceiling like a leak stain.

Clara introduced me to a sour-faced butler named Croft, who led me downstairs to where the servants lived. "Don't expect Buckingham Palace," he grunted. I opted not to tell him I was used to sleeping in a wooden box.

Deeper and deeper down the stairs went, until I realized that we had gone all the way underground. The servants' quarters looked to have been adapted from someone's private dungeon, with stone walls and a perpetual dusty smell.

"Is Rife Manor a very old house?" I asked as Croft led me down a snaking, barely lit hall.

Croft regarded me with a scowl. "If you're worried creaks and groans will wake you in the night, I suggest you get used to it. You're absurdly fortunate to have received this offer from the good Lady Clara. You're in no position to complain."

The room that awaited me was very small, and contained only a bed, an old oil lamp, and a small, cracked mirror on the wall. It all stank of dust, but it was a room to call my own, the first I'd had since I was a boy, and that made it wonderful.

"Lavatory's down the hall," said Croft, before closing the door.

Clara sent for me the very next morning. Her maid, a homely young woman named Henrietta, rapped upon my door to deliver the message, as well as some clean, folded clothes for me to wear. "Is the missus sweet on you or something?" she asked as I brought them to my bed.

"I wouldn't know." I unfolded the fine shirt, head low to hide the amusement I felt from the idea.

Henrietta frowned. "Mrs. Rife's been having an especially difficult year. For some time now, she's spoken of hiring a live-in musician to soothe her on her hard nights. I'd ask you to be mindful of her tender heart. And I wouldn't cross Mr. Rife neither."

"I am merely here to play music," I said. "I don't intend on doing anything underhanded."

Henrietta squinted at me, not believing a word, but led me upstairs to a sitting room regardless. My heart hammered so rapidly that I almost didn't notice when it skipped a beat. Sitting there by the window was Lady Clara, her light blue dress clinging to the curves of her torso. But even now I could not see her face, for she was staring mournfully out the window, as if waiting for sunlight to creep in through its semi-transparent drapes, even though outside there was only darkness and murk. "My lady," said Henrietta. "Mr. Schwartzenfeld is here to play for you."

"Thank you, Henrietta." Clara's voice was far more somber than it had been the night before, and she barely turned her head to acknowledge us. "Please, Caleb. Play me something...jubilant."

"Of course, my lady."

With the butt of the violin against my neck, I began *The Devil's Dream*, a common favorite at pubs. I waited for Clara to turn, for the opportunity to finally see her face in full. But no matter how enthusiastically I played, she barely moved. When the song was over, she said nothing, so I moved on to *Mist Covered Mountains*, making sure to stretch it out. Clara let out a soft sigh and finally went over to the tray Henrietta had left.

I was careful not to let my playing falter, even as I took in her face for the first time. Her features were soft, like she'd walked out of a painting—Millais's *Ophelia*, perhaps. She had somber amber eyes and trembling pink lips, her whole being fragile, delicate, and as lovely as I'd imagined.

But I also noticed, with some discomfort, an area on the side of her head where her skin looked to have darkened. A bruise? Either way, this jolly music had done nothing to improve her mood.

As Henrietta poured Clara a fresh cup of tea, I decided to risk transitioning into something that better matched her disposition. Many people feel that when you are morose, it is best to listen to something happy, but sometimes melancholic music can be more cathartic. And from the way Clara's slender hand quivered as she lifted the teacup to her lips, I sensed that catharsis was something she desperately needed.

I decided to play *Ashen Threnody,* an original composition I'd been working on for some time. It was a slow, morose song in minor, well-suited for such a dreary morning. I immediately sensed a change in Clara's demeanor, her breathing quickening until tears flowed from her eyes. Henrietta shot me a baffled expression, but Clara's grip on her cup was finally steadying. And as I reached the song's final chords, she let out a long, loud exhale of unmistakable relief, before turning to give me a teary-eyed smile.

"Thank you, Caleb," she said. "You knew what I needed, even though I didn't."

I could have never anticipated how intensely that smile hit me. It had all the force of a slap to the face. From that moment on, I was not merely attracted to Clara; I was bloody smitten. I found myself instantly lost in the throes of some unfathomably deep longing, as if my soul had latched onto hers like a leech. "Of—of course, my lady," I said, stumbling over my words.

Her brow quirked, as though amused. I wondered if she'd had any idea what her smile had done to me, and whether she, too, was developing an interest in me. After all, she had invited me to live with her. It was an easy thing to fancy, for if she did secretly harbor such affection, she would be in no more of a position to confess it than myself.

The door opened with a clang, and Sir Thomas strolled in. Clara's smile vanished, the sadness returning to her eyes.

Thomas was walking as if he was in a hurry to get somewhere important, but all he did was collapse into a seat. "Good, the help is already here. Get me some brandy, one of you."

"Isn't it a bit early for that?" asked Clara.

"I can bloody well drink when I like," said Thomas, planting himself next to her. His hair was disheveled, and he looked bitter enough to wring a puppy's neck. "Indeed, it so happens that I'm very much in the mood for one. Rudy refuses to have a rematch. He's comfortable sitting on his gains, and he knows that I could very well regain what I lost if he faced me again."

Clara lowered her head, something like a sigh escaping her lips.

Thomas glowered at her. "What?"

"Nothing," she said quickly. Too quickly.

Thomas's eye twitched. "Out with it. I'll not have you hiding your ill will."

Clara hesitated. "It's just... if I remember correctly, Rudy was embarrassed to beat you as badly as he did, and did not even wish to take his gains. He expressed fear that you'll gamble away your entire fortune."

"Nay, nay, he's afraid I'll take his!" Thomas clenched his fist, as if imagining it closing around Rudy's neck. Then he redirected his glare at Henrietta and me. "Why are you still here? Get me my brandy."

"Of course, my lord," Henrietta said, hurrying to the door and motioning for me to follow. I did, both reluctant and confused. Henrietta closed the door as soon as I was out and led me to the staircase. "I'd suggest heading back downstairs," she said quickly.

But I lingered at the top of the stairs, overcome by the sense that we'd abandoned Clara to the mercy of a hungry wolf. "Go!" said Henrietta, just before a loud *thud* and a woman's cry of pain echoed from the sitting room. Clara came rushing out, covering her face as she ran down past us, but not so well that I didn't see the fresh purple bruise.

Sometimes rage is hot, but what unspooled inside of me at that moment was ice cold. It spread like a blizzard, swirling from my heart until it had consumed me completely. My hands balled into fists as I marched back to the sitting room. Within, Thomas was wiping his knuckles onto a napkin from the tea tray, staining it red.

"Where's that brandy, boy?"

I contemplated getting his damn brandy bottle and smashing his face in with it. But I was five foot six and slender, while Thomas was six foot two and reasonably muscular. In a fair fistfight, I would most assuredly lose.

But this didn't need to be fair. Thomas might not expect an attack. An image flashed in my mind: Clara, gleefully running into my arms as I stood above her husband's corpse, crying "You saved me, Caleb!" before kissing my bloody lips.

Had His Lordship only bothered to look me in the eye, he would see the murderous hatred seething there. But Thomas did not look directly at me. To him, I was no different from a stool.

I hurried after Henrietta, back down to the dungeon-like passageway to the servants' quarters. "How often does this happen?" I asked.

Henrietta averted her eyes. "As I said, her ladyship is enduring a difficult time."

"*How often?*"

"If I said every night, or twice a week, or once a month, would it matter? It is enough to say her ladyship asks me to cover her bruises often."

I felt like my skeleton might jump out of my skin, charge back into that room and murder Sir Thomas in my stead. "How is this allowed to happen?"

Henrietta finally stopped and turned to face me, her eyes weary. "Do you think you're the first to ask such a thing? We had another maid who also asked questions last year, and she disappeared soon after. Scotland Yard never even looked for her."

"If all the servants backed Lady Clara together—" I began.

Henrietta let out a shrill, angry laugh. "And lose not just our jobs but quite possibly our lives? Consider Mr. Rife's friends, Mr. Schwartzenfeld. You went to that club, didn't you? You know what kind of men they are." Her voice lowered into a shaky whisper. "And you know what they would do if Lady Clara tried to go to the law about this. Even if she survived it, she would be wracked with scandal. None would believe her, not even with us at her back. We all know it, and we do our best to make our peace with it."

My fists trembled with rage. "Surely there's something we can do. That man—"

"Is rising through the ranks of the most powerful order in England," said Henrietta, her terrified eyes piercing into me. "Do not cross him, Mr. Schwartzenfeld. Better to find another job. I wish I could, if only to avail myself of this pain, but I cannot leave her. Not now."

Then she turned and went on her way, leaving me standing in the dark hall.

The rest of the week settled into a familiar rhythm. I would eat with the other servants, and answer Lady Clara's summons to play whatever she wanted for her. These summons might come during her own mealtimes, or when she was bored, or after parties full of dreadful aristocrats, who laughed freely and took no notice of the sadness in her eyes. *Ashen Threnody* quickly became a favorite of hers, and she requested it often.

I had every reason to continue this arrangement for as long as I could: regular meals, my own room, baths, daily opportunities to play my music, and of course my payment. At night I was free to go to the nearby pub and drink as I pleased. I had, in many ways, finally attained the stability I'd dreamed of since my father's death.

But night after night, Clara's sobbing echoed through the walls. I yearned to go up to her and whisk her away from this wretched place like a fairy tale princess from her tower. But Henrietta's warning rang in my mind, fusing with the impossible stage performance I'd witnessed at the club. Thomas was dangerous, perhaps in ways that were beyond my ken.

One night, it was he who called for me, summoning me to a sizable bathhouse separate from the main manor. Within was an enormous steaming pool, as large as some rooms. Thomas was already bathing in it, and he was not alone. A young woman was with him, laughing as he splashed her, then shrieking in surprise as she saw me before laughing once more.

"You sent for the fiddler?" she asked, covering her breasts with her arms. "Aren't you afraid he'll tell Clara?"

"Oh, my dear Petunia." Thomas came up behind her to rub her back and kiss her neck, his voice a low purr. "Surely you don't think she's unaware? Besides, Mr. Schweissenstein is not so foolish as to jeopardize his position here. Isn't that right, boy?"

More cool anger curdled in my veins, my grip on my violin becoming dangerously tight. The bastard didn't merely beat Clara; he went behind her back as well. I decided not to argue, nor correct his fascinating interpretation of my name. He was right; if I angered him, I would be back on the street. Thomas might even be able to ensure I became unwelcome at the club. I would never see Clara again, nor attain answers about what this club was, nor have any more prospects than I'd had weeks ago.

So, I did as I was told. I played for Thomas and his guest, torturous though it was. I selected a jaunty, vicious song, with a tune I could channel my hatred into.

I despised Thomas. Not just for his abuse and infidelity, but for having everything I wanted and squandering it. Thomas had come from old money, the owning class, and had not worked a day in his life. He'd done nothing to earn the wealth he'd inherited, and didn't appreciate a cent of it.

Meanwhile, I'd fought for my continued existence all my life with nothing to show for it. I had no assets to offer women: no wealth, no home. Even my body was too small to offer substantial protection. I was a failure of a man, and Thomas was my superior, though he had done nothing to earn it.

How wonderful it must have been to be wealthy. To reach out and grasp whatever and whoever you desired. To be one of the only people in the world with this elusive power. I hated them, but I also wanted to be one of them. Better than them. Richer, stronger, more respected, more beautiful. I wanted to make them feel the way they made me feel: like dogs at my feet, barking when I willed it. And as Thomas laughed and splashed his play toy without a care in the world, it was impossible not to feel that he deserved this fate most of all. I wished that my violin bow was a blade, and that Thomas's enormous bath was filled not with water, but his blood.

◆

When a week had passed, I traveled with the Rifes back to the Immortalist Club. They provided me with suitable attire and a mask to call my own, but Thomas was quick to remind me that I was still a Fledgling. "It will be some time before you can be a Collector," he said.

He brought with him a covered bird cage, and insisted on holding onto it himself in the coach rather than allowing me or one of the servants to carry it. Clara seemed keen to distance herself from the little cage, inching as far away from it as she could while Thomas whispered to whatever lay within. If any bird was inside, it was remarkably quiet.

When we arrived, a masked man was waiting for us in the theatre room, standing by the great stone basin, already half-full with blood. He held out a knife, and Thomas pricked his finger before handing the knife to Clara. Both left tiny drops of blood in the basin. The acolyte stared at me with his head slightly tilted, as if challenging me to do better, but I merely pricked my finger as they had.

We were then led to what looked like the nave of a church, with a vaulted ceiling and rows of pews. Most of those who sat were masked, but a few were not, and wore the same white tunics as I had my first week. Mother Pursha stood before us all, smiling as we took our seats.

"I'm delighted to see so many new faces," she said. "More who have decided to commit to the teachings of this order. You, who would learn the truths about this world and what lies beyond it. You, who wish to be prepared for what happens when the War in Heaven spreads here to Earth."

The audience remained silent, but Pursha let the dust settle before resuming. "We are on the precipice of a new era. An era of night. An era when the sins of the world are punished with a reckoning beyond comprehension. There are those who will cling to the desires of their mortal flesh and suffer greatly, but others, like yourselves, are willing to accept the truth. I can personally promise that you'll be rewarded for this courage."

It was nonsense, I thought; the same apocalyptic silliness that any religion peddled to control you through fear. Still, a chill licked up my spine like an icy tongue.

Later, I joined the Rifes and the other masked strangers on the second-floor balcony to watch new initiates cluster into the theatre room. The performance was as it had been before, giving me another opportunity to search for signs that any of it was fake. But even from up here on the balcony, it all seemed alarmingly authentic. We then returned to the social room with the painting of the hands reaching up from the endless red sea, where the established members gathered for dull, drunken chats, none of which seemed to involve the club's spiritual teachings. Instead, the members shared gossip and whispered predictions about who would next make Prominent, or which Fledglings might make Collector.

At this point we moved on, Thomas leading Clara and I to a bright red door flanked by masked guards who nodded at Thomas before opening it for us. Clara tensed, arms tight against her torso, and it didn't take me long to gather why.

The red door led to a series of candlelit hallways leading to all manner of strange rooms, and most of the guests who wandered through them were naked save for their masks. Many were fornicating on divans, beds, armchairs, and even the floor. Others huddled naked around enormous platters of chocolates, fruit, and malodorous cheese, gobbling the offerings with visible delight.

I might have been excited to have finally reached the long-awaited orgy room, but Clara kept her gaze down, clearly uncomfortable. Thomas's head rotated freely, observing the people on display: a woman who wore only gloves and stockings, her mask extending to an enormous poofy wig; an old man, body strangely full of life, chasing a girl who wore a deer mask through the hallways; a cabal of naked harpists, who were honestly quite good. Many of the bodies were wrinkled and gnarled, not the sort of people I'd have wanted to see in the nude, but sprinkled throughout were women of such youth and beauty that it was difficult not to stare.

Most of the wallpaper was dark red, but we eventually reached a chamber where a single mural stretched across every wall, making it feel as if we'd stepped into a strange landscape. It portrayed a ground made up of vague, lumpy shapes, rather than a flat track of dirt. Only upon closer inspection did I realize that they were countless bodies stitched together, all of them screaming under a scorched red sky.

The vista chilled me, for it brought to mind only one place: Hell. My throat closed, the memory of my father's death returning to the forefront of my mind. It was becoming harder and harder to pretend that the succubus had only been my imagination.

But if that was true, what did that make this club?

A large black door awaited in the center of the adjacent wall, incorporated into the mural itself. It was flanked by guards just as the red one had been. The black statue of a great winged goat loomed over it, growing out from the wall like part of the mural had come to life.

"Stay here," Thomas purred to me. "Enjoy yourself."

He was still carrying his birdcage, his other hand wrapped around Clara's waist, steering her to the black door. I was left alone in this strange place, a faint sense of nausea filling my throat.

I wandered the dark red halls, conscious of my every step. Was I in danger here? Some masked faces turned to stare at me in a way that made me feel unwelcome rather than lusted for. Others ignored me entirely, their gazes always pointedly averted, even when I stared for several moments at a time. Was it the fact that I was still clothed? Or did they know me for the stranger I was, even with the mask?

A woman sat in a chair not far away, nude save for her mask. Her body was perfectly endowed, with unusually large areolas, the hair shaved from her womanhood. My body tensed, excitement bubbling within me, and I willed her to look at me as I approached. But she did not meet my gaze, even when I was only a foot away.

Then someone pushed past me, so hard my shoulder ached: a tall, muscular man who stank of expensive perfume, his muscles glistening in the firelight. The woman immediately looked up at him, lifting her hand in invitation, and he took it, leading her from the room.

Any arousal I might have felt died. I was nothing to them. Furniture, just as with Thomas.

When Remy had told me of the orgies, I'd imagined myself indulging in them gleefully, but now that I was here, I felt only a profound sense of inadequacy. Not only was I painfully ill-equipped to face whatever dark powers churned at the heart of this club, I was also beneath these people in general. They knew it. Might even be able to smell it, given how long I'd been living in the streets, no matter how thoroughly I'd tried to scrub myself since moving to Rife Manor. Perhaps if I'd been born wealthy, I might have carried myself with more confidence. Perhaps if I'd been born taller, they would have come to me. And perhaps if I'd been stronger, I could have saved my father, and none of this would have happened to begin with.

A feeling of profound loneliness spread through me, eclipsing the fear, worsening with every crowded chamber I poked my head into. Each new room reinforced the sense that I did not belong, and never would, no matter what I did to distinguish myself.

"Cayyyleb?" came a slurred voice, and I turned as a masked young man approached me, his movements jerky, his limbs skinny, his little cock bouncing with every step.

"Remy?" I asked, recognizing the voice.

"It *is* you! Oops." His fingers hit his lips. "We're not supposed to say names here, are we? Well, welcome to the red wing I suppose."

Remy was twitchy and odd, clearly on some intoxicant. I doubted he was the only one.

"Not letting it all out, then? Are you ashamed of your body?" He tilted his head. "Or is it... do you feel like you were born into the wrong body?"

I recalled him asking me something similar when we were children, so many years ago. "*What if your body was not your body? What would you be, if you could become any-thing?*" I think I must have told him a dragon or some such nonsense. But I remembered something like disappoint-ment flashing in Remy's eyes, like I'd misunderstood him. Then he'd changed the subject instead of answering the question himself.

Now, I thought I had a better idea what he meant. "I thought I'd grow up to be stronger," I admitted. "Maybe a bit taller. Bigger arms. A bit less gut."

"Huh." In the holes of his mask, Remy's eyes shifted. It was not an expression of disapproval, or even disappoint-ment. "Well, I feel like that some days myself. But everyone else here is naked, so..." He shrugged dramatically. "When in Rome."

I had the sense that here, in this crowded wing full of people just as intoxicated as himself, Remy felt as alone as I did; uncomfortable, somehow, in a way that went beyond gentlemanly prudishness. Then a woman grabbed his hand and began tugging him away.

"Are you all right?" I asked.

"Never better!" he said, too quickly. Yes, of course he was, if it meant he didn't have to talk about it. He let the woman pull him into a chamber and was lost to the roaring crowd.

I circled back to the mural hall, just in time to see Clara walking out of the black door. Thomas was not at her side.

She made her way into a large room and sat on an unoccupied couch. When a nude, masked gentleman came up to her, she waved him away.

Something like relief flooded through me. I sat down beside her, and as she turned to see me, her shoulders relaxed a little. Around us, others continued to fornicate on the furniture and walls, moaning in ecstasy, but Clara and I merely sat there.

"Are you all right, my lady?" I asked, having to talk loudly to be heard over the moaning and music.

Clara hesitated before nodding. "We must wait for my husband. Fortunately, most who are here understand by now that I prefer not to join in." She looked over me, eyes lowering and rising through the holes of her mask. "I'd expected you to, though. Surprised you're even still clothed."

I forced a grim smile out of habit, even though she couldn't see it. "I don't expect anyone here wants me that way," I admitted.

"Oh, Caleb." Her voice was sympathetic, far more so than I'd expected. "Care not what these people think of you. All they recognize is nobility of the name. They cannot recognize nobility of the soul, for they have none themselves."

Soft wings fluttered in my chest. "You think my soul is noble?" It was not a word anyone had ever used to describe me before.

"It must be. Your music is an extension of your soul, is it not?" Her eyes glistened in the candlelight, visible through the holes in her mask. "The world could stand to have more men like you, Caleb. Ones with decency and kindness."

Her voice was nervous, almost tingly, and I realized she was sliding her hand slowly across the sofa toward me. I stared, afraid of what might result from taking it, but in the end I was compelled. Clara's hand trembled in my grasp before settling, and squeezing for good measure. I exhaled in relief. I felt much safer there with her beside me. Like I belonged. Like I wasn't some mangled street dog who would be better off being put down.

It only made my heart all the heavier.

"And... Thomas?" I asked. "What of men like him?"

Clara's shoulders sank.

"I apologize," I said quickly, but she shook her head, a forced smile in her voice.

"It is fine. I simply read too many novels growing up. Romances of men who would fight through Hell itself for the women they loved. It was hard not to hope for the same. But women of my station rarely have the luxury of choosing who they wed, and I've made my peace with that."

She withdrew her hand, leaving my own to grasp nothing but air. I wished that I'd never brought him up at all.

"I'm glad you're here, Caleb," she said, looking down again. "It would be all the more awful to sit here alone, rather than with a friend."

"Of course, my lady." I looked back at the entrance to the hall with the mural, and the black door waiting under the statue of the goat. "What was in that room, anyway?"

Before Clara could answer, a new voice cut in, startling me.

"How fortunate for you, Clara." Pursha was suddenly beside us, maskless, wearing her usual black habit. "To be allowed into that room at all is honor enough. But when your fine husband comes out, there is a very high chance he will have been accepted for the next rank within our order: Thrall."

Even with her face covered, Clara's stiffness gave away her concern.

"Oh, it will be such a wonderful boon to your household!" said Pursha. "He shall receive the first taste of what we offer before being taken under the tutelage of a Prominent. A gift from God Himself!"

Pursha leaned in close and whispered more into Clara's ear. I had to strain to make it out, and even then, some words were muffled.

"I'm afraid the Prominents do not feel that you're quite ready to ascend to this level yourself, and as such there will be some things your husband will not yet be authorized to tell you. I would ask you to respect this and understand that it is only because you are not yet ready. But do not think we are taking him away from you. Your husband is still very much yours. He is simply ascending to a position that will reap endless rewards for you both. So do not fret, my child. Celebrate! The night is young."

Then Pursha drifted away into the crowd, and Clara's shoulders sank even lower.

Thomas returned not long after, holding himself even more pompously than usual. Indeed, when we took the coach back to Rife Manor and removed our masks, I noticed that some of the creases of his face seemed to have smoothed out. There was a queer glimmer in his eyes, something bright and hungry. It was only then that I realized that he had not brought the birdcage back with him.

"How do you feel?" Clara asked.

Thomas smiled. "Absolutely wonderful."

CHAPTER FIVE

TRANSCENDENCE

CLARA SUMMONED ME THE very next evening. When I came to her room, a bespeckled man with a leather bag was on his way out. A doctor? I hurried in to find Clara lying in bed, a fresh bandage covering half her face and Henrietta holding her hand. "Do you think he believed me?" Clara was whispering.

"It doesn't matter whether he believed you, my lady. You said your truth. You merely fell down the stairs."

Clara turned her head, squinting with the one visible eye. "Is that our dear violinist?" Her voice was breathy, every word a labor.

My hands rattled at the sight of her. "My lady," I said, kneeling.

"Henrietta, may I have a moment alone with Mr. Schwartzenfeld?"

Henrietta gave me a piercing look, her jaw becoming tight—silently telling me to be very careful. "Of course, my lady."

It was a moment after she left before Clara was able to muster up the strength to say more. "I'm very clumsy, I'm afraid," she said quickly. "Please. Play me a song. That one from your first day here. Would you do that for me?"

"He did this. Didn't he?" My voice throbbed with cold, quiet rage. I was beyond the ability to control it; beyond any desire to lie.

"It was me. It was the stairs." Clara's voice had the shaking quality of someone who knew their lie was painfully obvious. "It's not...he's..."

I went to her bed and closed my hand around her own. I knew it was an enormous risk, but I needed her to know that I was there for her. Her hand was soft in my palm, and as delicate as a ripe peach. How dare Sir Thomas take advantage of that delicacy.

"You don't need to lie to me, my lady. Your secrets are safe."

She exhaled, voice shakier than ever, as if throttled by tears. A moment passed before she opened her mouth again. "He's stronger now. Stronger than I'm used to. It was just a single slap. Is... is he still out there?"

I looked out the window. It was dark, but I could just barely make out Thomas spreading birdseed across the barren field. He kept looking up, neck circling, as if searching the roof. I backed from the window before he could see me, returning my attention to Clara. "My lady, if there's anything I can do...if I can protect you, if I can make this stop..."

"No." It was not a word so much as a squeak. "Please. Do not cross my husband." Her hand trembled within mine. "Mr. Schwar—Caleb... you do not know how helpful your music has been for me this past week. If something were to happen to you on my account..."

I fixed her with a confident smile and closed her hand. "Nothing will happen, my lady. I promise."

I played *Ashen Threnody* for her. Then I went downstairs to prepare.

Thomas Rife was sleeping just a few floors up, and there was nothing to stop me from killing the bastard.

I skulked through the hallway, a kitchen knife in my hand. By now it was late, and so dark that I wouldn't even know it if I was being followed. Still, I had everything I needed to take charge of my destiny. A few quick strikes to the throat and the brute would be dead.

Of course, Clara, that beautiful angel, would be in bed with him. And when he screamed, she would wake up and see me. Logic told me that I should wear a mask, lest she report me to the authorities.

But I didn't want to hide who I was. I wanted her to know that I was the one who had saved her. I imagined her thanking me, and taking me as her lover, and eventually walking up the aisle to wed me, and kissing my lowly servant lips before her entire family: finally showing the love that I knew, hoped, or just desperately wanted to believe was there.

And if I merely ended up in jail instead, so be it. I refused to be a coward. I refused to watch Clara die as I had my father.

As I passed a window, I was met with a jagged sound, like claws scraping against the glass. The drapes were drawn, though, and I was in no mood to slow down and investigate. The bedroom was only a few feet away. I opened the door slowly, my throat dry with anxiety. Moonlight shone in through the drapes, ghostly and blue, too dim to clearly see the bed.

My hands trembled. I'd told myself that it was time; that I just had to face the hangman and do it, come what may. Clara deserved to be free, and even if she did end up hating me, even if she reported me to the police, at least she wouldn't be in such pain anymore. I stepped into the room.

"Henrietta? Is that you?"

The soft whisper emitted from the other side of the bed, gentle as a stream. The blankets shifted. She was turning to look. With the moonlight shining through the window, I would be just barely visible.

It was only then that my eyes adjusted enough to see only one shape in the bed. Thomas wasn't there.

I stepped backwards, out into the hallway, and pressed my back against the wall.

"Henrietta?" Clara repeated.

I considered meowing. I could do a fairly convincing imitation of Clara's cat Grumpsy. But for all I knew, Grumpsy might be in there with her already.

Instead, I hurried down the hall, and quickly noticed light coming from under a door to my left. Thomas's office. Would it be worth the risk of going in? It might be wiser to arrange a boating accident or spook his horse while he was out riding, so that it would throw him off and trample his head. But what if during my scheming, Thomas hit Clara again? What if he hit her so badly that she did not survive?

No, it had to be tonight. I opened the door and went in, hiding the knife behind me. Thomas sat behind a desk, scribbling away with a quill. He didn't even look up as I closed the door and plopped into the chair before his desk.

"I never gave you permission to enter my office," he said, voice calm and unconcerned. His eyes remained focused on the parchment before him, upon which he scrawled strange black symbols. A book was open to the side of his desk, showing many others. An occult text, I was sure.

"I never agreed to work for a man who beats his wife," I said.

"Have it your way. Tomorrow morning you'd better be gone." He finally looked up to glower at me. "This was always an absurd idea."

"I don't find that to be an acceptable solution," I said.

Thomas's face was still; an unimpressed bust of a man, so apathetic that I might as well have not spoken at all.

"You are a wretched man, Mr. Rife," I said. "Lady Clara is a kind, beautiful, tender soul. You do not deserve her. I demand you cease these acts of violence against her."

The hint of a smile cracked through Thomas Rife's face. He rose to his full height, dwarfing me, and fear at last coiled around my chest like a snake. With a quivering hand I extended the knife. "Stop right there," I said—then jumped from the sound of something hitting the window. A muffled squawk echoed through the room. Murky white shapes fluttered on the other side of the glass: strange, thin white birds.

Thomas walked slowly around the table. I got up from the chair, backing away, but he kept coming, slow and steady, his beefy fists at his hips, a cheery smirk on his face. Then, instead of coming for me, he approached the window.

"The Immortalist Club is very fond of ferreting out traitors," he said. "Vandals who are joining only to spy on them, or share their secrets to the unworthy. And I'm learning that there are many such secrets."

He opened the window, and the two white birds flew in and perched upon his shoulders. Their heads were bird skulls: eye sockets empty, flesh stripped away. Their wings had tattered feathers, but no flesh beneath them.

"What the Hell?" I whispered, horrified and confused, my hand rattling so badly that I dropped my knife. My back hit the door, but before I could turn and flee through it, Thomas was upon me.

"I'm going to enjoy what's coming very much," he said, pulling back his fist.

—◆—

When I opened my eyes, it was to pain: impossibly sharp, indescribably wretched *pain*. It was a pain so awful, so agonizing, so dizzying that none of my past injuries could have prepared me for it. I couldn't think. The pain was a storm, like a cyclone of my own blood swirling all around me, with my stomach in the greatest agony of all.

I tried to scream, but my mouth was gagged, and tasted of salt, copper, and bile. My vision was blurry, but I was vaguely aware that I wasn't on solid ground; my feet dangled free. My arms were stretched out to either side as if I were crucified. I was also naked... but as my vision came into focus, I realized that my clothes weren't all that had been stripped away.

My stomach was open, the skin peeled off and folded back. Red entrails were arcing out of me, festooning the wall to either side of me like garlands. Again I tried to scream, but again the sound was muffled by the bloody gag, and my jaws ached from the strain of being kept open. Blood and drool dribbled down my chin.

Below me was a stage, and dozens of masked people were clustered around it. The Immortalists... I was back in their domain, elevated over their stage. Ritualistic chanting echoed throughout the room, the different voices joining together to create a wall of sadistic white noise. I writhed, but my palms were pierced to the wall. I had to be hanging under the painting of the satyr. Maybe if I pulled hard enough, I could yank myself free and fall down to the floor, but no matter how hard I struggled, I was not strong enough. All I did was dig the nails deeper into my palms.

Below me, a naked woman had gotten up onto the stage, her head covered by a disproportionately large goat mask. She appeared to have wings: huge, sweeping bat-like things, but these were not fake like the mask was. They flapped and stretched just as a bat's might, their ends curling inwards and then out again.

She danced as my blood rained down upon her, her movements slow and graceful, matching the beat of an unseen drum. Her breasts swung, and her wings whistled through the air. My head throbbed, so overwhelmed it felt like a crack was running through it. I wanted to believe this was a nightmare; that this was impossible. My guts were outside of my body, and more of me was falling out with every passing second, and I couldn't even scream because of the bloody gag.

Caws joined in with the chanting, and I became aware of Thomas's two crow skeletons circling above me like vultures. They began pecking at my guts and open wounds, sending more blood gushing down, painting the goat-masked woman with a torrent of crimson rain. A masked man joined her on the stage, and undid the sash of his robe to reveal his wrinkled, corpulent body. He went to the woman, and she lowered to her knees, still moving in a rhythmic fashion. More figures joined them on the table as well, more gnarled men and even some women as well, all becoming entangled as they made love, their skin dappled with my blood. Some opened their mouths wide, revealing sharp fangs. They stuck their tongues out to taste my falling blood, grinning and gargling in delight. They were eating me, drinking of me, making love beneath me...

One of my entrails snapped free from my body as one of the skelecrows pulled hard. The other began fighting for it, and the two began snapping at each end, slashing the pink tissue to ribbons. Vomit rose up my throat and flooded my mouth, only to hit the gag and have nowhere to go but back down. I choked, unable to breathe. I was drowning, my clogged throat feeling a repulsive itch, my stomach empty and yet so full of pain, the room echoing with moans and squelching and the cawing of the undead birds.

The dancer was now on her back. Her goat mask had fallen away, and I saw that it was Mother Pursha. Without her habit, her sea of black hair had been revealed, along with a pair of long, gnarled horns, like those of a ram. As the man rutted into her, she looked up to meet my eyes and gleefully licked my blood off her lips before reaching to stroke a man at her side.

Then the man rutting into her pulled off his mask: Thomas, looking at me with a cruel grin of his own, revealing monstrous fangs.

This time, it was a scream of wrath that the gag muffled. It was as if every ounce of blood I'd lost had been replaced with rage. Clara was in danger. Even more than before. I had to kill him...had to save her, no matter what.

The bone crows came for my eyes, their sharp beaks each piercing one like daggers, blinding me. Wet plops filled my ears as they pulled my eyeballs free.

The next stabs were into my throat, and then I was gone.

PART II

SCRAWLED ON THE WALLS

CHAPTER SIX

THE RED SHORE

L OOK UP. WE'RE OUT of space, so let's switch to the walls. Perhaps my blood will help cut down on the sounds echoing from beyond this room. It's a mad thought, but please allow me this one delusion.

My skull aches from the countless screams penetrating the walls around me, but it's better this way. Better, because when my neighbors become quiet, it's easier to make out the sobbing: an all-too-familiar voice, crying as if right beside me, full of such utter pain that I'd cut off my own ears to silence it. They knew what they were doing when they chose that voice. Oh yes, they knew that out of any, this was the one that would drive me to madness.

These walls need decorating anyway, so why not turn them red with my tale?

It's rather fitting, since an endless salty red was also all that I saw when I first fell down to the world below. I was submerged in it, choking on it, my open mouth flooded with its metallic taste. It tunneled into my nostrils, clung to my lungs, clotted against my skin, and stung my eyes. I felt like I was drowning, but I didn't die. I was merely caught in the perpetual *feeling* of drowning; of desperately gasping for air, and finding none, as liquid filled places it was not meant to fill.

I was naked. My body was whole, but covered with bruises and scars. There were vague, murky shapes around me: the dark silhouettes of other people, thrashing in the endless blood. They were as naked as I. Some had pieces of their flesh hanging in strips or were covered in gaping wounds. More descended around me, falling from some unseen place.

Others were being pulled down. Bubbles escaped their mouths, their screams taken by the sea. Something tickled the soles of my feet, reaching for me...

I kicked my feet and thrashed my arms to rise higher, ascending through the red water. Enormous black tendrils lashed up around me, barely visible in the crimson sea. I swam higher and higher until I'd passed them, and broke through the surface at last. I gasped for air, howling desperately in and out, and swam madly across the surface, lest the thing below catch me. It was dark, but not so dark that I couldn't see. Enormous distant flames flickered in the horizon.

Thousands of miles above me was a black stone ceiling that spanned farther than I could see. I was underground, far from the light of day. More figures were falling down through tiny holes scattered across that great stone sky, and a choir of screams echoed through the salty air.

I continued thrashing away from where I'd fallen, my hair dripping more salty blood into my eyes. The red water went on for as far as I could see, a veritable ocean peppered with small black islets. A splash erupted several yards away as another figure crashed into the blood, and more wailing bodies soon followed.

Then a new shape swooped down, black enough that I didn't spot it until its claws had already hooked into me. It lifted me high into the air and out of the blood. I screamed in pain and tried to break free, but the thing's enormous claws were fully embedded in my shoulders, their bloody tips sticking out through the front. It was like a huge bat, each wing three meters wide, its body so scrawny I saw the jutting of its bones. It was mostly bald, its skin covered with scars. It had no eyes, and its huge, drooling mouth was outfitted with ever-clicking mandibles.

I kept writhing to free myself, even as we ascended high enough that a fall would break every bone in my body. Another giant bat swooped above the one that had me and bit into its wings, perhaps hoping to steal me. The first bat-thing dropped me, and as I fell, the two beasts collided above me in an aerial battle. My ears rang as I plummeted, blood rising to my head even as it gushed from the wounds in my shoulders. Worse, below me was the shore of a black isle, and there was no time to veer away.

I crashed into stone. Cracks reverberated through my entire body: fresh, sharp pain rupturing through me as my limbs crunched, crumpled, and popped from their sockets. One of my ribs was stabbing out through my chest. My neck had been snapped, rendering my head immobile. I couldn't even scream.

And yet, despite all the pain, I was aware and conscious. I had been injured in ways that should have killed me, but even after hours had passed, I remained.

The answer, of course, was obvious. I wasn't dying because I was already dead. Thomas and his club had killed me, sacrificing me to whatever darkness they served. And it didn't take much imagination to realize where I'd ended up.

It was not a conclusion I reached willingly; indeed, the thought was almost as painful as my wounds. I'd never wanted to believe in life after death. It had always struck me as a preposterous fairy tale that people clung to, to feel better about the nothingness waiting on the other side. The demon who'd claimed my father's life had seemed no less illusory, her sheer impossibility providing further proof that the human mind was fallible.

But there was no denying the dark world around me, nor the grievous wounds that I should have never been able to survive.

I faded into unconsciousness, and when I next opened my eyes, the pain was numb. My limbs seemed to have cracked back into place, and the torn flesh had repaired itself. But my skin was stained with blood, and the ghosts of old wounds raked through my body.

Blood is not like water. It's thicker, stickier, and full of strange textures and clots. Clean water brings and preserves life, while blood beyond the vein reeks of death. It does not simply drip off you as water does; if not immediately washed away, it clings to everything it touches, a permanent mark. So it was that I remained coated with crimson residue, baptized in the putrid crucible of Hell.

A loud horn sounded in the distance, and was joined by the dull thunder of many feet, or perhaps hooves. My body ached, reluctant to move, but the tumultuous rumbling was only getting louder. With a groan, I forced my frail, naked body to its feet and turned around to see blurry figures in the distance: dozens of naked men and women charging toward me. And behind them...

My throat closed. Riders formed a line across the horizon, a line that was growing closer with each second. An enormous plume of dust rose behind them like a great black storm. While the figures were distant, even from here they did not seem human. This was no mortal legion, but some unfathomable army of the damned.

Before I knew it, an old man had already passed me by, wheezing, his flesh covered with dirt and scars. Another loud horn sounded, and I bolted along with him, the rocks sharp against my feet. I tried heading back into the bloody water, but huge tendrils erupted from those crimson waves and slapped against the shore, tips landing inches from my toes. Hook-shaped teeth stuck out from the suction cups, eager to taste my flesh. There was nothing to do but keep running along the shore after the old man.

The other naked souls caught up with us, but the cavalry was getting closer and closer. It was a motley group of hundreds, and none looked entirely human. Many had horns, and a few also had wings. Some wore horrific beast skull masks. Others grinned with sharp-looking teeth...like Thomas's, I thought, my gut souring. Some of the cavalry rode horses, while others sat atop massive goats or monstrous hounds.

A caged wagon full of people trundled in the back, but other riders carried huge rope nets containing people who were pressed tightly against one another. I glimpsed riders punching one another, trying to slow each other down. This was not an army but rather hundreds of competing individuals, each trying to claim whatever bounty they could.

Something whistled past my head: a spear, thrown by a horned woman who rode an enormous goat. The spear landed in a young boy running to my right, and he wailed in pain as he bit the dirt, only for another spear to hit his head. As the rider passed, she lifted him up and tossed him into a basket at the goat's rear before throwing another spear at a man up ahead.

Racked with pain as I was, every step felt wretched and deliberate, and every heaving breath reminded me of the blood still bubbling inside my lungs. Some of the other runners split away, heading into a forest of great white trees. I joined them, thinking it might be easier to escape our pursuers with cover. It was very cold here, and the thundering of the cavalry remained at our heels. Worse, my own body was failing me. The pain from my last death, the fresh cuts on the soles of my feet, and my general exhaustion were simply too great to bear.

I came to a stop, wheezing for air, my muscles throbbing with every breath I took. I glanced over my shoulder, checking if the cavalry had caught up, but it was impossible to see through the pale foliage. Only then did I look at the trees long enough to notice that they weren't made of bark, but rather...bone.

"W-wait!" shouted a voice. "Turn back!"

I turned to see a man tied to one of the trees, a red sigil drawn on his forehead. Other trees had bodies strapped to them as well, their heads hanging, unconscious. Each of them had the same red sigil on their foreheads. A single voice's incomprehensible chanting echoed through the glade.

"Get out!" shouted the tree man, his eyes bulging. "Get out before the necromancer comes ba—"

Then he screamed, and he and the other captives began to vibrate. Even the bodies that had appeared dead stirred, their eyes and jaws wrenching open from some unholy force. As the chanting became more intense, each body's skin tore, cuts appearing all over. The man who had addressed me screamed as more and more of his skin peeled away.

It should have revealed red meat, but the thing that hung there was almost as white as the tree. But it was not a skeleton either. It had bone musculature, with ball-and-socket joints like a mannequin. The man's head had become a skull, and his chest was not a rib cage, but rather an entire torso with solid bone where meat should have been. The same was true of the other bodies. The chains broke away and the bone monsters fell upon the piles of discarded flesh, only to rise back up as if compelled by strings. I shivered, immediately reminded of Thomas and his birds.

The chanting ceased, and a cloaked figure lurched toward me through the woods. "Ah, a fresh new soul," croaked a reedy voice. "What do you say to becoming my puppet for eternity?"

Panic surged through me and I bolted again, deeper into the bone woods, only to come to a high cliff leading down to the shore. I saw it too late and tumbled off, hitting stone after stone on my way down. My vision blurred, my bones cracked, and my limbs snapped in the wrong directions yet again. The last thing I was aware of was crashing back into the crimson sea.

◆

Once again, I opened my eyes. I had washed up onto another black shore. I don't know how far the crimson tide had carried me, but it appeared to be a smaller island than before, and I did not see another land mass nearby.

As before, my body's worst wounds were healed: the limbs were bent back into shape, and I seemed able to turn my head, maybe even stand. But throbbing aches quaked through my skull, and I was covered with open cuts and stinging scars, many of which had flies burrowing into them. I tried to swat them away and brush them off, but many just burrowed in deeper.

Above me loomed an enormous cathedral-like building, which looked to be made out of bones. On the wall above its front doors was a massive skull, formed of countless normal-sized skulls affixed together. Dozens of men, women, and even children hung screaming from the outer walls just as I had in the Immortalist Club. Sickly thin bat beasts crawled along its side and wove between the hanging people, sniffing them before gnawing off ribbons of flesh. Other prisoners were being gorged upon by enormous black crows.

Strangest of all were the crosses. Everywhere I looked, I saw bones arranged into Christ's symbol. I was baffled. I knew this was Hell. It could be nothing else. So, who was building cross after cross with the bones of the dead?

Such questions seemed of little consequence just then, however. I had to flee. It wouldn't be long before one of those beasts spotted me. I sat up, only for a spear to lower before me, inches from my throat.

It was a satyr, riding atop a huge hound-like creature with a mouth large enough to swallow my entire head whole. It stared at me with bright red eyes and drooled, its blood-stained jowls lifting to reveal foot-long teeth. The rider let out a low whistle, reminding the beast who its master was.

Ram horns protruded from his head, his feet were hooves, and his nose and mouth seemed strangely pushed out. This was not a mask like what Pursha had worn, but the genuine artifact, with the same disquieting horizontal pupils as the satyr painting at the club.

Most troubling of all was the all too human intelligence in the rider's gaze. A crucifix hung around his throat, a tiny Jesus Christ hanging on it. The satyr smiled at me in satisfaction, maybe even relief.

Then he lifted a net.

"Wait—" I choked out as the net hit me. I scrambled, tried to claw myself free, but only became tangled. Sharp pain exploded in my rump as the rider stabbed me with his spear. He chuckled, circling me on his hound, whose paws, I realized, looked like human hands with bear-like claws instead of fingernails.

I screamed and thrashed but could not get free. The rider slammed the wooden handle of his spear against the back of my head. The net weighed me down, biting into my wounds. My struggles were useless.

The satyr kicked his hound with thorny spurs and it sped up the hill, yanking me along after it. Every jagged rock in my path only opened more of me: slicing my cheeks, bashing my nose until it was flat, and cutting up my arms.

Thomas did this. That was the thought that repeated through my mind over and over. Thomas and his cult had murdered me. Thomas had brought me here. Thomas was the one who deserved to be suffering, not me.

This I vowed: I would send Thomas Rife here in my place. Whatever pain I endured, he would suffer tenfold. I did not yet know how I would achieve this, but my very bones hungered for vengeance. And Clara, poor Clara, she still needed to be saved from him.

The satyr dragged me across a shabby wooden drawbridge and through the cathedral's bone gates. Inside, the walls were either covered in bones or formed from them. The roof had crumbled away, but a staircase led up to other stories, each of them containing huge cells full of naked mortal souls covered with open wounds and fetid scabs. Most of them shivered, for it was terribly cold, the shore's wind nipping at us through the open gates and ceiling. In the center of the bottom floor was a stockade, its iron stained with red crust.

The satyr brought me to the first cell's door, then dismounted to pull me free from the net.

"Let me go," I hissed, trying to swing at him, but he kicked me hard in the ribs. Pain crackled through my entire body. My agonized grunt was barely audible over the choir of screams and crashing waves.

"I'm gonna need you to go on in, lad," said the satyr, smiling down at me.

"Wait," I forced out through clenched teeth. "I'm not supposed to be here." Yes, that was what I had to do: focus on my rage. It would keep me alive...or as close to alive as I could be.

The satyr lowered his spear to my throat. "If you don't go in, I can make things very miserable for you."

"I'm already dead, aren't I?" My voice cracked, tears joining the blood.

"You think that means you can't suffer?" The satyr's goat lips pulled back to reveal large yellow teeth. "I can cut off your cock and make you eat it. I can bend you over and punt your arse until it bleeds. I can eat you one piece at a time to make you experience every inch of my intestines. You would regenerate from my feces and stink of me for years."

The cell door remained open, the satyr's dog growling beside it. A dozen or so men remained inside, naked, terror in their eyes. They might have been enough to overwhelm the satyr, but not a single soul ran or attacked. Some looked away. Others had the blank stares of terrified animals.

I was weak, barely able to move, and even at my full strength, I would have been no match for this monster and his hound. But I was also furious at the thought that I'd been murdered. Rage blinded me as much as the blood dripping into my eyes. So I spit on the satyr's hoof and growled, "Do your worst, you goat-faced fuck."

The satyr grabbed me by the throat, his thumb hooking into a wound. I wailed, but that was nothing compared to the agony that followed. He dragged me in front of the other men and shoved my face hard against the rocky ground. I saw nothing but blood as my face hit stone over and over. Then the satyr lifted me up into the air and punched his fist through my chest. That huge hand crashed through my ribs, shattering them, before pulling something free, filling me with a sense of something wrong, something missing. The satyr's hand was coming out through my back, chunks of my shattered ribs sticking to his hairy wrist, his gnarled fingers clutching my still-beating heart. I could feel his forearm plugging the hole he'd formed, his wiry hair tickling my insides.

The pain was unimaginable. I wanted to beg for death, but I could not speak, could not think, could not even remember that I'd died already. And even then, more fresh pierces of pain bloomed across my arm as the hound bit down and pulled, the skin stretching and tearing to reveal scarlet musculature, until it ripped free from my shoulder. The hound inhaled my flesh, and even though the arm was severed, I still felt each and every laceration as it tore all the way to the bone.

The satyr pulled his arm back out through the sore tunnel of flesh he'd made in my chest. He held my beating heart before my eyes and squeezed until it exploded, blood dripping between his fingers. Even then he was not done, for he bit off my ear and swallowed it whole, and I felt every moment of its passage down the bastard's throat. I heard the beating of his heart, and the repulsive, gassy gurgles of his stomach, and crawling sounds like an army of wet worms. Then came a burning sensation as his stomach acid dissolved my ear's tender cartilage.

Then the satyr dropped what remained of me onto the cold floor. The hound, having reduced my arm to bones, closed in on my leg.

⸻ ◆ ⸻

What might have been a month later, I sat quivering in a corner of the cell. I couldn't smell myself without smelling the satyr and his hound. My skin, while fully reformed, felt like a fetid, moldy shirt. My throat was chapped and dry, but there was no water anywhere. I was so hungry that I could have sworn I was starving to death, but nothing killed me. Not for long.

The floor was riddled with bloody puddles, some fresh and wet, others dry and sticky against my feet. There were a dozen or so men in the cell with me. One leered at me like he was considering eating me. Another huddled in the corner, tugging his manhood, trying not to meet any-one's eyes. Several of them prayed, endlessly calling out to God in various tongues. But most just hung their heads, as if they'd long since given up.

Right then, I felt ready to give up, too. I wanted to die; *truly* die. To no longer exist in any world that might hurt me.

"How...do we...make it stop?" I whispered.

No one responded.

"How do we make it stop?!" I repeated, my voice breaking even more as I tried to raise it. "How do we just...die?"

I looked at the man beside me. Then at another. Nei-ther looked back.

Finally, one spoke. It was a bald old man with dark skin, a scruffy white beard, and a huge scar beneath his eye. "We cannot die," he said, sounding as hoarse as myself. "We are already dead."

I lurched over to the old man. The other souls let me push through them, their wills so stripped that they did nothing but stand there. "Can we get out?"

"We cannot get out. Not even through prayer. We are already damned." The old man's eye sockets sagged, revealing the red flesh beneath. His gaze did not meet mine, even as he spoke. "What does it matter? We'll all become husks, in the end."

"Husks?"

He jerked his head at the vacant-eyed people around us. The ones who weren't leering or praying. The ones who had been reduced to animals.

"No." I tightened my fists, as if my anger would help protect me. "I will not. I refuse to let my mind go."

The old man closed his eyes, as if this was the closest he could come to expressing pity.

"Enjoy it while you still can. Before centuries pass and you forget your memories, and how to speak, and what life felt like. Before you forget your very name." His voice became a croak as he added, "Sometimes I envy the husks. It must be easier when you no longer want to keep fighting. When you can just...let go."

Looking at the lost souls around me, I could only feel dread and pity. "What of the walls?"

"The walls?"

"The skeletons. Why don't they grow back?"

The old man's eyes raised, examining the bones around us: the skulls, the ribs, the piles and piles of human remains.

"Reapers," he said.

"Reapers?"

"The skeleton things. They stop moving when their necromancer dies. Yes... yes, it must be dead Reapers."

Again, my mind traveled back to Thomas's birds. If he died, would they cease to move as well?

"Are you saying the monsters here...can die?"

The old man hesitated before nodding. "It is not easy, but... it is possible."

There was hope. I regarded the husks once more, wondering whether they'd already tried fighting back too many times, or had simply given up. Whatever happened, I could not let myself become like them. I could not give up. I had to cling to my anger, my hatred, my purpose.

I lowered my voice. "If they can die and we can't, then why are we not fighting back?"

The old man shook his head. "If we killed the satyr holding us, there would be another just like him."

"Then we'll kill him, too," I said.

"Forever and ever?"

"Why not?"

Again, the old man shook his head. "I've been here longer than I was alive, and I lived a long, healthy life." He gestured to his wrinkles. I imagined that his body was wracked with all the pain he'd felt while alive at that age. Was it better to die young, as I had?

I pointed up, my jaw as set as my will. "I have unfinished business up there. There's a man I need to kill. A woman I need to save. There must be a way..."

The old man's eyes looked on the verge of tears, so full of pity that it hurt my chest. "Give up your dreams, boy. There are only nightmares here."

Then we silenced, for the satyr came by, and we did not wish to draw his attention further.

There was no rest to be had. The satyr did not give us work, so we could find no Sisyphean satisfaction from our efforts. We merely stood there, collectively going mad, pushing each other around, often attacking each other from sheer madness. We frequently tried to eat one another. A man to my left kept going for my ears until I bit off his nose, and ended up puking it back up. Some were repulsed and moved away. Others wandered into the puddle, too broken to care about stepping in it.

The one thing keeping me sane in that wretched place was my desire—no, my *need*—for revenge. I did not know how much time had passed, nor what had occurred on Earth since I'd been gone, but such details were insignificant to my goal. I had to make Thomas hurt, and I had to save Clara from him.

My thoughts also traveled back to Remy. I wondered how much I should blame him for this; whether he'd had any idea how twisted that cult really was. I was angry and tempted to add him to my list of people I wished dead along with Thomas and Mother Pursha, who'd danced and fornicated under my raining blood. But I knew not whether Remy had even been there that night. As far as I knew, he wasn't even a Thrall yet.

Either way, the question remained: how could I get back? It was not just that I couldn't escape from Hell; I couldn't even escape from my own cell. Sometimes the other souls would try to break through the bars of our cage: rattling them, punching them, biting them. But all that did was crack their teeth and open their skin. The bars were too strong.

The husks around me frequently collapsed from dehydration or starvation, but they would always get back up eventually. I imagined they were returning to how they'd been when they'd died, no matter how old or sickly. It never ended. There was no release to be found. No calm. No hope.

Well, there was one hope: the hope that we wouldn't win the Satyr's Lottery.

The satyr would periodically peruse the cells, carefully considering those within as if trying to decide which book to pull from a library shelf. He would eventually select someone, bring them out to the stockade on the bottom floor, and use it to bind their wrists and neck. Then he would torment them. He often went for the most attractive souls or those who had the most life in their eyes.

While his gaze was not without pleasure as he did this, more than anything it held an intense look of concentration. He seemed to be studying his victims, analyzing their screams or the ways their faces contorted or how long it took them to break. Eventually, he always brought the remains of the person back to the cell, eyes narrowed, as if met with a challenging decision.

My time came soon enough. As before, I tried to fight, but the satyr effortlessly subdued me. He bound me to the stockade and removed my nails one by one, first from my fingers, then my toes. Just as I thought it was over, he began flogging me with a bladed whip, his crucifix bouncing with every lash. It went on and on; a thousand cuts, a thousand bleeding wounds. And with each new blast of pain, it became harder and harder to remember myself.

"That's it!" he roared as I screamed. "Give in. You're weak."

"I'm not weak," I tried to snarl, but my voice was broken and unconvincing.

"You'll forget your own name soon enough," the satyr hissed into my ear.

Again and again, I promised myself that I would not. That no matter what it took, no matter what I had to do, I would escape this wretched place. Thomas would suffer and die at my hands. I would save Clara from his evil and, if she would have me, I would love her as she was meant to be loved. That hope—that desperate, wretched, all-consuming hope—was all I had to sustain me.

My punishment at last ceased when a frail woman managed to escape her cell. She tried sneaking past the satyr, and even made it to the door before he spotted her. Then he decapitated her and fed the head to his dog. Frustrated, he untied me and dragged my limp body back into my cell.

I couldn't shake the thought that we might have a chance if we all tried to rebel and escape at once, but few of my fellow captives responded when I spoke to them, some because they were husks and others because they were from other countries or eras and did not understand my modern English tongue.

The first meal I had in Hell was the old man who had spoken to me. It was after he won the lottery. His frail body had caused him to break quickly during his time in the stockade, so the satyr decided to carve him up and roast him using a large pyre. He offered me a chunk of the resulting flesh, and my mouth could not help but water; it was food. Others around me were already eating, moaning with pleasure as they sank their teeth in. The first bite felt like being reborn, like having a taste of Heaven. I inhaled the rest of my share, and when I was done, I licked my fingers, wishing I felt more guilt over it than I did.

Eventually, the old man's body regenerated, piece by tiny piece. He didn't stop screaming for a long time after that. He could speak no words, and seemed to have gone completely and utterly mad. The satyr cracked his neck to shut him up, an effect that lasted no more than a week. When that too had passed, the satyr cut off his tongue and threw it into the sea.

By the time the old man's tongue had regenerated, he was used to being silent, and no longer had the will to scream. He merely stood frozen like a mannequin. I feared he'd become a husk and that I, too, would end up as one sooner than I hoped.

"You see?" I asked him, when the satyr had gone upstairs. "It doesn't matter whether we do what he says. He will torture us regardless. So why not do something to bloody well earn his wrath?"

The old man said nothing. His back was to me, a ragged canvas of scars.

"We should work together to kill him," I pressed. "To be free."

The old man slowly turned his head to look over his shoulder at me, his jaw hanging, teeth crooked.

"I know you're still in there, old man," I hissed. "Don't abandon me now."

The old man gave me that pitying expression again. Then he shook his head.

"I know you want to give up," I said through clenched teeth. "But you can't. You hear me? You can't!" A lump formed in my throat. "You're the only one here I can talk to. The only one who still has anything left of himself. Please. Please." I scrambled before him, grabbed his leathery hands. "I need you to hold on so that we can fight back."

His face scrunched up, quiet sobs escaping him, though his eyes remained dry from dehydration. "I tried," he finally said, his voice sounding even more weary than it had before. "I tried fighting back, with others. We all tried. There was no point."

"There is more point than this!" I said. "You said it yourself: demons can die."

"There are worse demons than him. Some a hundred times more powerful, and two hundred times more cruel. And the more of them you kill, the more they come for you. This satyr is a lesser evil."

"A lesser evil?" I scoffed, showing him my hand, the nails still not fully regrown. "After all he's done to us, how can you say that? What's your name, you doddering old fool?"

The old man appeared startled. None of us had exchanged names before. We didn't wish to see each other as people; to start caring about each other would make everything even worse. It was an unspoken but mutually understood rule, and asking this man's name felt like breaking a great taboo. But I was angry and I wanted to know. Slowly, he shook his head.

"Do you even remember?" I asked.

"I...think so," said the man, his gaze uncertain. "It's... hard..."

"Tell me," I said.

"Eh...El..." He trailed off, shaking his head, the glimmer of clarity leaving him.

"Don't let it get away!" I hissed. "Reach out for it. Reclaim it! *What is your name?*"

"*Elias!*" the old man bellowed, as if he was only just remembering his name himself; as if he had intentionally locked it away. "Elias," he repeated, more calmly this time. But even now, the pain remained in his eyes. I wondered how long it had been since he'd spoken it aloud.

I squeezed his hands. "Good Sir Elias, I am Caleb Schwartzenfeld, and I am your brother in arms."

Elias stared at me, eyes wide as plates, and trembled with both excitement and fear. He might have said more, but the clip-clopping of hoofs silenced us. The satyr was coming back down the stairs.

"MORTALS!" he bellowed, his voice a soul-quaking echo. "I've selected twelve of you to come with me on a voyage. We shall depart immediately."

From each cage he grabbed a few of us and made us wait by the stockade. His huge hound guarded the gate, drooling as if eager to devour anyone foolish enough to run.

To my surprise, I was among those chosen. The others included the thin woman who'd tried escaping before, a strong, bearded man who was easily as tall as the satyr but held himself with a shy cower, and a little girl in a faded sack-like dress, whose eyes held the wisdom and patience of someone far older than she looked. Elias was also chosen, even as he screamed, "Don't take me! Don't take me!"

Some of the other prisoners stirred at this, mumbling or rattling the bars.

"Rather kind of you to take us on a cruise," I said to the satyr. "I think I'll quite enjoy the fresh air."

"Will you, now?" The satyr grinned, and somehow, I instantly knew that the voyage before us would be anything but pleasant.

***

It's fascinating, reliving these memories of my early days in Hell. The torment seemed so dreadful at the time, and I suppose it was, from a certain perspective. But compared to what I have endured since, especially since I took up residence in this little room, it all feels so...rudimentary. Every time I think there is a limit to how vile or imaginative punishment can be, I am always humbled by a reminder of how much worse it can get. I've become enlightened in ways no one should have to be enlightened, learning first-hand that there are infinite ways for skin to be maimed, folded, and deformed.

The visitors who come into my room have the minds of scientists, continuously experimenting to find the optimal way of making me suffer. But they are also artists, and my body is their canvas. The constant echoing screams from the adjacent cells remind me that I'm not alone, but my neighbors are too far away to call out to, and my throat is always too dry. Besides, the visitors love to take my tongue, lips, and teeth.

They certainly know I am writing by now. Indeed, they encourage it. Perhaps they understand that sooner or later, I'll have to relive my worst memory of all.

CHAPTER SEVEN

LADY WEAVER'S MANSION

THE SATYR TOOK US onto a great wooden longship he had tied up around the back of the island. Its name had long since been rubbed away, like those of so many of my fellow passengers. The satyr chained us to either side of the ship and made us row. His hound paced between us, tail flicking irritably, its hair a nest of barbed wire.

The air stank of metal as we set sail. The bloody water crashed against the ship's outer walls—loud enough, I hoped, to mask quiet conversation. The satyr watched us from the rear, puffing on a cigar as if the air didn't stink of smoke enough already.

"Psst." I made eye contact with Elias, then with the thin woman. "We should break free," I whispered. "If we all do it at once, we can throw him overboard and escape."

Elias's eyes pointed stubbornly down, focused on his rowing. The frail woman squinted, understanding but not yet agreeing. She eyed the hound, who lurched past us, drool hanging from its jowls in thick slimy strands.

"Stay your mouth," barked the satyr. "I want them in good condition."

Good condition for what? I didn't want to remain on this boat to find out.

"What's your name?" I whispered to the thin woman. "I'm Caleb."

She hesitated. "Jeanne." She had a thick French accent.

"Look, Jeanne, wherever we're headed, it's nowhere good. And there are more of us than there are of him."

"You have no idea how many times I've tried. There's no point." The woman's voice was as frail as her body, but there was a blazing fury in her eyes. No, she wasn't broken like some of the others.

"There is no point in giving up, either." It was the little girl this time, her nostrils flared, messy black hair tumbling in the wind. "Anika," she said, nodding her head at me. "I've been like you, Caleb. And like you, too," she added to Jeanne. "It never gets better. Not really. But I've learned that hope can give you the illusion that it will. And sometimes, that illusion is enough to help you keep your mind. Because when you lose it all, when you become a husk... that's when they win."

Some of the others were stirring, listening as they rowed. The huge man looked up, his haunted features hanging slack.

"If just a few of us fight back, then others will join in," I said to Anika. "All a fire needs is for someone to strike a match."

"Shh." It was Elias this time. The satyr was walking back to us, checking us over. He grabbed the little girl's chin, made her look up at him, and grinned at her scowl.

"Spirited. They'll like that."

He turned to me, and I glowered.

"Yes, yes, keep doing that," he said, chuckling. "That's what we want. Life! Fire in those eyes. It means there's still something in you left to take away, unlike those miserable husks." He side-eyed a few of my fellow captives before looking back at me with those horizontal pupils, rubbing his goat chin with satisfaction. "Yes, I think I'll fetch a fine price for the lot of you."

I jerked my chin at the crucifix hanging around his neck. "Doesn't that hurt you?"

"Why would it?" The satyr was unblinking, showing no signs of discomfort. "It gives me hope that even one such as I may find redemption."

"But you're a demon. You torture us. You're planning on selling us."

"You are sinners," said the satyr, smiling. "Why else would you be here? Your suffering is God's will."

"You enjoy it," I hissed. "I see it in your eyes." The others were watching us, now: Jeanne, Anika, Elias, even the huge man.

The satyr was unfazed. "I take pride in my work. I chose this path because I am good at it and God will reward me one day. You think I want to be here?" He gestured to the broken world around us. "You think I like living on that rock? No. It's simply a place where a lot of souls fall, so I can meet my quota. I've been saving up, you see. For the migration."

He wasn't apologetic, but something in his voice told me he expected us to forgive him; to see him as not such a bad man. Another victim of Hell, who had no choice but to torment us.

It occurred to me that this bastard was probably quite lonely. He had no one to talk to but us: his merchandise, who he had so carefully broken just enough that we'd obey him. I decided to humor him. If he kept talking, maybe he'd reveal a weakness to exploit.

"What migration?" I asked.

He looked at me like I was a fool. "Why...the migration. *The* migration. Bah. You think a common goat like me has any chance of getting out of here if I don't save up? Right now, only the pretty demons get to go up. The ones who blend in. The more monstrous looking of us are trapped down here. But once those doors open, once they no longer have to pretend... maybe then I can finally get out."

"What do you mean, out?" I asked. Then I realized that it could only mean one thing: that his goal was likely the same as mine. "You want to go to *Earth?*"

Again the satyr gestured to the red sea, his upper lip raised in a sneer. "Why would I want to stay here, brushing away scadbats and vultures? Why stay in a place where time has no meaning, where no crops can grow? I'm a satyr, not a vampire or lilitu. I must eat real food, just as you mortals do in life. Indeed, I happen to enjoy eating very much. But what's there to eat here, other than you, or the beasts?"

So there *was* a way out. If this satyr knew what he was talking about—and admittedly, I could not be sure he did—there was a way to return to Earth. My fists clenched. "How?" I croaked.

The satyr's chuckle sounded like a bleat. "Never you mind, boy. You'll still be down here with all the rest of your lot. But me, if I can make enough to afford a ticket to Earth, I'll be able to have it all. Grapes, potatoes... *strawberries.*" His eyes glimmered with some deranged hope. "All the wonderful things you can't find down here."

A dry, sour taste filled my mouth. "You've been torturing us...for *strawberries*?"

He pulled a cigar from his pocket, lit it, and took a long puff. "I feel that I deserve the finer things in life. I may have been born a commoner down here, but in my heart, I have always been nobility. Even my mother always told me that I was bound for great things. No, I don't belong down here. I belong up—up—*up*—" He sneezed, smoke exploding from his nostrils and nearly setting the boat on fire. He removed a handkerchief from his belt, blew a new black stain into it, scratched his hairy butt with it for good measure, and then hung it back on his belt. "Up above," he finished, pointing with the cigar. "On Earth. Where the other gentlemen are."

"Gentlemen," I repeated, eyeing the handkerchief's many stains. "Indeed."

The satyr rubbed his wet nose with the back of his hand. "It'll benefit us both if you impress them. Who knows? Perhaps Lady Weaver will take a liking to you."

"Lady Weaver?" repeated Elias, his voice hoarse. He finally looked up at the satyr, eyes swimming with terror. "Not her. Not the Flesh Weaver..."

The satyr let out another soft chuckle and returned to the helm at the stern, adjusting the wheel without ever fully taking his eyes off us.

"You know who this Flesh Weaver is?" I whispered to Elias.

He nodded grimly, panic in his eyes. "We do *not* want to be sold to her."

"Then we should break free!" I slammed my wrists forward, rattling the chains. The hound growled at me, but I knew that if I could just get the others to fight back, we could beat the satyr and his hound both. He'd gathered the twelve most lively souls. Didn't that also make us the twelve who were most likely to rebel?

"Come on!" I hissed. "Rattle them! We have nothing to lose!"

But no one else would. Not even Anika, Jeanne, or Elias could muster up the courage. None of my fellow captives believed we could win, even though many of us knew what was waiting for us if we didn't.

The hound brought its face inches from mine and growled once more. Fear took hold of me, freezing my limbs. Part of me wondered if maybe everyone else knew something I didn't. After all, I was new to Hell. Many of the others had been here far longer than I.

"Right." The satyr looked down at me, arms crossed. "You'll be the prow, then."

He tied me to the prow for the rest of the journey, like I was a wooden mermaid. The icy blood waves splashed against my skin, got into my eyes, and violated my nostrils. For hours I was lashed by thorny tendrils, taunted by harpies, and harried by more huge, bloodthirsty bats. But my greatest enemy was my own weight, putting an ever-worsening strain on my arms.

The satyr stood atop the bow, grinning down at me as he smoked his cigar. "You'll understand, sooner or later," he said. "Maybe you'll even be in my shoes someday, once you decide to make a name for yourself. You think us demons are the only ones who break 'em down and sell the remains?" He chuckled, shaking his head.

"Fuck you," I rasped out. Some of the salty blood had splashed into my mouth, but it had only left me thirstier.

"This place will take your soul," said the satyr. "Whatever goodness you once had will drain away in the wake of your desperation. The memories you once cherished will fade. Before long, you won't have anything left of who you once were. Not even your name. You'll be nothing but an animal."

"I am Caleb Schwartzenfeld," I whispered to myself. "*Caleb Schwartzenfeld.*" I could not, *would* not, forget that.

Yet already I feared I no longer knew what that meant. The things that made me who I was—my violin, for starters—seemed so distant, now. I'd been molded by the circumstances of my life. Now that I was reborn in Hell, would it not mold me just the same?

Hours later, we reached the shore of a large body of land that stretched as far as I could see in either direction. Before us was a great city, complete with a sizable dock. Yes, a *city*. Not nearly as large as London, but a city nonetheless. Buildings. A town square. More people than I could count.

Even in my debilitated state, it astonished me to learn Hell could contain such a place. Fanged soldiers with horned helmets and black armor were waiting at the pier, and helped the satyr remove me from the prow. I wanted to collapse, but I was forced to my feet, my open wounds leaving trails of gore behind me as I slumped slowly into line with the others. The soldiers marched us from the boat to the cobblestone streets, ensuring none of us could try making a run for it. The satyr took the lead, riding proudly atop his hound into the city's mouth.

Everywhere we looked, we saw demons. A pale man rode in a carriage toted by horned monster horses. A huge bone beast lashed mortals with a flaming whip. A bored-looking winged woman watched us from a balcony, cooling herself with a fan that looked made of skin.

The mortals outnumbered the demons five to one, but were in agony: standing in row after row of rusty old cages, hanging from archways, struggling as they were loaded onto ships, and being forced to sweep the streets just as I'd done so many years in life. I almost felt like I was home.

Why was no one fighting back? My hope withered. If all of Hell was like this and not one mortal rebellion was successful, then maybe they were right. Maybe there really wasn't hope.

No. I clenched my fists and jaw, even as they shuddered with pain. Anika was right. Giving up would mean letting them win. They wanted us to believe it was hopeless because that was how they controlled us. And I would not be controlled.

They marched us up a long road to a towering mansion on the tallest hill in the city. The satyr had to leave his hound outside, but once he'd done so, guards opened its double doors to reveal a grand ballroom, where a gala was afoot.

I gaped, even more amazed than before. The opulence on display was staggering, making it abundantly clear that not all demons lived in the same squalor as our satyr. The fiends here had wealth to rival London's worst and richest. They were dressed as aristocrats, their wings and horns bejeweled with gleaming rings.

The demons danced in pairs and lounged on red satin seats and drank from glasses of scarlet liquid—bloodwine, I would later learn it to be called. Several had hellhounds of varying sizes, from a hulking horned thing to a tiny squirrel-like whelp whose disproportionately huge eyes quivered with rage as we passed.

Mortals served bloodwine on trays, wearing the attire of butlers and maids. String music echoed through the walls, ever so slightly off-key. A pair of curved staircases led up to higher balconies, where more demons loomed: more satyrs, fanged pale people who I presumed to be vampires, and even a woman who I could have sworn was part maggot. Her skin was shiny, white, and gelatinous, and stuck out all the more thanks to her red dress with its oversized frilled collar. A huge black stinger protruded from her abdomen. She had six pitch black eyes, all of them focused on the huge, cowering man treading silently with me.

Then I saw the figures hanging from the ceiling, all of them tied up in thin red threads, their eyelids and lips sewn wide open.

"We have to get out of here," I hissed to Elias, who stood behind me in line.

"How?" he croaked.

I didn't want to admit it, but I wasn't sure yet. There were an awful lot of mortals around, but the demons here looked far bigger and nastier than any I'd seen yet. "Maybe one of us can create a distraction," I said. "We just have to light a match..." The room was lit with hundreds of candelabras, each flickering flame an opportunity for escape.

"That will only upset them," said Elias, his eyes and voice dead. "It's better, when we don't upset them."

"Just pass it down," I whispered. I knew I'd have to be the one to trigger it; no one else had the will. But I could only hope that the others would follow suit this time. Perhaps they had no reason left to fight, to live, to keep trying. I *did* have a reason: my vengeance. No matter how weak I'd been in life, it would fuel my will in death.

But my body was so racked with pain that I barely had the strength to walk.

The satyr led us to a gaggle of demon women sitting in a circle of well-cushioned couches, all of them dressed in elegant bustle dresses and gleaming jewelry. The most distinctive figure was a pale, bald demoness, her heels resting on a coffee table before her. Her fingers stretched into long, red needle-like tips, one of which was stirring the bottom of a full glass. Her features looked like a wax impression of a woman: stretched, simplified, and wrong in ways I could not quite put my finger on.

As Elias and Jeanne whispered to the souls on either side of them, the satyr approached the strange demoness and bowed elaborately.

"My dear Lady Weaver! I am ever so excited to show you my latest crop."

"Let's make this quick, Ferdinand. We may have forever, but that doesn't mean I have all day." Lady Weaver had the voice of an embittered grandmother, her red lips pursed. She tapped those too-long fingertips on their armrest, appraising us hungrily: unblinking, unimpressed, and yet giving her undivided attention. Her gaze narrowed as it focused on Elias, upper lip lifting into an expression of disdain. "Fortunately for you, I find myself unusually low on chattel at the moment."

The satyr's face softened into a look of concern. "Oh, dear. Whatever happened?"

"Pestilence." The word ripped from Weaver's mouth like a fish from its hook.

The satyr's expression turned graver at that. "I thought she was only a rumor."

"On the contrary. Because of her, I had to flee my summer home in the Patchwork Sea last month." Weaver's nostrils flared. "All my plants died, rotting from her very presence. My guards there fell under her spell. I would have too, had I not fled. After all the work I did to create that lovely blanket over the land..." She sighed miserably. "I hear the Blood Saints are after her, so hopefully I'll be able to return soon. Oh, how sad it is to suffer such poverty."

"Indeed. With that in mind, allow me to present my latest crop." The satyr gestured to us with his arms, eager to change the subject. "I think there are some that you and your friends will especially enjoy. There is even a child. An old soul, if you can believe it." He nudged Anika before him, even as she glowered at Weaver. "I think you'll agree she's a terrific find. A real diamond in the—"

"I shall decide for myself, thank you," said Lady Weaver. "The question is, how long will it be before I get bored of torturing them? And then I have to find another buyer so they're not sitting around taking up space. It's an awful lot of work, Ferdinand."

"Indeed?" said the satyr, a sparkle appearing in his eyes. "Well, in exchange for a small commission, I'd be willing to help you find a second buyer when you get bored of these fine specimens—"

"Oh, it is ever so much work," sighed Lady Weaver, placing the back of her hand onto her forehead. "My poor head hurts just imagining it, especially after the tragic loss of my summer home. Taking these considerations into account, fifty silver for the lot seems quite reasonable, don't you think?"

The satyr hesitated, his eyes making it very clear that he'd hoped for more. "Well—"

"Oh, I'm delighted to hear it!" Lady Weaver beamed. "Some merchants, you know, are less reasonable. We have no use for unreasonable people here, Ferdinand. Indeed, we make sure they never bring their unreasonable-ness anywhere else." She crouched down before Anika and clutched her cheeks with her needle-thin fingertips. "What's your name, little thing?"

"Not yours." Anika glowered, even as her cheeks bled.

Weaver grinned, her white lips stretching like taffy to reveal needle-thin teeth. "You think keeping your name secret somehow protects you? All it does is give me the chance to give you a name of my own choosing. What do you think, Ferdinand? Should I call her...Pincushion?"

Weaver's friends tittered with laughter.

"A fine name, my lady," said the satyr, bowing. "I think these souls will keep you entertained for a long time. For example, we have this giant of a man." He put his hands on the shoulders of the muscular man whose head still hung miserably. "Why don't you tell the good Lady Weaver your name?"

The huge man swallowed, then mumbled something too quiet to hear.

"Is he missing his tongue?" asked Weaver. "Speak up, boy."

The huge man's throat bobbed, his gaze fixed to the floor. "...Duncan."

"And so obedient!" The satyr parted his lips in amazement, before lifting a fist. "Imagine, Weaver! Your own gladiator, willing to fight for you in the Wrathful Arena. Duncan, the Undefeated! But perhaps you also desire a more distinguished victim?" The satyr put his hands on Elias's shoulders next. "An old man, who longs only for death? You could think of him as your father. You could pull him apart and remake him in a way you like better."

"Indeed, I plan to." Weaver cooed, her eyes lighting up. "So good to see you again, Elias. I hope you understand now that there is no point trying to run from me?"

Elias's face was just barely contorted, a sheen coating his eyes. But he kept his gaze low, just as Duncan did.

"I take it he already belongs to you?" The satyr grinned. "Then he is yours, on the house. But I would hope you'll consider the rest of my crop as well. Consider this strapping young soul." I jumped as the satyr gripped my shoulders. "He only just landed in Hell three months ago. He's barely suffered at all. Practically a virgin." He winked, grinning as he pulled on my chin, forcing my head to turn. "And what a handsome young man. Don't you just want to slice him up?"

I jerked my shoulders out of his grasp. Weaver and her friends cackled, delighted by my resistance.

"He *is* fresh," said Weaver, dragging a needle-finger down my chest, teasing the cuts left. "But recently wounded, too."

"Yes, young enough to still be a rebel," sighed the satyr, voice full of lament. "I had to put him in his place, you understand."

"Does he have any talents?" asked Weaver. "Skills from his life that have not yet faded?"

The satyr whipped his head to face me, commanding me to answer with my eyes alone.

I swallowed, even though my mouth was utterly dry. "Violin. I can play the violin."

"Briony, bring him a violin," Weaver whispered to a mortal maid standing behind her chair. "The orchestra should be able to part with one." She kept her eyes on me even as the maid left. "This shall be most interesting. If he's any good, it would be delightful to cut those fingers off and watch him try to do it without them."

Somehow, this made my guts squirm worse than more substantial injuries. I absolutely detested the thought of losing my ability to create art, even if only temporarily.

"Do we have a deal, then?" asked the satyr.

"There's no need to be so hasty, Ferdinand," said Weaver, waving her hand dismissively. "Let me watch him play first."

Cold sweat broke out on my brow. I was all too aware that this could end in disaster. We did not know this mansion, nor the city as a whole, and both were filled with demons. I was also beginning to understand that this place could always, *always*, get worse in ways beyond my capacity to imagine.

But demons could die. We couldn't. It didn't matter how badly they hurt us; we would survive it all.

And that meant there was no reason not to fight with everything we had.

Weaver's maid returned with a violin, and the satyr unlocked my chains. I took a moment to take in the beautiful instrument: its smooth wood, its delicate, curvy shape... even the smell of it made me feel more at ease. I almost felt that even if this whole plan went to shit, at least it led to me getting to hold a violin one last time.

I brought bow to string, mirroring the dance floor's ghostly melody. The instrument was perfectly tuned, and the sound that came out was butter smooth. I let all my sorrow bleed into the strings. I even fancied I might make a demon cry. All the same, I eyed Elias and Jeanne, letting both know that it was now or never. Weaver stared at me, transfixed, but any moment she might decide to take my fingers off instead.

"NOW!" I barked, lancing the violin bow into the satyr's eye. He screamed, and blood gushed out between his hairy fingers. Then I felt a fresh, powerful impact against the back of my head, and collapsed to the floor. Above me stood one of the soldiers, blood dripping from his fist. My vision was already blurring, the room spinning. And the back of my head felt so, so wet...

"It's a rare treat to meet a soul with spirit," Weaver cooed, stepping over me. "I shall delight in breaking it. What do you all think? Should I make him a host for Resimira's broodlings?"

The maggot woman approached from behind, her abdomen throbbing excitedly. "Nay, sister. I'd not have my children grow up shrimpy like him. They deserve a bigger baguette..." Her all-black eyes remained focused on Duncan.

The satyr pried the violin bow from his eye with a cry of pain. He reached to cover it, but the blood gushed out between his hairy fingers. Darkness spread through the corners of my vision, muting whatever satisfaction I might have felt. Jeanne and Elias had not moved. They remained standing there, shaking and averting their eyes. Fighting back had only made things worse for me, ensuring the fiends would torment me even more ruthlessly than before. I would be tortured to death over and over again for all eternity, with no end in sight.

"Oh, I know!" said Weaver, eyes gleaming with excitement. "Why don't we stitch him to the edge of the Patchwork Sea once we've reclaimed it? He can become a part of my life's work..."

Suddenly one of Weaver's friends let out a shriek, pointing behind her. Anika was standing by the wall, having somehow gotten free of her chains. At her feet was a fallen candelabra, and fire was already spreading over a nearby rug. The fearless girl shot the satyr and Weaver a spiteful grin.

Excitement surged through me. Someone else had actually fought back. And I knew, with sudden certainty, that this would encourage the others as well. The demons were distracted, staring at the blaze in disbelief. The satyr gaped, jaw lowered, wounded eye still bleeding. This was my chance. My one and only chance.

I pulled myself to my feet. A chain still hung loose around my wrist, so I grabbed the other end, got behind the satyr and pulled the chain up against his throat, choking him. Jeanne grabbed the keys from his belt and worked to unlock her cuffs, kneeing him in the crotch in the process. The satyr gasped for air, tongue sticking out, remaining eye bulging.

"Guards!" shouted Weaver, but Jeanne was already uncuffing the other captives. Demons and mortals alike were already running from the rapidly spreading fire. Some of the captives bolted right away, while others simply stood there, confused about what to do.

The satyr elbowed me in the face and wriggled free as I recoiled, blood spurting from my nose. "You think you can fight me?" he asked, nostrils flaring.

"Aye, bitch!" I snarled, spitting blood into his good eye. The satyr was stronger and I knew it, but he could die. I couldn't.

He punched me in the gut, but Duncan was suddenly beside me, clocking the satyr in the jaw. Behind him, Elias walked backwards, staring in fascination. Duncan punched the satyr over and over, his massive fist slamming back and forth like a hammer. The satyr began to cower, but still Duncan punched, until a loud crack sounded through the room. Then the satyr fell to the floor, one dead eye open.

Duncan panted, covered in blood. A fundamental shift rippled through the room as everyone who remained realized that he'd just killed a demon. A waitress dropped her tray of glasses. Weaver's maid fled. The tiny squirrel-like hellhound yapped furiously at us before running away.

Then two bigger hellhounds charged toward us, each one frothing at the mouth. "RUN!" I screamed, fleeing in the opposite direction of both the fire and the hounds. But Duncan positioned himself before one, even though it had to be twice his weight, and plugged its mouth with the wrist of his huge arm. The beast growled and gargled as it shredded his flesh, but Duncan stood his ground, while using his other arm to punch the beast's eyes. The other hound was still coming for us, though.

Jeanne, Elias and Anika ran alongside me, all four of us desperately trying to dodge the hound's rapid lunges. Jeanne stood between it and Anika, protecting her tiny body. I reached a window and tore open the drape, but found only bars on the other side. The next window was the same.

Weaver cackled and rose to her feet, stilettos clicking against the marble floor. "You think I'd give my servants easy ways out?"

Her friends, along with most other demons, had departed out of fear from the fire. However, the maggot-like demon remained. Her fat abdomen bounced as she approached Duncan, who was still grappling with the first hound, his bloody wrist between its jaws.

The other hound lunged for me, and I shoved the violin between its jaws. I hated the thought of damaging such a beautiful instrument, especially since I didn't know when I'd next get to play one, but I didn't have big arms like Duncan did. "Hurry!" I shouted to the others. "Find weapons!"

Jeanne led Elias and Anika through the nearest door, which was between the two staircases. Weaver walked slowly, even languidly after them, like she had all the time in the world, even though the fire was spreading closer and closer to us, traveling across the drapes and furniture.

"You think this is my only house?" she asked, as she followed Jeanne and the others through the door. "I'll just make you all rebuild it."

The hound fighting Duncan suddenly yelped, for the ever-encroaching flames had reached its tail, and now the fire was spreading across its fur. Then Duncan let out a fresh cry of pain as well, for the maggot lady had pierced his side with her abdomen's stinger. She giggled in delight, her abdomen throbbing like a heart. Duncan pried himself free and limp-ran backwards, blood gushing out from the hole the stinger left behind.

My hound chomped down on the violin, splintering it thoroughly, so I bolted again, colliding with Duncan's huge form. Even while limping, Duncan was faster than me, and had managed to outpace the bulbous maggot lady. The hound charged for us again, splinters in its tongue, but a flaming rafter landed on it from the burning ceiling, pinning it to the floor.

Flames blocked the front door and stairs, so there was nowhere to go but through the door after Weaver. If she'd headed that way, it might offer a way out rather than a dead end; a back door, perhaps. Duncan and I hurried through and emerged into a long, dark hallway, although in truth it felt more like a tunnel. I couldn't see what lay ahead; it was too shrouded with darkness. The sound of crackling flames continued to haunt our tail, and it wasn't long before the door behind us creaked open again, followed by the rhythmic thud of the maggot lady's abdomen.

"Don't run too fast!" she cooed. "I want to watch it while it happens..."

"Don't slow down!" I hissed, but Duncan's face grew concerned.

Deeper and deeper we went. Just how long did this damn hallway go? I realized there was a very slight downward curve. We were descending. "This might have been a mistake," I admitted. "I'm not sure this leads out..."

Behind me, Duncan let out an awful groan. I turned to find him holding his stomach, his face contorted in pain.

"Maggotis demon," he muttered.

"What?" I asked.

Cooing laughter echoed from behind us.

"Come on, mate!" I grabbed Duncan's hand and pulled him onward, but he ended up slumping his arm around my shoulder, the entirety of his weight almost crushing me to the floor. We trudged slowly on, likely even slower than the maggot lady now.

"Maggotis demon!" he repeated, voice choked. Multiple bulges were swelling on his body, pink with irritation. "They breed by..." He coughed, unable to keep speaking.

The maggot lady's laughter closed in around us, louder now, closer. "Hurry!" I said, just as Duncan began screaming in pain. The bulges on his body distorted, like things were moving beneath the skin.

The other end of the hall was finally within sight: an open door, leading to a circular chamber with bone walls. I couldn't see what lay within. "We're almost there," I said, just to give Duncan some hope.

"Keh...kill me!" he choked out, even though none of us could die anymore. His pain was so overpowering that he was past the point of clear thought. I couldn't help but feel like I'd let him down. If only I were stronger. If only I had been able to simply drive my fist through the face of every demon in our path, and ensure they fell. I envied the demons for their strength, power, and wealth. It was an envy even more overwhelming, and even more hungry, than the envy my mortal self had felt for men like Thomas Rife.

"Just a bit further," I said, charging into the room. There was indeed another door on the other side of it, and it even had a window leading out. But between it and us was Lady Weaver...and Elias, Jeanne, and Anika. Elias had his back against the wall, too frozen with terror to keep running, while Jeanne and Anika were strung up in red thread. Jeanne was on the floor, flat on her belly, her legs and wrists tied above her head. Her eyelids had been sewn to her brows, forcing her to stare, while Anika's arms were sewn to the sides of her sack-like dress. Weaver was inching her needle-like fingertips closer to Anika's eyes when we stumbled in.

She turned and faced us. "I see you've decided to join in the fun."

"Fock," Duncan moaned as something sharp stabbed up from the center of one of his tumors, tearing open a hole. An infant's high-pitched squeal filled the chamber as the creature crawled out. It looked like a human baby, but the size of a rat, with too many eyes and six spindly sharp-tipped limbs. Duncan keeled over, screaming in agony. His second tumor ruptured, and another maggot baby popped out of him, followed by a third, and a fourth, all of them giggling as they skittered over his body.

Even Weaver winced. "Damn Resimira...never did know when to respect when souls are *my* property!"

The maggot babies took bites out of Duncan's arms and legs, only to spit them out with repulsed "BLEGH!" sounds. Then they focused their eyes on Weaver. Bloody drool dripped from their all-too-human lips.

"What?!" Weaver exclaimed, but one had already launched onto her, skewering her with its sharp limbs and giggling as she shrieked in pain. The other maggot babies followed, knocking her to the floor, sinking their teeth into her pale flesh, and gleefully tugging until pieces ripped off. Weaver screamed and writhed as the tiny things feasted on her body. She managed to slice off one's sharp limb, causing it to fall to the floor.

With Weaver distracted, I ran to Jeanne. Anika grabbed the fallen limb, and sliced through the threads binding their arms and legs. Duncan was still groaning on the floor, the skin on his sides and stomach looking like popped balloons. Jeanne and I ran to help him up.

"ENOUGH!" Weaver screeched, lurching to her feet, grabbing the spider babies and tossing them against the walls, where they splattered like eggs. Then, still standing between us and the exit, she lifted a claw. Red threads wormed out from her palms like tentacles.

"Yes, enough," Elias said, finally stepping away from the wall, a fire blazing in his eyes. "Enough! ENOUGH!"

He ran at Lady Weaver, letting her needle and thread pierce his chest so he could get close enough to grab her shoulders. Then he whirled her around and pushed her away from us with a wail of rage. Weaver stumbled backwards, no longer blocking our way out but far from defeated.

Suddenly, the maggot lady came charging into the room, her entire body engulfed in flames. She was like a huge torch with legs, screaming in pain, her skin already blackened, swelling, and popping.

"Resimira!?" said Weaver, baffled as the flaming maggot lady charged closer.

"I WAS TOO SLOW! I WAS TOO SLOW!" Resimira shrieked, just before colliding with Weaver, setting her aflame as well. Both screamed as their flesh burned away to nothing.

The rest of us didn't need any more reasons to bolt. We ran through the door, taking Duncan with us, and out into gardens that were also on fire. We surmounted the fence, only to find the fire had spread to the rest of the city as well. Demons and mortals alike were yelling in pain as they were cooked.

In the thoroughfare before us, a large group of mortals marched on, torches in their hands, spreading more and more of the fire. Somewhere in that crowd, a woman pounded on a drum, and a man shouted "KILL THE DEMONS! SAVE ANY MORTALS YOU SEE!"

Elias, Jeanne, Anika, Duncan, and I gaped. The rebellion had begun. We joined the crowd, instinctively feeling ourselves become one with it, made singular by our rage.

"That's him!" said a woman in the crowd, pointing at me—Lady Weaver's maid, I realized. "That's the man who stabbed the satyr in the eye. The man who started all this!"

"I barely did anything," I said, feeling oddly embarrassed. "Duncan did the most damage. And Anika started that fire."

"He was the one with the plan!" Anika piped in. "The one who got everyone fighting. I only found the courage to set the fire because he convinced us we had a chance."

"Aye, it was him!" Elias added, grinning like he was a new man. There was more life in his eyes than I'd ever seen before. The fire of the city reflected within them, orange and beautiful. "Lead them," he said, shouldering my part of Duncan's weight. "Go."

"It's—I—" I stumbled over my words, strangely overwhelmed. I didn't want credit for a rebellion. Rebellion had not been my goal; returning to Earth was. But within the faces of my companions was something that I'd not seen in a very long time: hope. Even Jeanne, whose eyes were sewn fully open, beamed at me with encouragement. And who was I to argue with that?

I hurried through the crowd, weaving my way through until I'd reached the front, where a chaotic battle was afoot. More demons were charging at us with swords and axes. But we had flaming pieces of wood, axes, shovels, hammers, knives, and sharp limbs cut off from the demons we'd already slain, and the fear was gone. None of us cared about the wounds we'd accrue, so we marched on, facing the bullets, the fire, and the stab wounds. My eyes were dashed with soot and something blasted through my arm, but I marched on. "FREE US! FREE US! FREE US!" chanted the souls behind me.

We climbed to the highest street in the city, so that all could see us marching. Demons fled in terror to the docks, but another mob was waiting to swarm them. Some demons leaped into the red sea, while others were stabbed or pummeled to death. Others ran into burning buildings and were scorched alive. More and more lost souls realized, finally, what power they had. Even though the city was burning, we could build something new from the ashes. Something better. Something beautiful.

Yes, the city was ours. It was a certainty shared between us in that crowd, some collective understanding that no one could deny. Anika ran beside me, and when we reached the highest point, I brought her atop my shoulders and we both raised our fists high.

I don't think Hell had ever heard so many wails of joy as it did in that moment: an entire city, crying out with relief. We were united, and for the first time since we'd died, we were without fear.

CHAPTER EIGHT

BLACK HEAVEN REBELLION

BARBECUED HELLHOUND IS TASTIER than you might think, at least when you're starving. It's rather gamy, but has a rich, smokey flavor not unlike bacon. I found that out during the celebration, when the fires had settled down and most of us had regenerated. While we didn't need to eat anymore, we still felt awfully hungry.

My companions and I ate heartily around an isolated bonfire on the shore, a small crowd surrounding us. A few people whispered to each other about what they'd heard about me. Others brought me trinkets. A youth named Timothy all but hovered at my side, constantly asking what I needed to the point that it annoyed me. He must have been no older than fifteen in death, and possessed so much youthful exuberance that he couldn't have been in Hell for very long, either. He looked at me with wide eyes, like I was some kind of god. "Thank you again for all you've done for us, sir," he kept repeating, as if my attention was the one thing keeping him sane.

"Of course," was all I could muster out. It was all quite embarrassing. They were acting like I was their leader for sparking it all, but I hadn't done this for glory. I'd done it for revenge. But I kept mum on this as the celebration went on, and simply tried to enjoy the rush of victory. It was the first time in a long while that I could remember feeling victorious about anything.

"What now?" asked Duncan, beside me. "Do we remain here?"

"Oui," said Jeanne, her eyes now free from the Weaver's threads. "We took this city. It's ours. With it, we could make Hell livable."

Anika frowned. "Some demons may have escaped the fire. What if they return with others?"

"It is possible," said Elias, his voice grave. "But we killed a great many, and there is uninhabited wilderness for miles around here. I know this; I used to travel with Weaver back and forth to her summer palace."

Jeanne scowled. "If we run about like toddlers without direction, we'll run into other fiends for certain. Better that we defend ourselves here, where we have the upper hand. Let us rebuild this place and turn it into a fortress. It could be years before they come for us. Hell is disorganized, with far too many people to govern. The demons have no grip on it."

I chewed on that. "It sounds to me like the demons don't really have any idea what they're doing here."

"No one has any idea what they're doing here," admitted Elias. "But that doesn't stop them from coming. Some demons seem to have a knack for finding unowned souls. It's like finding unclaimed land. If there is no demon torturing us now, then there is no competition. We're easy pickings."

"There is more to fear than just demons," said Duncan, brow furrowed, his beard blowing in the wind. "A group of wandering mortals might be just as eager to enslave us as the satyr. And they cannot be killed."

The strong man's scars told the story of one who had endured much. But Jeanne's expression was already one of cold disdain.

"We should not mistrust our fellow souls when we are hunted by those who have given theirs up," she said.

I frowned. "What do you mean, given theirs up?"

"Why do you think they can die when we cannot?" She gestured around her. "They were like us, once, but they chose to become demons instead. They gave up their souls."

Now that was a curious idea. Most curious indeed.

"Is that really possible?" I asked, leaning in. "Can mortal souls truly become demons?"

Anika's eyes narrowed, watching me very carefully.

"The fiends are choosy about who they turn," said Elias. "They don't want to taint their bloodlines with those they see as undeserving, and can be dissuaded by anything from your accent to the color of your skin. But every so often they see something in someone and decide they're fit to join the ranks of the monsters that once tormented them. Some believe they will get a better life from it. Some even say that demons can return to Earth."

Excitement sparked in my chest. Becoming a demon was no little thing to accept, and I wanted to dismiss it as the others did. But even then, the idea prickled me.

What if I *did* become a demon? I would be a person of power here in Hell. Safer. Stronger. Possibly able to return to Earth and have my revenge.

I wanted to know more, but could not ask my questions without raising suspicion. Instead, I decided to ask another question that had been bothering me. "Why are you even here, Elias? You don't seem so bad. What's your big sin?"

Elias shrugged. "I wouldn't know."

"Were you ever unfaithful to your wife? Killed anyone? Stolen anything?"

"Never. I worked hard. I was a dutiful husband. I never struck my wife or children. I turned the other cheek. Here I am."

I turned to Duncan. "And you?"

"I fought and died in the Crusades." Duncan shrugged. "We were told that we were fighting for God. That simply by fighting, our sins would be wiped clean."

I looked at Timothy, still hovering just outside the circle. "And you, Timothy?"

"I-uh-I stepped on an ant once," the boy stammered, clearly overwhelmed by the acknowledgment.

"An ant! Hellfire and eternal punishment!" I all but rolled my eyes. "What about you, Anika? You were, what, six when you died? Can't have done anything too bad."

"Seven," said Anika. "And no, I don't believe I did. I have encountered some that tell me it's because I had never learned the Christian god you speak of, and as such I did not worship him. But I have met countless men like you, Duncan, who did but ended up here anyway."

"It seems God has never made a child that didn't disappoint him," said Elias.

"Or perhaps none of us believed in the right gods," said Anika.

I frowned. "What about you, Jeanne? Did you sin?"

Jeanne's face soured. "I killed a man who attempted to take me by force. I suppose that was enough."

"That isn't bloody worth going to Hell for! What's wrong with this place?" I looked up at the distant stone sky, my upper lip raised in disgust. "Is it just me, or is this whole thing a little absurd? None of us deserve to be here. We should be up there." I pointed up and swished my finger around. "In that...other place."

Elias looked down. "There is no other place, Caleb. During my time in Hell, I've met countless priests and nuns. I've met saints who cried out to God and wondered what they'd done wrong. I've met children, so many children, far too young to have ever sinned. I've met babies—every miscarriage, every infant who perished in a harsh winter, infants who were baptized and whose parents loved them very much. There is nothing up there, Caleb. This is where everyone who dies ends up. It was all a farce." He exhaled, nostrils flaring. "But you know what? I still would have done what was right had I known all of this. I didn't need God telling me it was wrong. I wanted to be good because it was right, not because I was afraid of coming here."

"You *really* shouldn't be here then," I said, smirking. Based on his logic, everyone who had ever lived ended up here: every historical figure, every king, every famous artist or writer. If that was true, Hell had to be unfathomably vast. Far vaster than Earth.

I wondered if my parents were down here somewhere. If my father was wandering these wastes as a husk, or if my mother was being dragged into the River Styx again and again. I was tempted to look for them, but was it even possible to find the souls of lost loved ones in a place that only wanted to bring you pain? I could search for thousands of years and never find them.

"Some say that Hell is created from the nightmares of mortals yet to die," said Anika. "A composite of the underworlds we see in different faiths. I grew up being told of a cold place called Kuzimu, and indeed some parts of this place are so cold your teeth will shatter. We've seen the fire and punishment of your Christian Hell and the endless red of the River Styx. I've heard rumors of the Four Horsemen, such as the Pestilence that Lady Weaver mentioned. Even tales of a grand hall where men gather to do battle again and again, caught in an endless cycle of war and hate, wishing always to kill their enemies but unable to do so."

"Then perhaps this is merely a greater test," said Jeanne. "If God judged us on Earth, why not here as well, by forcing us to endure our worst nightmares? To seek happiness here rebels not just against the demons who torment us, but God as well. Perhaps this is the only way we may find the Heaven we deserve: by making it for ourselves. And we have eternity to do so." She smirked at me. "Think of it. There's nothing left to lose here. Nothing else to hope for, save God's forgiveness."

I frowned, far from convinced. "But there is no sign of God here, any more than there was on Earth."

She gestured broadly with her arms. "One might say the signs are everywhere. All around us, for those with the eyes to see them."

I shook my head. "That's what they said about Earth, too."

"Or perhaps the Cardinals are right, and this is what has become of Heaven," said Duncan.

We all looked at him, baffled. "What?" I asked.

"The Cardinals. The ones trying to bring order to this place with their Blood Saints." Duncan kept his eyes on the fire. He sounded anxious, like he was ambivalent about bringing this up. "They have churches. Huge black buildings of stone that they claim can offer salvation. The Church of Black Heaven states that we are in Heaven now, but it has been ravaged by sin. Now it is we mortals who must restore it to its former glory, by submitting to the punishment that awaits us." Duncan's voice was oddly reverent, as if he genuinely wanted to believe this, despite his doubts.

"Some Heaven this is," I said. "What about all the demons crawling around?"

"Angels," said Duncan. "Angels corrupted by the sins of men on Earth. They tried to absorb sin from mankind, but in the process were changed by it. Emperor Riven claims that Heaven was ruined because of us. That is why we must let them punish us. This...saves them. Purges the evil from their system. And over time, if enough of us willingly accept the sacrifice—"

"It's nonsense, Duncan," said Elias. "I was punished by Lady Weaver for over a century. She tortured more than I could say, and not once did it seem to redeem her. Indeed, she took great delight in it."

"I know. I know." Duncan's face scrunched up. "But what if it's true? What if, after thousands of years, this place becomes the Heaven we were promised? None of us belong in Hell. Maybe the issue is that so few submit willingly. Don't you see? This being true would give us power. It would mean we have the power to make this into Heaven."

"Maybe we already do," said Jeanne, reaching to grab my hand. "Look at us. We freed this city. We can rebuild it.

And we can live forever. We can do whatever we like!" She laughed, and then without warning threw herself upon me, lips smashing into mine. I was baffled; she hadn't seemed to be flirting with me at all before. Again, I felt hot from embarrassment, but no one cared. Everyone was eating and relaxing and speaking to one another, introducing themselves to one another. So, I decided to enjoy the moment. I melted into the kiss and held her body tighter against me.

Jeanne led me to an empty home that was still intact. She threw me onto a barely cushioned bed and climbed on top. "Do you know what the one perk of Hell is?" she asked. She kissed me again, then pulled away just long enough to say, "You can't get pregnant."

She was filthy, covered in cuts and bruises, and her brown hair was messy and tangled. But at that moment, to me, she could have been the fairest maiden in the world.

⸺◈⸺

After we were done and she was asleep in my arms, my thoughts wandered to the future. Jeanne wanted to remain here, and it seemed exceedingly wise to do the same. No matter how far I ventured, I couldn't expect to find what I sought. I could travel for eternity and not find a way back to Earth.

Besides, Jeanne was wonderful, possessing a fire most other souls lacked. And she wasn't hard on the eyes—by Hell's standards, anyway.

But then I wouldn't get my chance at vengeance.

Already, the rush of victory was fading. I didn't feel any stronger, nor more secure. All Thomas had to do was hit

Clara hard enough, just once, and she would end up plunging into this miserable afterlife just like me. I didn't want that for her, and every moment I spent here increased that risk. Every moment I remained weak, powerless, mortal...

I shook my head, surprised. It should have bothered me, how quickly I'd warmed to the idea of becoming a demon. The others certainly would have never agreed. I didn't even mind the thought of becoming killable again, permanently this time, if it meant I could have my revenge.

Still. It seemed best to remain until I knew where else to go. I sighed, my arms wrapped around the sleeping Jeanne. When I fell asleep, my dreams were haunted by the clinking of chains.

CHAPTER NINE

BYZANTIUM

"SO THIS IS OUR city, now." Elias's voice was distant, even confused, like he expected to awaken from a dream.

We had joined together in the center of town to discuss what to do: me, Jeanne, Elias, Duncan, and Anika. We who had led the rebellion. Even though we were once again sitting around the bonfire, our bleary eyes made it feel like morning.

"Ours," Jeanne agreed, arms crossed. "To build anew, as we see fit."

"Does anyone here actually know how to run a city?" asked Elias. "What should we make of it? Who should rule it?"

Jeanne's eyes narrowed. "No one. No masters. Everyone does as they will. After all, we cannot die, and we have nothing to steal from each other. If someone commits an offense, we can decide how to punish them."

"Isn't that a rather...antiquated way of doing things?" asked Elias. "Laws came into being for a reason, Jeanne. You cannot expect crowds to be wise."

119

Jeanne's eyes flashed with rage. She stepped over to Elias, body puffed up like she meant to strike him. "Then whose wisdom are we to listen to? That of a king who cares only for building his harem? A court that listens to whoever pays them? Soldiers who beat anyone who speaks ill of their lord?"

Elias lifted his chin, remaining calm. "I was a man of knowledge, Jeanne. I spent my life studying the human body and experimenting with ways to heal it. And do you know what my people did to me? They accused me of witchcraft and burned me alive."

"You're a doctor?" I asked, surprised.

"Was," said Elias. "Here, I'm afraid my skills are quite useless."

"Perhaps this whole conversation is proof that we should come up with *something*," said Anika. "What if you come to blows over this discussion? How would we have decided who to support?"

"You'd support whoever you wanted," said Jeanne. "It's not like we can kill each other." She kicked some dirt into the fire, causing it to erupt with a fierce blaze. "You think you ought to be king, then, do you, Elias?"

"On the contrary," said Elias. "I feel we should be ruled by the one who is ultimately responsible for our freedom. The one who convinced us all of this cause in the first place."

All eyes turned to me. I shook my head, my cheeks burning. "No. You all fought back, too. If I'd done it alone, it would have never worked. I can't accept this."

"That's why it should be you, Caleb," said Elias. "Anyone else would seek that power."

By now, dozens of onlookers had gathered around us. Some let out shouts or murmurs in agreement with Elias. My throat dried, anxious and embarrassed. How was I to tell them that I'd only fought back for my own selfish purposes?

"What do you all say?" asked Elias, turning to the others.

Cheers from the crowd. "Aye!" Timothy piped in, his voice the loudest of all.

Jeanne's upper lip raised. "All right. If we've got to have someone in charge, it might as well be him. Especially if that means I get to have my say, too."

"He has my support," said Duncan. "He brought us here. Only right that he gets us out."

Young Anika studied me, her gaze more suspicious than the others, like she could see the darkness hiding under my skin. "And how would you rule?" she asked.

"Ideally, I wouldn't rule at all," I said, grinding my teeth, but this only caused the crowd to murmur in reverence, seemingly even more impressed than before. "I know nothing of ruling! You want to come to me for advice or ask me to make decisions? I can do that. But I don't rule any souls, not here, not anywhere. I won't."

Unfortunately, the crowd only cheered louder at this. It had clearly been decided. I was to be this place's leader, whether I wanted the job or not.

"Well, I can't very well lead this city if it's burned down," I said, searching for any excuse to relieve myself of the responsibility.

"Then we can rebuild it!" said Duncan, and again everyone cheered.

"We can build it how we like," said Anika, eyes lighting up at last as she, too, felt the excitement.

"We need a wall around us for defense," said Jeanne. "And a barracks for soldiers."

"A library," said Elias, actually smiling at the thought. "Surely even here there are books."

"All of you are missing the obvious," said Duncan. "We need a tavern!"

"What, with no alcohol?" I asked, baffled.

"We shall find some!" proclaimed Duncan, earning more cheers.

"We will need more wood," I said.

"The Deadwoods are nearby," said Anika. "We can harvest from them. Just be careful not to touch the trees that have faces. They were once people, and their splinters will turn you into a tree as well."

"And what if other demons find us?" I asked.

"We shall fight them back!" Jeanne roared, and everyone cheered louder than ever at this.

I stood there, flummoxed. One by one, every concern I'd voiced had been dismissed. I feared that arguing further would only anger them, turning them into enemies. I sighed, shook my head, and accepted that getting out of here might take longer than I'd thought.

"What should we call it?" I asked. "Can't very well have a city without a name."

Jeanne thought a moment before saying, "Byzantium."

I doubted that everyone in the crowd understood the reference, but it made sense to me. A place for souls to find rest. That was what it would have to be, with or without me.

"Byzantium!" Duncan roared, fist in the air, and the crowd followed suit.

And before I could even blink, the reconstruction began.

The Deadwoods turned out to be an enormous forest of tall, grey trees. Many indeed had eyes and mouths that looked carved into them. They lurched with painful, bark-stretching screams, but seemed incapable of forming words. I accompanied the first lumber group to the edge of the Deadwoods, avoiding the ones with faces as Anika had instructed. We returned with as much wood as we could carry.

Slowly but surely, Byzantium took form atop the ruins of what came before: towering walls for protection, a bell tower to warn everyone if we spotted enemies, weapon forges, Jeanne's barracks, and even Elias's library. Without any fear of death, many happily volunteered for dangerous construction projects. Some insisted, despite my arguments, on reconstructing the remains of Lady Weaver's Mansion into a palace for me and Jeanne. There were thousands of souls here, many of them craftsmen in life, and they brought those skills with them into death: stone masons, woodworkers, smithies, all of them eager to rebuild, to make death a bit closer to life. Soon our army was outfitted with not just blades, but also rifles with bayonets.

We even discovered a basement in the ruins of Weaver's Mansion where a chest full of silver coins awaited. "Silver!" Elias exclaimed, excitement in his voice as he picked up a palmful, letting the coins leak out from between his fingers.

"What use is coin to us?" asked Jeanne. "We've no intention of trading with the fiends."

"Silver is lethal to demons," said Anika, sharing Elias's excitement. "They don't heal cuts from silver wounds. That makes it the most valuable metal there is down here."

"We can smelt it down," said Elias, the corners of his eyes moist with relief. "Coat weapons with it. Don't you see? This could give us an edge if they attack!"

And so we, Byzantium's founders, were soon equipped with silver weapons. Jeanne requested our forge to create a mace with silver spikes, while I asked for a knife with a blade made entirely out of silver. Still, I made sure to ration some silver for later. Money was probably a good thing to save, even here.

I write about all this as if it happened overnight, and while that is far from the case, time is different in Hell, distorted by our inability to count the hours or days. Even now as I write about it, I'm compressing a great swath of time to a few pages, simply because this is all that I can remember. And yet even these memories may be discolored like an infected wound, altered by my own deep longing for forgiveness.

It is the truth. I know it. I feel it in my heart. But I have lied to so many. Have I lied to myself, just as convincingly, through omission if nothing else? Have I strung together these disparate memories into some clean narrative to justify my deeds, every word carefully chosen to mitigate my vileness, to myself if no one else? After all, I have nothing else to hope for in this place.

Back then, though, we did have hope. The rebellion had awakened a new zeal in us, and even without the promise of monetary payment, many did the best they could to help in one way or another. Having burned what lay before down, we rebuilt it how we liked, every citizen having their say in what was needed.

Arranging it all kept me enormously busy. Again and again, I would tell myself, "Tomorrow night, I will leave."

Yet again and again, I would delay, unwilling to abandon my responsibilities. *As soon as the wall is completed. As soon as the tower is finished. As soon as I know how to find a demon who might turn me.*

I felt, on some level, that abandoning Byzantium would make me a failure as a man. To seek out its enemies and join their ranks would betray the people who had come to see me as their leader.

But to stay would make me no less a failure, for it would mean turning my back on my vow, abandoning Clara to Thomas's cruelty, and letting my enemy go unpunished.

I could accept neither, so in my ambivalence I remained—hopeful that in time, my path would become clearer.

Every time I closed my eyes, I expected to awaken to fire, or pain, or the ringing of our bell. But day after day passed, and we went unnoticed. Surely, Hell was full of demons, but all around us were great, empty swaths of seemingly deserted wilderness.

Still, we all knew it was only a matter of time. We had rotating guards for the perimeter, ensuring there were always people on duty. Jeanne established scouting parties to check our surroundings. Secretly, I hoped they might really find a demon so that I might interrogate it, perhaps force it to turn me. But as the months passed, we remained unnoticed.

Meanwhile, Duncan led a group further into the Deadwoods in search of fruit or other provisions. There were none to be found, but they did find weeds, which Duncan fermented to make some truly foul alcohol. It tasted like ash, and indeed some vomited from the first sip, but it was nonetheless possible to get drunk off it. Duncan was quite pleased, and wasted no time in constructing a tavern.

Jeanne approved of the idea, for alcohol would mean fights. "We can improve our fighting skills," Jeanne explained. "Tournaments. Training sessions. Weedbeer for the victors. Then, when we are attacked, we will be ready."

"And what will you call it?" I asked.

Duncan's eyes gleamed. "I once met a stranger who believed that one day, he would go to a great mead hall where everyone fought, but no one died. We shall call it what he did: Valhalla."

Valhalla was not simply a tavern. It was a gathering place for our city's warriors, where we would fight to the death again and again, and always wake up the next day.

"No restrictions!" crowed Duncan during my first fight with him, as he raised a table leg to clock my head. "No consequences."

Another hit and I was down, waking up only to see him towering over me, guzzling his disgusting weedbeer like water.

After I recovered, I attended one of the training sessions he hosted. Almost everyone in the city showed up to one sooner or later, for we all knew that demons might one day find us.

"You want to start by taking out their weak spots," said Duncan, poking spots on my body. "Joints. Feet. Crotch. Eyes. Gaps in their armor. Wherever they can be distracted, weakened, disabled."

I learned much from my bouts at Valhalla. I hoped that rigorous exercise would strengthen me, but even after months of constant fighting and manual labor, my muscles did not grow. This may have been because of my utter lack of nutrition, but it also might have been because I was dead. No matter what I did, my body returned to how it had been when I'd died. Yet again I found myself envious of demons, whose bodies were gifted with unnatural strength without them even trying, while I worked endlessly in pursuit of strength forever beyond my grasp.

I could not rely on strength the way someone like Duncan could. Instead, I had to learn how to fight with intelligence and unrelenting viciousness, analyzing the best, most effective places to strike. I learned to channel the rage I felt about my body into a bloodthirsty fearlessness. I couldn't die, but neither could anyone else, and that meant I didn't have to hold back. I could play dirty: going for the eyes, the balls, grabbing them by the hair. I imagined every opponent was Thomas, who I knew—if I was fortunate enough to once again face—would dwarf me as much as anyone else.

Eventually, I was able to topple even Duncan, to the surprise of everyone in attendance.

But not everyone was ready to strike killing blows, even though we all knew we would survive. A small woman named Ji couldn't seem to muster up the courage to do more than a gentle pat to her opponent's chest, and even that made her giggle with embarrassment.

"We need to teach them how to face their fears," said Jeanne, as we watched the fight from the sidelines. "Facing another person, it doesn't feel real. We need to show these people they can win even when they're terrified."

"Didn't they already do that when we rebelled?" I asked.

"That was once. We need to reinforce it. Besides, I wager that not everyone fought."

By now, our scouts had informed us of a waterfall in the Deadwoods. It was easy to reach, and not so high as to be deadly even if we'd found it in life. Both it and the lake below were as crimson as the sea. Dozens of us stood on the shore at its peak, looking down at the pool. I would be lying if I claimed not to be afraid. Even knowing that it wouldn't kill me, imagining the fall made me dizzy. But Duncan stood before us all and said, "We shall all jump today! Some of us may be wounded, but every wound shall heal. We have spent so long thinking of eternity as a curse, but what if it's a gift? What if it means we can survive whatever this world throws at us? We can fall. We can die. We can break our bodies over and over and always get back up. No consequences!"

Though it was hidden in the bushels of his beard, Duncan's grin was infectious. Even I felt something of a rush as he waded into the stream. The water went up to his knees, and while the river was wide, it was not so rapid as to topple him. He approached the drop and turned his back to it, arms folded across his chest. Then he fell backwards off the waterfall. We surged to look over the cliff and watched him splash into the bottom—only to break the surface moments later, still grinning, lifting his fist to show he was fine.

Mirroring his expression, Jeanne dashed into the water and leaped over the edge herself. She too was fine.

That was all the bulk of us needed. The most excited rushed to the cliff all at once to take the plunge, followed by more hesitant clusters. Even Timothy gave me a sheepish grin before joining the charge, checking to make sure I was watching.

I waited to go last to ensure no one would be left behind. Soon, only Anika and I remained. Anika scowled at the cliff like it was some beast that had wronged her.

"Stupid," she said. "I have been here for thousands of years. There's no point in fearing one little cliff."

She looked enviously at those splashing gleefully in the water below. They had become like children, and poor Anika, an eternal child herself, seemed to resent them for how easily they'd taken the plunge. Her fists trembled.

"You died by falling, didn't you?" I asked.

She nodded stiffly. "Traveling with my family above a narrow ravine. Refugees, we were. I slipped. Fell down into the pass. Then fell down here. No good things come of falling, it seems."

"Then why did you come?" I asked.

She exhaled loudly. "I swore to myself I would. I can't let this control me anymore."

"Would it help if we jumped together?" I asked.

Though her lip remained curled with disdain, Anika nodded.

"Here," I said, picking her up and hoisting her against me, heavy though she was. Then I waded into the water. Anika clung to me tighter as it splashed her rags.

"Please don't let go," she squeaked, closing her eyes.

"I won't," I said. "I'm going to approach the drop now. I'll let you know before I jump."

I stepped to the edge of the cliff. Anika tightened her squeeze, breath rapid with panic.

"Wait."

"You want to turn back?" I asked.

She pulled back enough to look me in the eye, her gaze fierce. "Put me down. I need to do this myself."

"Are you sure?"

"Yes."

I lowered her into the water, which went up to her chest. Anika glowered at the drop before us—then jumped. I followed.

The impact of the water hurt, but soon I was submerged in the comforting warmth of the deep lake. Anika was submerged nearby, eyes still wide with terror, rubbing her limbs—likely from pain. I swam to her and took hold, swimming up so we could break the surface together.

Dead or not, it was an enormous relief to gasp for air, and I couldn't help but grin again. Anika wailed in horror, but breathed, and breathed, and after a moment, relief filled her face. "I did it. I can't believe I did it." I shared her strange bliss. It was like a baptism; like being reborn.

Our eyes stung from the salty red water, but we couldn't help but all play there: splashing, racing, competing to see how far down we could go. A few of our number were mildly wounded, but Duncan had been right. There were no real consequences. We could do as we pleased here in Hell.

When we'd had our fill, we took to the shore and journeyed through the woods back to Byzantium. We were all in an unexpectedly fabulous mood until Jeanne brought her fingers to her lips, silencing our chatter, and pointed to our left. The web of branches was challenging to see through, but in the distance, there was movement. Multiple armored bodies.

"Soldiers?" I whispered. I couldn't see them clearly, but the distant voices didn't all sound human.

We passed the message along down the line, and hurried back to Byzantium as quietly as we could. I think we all breathed in relief as we reached it. The danger seemed to have passed for now, and we could go back to riding the high of having faced our fears. We were stronger now. Reborn. And with Duncan's training, our warriors were becoming more formidable every day.

But even then, I had the terrible feeling that our troubles had only begun.

131

CHAPTER TEN

THE COMMEDIA DELLA MORTE

TIME PASSED, NOT IN days or nights, but it passed. I worked with the other souls to rebuild the burned buildings, trying to bury my uncertainty under the labor.

By now, I was trying to convince myself that it was enough. Returning to Earth was a ridiculous dream, and I believed that I'd be happier giving it up entirely. I'd only known Clara for a week, and I'd spent far more time among my fellow rebels than that. It should have followed that I could forget about her, and Thomas, and the entire world I'd left behind.

And yet the desire for vengeance continued to gnaw at me, like a tick in my mind. It nibbled when I lay awake, trying to sleep. It burrowed when I worked with my hands. Whenever my mind was not occupied with some intellectual problem, it would be there to plague me with thoughts of rage.

Eventually, Duncan decided to leave. "I must seek out the truth," he told me. "I wish to learn what this place is, and I don't think I will find my answers here."

He said his goodbyes. Then he turned around and sprinted across the blackened wasteland before diving into the crimson Styx.

I tried to push away the envy coiling around my heart. I should have been the one fleeing, not him. But without a clear destination, how long would it be before I was captured by another demon? No... better to stay here. I fancied that one day, I might even be able to forget the dream of vengeance and accept my new home for the opportunity it was.

"I wish I could join him," admitted Elias, watching Duncan's increasingly distant figure. "Had I died a younger man, I would run through Hell forever. But I died an old man, and I can't run at all."

"I'm sure you could outrun me," I said, eager to be distracted from my thoughts. "Come on. Race you to that pillar over there."

"Oh, don't," said Elias. "I know you. You're just going to move really slowly."

I grinned. It was like he'd read my mind.

Instead, we took a long walk around the walls surrounding the city, inspecting our defenses. "Never did figure out what to do about flyers," said Elias. "Succubi, incubi, imp scouts..."

"That's what the bows and arrows are for," I said.

"Arrow wounds are like bug bites for most demons. Though that may be the old familiar despair trying to drag me back down." Elias sighed, coming to a stop. He seemed to be lost in thought, his gaze traveling back down to his bare feet. "Sometimes, I still can't believe Lady Weaver is truly dead. I spent so long with her that part of me almost mourns her. She... it sounds dreadful to say. But she saw something in me that no one else did. I have always regretted dying an old man. Living in this weak, wretched body for eternity. But she looked at me as though I were young again. Saw my body as something beautiful. Her perfect canvas. She said the wrinkles and hanging flesh added texture."

"She was an artist?"

"A most methodical one. The torture she inflicted upon me was not merely out of sadism, but rather to make me into her art. Each tender laceration brought me closer to her vision for what I could be: my wrists laced together behind my back, my lips sewn to muffle my screams, my eyelids sewn to my brows so that I had to watch her work. She'd call me beautiful. And yet she was never entirely satisfied with her work, always finding some little thing to gripe about: a stray thread, uneven lacing..."

I knew this all too well. When I performed, I would always get hung up over getting a single note wrong, even when no one else noticed. I laced my fingers tightly, uncomfortable with this commonality. "I'm sorry, Elias."

He shook his head, a single tear dripping down his cheek. "There is no reason to miss her. I tried for years to escape from her. And yet, on some level, I wanted her to finally make the perfect version of me. Not just because I thought she might finally stop, but also because then I might have value to someone, becoming something more than another useless wandering soul. If I'm honest with myself, her rare smiles were the one thing keeping me going for a long time. But perfection is a lie, Caleb. Even Byzantium's defenses will remain imperfect, no matter how much we try to make them so."

Duncan had been our strongest warrior, and the city felt more vulnerable without him. But as time went on, more warriors came to join us, many already bearing weapons, swelling our population from perhaps two thousand to roughly five thousand.

The strangers said Duncan had told them of Byzantium: a city that represented the hope for Heaven, even in Hell. Word was spreading. The strangers swore to help us build and defend the city. Many brought gifts to pay for their entry: horses, dogs, firearms, compasses, and books.

I was confused by the animals until Elias explained it to me one day when we were organizing books in his library. "Demons import animals and possessions from the land of the living," he said, placing a thick volume onto a shelf. "Livestock, cats, clothes, whatever suits them. But as far as I have seen, the souls of animals do not come here after death. When they die here, they do not get back up."

"More's the pity," sighed Anika, overhearing us. "I wouldn't say no to a nice immortal cat."

"How do they do all this...importing?" I asked.

Elias shrugged. "No one knows."

"If they can bring things back and forth, that means they have a way back and forth."

"None that the dead are allowed to cross, I'm afraid. And we are the dead."

As always, I was left with more questions than answers about the nature of the underworld, but few others in the city were preoccupied with such concerns. What mattered to them was that we were growing in size, population, and power.

In time, our army even had enough horses to form a cavalry.

"You see?" Jeanne asked me one night, as we curled up together after hours of work. "Even strangers know this place can become Heaven."

I stared into the darkness, my arm wrapped around her, wishing the feeling of her body against me brought me comfort. But I merely felt pressure. Even my arm ached, yearning to be loose.

"Why are you so sad?" Jeanne asked, running her fingers through my hair.

Was I that obvious? I could not tell her about my yearning to escape; about how even now, with my arms around her, I was fixated on Clara. So instead, I whispered the doubts I thought she'd better understand. "What if we aren't the first? What if others have done this before?"

Jeanne frowned. "So what if they did? We are doing it now, and I'm the happiest I've been since I was alive. We can do whatever we want. Swim in deadly tides, jump off endless cliffs. We'll survive, always."

I held her tighter, but the mood did not pass. Ever since Duncan's departure, it had become harder to shake the feeling that I did not belong here. I was wasting my time.

⸺◆⸻

I tried to move on. Truly, I did. And some nights, I actually managed to forget about my oath of vengeance. My responsibilities as Byzantium's leader had become all-consuming, leaving little room for anything else.

But other nights, I would awaken haunted by flashbacks of my death, visions of Clara's own, and fits of rage so overwhelming I'd get up to smash my fists into the wall.

No, I could not stay here. I could not let this city seduce me. There was work to be done, and my soul would not rest until I completed it. I had to find a way out. Had to find a way to become a demon and return to Earth. But how?

Now, in my cell, I wonder what trajectory my eternity might have taken had I not been so gripped by this festering rage. Whether it would have turned out any better. Whether I could have learned to love Jeanne, who I'd been with for months, maybe even years, in comparison to the single week I spent in Clara's company. But one never knows what they have until it is lost, just as one never truly knows who they are until it's too late.

It all changed the day our scouts called me to the wall to inform me of an approaching caravan. There were four horse-drawn wagons, but the horses appeared to be skeletal. So did their drivers. "Reapers," I said, watching them through the spyglass. "Have the men prepare for combat."

"Wait," said Anika, peering through a spyglass of her own. "That's not a war party. The wagons aren't armored. They don't even look armed."

"Why else would they be coming?" asked Jeanne. "It could be a trick."

"Maybe it's a merchant," said Anika. "A necromancer who uses his Reapers for labor rather than war."

"Who has even heard of such a thing?" scoffed Jeanne.

"Can't be too careful," I agreed, motioning to our soldiers to stand at the ready atop the battlements. They aimed their rifles as the Reaper caravan neared.

The front wagon stopped before the gate, and the Reaper driving it jumped down, bone feet hitting the sand. He scratched his skull as he looked up at us, a motion that baffled me. From what Jeanne and Elias had told me, Reapers moved in simple, puppet-like motions. They did not scratch themselves or express confusion. Still, I wondered if an especially advanced necromancer could command one to do so, in an effort to make it seem more human.

Then the Reaper said "Greetings!" and waved his hand broadly.

My jaw could have hit the ground.

"What the fuck?" said Jeanne, just as shocked. "Reapers don't talk."

I squinted down at the creature. "Hello?" I said, waving my hand back.

"Would this be the city of Byzantium?" The Reaper's voice was creaky, but oddly jovial—even friendly.

"Who wants to know?" I called.

"Ah. Forgive me." The Reaper bowed deeply, his hand zooming out from beneath his stomach to stretch high into the air, just as his face dipped low enough to reach the ground. "I am Rumpelstiltskin Von Heinrichson, and behind me is my troupe: the Commedia Della Morte, the one and only Reaper theatre troupe on Black Heaven or Earth. We've come searching for the mortal city of Byzantium to offer our services."

"What services?" I asked, jaw tight.

"Why, the greatest service of all," said the Reaper, with another low bow. "Entertainment!"

"What the fuck?" Jeanne repeated. "Right, this is definitely a trick. Guns at the ready, men."

"Wait!" said Anika. "Let's at least hear them out."

"These are not normal Reapers," said Elias. "When a necromancer transforms a corpse into a Reaper, the person it once was ceases to exist. They lose all ability to speak or think for themselves. They are puppets for the necromancer. And when that necromancer dies, they crumble into a lifeless pile of bones."

"Aye, our circumstances are unique," said Rumpelstiltskin. "We would be delighted to tell you all about it if you let us into the city."

Another Reaper joined at his side, having apparently stepped down from their own wagon. This one was wearing a faded purple dress that drifted in the wind. "We promise we won't be any trouble," it said. "Your men may search our wagons if you'd like. Just please be gentle with the costumes. Some are irreplaceable."

A woman's voice. It was theoretically possible for a necromancer to speak through their Reaper puppet, but two voices from two separate Reapers?

Jeanne led a squad to give the caravan a thorough inspection, and returned with a glimmer in her eyes.

"Barely any weapons. Only a few swords and maces to defend themselves with. They are, however, carrying food and alcohol. Real alcohol, not that swill Duncan makes."

"Truly?" I repeated, suddenly all too aware of my hunger and thirst. I hadn't had real food since I was alive, unless Elias or hellhound meat counted. And *real alcohol?*

"We'd be happy to trade if you've got any silver," Rumpelstiltskin called up. "Theatre may be our passion, but it doesn't pay the bills half as well as drinks. We've a fine selection imported from the land of the living, enough to get half the city drunk. Maybe the entire city, if you share. And the food, while not as fresh as you might like due to our weeks on the road, has not yet spoiled either."

My stomach growled, and it was hard to not feel curious given the bizarre nature of it all. "Let them in," I said. "We greatly outnumber them. If anything happens, it's on my head."

We opened the gates. Then we had a party.

Valhalla was packed. The Reapers performed circus acts: juggling each other's heads, tight-rope walking, even singing and music with a harp. Alas, they had no violins and did not let me join in their playing. But my disappointment was softened when they donned Commedia dell'arte masks, and performed the silly plays with such zest that I almost forgot they were Reapers.

Some in the crowd gave into the merriment right away. Others watched uncomfortably, weapons still in hand, waiting for any excuse to attack. Rumpelstiltskin ignored the hostility, seemingly understanding why so many would be suspicious. His prices were more than affordable, and he even donated some old books to Elias's library, stating that they would be better appreciated here.

The food was rationed out, leaving me with just an apple. I devoured it as quickly as I could, barely even conscious as I took bite after bite, the hunger overtaking me. Before I knew it, it was gone. While others were savoring their food, I had not. Worse, my stomach seemed to have forgotten how to work and soon felt bloated with acid.

"Another kind of torture, isn't it?" said Rumpelstiltskin, something of a grin in his voice even though he had no lips. Up close, I could hear that his voice had a slight echo as it emitted from the cave of his skull.

"Will you tell us what the hell you are, already?" asked a drunk Jeanne beside me, her voice slurred, eyelids limp.

Rumpelstiltskin let out a dry cackle. "We used to be the puppets of a necromancer. I don't even remember those days, for *I* didn't exist then. But our necromancer became plagued with thoughts of death, and over time grew obsessed with the notion that he could not be an expert on death magic without actually dying. So one night, he ordered us, his Reapers, to devour him. His brain, his heart, his spleen...every inch of him. And in so doing, we gained sentience. Seemed to be his way of thanking us for all the work we did for him for...oh, five centuries or so. I know not whether the person I am now has anything in common with who I was in life, so I took a new name. Rumpelstiltskin. The name one can never guess, for a past that cannot be found." He jerked his head in the direction of a juggling Reaper whose skull was painted with colorful makeup. "He goes by Faust." Then he gestured to a dancer with bone fairy wings, obviously fake. "And she goes by Mab."

"Don't you wonder who you were in life?" I asked.

The Reaper shook his skull. "What would be the point? The man I was died long ago. This frees me to be someone new. Whoever I want to be, in fact. This city you've built seems to be similar. Whoever you were in life...your sins, your regrets, your dreams...none of that matters now. And as most of us have unhappy lives, is another chance not something to welcome?"

I considered his words, and found myself struck with an anger I could not explain. He was right, and part of me hated him for it.

"Besides," he added, leaning in close, "better to enjoy freedom while you still have it."

My hand went to my belt, where I'd sheathed a crude knife, but Rumpelstiltskin raised a bone palm in reassurance.

"We have no intention of revealing your city's location," he said. "But mortals have done this before, and it rarely lasts long. The Blood Saints make sure of that. And I fear a sizable brigade of them is nearby."

"The Blood Saints?" I repeated.

Rumpelstiltskin nodded. "Demonic soldiers who serve the Church of Black Heaven, and its leader Emperor Riven. It is said that they will allow anyone to join their ranks and become a demon themselves. I cannot say whether they will ever find you, but if word of your city reached us, then they may have heard of it as well."

I remembered the soldiers in the forest. Something sparked in my chest, as volatile as the acid in my belly. "When was the last time you saw them?" I asked.

"Roughly forty miles south, a few nights ago."

That was further away than the Deadwoods. They'd been moving in the opposite direction from us. This was good for Byzantium, but it brought a dry feeling to my throat. "Are they looking for us?" I asked.

"I believe they have another query," said Rumpelstiltskin. "Something of far greater concern than mere mortal rebels."

Jeanne made a face. "What could an army of demons possibly fear?"

"The Four." Cool air hissed through the cracks of Rumpelstiltskin's pearly whites. He looked left and right, then lowered his voice. "The underworld houses four horsemen. Two are allied under Riven's banner. The third has disappeared. The fourth rides rogue somewhere here in the underworld. Pestilence, her name is, and Riven is rumored to be hunting her. He seeks to reclaim her power for himself."

I furrowed my brow, remembering Weaver's mention of Pestilence invading her Patchwork Sea.

"How would we know this Pestilence?" asked Jeanne.

Hollow though Rumpelstiltskin's eye sockets were, they still seemed to pierce us with their gaze. "If you're lucky, you'll never find out. Either way, you had best be prepared. It is possible the Blood Saints will find you while they search, and should they learn of this place, I guarantee they will breach its walls. Especially given that this is no ordinary brigade." He lowered his voice and looked around us, as if frightened he might be overheard. "It is being led by one of Riven's most infamous ritualists. A Cardinal, high in the ranks of the Church of Black Heaven. An incubus they call Salem Sotirios."

I did not recognize the name, but the very air seemed to shiver as Rumpelstiltskin spoke it. "A ritualist, you say?"

"One who can alter reality through magic. Sotirios is rumored to be a man of unfathomable power and unspeakable cruelty, possessing all the beauty of Lucifer himself, but a heart blacker than a starless night." Rumpelstiltskin's grim tone clashed with the perpetual smile of his teeth. "I do not fear most, but I fear him."

"I don't," said Jeanne, scowling. "What more can they do to us?"

"What more?" Rumpelstiltskin let out a dry, humorless chuckle. "Punishments of malice beyond what you or I could imagine, I can promise you. That is something I have heard often in my years of traveling. Here in the underworld, it can *always* get worse. Have you heard of Tartarus?"

Jeanne and I both shook our heads.

Again, Rumpelstiltskin hesitated. "Imagine a prison larger than most cities. The Church of Black Heaven created it as a place to house their enemies, from mortal rebels to powerful demons. Over time, it has transformed into their effort to bring law to the underworld, and ensure no souls have the strength to rebel. Tartarus is said to be far worse than the rest of Hell. There is no chance of escape. No chance of freedom. Only cruelty so exquisitely awful that even the strongest warriors lose hope. If you've got even an ounce of life left in your soul, Tartarus takes it away. It is the very worst of Hell, and it remakes all its prisoners into its own image."

"They won't break me," Jeanne snarled. "I will bow to no man ever again."

"For your sake, my lady, I hope that is true." Rumpelstiltskin bowed deeply, then turned to address the room. "Byzantium!" he bellowed. "What do you all say to witnessing an all-Reaper performance of the Scottish Play?"

⚬

As charming as the performance was, I found myself unable to focus on any of it. I was too haunted by Rumpelstiltskin's words; by the knowledge that the Blood Saints lurked somewhere just beyond our gates. It must have been them in the Deadwoods.

Rumpelstiltskin's troupe departed not long after, much to Byzantium's sorrow. We had drained their stock of alcohol, but Rumpelstiltskin promised to return with more someday. "Should you still be standing," he added, with a hollow laugh.

"We should not ignore his warning," I told Jeanne, as we watched him leave from the gate. "We should scout. See if we can find these Blood Saints before they find us."

Jeanne shook her head. "They seem to be heading in the other direction. Why draw their attention? Our scouts could get captured."

"It's worth the risk if we find out where they're camped," I said. "And how many of them there are. We're armed now, and stronger than we were before."

She scowled. "Fine. But I'm joining the scout party."

"As will I," I said. I wanted to see these Blood Saints myself.

Jeanne and I took horses for a ride beyond the walls, bearing rifles with silver bayonets. To my frustration, we were joined by Timothy. The cheery boy continued to idolize me, no matter how uncomfortable this made me. "Honor to ride with you, sir," he kept saying, bowing his head low each time.

I told myself that I would kill any Blood Saints we found, but deep down, I wasn't so sure. Some hunger in me had awakened—some desperate certainty that they could bring me closer to accomplishing the dream I'd promised to never give up.

We headed south, crossing over ashen black soil with scattered dead foliage and the cawing of distant, enormous ravens. The wind was heavy, stinking of sulfur, and the edge of the Deadwoods remained always at our side, some of the trees bearing the faces of those who had joined their ranks.

All too abruptly, I noticed another group of riders in the distance: three to our three, all of them wearing gleaming black medieval armor and horned helmets. One pointed and whistled, and the entire trio rode toward us in a furious gallop, drawing blades and axes. Mud splattered beneath the hooves of their steeds.

I unholstered my rifle, aimed for their heads, and fired. My aim was rubbish. Jeanne was able to shoot one in the arm, but he remained on his horse, seemingly unbothered. Timothy forgot to undo the safety and squeezed the trigger pointlessly in a blind panic.

The riders let out shrieks of excitement as they closed in on us, forcing us to resort to melee. The helmets didn't cover their pale faces, which would have been human were it not for the fangs. Vampires then—like Thomas. Their armor covered them head to toe, with the faces the only visible weak point.

"Go for the faces!" I roared, holding the rifle like a blade. Timothy did the same, while Jeanne stashed her rifle and readied her silver-spiked mace instead.

We met the warriors blade to blade, with a fearlessness that seemed to astonish them. One froze in shock as Jeanne barreled toward him and bashed him off his horse. Even as he fell, he swung his battleaxe into Jeanne's horse, causing the steed to neigh in pain and topple to the ground, trapping one of Jeanne's legs below it. Jeanne roared in pain, pinned to the ground, bones no doubt crunching under the dead horse's weight.

I sank my bayonet through the other soldier's face, downing him. A rush surged through me; the silver was working. The fiend was dead, and I wagered we could kill the others, too. I slapped the soldier Jeanne had faced with my rifle's butt. He toppled to the ground beside Jeanne, who slammed her mace into his skull until it caved in, the silver-coated spikes ensuring he would never get up. The air already stank of blood and dirt, pungent enough that I wrinkled my nose.

The final soldier had been busy stabbing Timothy in the chest, but upon seeing his squadmates fall, he opted for retreat, galloping in the direction of the Deadwoods.

Jeanne tried to pry her leg out from under the dead horse without success. More bone crunching sounds echoed, and she let out a blood curdling scream. "Get him," she grunted. "You can come back for me."

I hesitated, afraid of leaving her behind, but it could not be helped. The final soldier might tell the others about us. So Timothy and I gave chase, breaking through the tree line.

While I feared for Jeanne, I also felt a strange rush of power, excitement vibrating through my body. Duncan's training had improved my fighting skills. I'd killed one soldier, wounded another, and now the third was running from me. I clenched my teeth, eager for more of this power, for the rush to continue. I sped up, hoping to catch the demon first. If I could just talk to him... if I could find out whether Rumpelstiltskin's words were true, and the Blood Saints really *did* turn anyone who joined them...

Beside me, Timothy was in awful shape. Blood flowed freely from his chest wound, and he coughed some up as well. He grimaced in the direction of the soldier, red in the cracks between his teeth.

"Hold back," I told him. "I can catch him."

But Timothy kicked his horse to make it speed up. "I'll get this one, sir!" he called. "I'll be strong like you. Just you wait!"

He surged before me, caught up with the demonic rider, and leaped from his horse to barrel into the rider. Both tumbled to the ground, the demon's steed fleeing, but the vampire quickly regained control, rolling on top and pummeling the boy with a shining black gauntlet, knuckle spikes tearing scarlet trenches through Timothy's cheek. The boy screamed in pain, the sound so high-pitched that it made my blood boil. He wasn't just in pain; he was absolutely mortified.

"HELP ME!" he cried. "HELP ME, SIR!"

I got off my own horse and stormed over, grabbing the vampire and pulling him off the boy before stabbing him with the bayonet for good measure. Timothy's face was a mess, covered in deep cuts, weeping as he bled.

"Are you all right?" I began.

Before Timothy could answer, a woman's tingly laugh echoed through the woods. It sounded innocent and gentle, even though it could not be.

"So fierce." The voice velvet smooth, the sort that could only belong to a beautiful woman. It also seemed to come from somewhere above me.

"Show yourself!" I whirled around, but I didn't see her.

A soft laugh echoed from the darkness between the trees ahead of me. "I'm right here."

I could not help but turn and pursue it. Timothy let out a pitiful wail behind me: "Please...don't...leave me, sir...it's got to be a trap..."

The boy was probably right. The demon might capture me, interrogate me. But I could not let this opportunity go. "We can't let her return to the others," I hissed. Yes, that was the excuse I could make, both to him and myself. Besides, there was no time to think. I charged into the foliage, even then knowing it was sloppy of me to not finish the vampire off; that I should have made sure, for Timothy's sake, that it wouldn't get back up. But I was blind, eager.

Further and further away I stomped. The sound of leathery wings echoed through the woods, mingling with the chirping of unseen crickets. Something zipped past me and touched my back, and I whirled around again, seeing nothing. Another laugh echoed all around me. The forest spun, the trees blurring together until she emerged before me: a naked woman. A beautiful naked woman with a slender hourglass figure. Long, shining brown hair billowed from a wind I did not feel. And her face...

Clara?! I froze, refusing to believe it was her. And indeed, the longer I stared at those sensuous features, the more I realized they were not quite like Clara's. This woman's lips and eyes were larger and more sensual, as if Clara's had been combined with those of heavily made-up burlesque dancers I'd seen earlier in life. Her beauty was perfect in a way that made it difficult to believe. Many souls here in Hell were naked, but this woman had a body that invited attention: that rare mix of slender and curvaceous, with clear, perfect skin compared to the dirt and grime of the rest of us. I almost didn't even notice the bat-like wings sprouting from her back.

It was as if someone had reached into my mind and pulled out my idea of the perfect woman—the kind who would have never looked at my short, frail form under normal circumstances. And yet her amber eyes were fixed on me with disarming intensity. As if she knew me.

What if it *was* Clara? What if while I'd been tortured in Hell, Clara had become a demon like Thomas?

"Who...are you?" I choked out.

She smiled at me, her head tilting. "Relax. I'm not here to harm you." She even *sounded* like Clara. Her full red lips hooked into a smile, and she was suddenly close enough to put a soft hand on my arm, lowering it. A sweet, intoxicating scent filled my nostrils: some dizzyingly rich pheromone, pulling me to her like a rope around my neck. I tried to aim my rifle at her, but my hand became limp, dropping the weapon to the ground.

I stepped back, terrified by the intensity of my desire.

"You...won't...take me," I forced out, but I didn't believe my own words. The woman let out another quiet laugh, this one sending tingles up my spine. I stumbled to cover myself, for her appearance had excited me in an all-too-visible way.

"Such spirit. What's your name, brave soul?"

My breaths were louder than the crickets, now. "Caleb."

"I think we've gotten off on the wrong foot, Caleb. Indeed, I want to help you." She circled me, her body inches away. "You have spirit. Passion. Potential. Given the right strength, you could be...formidable."

"What do you want from me?" I whispered.

The woman's smile widened. She leaned in close, lush lips brushing against my cheek on their way to my ear. "I think you'd make a wonderful incubus," she hissed, her breath warm against my neck. Her hands slowly, ever so slowly, slid down my chest. "You'll gain wings, and the power to enter dreams. Your beauty will blossom. Your heart will stop. And you will feed...over and over again."

Again, there was that corpse flower of hope, blooming before I could stop it, no matter how fetid it stank. "Would I get to return to Earth?" The desperation in my voice betrayed just how easily she could convince me. I think it was the first time I could truly admit to myself how unsatisfied I was in Byzantium or how badly my heart still burned for vengeance.

The woman tilted her head, eyes pinching slightly, but her smile did not waver. "Perhaps something could be arranged. You have unfinished business there, do you? A long-lost love? Family you wish to see again? Or perhaps an old enemy?"

This time it was my eyes that betrayed me. The woman's lips opened to reveal her perfect teeth, something nearly impossible to find even in life.

"That's it," she said. "You want revenge." She continued to circle me, surrounding me with that intoxicating aroma. "What will you choose, when the time comes? Rebellion? Or revenge?"

My hands trembled, aching to grab her. I needed her closer...needed to be inside her...

Another blood-curdling scream echoed from behind me: Timothy. I surged back the way I'd come to find the vampire had risen back up. He lifted Timothy to impale him onto a tree branch. Timothy writhed and tried to break the branch midway, but its tip snapped off, blood spurting out. The face on its trunk let out a wood-creaking groan, more blood leaking out from its eye and mouth holes.

The boy froze, mouth opening in a silent scream. Immediately, the skin of his arms began to open, splitting and falling away to reveal grey bark beneath. He was turning into wood.

A burning feeling spread through me. I knew I had only myself to blame; that I'd been the one to run off after the demon woman, abandoning Timothy to this fate. But that made it all the easier to blame the vampire instead.

I'd foolishly left the rifle behind, so I grabbed a rock from the ground and slammed it into the vampire's face, again and again. "Where are the rest of you?" I asked. Below me, the demon sputtered, blood welling up from its nose. It had to be strong enough to throw me off, but it looked astonished to see a mortal fighting back. I slammed the rock down once again to disorient it before it could recover. "*Where?*" I repeated.

A terrible thirst had awakened within me. I wanted to kill this thing, but I also wanted to know where the rest of the army was camped, so I could...fight them, right? That was what I told myself: that it was all just to ensure the safety of the city. But deep down, I also understood that all my slow-boiling rage had finally bubbled to the surface, and this shitty little vampire with its shitty little fangs was another step toward my vengeance. I didn't care how deep down this staircase took me, provided what I wanted lay at its end.

Eventually, the vampire stopped moving. This time, there was no rush of victory.

As I stood up, panting, Timothy's change was almost complete. His arms and hair had transfigured into branches, and his skin had puddled around his roots like a tattered blanket. Soon, all that was left of him were holes for his eyes and mouth in the trunk where his face had once been, each gash dripping blood. A crushing feeling settled in my soul. He'd idolized me, and I'd let him down to pursue a demon woman.

Now she was gone. The air was clear of her pheromones, and my head was clearer as well. Shame coiled through me for even considering her offer. Jeanne, Elias, and the others would never forgive me. I wanted to ignore the brambles of yearning that she'd fostered within me.

But did I really owe Byzantium my loyalty when I'd only done this for selfish reasons to begin with?

⚬

It did not take me long to find my horse, but Timothy's was gone. I returned to Jeanne, and was relieved to find her still there, if in great pain. Together, we were able to pry her legs free, and I managed to help her up onto my horse's saddle. She groaned in agony the entire ride back.

"Where is that boy?" she managed to grunt at one point. I shook my head, a great weight falling over me, already ashamed of what I'd yet to admit I was going to do.

Chapter Eleven

The Blood Saints

"A RAIDING PARTY?" ASKED Elias. He, Anika and I stood in the bedroom of Weaver's half-rebuilt mansion, Jeanne lying on the bed.

"Is it not the best solution?" she grunted, eyes still inflamed with rage. "A team of our best, all armed with silver. Strike them before they find us."

"The best solution would be further reconnaissance," said Elias. "We don't know how many soldiers they have, or how strong those soldiers might be. You surprised those scouts, but demons are uniformly stronger than we are."

"Wrong," said Jeanne. "They can die, and we cannot."

"That doesn't mean they can't completely overwhelm us," said Elias. "There could be powerful monsters in their ranks. Warriors twice your size."

"They could also have imps or harpy scouts," said Anika. "And now that one got away, they undoubtedly know we're close."

"Exactly!" said Jeanne, sitting up in excitement, only to groan from pain and lie back down again. "An attack may be imminent. We should strike as soon as possible. Tomorrow, after we've gathered enough of the men. What do you say, Caleb?"

My lips thinned. "Let me think on it."

Anika watched me closely. Her expression was difficult to read, but it gave me the same sensation as feeling watched while walking in the dark.

Elias exhaled through his nostrils. "This is not a decision to be taken lightly. We cannot let them take this city. We are nearing a thousand souls, and every week more join us. I suppose it was only a matter of time for demons to come searching, but the dream of this place cannot be allowed to die."

The texture of his voice spoke louder than his words. This city, and the rebellion it stood for, meant everything to him. It had transformed him from Weaver's meek, fragile victim to the noble scholar he'd been in life. I was responsible for him; responsible for everyone here. The burden made my entire body ache.

After Jeanne healed, I accepted her demand to make love, but it was passionless, like we both knew something was lodged between us. All the while, I closed my eyes and thought of the woman from the woods. Even after I fell asleep, I dreamed of the demon woman drifting down to meet me, her naked body soft as it pressed against my own. Then my eyes shot open, and I was back in that decrepit bedroom, my thin, frail arms wrapped around Jeanne. My manhood pressed against her, throbbing insistently for another release.

I took care of myself, unwilling to awaken Jeanne. I was ashamed to have let the demon woman get under my skin; ashamed that even now, I desperately wanted to return to her and accept her offer. The secret weighed heavy in my heart, threatening to punch its way out if I ignored it. But there was no one I could tell. No one who would possibly understand without judging me for it.

I decided to clear my head with a walk. With the hours still undefined, I was not the only soul in the streets. A few of them waved at me, jerked their heads up in greeting, or called me to join them for a drink. I was still limping from my wound, which made me unable to hurry out of their purview. "Mr. Caleb," said an old woman, catching up to me with a tree branch for a walking stick. "I don't know whether we've been introduced, but my name is Abigail, and I'm a stonemason. I've been wondering how you'd feel about a statue?"

"A statue?"

She beamed. "For the town square, Mr. Caleb. Everyone in this city knows they have you to thank, after all."

It was like a blade stabbing into my gut. "We can discuss the idea later," I said, forcing a smile. The old woman nodded in understanding, letting me pass.

I continued mulling it over as I slouched, almost drunkenly, to Elias's library. I wanted so desperately to do the right thing, but what even was the right thing when every path led to ruin? The plan of attack seemed like a worse idea the more I thought about it.

This place will burn anyway, whispered a little voice in my head—a voice that sounded much like the woman in the forest. *Sooner or later, someone will find it. So why not join the stronger force? Why not pursue your goals? Why not confront the Immortalist Club, and save their future sacrifices?*

Then Clara's words echoed in my mind: *I simply read too many novels growing up. Romances of men who would fight through Hell itself for the women they loved.*

That was what a real man was to her. It was what I wished to be. And what would I be if I stayed down here while she suffered in the world above?

I reached the library's door. It was already open just a crack, a sliver of torchlight emanating from within. But as my hand neared the knob, a voice echoed out:

"Believe me or don't, but I am all but sure."

It was Anika, her voice strained with worry.

"He wouldn't," Elias said. "He's a symbol of this place. He knows how much he means to it."

"I have been here longer than you, Elias, and I know when a man's heart isn't in what he claims. I am not saying we should string Caleb up, but we should watch him. Ensure he does not betray us."

"Anika, he is our leader."

"I know, but please watch him. My instincts about these things are rarely wrong. Especially when I know, but don't know *how* I know. That's when they're most right of all."

I hid in the shadows behind the door as it opened. When Anika had disappeared down the street, I went in and found Elias leafing through a misbegotten volume by candlelight, brow furrowed in such obvious concern that I doubted he was taking in a single word.

"Good evening, Caleb," he said, without looking up.

I felt dizzy, delirious, as if I were still dreaming of the woman from the woods. "I...crave your council, old man."

"Go on, then." Elias sounded very tired, as though he was being woken by a child who was afraid of monsters under the bed.

I crouched low and closed my eyes, unwilling to jump right into it just yet. "Demons... you said they were all once human souls?"

Elias closed the book and finally met my eyes, his own pinched—wondering, perhaps, whether Anika had been right about me after all. "Yes," he answered.

"Then does becoming a demon make you wicked?"

His brow furrowed. "They say that becoming a demon makes it more difficult to not indulge in your viler tendencies. Perhaps there are good demons out there, but I've yet to meet one, unless Rumpelstiltskin counts. What's this about, Caleb?"

I hesitated, then finally let it out. "There was a demon in the woods. A woman. And she came to me in my dream, after."

"It was a succubus, then. Lilitu. Caleb, whatever she said, you cannot trust it. Demons are monsters. Even lilitu, no matter how human they look. They lie. They seduce. They feed on our very souls. That's why they're so beautiful, Caleb: it helps them kill."

"You don't understand." My hands were shaking, upset to have my decision questioned before I'd even made it. "She offered to make me like her. It... it could be my only chance to return to Earth and get revenge on the man who killed me." Crooked laughter tumbled out of me, surprising even myself. "It's almost too perfect."

Elias looked at me as though I'd just confessed to butchering children. "Surely you don't mean to accept this offer?"

I laughed again. I couldn't help myself. "What else is there to do? Wait to be captured and tortured once more?" Even though I knew it would never happen, I wanted Elias to agree, to sympathize. Not to give me this look of disappointment.

Elias studied me, lips thin. "Caleb, do you feel that you are...better than other people?"

"No."

"Then why do you think you deserve better?" He swept his cracked hands through the air in a slow arc, gesturing to the bookcases we'd spent so much time filling. "We are building something here. A city in the underworld where people can be free and happy. We even have silver to defend ourselves with. It is far better than most souls will ever experience in this place. Better than any of us could have dreamed of. And it is still not enough for you?"

Frustration creeped into my voice, building up under my skin. "You speak as though this underworld is just. As though the constant torture is what we deserve."

"You know I don't think that, but it is the fate that befalls us all. We all die, we suffer in death, and we give up what mattered to us in life. Why should it be any different for you?"

"Because I refuse to accept it if it means denying my goals." I was just short of yelling by now, probably blue in the face from all the rage I felt. "I refuse to relinquish my true dreams, and will stop at nothing to attain them. Is that not worth something? Does that not make me stronger, more worthy, more deserving?"

Elias looked more tired than he had since before we'd broken free. "Do you truly think the people out there aren't trying their best to improve their circumstances?"

"Yes, I do," I said. "I've seen how they accept their lot, until someone like me comes along to inspire them. You accepted yours, don't forget."

His face distorted into a look of revulsion. "I know you didn't rebel just to get the attention of these demons. I *know* you didn't," he repeated with a glare. "But that's what they'll say. You are a symbol to these people, Caleb. You gave them hope, and that hope will vanish if you turn your back on everything we've built. This rebellion will crumble. Letting those fiends corrupt you will corrupt everything we've done."

"There's someone on Earth I have to help," I said stiffly. "Someone I have to save. And someone I have to kill as well."

"The people *here* need your help," said Elias. "Look around you, at the souls outside these very walls."

My jaw clenched. I was tired of justifying myself. "Look, old man, my choice has no bearing on what happens to the rest of you. The rebellion is pointless. It was always pointless. You yourself always said that they would catch us eventually."

"I did," Elias admitted, his voice heavy with remorse. "I've been in other rebellions, and they've all failed. But Caleb, this one feels different. It's changed me. Changed all of us. With enough time, we could become an army that even the Blood Saints fear."

My shame was all but gone, now, his lecturing only solidifying my belief that becoming a demon was the best possible option. I did not want to stay here to be a hero to those without hope. I wanted to get back up there, to the world I knew. To stay here would be to admit defeat.

It would make me a failure as a man.

There was but one way out. I had to be ruthless. So determined that I could not let anything, even my own conscience, get in my way. I closed my heart and said, "I am getting out of Hell, and I don't care how many people I have to kill to do it."

Elias's eyes sagged almost as much as they had when we'd first met. "How can you be so prepared to give up your humanity? It would be tantamount to giving up who you are."

"Maybe I don't like myself," I said. "Indeed, maybe I *despise* myself. Maybe I seek to end myself, and become someone else instead."

"Do you really think becoming a demon will make this self-loathing go away? Stay with us, Caleb. Help us. If you wish to like yourself, then become someone worth liking, by helping those who depend on you."

I shook my head. Elias didn't understand at all. He still thought happiness could be found here, and this would be his ruin just as it would be Jeanne's. I was under no such illusions.

"What about Jeanne?" asked Elias. "She believes in you. She might even love you."

Something akin to disgust brewed in my throat. "She loves the symbol you speak of, not the person I truly am."

"But you could be that symbol," Elias pleaded. "If you only allowed yourself to be."

I looked down, the hooks of shame finally settling in. The conversation was going in circles, and trying to argue for my cause further would accomplish nothing. "You're right," I admitted with a sigh. "I'm sorry, Elias."

His eyes remained pinched, but his smile was warm. "To-morrow, we will fight those demons off. Then all will know Byzantium refuses to be conquered."

Then he embraced me like a brother. That was good. It meant he couldn't see the emptiness in my gaze.

"Are you sure you want to go out alone?" asked the men at the gates.

"I'll be fine," I said, tugging on my horse's bridle. "I simply desire to take some air." An absurd expression, given how smokey it was, but I said it regardless.

This I have learned: a sufficiently strong desire always trumps fear or shame.

Before exiting the gates, I took one last look at Byzantium's defenses, gauging whether they really had a shot. Roughly two thousand soldiers, decent enough walls... they weren't the worst chances. Something in my gut told me that no mortal force would ever be enough, but in retrospect, I wonder if that was just what I wanted to believe. It was easier to proceed if I told myself it wouldn't matter anyway.

I left the city to its squalor and its doomed ideals and rode south. I'd brought with me no large weapons, lest they think I meant to fight them, but hidden at the rear of my belt was my silver knife.

The wind caressed me as I rode, a pleasantly cool bite. This was the right decision. It was the only way to avenge my death. To save Clara, assuming I wasn't already too late. To bring Thomas and the Immortalist Club to justice, so they couldn't hurt anyone ever again. Additionally, I found myself obsessed with the thought of seeing the succubus again, and finding out whether she truly was somehow Clara, or merely resembled her.

I traveled further and further south until I found the Blood Saints' camp. It was a veritable city of tents, illuminated by torchlight, the air echoing with the thunder of drumbeats. Soldiers sat in circles around fires, laughing, drinking, and sharing pieces of red meat. Some drank from their mugs, others their horned helmets. Not far off, a group was cleaning weapons and armor, an overseer with a large hot iron brand watching them with twitchy, beady eyes, as if eager for one to make a mistake.

A horn sounded, and I looked up to see a figure standing atop a mobile tower. The soldiers before me all turned and rose to their feet, swords and axes at the ready. I dismounted and held up my hand to signal peace.

"Where is your leader?" I asked.

One demon jerked his chin at me, inviting me deeper into the camp. As I followed, another demon yanked my horse's bridle from my hand and led it away, laughing as it whinnied in terror. I hadn't expected them to simply accept me, as though they already knew that I belonged there. As though they could smell the darkness growing within me. One satyr even lifted his mug, gave me a toothy smile, and gestured to a keg with a severed head sitting atop it.

More soldiers surrounded me as we ventured deeper into the camp. They shoved me along, and tried to make me jump with shouts and sudden grabs. "Fresh meat!" one cackled. "And it came willingly!"

Nearby, a smithy ground a sword against an iron wheel, sending sparks into a satyr's drink. The satyr rose up and slapped the smithy's face into the still-whirling wheel, shredding his features. As the smithy screamed, the beady-eyed overseer rushed over and gutted the satyr, who stabbed the overseer right back. Some onlookers roared with laughter, while others shook their heads with visible exhaustion as they trudged over to clean up, as if they'd done this thousands of times before.

Deeper in was a bonfire. A demon beat an enormous drum with cylindrical sticks, the reverberations so loud that I half expected the ground to crack open. Silhouettes danced to his rhythm, both men and women, the firelight winking between the slashes of their wings. Some had horns or spade-tipped tails that swayed like hypnotic serpents. Pendulous breasts swung and cocks flapped, flaccid but terrifyingly large. These had to be the lilitu Elias had told me of. Their bodies were so perfect, and their movements so graceful, that I was utterly spellbound until the soldiers nudged me onward.

They led me to a large tent, where several figures stood around a table, a map unrolled across it. The tallest figure was an incubus with long, flowing black hair, and features so wickedly handsome that even I felt a twinge of uncomfortable attraction. Massive bat wings stretched out from his back, casting shadows across the rest of the tent. His armor was more elaborate than that of the others, with beautiful indentations and plenty of dark red stains.

Across the table from him stood a satyr. This one was far taller and bulkier than the one that had caught me, his body coated in dirty white hair. Four gnarled black horns spiraled out from his head like misshapen tree branches. Both men hovered over the map, brows furrowed as they moved figures across it.

"Captain Thaddeus," said the demon who had led me there, crouching in submission.

The satyr turned, horizontal pupils thinning. "I'm busy, Brindle." He lowered his voice and added, "*That man there is Cardinal Salem Sotirios.* He is not someone to interrupt." Fear clenched the captain's voice. The incubus behind him did not look up.

"Apologies, captain. But I thought you might want to know that a mortal has come willingly into our camp." Brindle grinned to reveal sharp, triangular teeth.

I lowered myself into a crouch beside him. Laughter rumbled from the soldiers around me. "He knows his place after all," one snarled, spitting onto the back of my head. I took a deep breath, determined to endure it all to get what I wanted.

Something touched my back, and I turned to see the beautiful succubus, her skin rippling in the firelight, smiling like an eager courtesan. "Delighted to see you've joined us." Her face reminded me so much of Clara's...

"I haven't promised to join anything yet," I said through clenched teeth.

"But you're here. You're showing us the back of your neck. Does that not make it clear where your loyalties lie?"

"Who is this, Kaeru?" rumbled the satyr, finally noticing me. The woman beside him was gone.

"His name is Caleb," said the succubus. "Won't you grant him a moment of your time, good captain?"

Kaeru? Even her name reminded me of Clara. But it couldn't really be her, could it?

I lifted my head enough to meet Thaddeus's golden goat eyes. "It is an honor to meet you, Thaddeus. I... I'm here to join you."

Laughter rumbled from the demons around me. "What could you have to offer us?" asked Thaddeus, an ever-so-slight bleat in his booming voice.

"I can fight for you," I said. "I just... I have to become a demon."

It scared me, how unflinching my voice was; how certain I'd become that this was the only way.

Thaddeus's goat lips peeled back into a cruel smile, showing teeth sharper than any goat should have.

"Caleb is the one responsible for butchering our scouting party," said Kaeru. "You did say you wanted to find him, didn't you?"

The war drums thundered in my ears, my blood surging as fear took hold of me. Thaddeus grinned and crouched down before me, looking at me with renewed interest. "You're saying this little mortal has killed multiple demons? Are you positive it was him, and not Pestilence's ghouls?"

"I saw it with my own eyes in the Deadwoods," said Kaeru.

I trembled. "I apologize for killing your men, captain. Please, let me make it up to you. If I can kill your kind even now, imagine how strong I'll be as a demon."

Thaddeus's horizontal pupils bored into me. "Oh, I'm imagining something else entirely right now. Like just how much I can punish you while you're still mortal..."

"Wait." Salem Sotirios's voice cut through the air like a knife, a quiet bark that somehow silenced us all. "Ask him if he knows where Pestilence is. She may be hiding among mortals."

In that moment, I understood. This was the man I had to impress. The one who would, in the end, decide my fate. "Pestilence?" I repeated.

Thaddeus glowered, his eyes moving sideways as if to direct the glare at Salem, but he did not dare turn his head. "Have you seen a rider with a plague doctor mask?" he asked me. "One with the long beak. It would be a woman. Her horse looks like it's rotting."

I hesitated. I knew Pestilence was in the Patchwork Sea, but had no idea which direction that was. I also knew that if these demons searched the direction from which I'd come, they would find Byzantium. Sweating, I decided to risk it.

"She's in the Patchwork Sea," I said. "I saw her there."

Salem finally looked up from the map, meeting my gaze. "The Patchwork Sea? To the south?"

"Yes." I nodded hastily.

"You're sure?"

"Yes."

Salem smirked. "From which direction did he enter the camp, Brindle?"

"From the north, sir," said Brindle, leering at me.

"From the north, you say? How fascinating. If you came from the south, then why did you enter our camp from the north?"

I stood there, flabbergasted. "Must have gotten turned around."

"Turned around?" Salem's brows knit in a perfect parody of concern, the corners of his mouth tilted up.

"It's easy to get lost here," I mumbled. "It's dark."

"Oh, yes, very easy," said Salem, nodding in understanding, but his eyes gleamed maliciously. Everyone was staring at me, now, waiting with bated breath.

"I'm fucked, aren't I?" I croaked.

Salem's handsome face split into a ruthless grin. "Do as thou wilt, Thaddeus."

"Wait!" I screamed, but they were already grabbing my shoulders, pulling me to my feet. "She's there! She's at the Patchwork Sea!"

Thaddeus grinned. "Quarter him."

"She's there!" I repeated, but the soldiers were already carrying me to the stables. There, they chained my limbs to the ankles of horses, one of which was my own. I looked desperately for Kaeru, but she seemed to have gone. Brindle, the demon who had led me there, approached with a torch. He grinned and took his time inching the blaze closer and closer toward my horse's tail.

Oh, I'd been a fool for coming here. I closed my eyes, preparing for another painful death, followed by another, and another after that. I would be this army's toy, now: theirs to torture and kill again and again. The horses grunted anxiously, sensing the torch's ever-closer heat. I felt the slightest tug on my wrists and ankles...

"PESTILENCE!" someone shouted in the distance.

Brindle stopped, uncertainty crossing his face.

"We've spotted Pestilence!" the voice repeated, louder this time. A trio of demons charged into the camp on horseback. "She rides south of here, in the Patchwork Sea!"

Brindle furrowed his brow at me. Thaddeus and Salem both looked up.

"Untie him," Thaddeus said. "Let's see how well he fares." The captain grinned at me again as Brindle reluctantly undid my bonds. Then he raised his voice and shouted, "WE MARCH!"

A horn sounded. Everyone in camp stirred and grabbed their weapons and armor.

"I could cast my draconis ritual," Thaddeus said to Salem, the both of them already on the move. "Fly above. Burn her and her entire horde."

"The emperor wants her alive," said Salem firmly. "Wounded is fine. But burning her..."

"I doubt a blast of fire would be enough to kill her," said Thaddeus. "We speak of Pestilence, after all."

"Do you want to risk the emperor's wrath?" Salem asked coldly. "Save it for when we can leave no survivors."

Once more the soldiers closed in around me and pulled me up, forcing me to join in their march. Some patted my back, others continued to snarl, and a few slapped my rump. Behind me, Captain Thaddeus was barking more orders. The war drum beat louder than ever as the drummer joined in the march, riling up the other soldiers. Their armaments ranged wildly: melee weapons, shields, firearms, small explosives... it was a strange hodgepodge of different eras, as if an army from the dark ages had picked up a few modern weapons but not yet consistently adopted them.

Something caressed the top of my head. I instinctively looked up to see Kaeru, flying above with a grin. "Have you any experience in battle, Caleb?" she asked. She was wearing black leather armor, fully covered from head to toe, currently slipping a leather glove onto her hand.

"Not enough," I admitted. "How do I get armor or weapons like everyone else? Can I even get my horse back?"

Kaeru laughed. "I doubt you're strong enough to wear plate mail." She flew on ahead of me, into a cloud of red fog.

Up ahead, the cavalry also left us in the dust. Squeezed shoulder to shoulder within a thick crowd of infantry, there was nothing to do but march on—I wouldn't have been able to turn around or wriggle out if I'd tried. The demons on either side of me glowered when I tried to meet their eyes. One looked human enough until he showed his fangs, while the other appeared to be a satyr, though most of his hair had been shaved, revealing an awkward, gangly bald goat head of saggy skin flaps. Trying to fight my way out would only get me captured. No, I had to make use of this situation. I had to find a way to impress Salem or Thaddeus. Whoever this Pestilence was, I had to be the one to bring her in.

I heard the Patchwork Sea before I saw it: the ceaseless groans of pain from hundreds of thousands of mouths. The "sea" had no water to speak of. Rather, the land was made out of countless souls who were stitched together. Their arms and legs had been attached to their sides, fingers stitched together into flippers, flippers stitched to their neighbors. Their mouths and eyes, too, had been sewn shut, but it didn't stop them from writhing and letting out muffled moans as they felt the impact of our feet. It was another sight I recognized from a painting at the Immortalist Club.

"Look at them," said Brindle, amusement creeping into his voice. "Can't even pull away without ripping off their skin."

I imagined cutting every last one of these people free and leading them back to Byzantium, to freedom, but I had forsaken that place, and now I was marching with its enemy, surrounded by people who would never think to show such compassion.

Muffled groans emitted from underfoot, for the people sewn together below us were all too conscious; they just had their eyes and lips sewn shut. A few demons stomped hard to break the noses, eyes, or genitals of the people they walked over. An infant's muffled cry echoed from not too far away.

"Fuck you!" a man beneath me shouted as I stepped on him. His lips had somehow come unsewn, and his voice was filled with vitriol.

An explosion sounded somewhere in the murky distance ahead, followed by a terrified neigh. A horse sailed over my head like it had been launched by a catapult. It landed on soldiers at my rear, crushing them. Screams of terror and pain erupted from the red fog before me, combining with the thunderous war drum, and the clanking of metal against metal. When I looked in the eyes of the demonic soldiers, there was a glaze of fear. Already, I could taste blood in the air, mingling with Hell's ever-present stenches of soot, smoke, and sulfur.

One nauseating stench cut through the others: vomit. A hole had appeared in the formation ahead, for a soldier was on his hands and knees, vomiting out blood in ceaseless, uncontrollable geysers. He sounded choked, like he was drowning. Then I spotted another soldier vomiting just as profusely, and another, and...

In a flash, a rider with a long-beaked mask bolted past me, outstretched hand missing me by inches before she crashed through the soldiers at my side. I caught only a glimpse of her horse's face: bulging white eyes that looked ready to pop from their sockets, a neck that held too much skin, long rodent-like teeth forming a spine-tingling grin.

The vampire to my side let out a scream, holding his shoulder where the rider had touched him. His armor had melted away, revealing a terrible black mark. The black skin bubbled, popped blood, and the vampire fell to his knees. Then he vomited a scarlet torrent onto the quilt of mortal souls.

"GET HER!" echoed Thaddeus' voice as the rider circled back and broke through us again, sending more Blood Saints reeling to the patchwork ground.

I couldn't see where Thaddeus was, nor where the rider had gone; I was still lost in a throng of armored beings. I spotted a fallen sword at my feet and grabbed it before I missed my chance. It was heavy and already stained with blood.

An incubus fell straight down from the sky, crushing some soldiers to my left, a huge spear sticking through his chest. The scarlet fog ahead became filled with disfigured silhouettes, lurching and groaning like wounded men, and somewhere behind me a woman let out a terrified shriek, followed by a wet splatter sound.

"KEEP MARCHING!" Thaddeus bellowed.

There were still soldiers on either side of me, going for as far as I could see, thousands in every direction. There were more gaps in the formation now, and the enemy line's warped silhouettes grew closer and clearer. This wasn't a hunt for a single rider; it was a battle. And I had the feeling we were already losing.

The enemy line broke through the fog and shredded into the soldiers several rows before me, their blades breaking through the armor and sinking into flesh. They wore the same armor as us, but their faces were sunken, distorted, bleeding from their eyes and mouths. *Ghouls*, I thought.

"Hold the line!" Thaddeus barked from somewhere ahead, but the line was tearing like paper, the ghouls penetrating deeper and deeper. The soldier before me fell, and a ghoul stepped into his place. It was a former incubus, but his skin was so thin around his skull that I almost thought him a Reaper. Chunky red liquid dribbled down his chin, and the leathery membrane of his wings was shredded with holes. He clumsily lifted a battle axe and sliced it down toward me. I jumped backwards, colliding with the demon at my rear, but narrowly avoiding the axe's swing. It lodged into the stomach of a corpulent stitched mortal lying flat below us, who let out a wail of pain. While the ghoul-incubus was keeled over, I stabbed his head with my sword, causing him to fall limp. But more ghouls were lumbering forward, and all around me Blood Saints battled ghouls of their own.

The rider overlooked them all from a distant hill, her ragged black cloak billowing in the wind, her face hidden behind a black leather bird mask. Her horse grinned at me, drooling blood, its off-white body covered in vile-looking wounds. Flies buzzed around the creature, and a long, snake-like tail lashed the ground with a thorny tip. Excess skin hung from its neck like jowls.

A small black object sailed over my head from behind. It landed in the cluster of ghouls before me and erupted like a stick of dynamite. Blinding light threw me back with terrible force, and I was not the only one. I landed painfully on my back, my face hot from coming so close to the fire, eyebrows singed, entire body stinging from fresh pain. And whereas before there had been ceaseless, deafening noise, now I heard nothing—nothing but an awful ringing sound.

My eyes stung. I wiped blood from them, smearing it across my cheeks. My hand collected bits of bone, maybe teeth. I didn't seem to be wounded, but it hurt terribly. I stumbled to my feet and whirled around, sluggish and clumsy, ears still ringing. The line had broken formation and scattered, silhouettes in the red fog. More horses thundered across my field of vision. The rider? Or our own cavalry?

Slowly, my hearing began to return: screaming, gunfire, blades clashing against armor, wails of pain from the mortals stitched beneath. Another, closer explosion ruptured the air, and I ducked, instinctively covering my head as a torrent of gore splashed, the soldier who had been there a moment before suddenly reduced to red mud. I scurried away, still covering my head in terror, only to notice more shambling silhouettes in the red fog coming from all around me this time. The bald satyr dashed past me, back the way we'd come, blind with terror.

I stumbled and fell onto my rear, right beside the vampire who the rider had touched. He was still on hands and knees, but no longer vomiting. Instead, he let out little whimpers before rearing up, body twitching. His exposed shoulder seemed to be rotting, and blood leaked from his eyes and mouth. His face had grown excessively gaunt, like all the meat beneath the skin had drained away. His jaw lowered hungrily, strands of red drool connecting his fangs, but his eyes were empty of emotion. There was no maliciousness; no desire to threaten. Merely an exhausted, apathetic hunger.

Backwards I crawled, desperately trying to get away, but more ghouls were emerging from the fog, their groans a symphony that joined with the drumbeats. My hand nearly fell into a mortal's snarling mouth, the same angry man I'd stepped on before. "I'll fuck you up!" he shouted. "You mark my fucking words! One day I'll rip free of this, and I'll find you and tear you limb from limb!"

I managed to stand and clumsily swung the sword at the vampire ghoul, but it only became lodged into the creature's neck. It reached for my naked flesh, skin rotting and falling away from its gnarled fingers. I left the sword behind, ran, and quickly found another. More and more of the Blood Saints had fallen, and the ghoulish horde's numbers had only increased. I bolted through the red fog, trying to avoid the ghouls in my path and the bloody pools forming on the patchwork flesh.

A horse began running alongside me, no rider on its saddle. I grabbed hold of the bridle and kicked off in a desperate scramble to get atop, but I damn near fell off in the attempt. I kept hold desperately, even as my arm screamed for release, and pulled myself up with all the strength I had. Then I rode, exhaling in relief, trying not to be terrified by how quickly we were rushing through the fog. The air remained a deafening choir of groans from the ghouls, cries from the soldiers, and shouts of pain from the faces beneath our feet. It was all made worse by the inescapable odors of blood and death.

I reached down to the side of the saddle in search of more weapons and found a pair of iron cuffs bound by chains, along with a small black iron ball. One of the explosive devices, I wagered.

Then I saw her, through the veil of fog: Pestilence, still on her horse atop the flesh hill. There was a pile of quivering bodies at her horse's hooves, indistinguishable from those that formed the Patchwork Sea. Other Blood Saints were targeting her already: horsemen charging at her, swinging swords much larger than mine, but she dodged their blows and jabbed her hand forward lightning-quick, sending them falling off their horses to vomit their way into her army's ranks. Her horse ripped into a few soldiers with its rat-like teeth, that long neck bulging as it gulped down chunks of their flesh.

A satyr with a rifle kept his distance as he fired again and again. Pestilence galloped on in pursuit, apparently unharmed by the bullets zipping through her chest. Soon she was before the satyr, her rotting horse rearing up on its hind legs to clobber him in the face. After that, it was easy for her to reach down and strike his forehead with her palm, ensuring he too would join her sick horde.

My horse pivoted in terror. Perhaps I should have listened to it. Why not use this opportunity to flee the battlefield? In the chaos, I might break free of the demonic army and return to Byzantium.

But as formidable as Pestilence was, I knew she could not kill me. And I had noticed that the mortals forming the sea below us had not become ghouls like the demons had. Maybe I could touch her without becoming a ghoul too.

I tried steering my horse back to Pestilence, but it flat-out refused to turn. I jumped off, my ankles crunching painfully as I hit the ground. I was not used to such maneuvers, and my body remained frail and weak. But didn't that mean I had nothing left to lose? I limped up the hill, each step painful, inching closer and closer to Pestilence, my grip tight around my sword.

Pestilence looked down at me, flies still buzzing around her. This close, I could see her bare hand at last: scabby, twitchy, drained of color save for the red welts and purple boils and rotten holes where the flesh had burned away. Just the sight of it made my stomach turn. Her horse gave me a rodent's grin, hairless tail lashing the fleshy ground in warning. "Oh yes," it hissed in an all-too-human voice. "Do come closer. I would so love to taint you..."

They came down the hill toward me in a steady canter. Both horse and rider carried such a repulsive stink that I tasted it even with my mouth closed. I had to stop myself from covering my mouth, half certain I'd vomit even without her touching me. Worse, I was alone. While the red fog around me was filled with the silhouettes of clashing warriors, the remaining Blood Saints were too busy fighting the ghouls to join me against their leader.

"How many?" The rider spoke in a disharmonic feminine croak, thick like her throat was clogged. "How many of you must I infect for Sotirios to show himself?"

Was that a twinge of regret in her voice? Or perhaps yearning?

"You want Sotirios?" I asked, jerking my chin high. "He's up there."

Pestilence turned with a desperate gasp, but her steed was more cunning, lunging for me as I threw the explosive ball. It erupted beneath them, launching the rider from her steed and the steed onto its side.

Pestilence recovered immediately, pushing up from the ground and rushing toward me, scabbed hand outstretched, the skin of her palm bubbling like water. Her mask had fallen off, and I could see her face was just as deformed and disease-ridden. Her nose had rotted away, her cheeks were covered in throbbing boils, and one of her eyes was slightly larger than the other. I also noticed that her extended arm was longer than the other, with a bulbous, swollen wrist. Behind her, the strange horse reared up. It elongated its snake-like neck, the extra throat skin tightening against the musculature.

I raised my sword, but Pestilence was already grabbing my arm. The pain was immediate and dizzying. My skin shrank against my bones, moving became harder than ever, and Hell, despite its eternal humidity, suddenly seemed frigid. Pestilence's horse laughed, its long serpentine neck swaying as it neared. Acid climbed up my throat, a salty taste filling my mouth.

What if I became a ghoul after all? What if the mortals at our feet hadn't turned simply because she hadn't touched them with her bare hands, or hadn't willed it? It didn't matter, I decided. This was my one chance. My *only* chance.

"You can't kill me," I growled, voice a quiet rasp, each word a lash inside my throat. "I'm already fucking dead."

Pestilence let go of my arm, leaving a bubbling welt behind, then gripped my neck. She squeezed, but even as my body became increasingly skeletal, I managed to raise my sword and plunged it into her chest. It was shockingly easy, for her flesh was butter-soft from all its wounds. She stumbled, but kept her grip around my throat. I doubted the sword had actually harmed her—the bullets hadn't—but it allowed me to get closer.

My hand shook, just skin and bones, but I used the last of my strength to slap one handcuff around her wrist, and its mate around my own. "You're...coming...with me," I choked out, twisting the blade.

Talking was so painful that I almost didn't notice her rotten horse charging at me. I might have yanked the blade free and lanced it through the beast, but a fit of coughing took me, painful and dry as sand, my punishment for trying to speak. Pestilence pulled a knife from her belt and stabbed it through my wrist, trying to cut herself free, but by then I was already in so much pain that I barely noticed more. Trembling, I pried the knife from her grip, pulled it free from my flesh, and threw it at the charging horse. The blade landed in its throat, but it kept coming.

More figures emerged around us: other Blood Saints, closing in now that Pestilence was finally off her steed. Fear and pain flashed through Pestilence's eyes. "Run, Alastrim!" she yelled.

The horse halted its charge and stared at her.

"Run!" she repeated. "Don't let them take your bridle! I'll find you!"

The horse hesitated, let out a growl, then lowered its head in submission and pranced off, leaping over some of the soldiers and disappearing into the smoke of war.

As the Blood Saints surrounded us, Pestilence fell to her knees, head sinking in submission. Her hand fell away from my wrist, and it was like being born again. Air finally returned to my lungs, and while I remained more skeletal than I'd ever been, some of the pain was ebbing away.

"He has her!" someone shouted. "He has Pestilence!"

A huge shadow passed over us: Salem Sotirios, landing just beside me, arms crossed as he looked upon Pestilence's pitiful form, the tip of my sword still sticking out her back.

"Go after her horse!" he barked at some of the men. Scowling at her, he lowered his voice and added, "Fine. I'm here. Now will you stop this silly game?"

Pestilence made a sound like a thick, hollow gushing of air, the closest she could come to sniffling with the rotten hole where her nose had been. "This wasn't how I meant for things to go," she said. "Salem, I..."

"Stand your ghouls down or I'll never speak to you again." Salem turned to me and added, "Take her back to camp."

Then he kicked back up into the air. Pestilence watched him go with a heartbroken expression, then sighed and hung her head. "I surrender."

Chapter Twelve

Unholy Baptism

T HE MEN HAULED PESTILENCE back to the camp. A huge cage was waiting in the back of a wagon, a bloody red circle drawn on the wood around it. As the only mortal there, and therefore the only one immune to her control, I was also responsible for chaining her to a pike so that she wouldn't get close enough to the bars to stick her hands through. Pestilence went along with it all reluctantly, saying nothing.

Once she was safely secured, Thaddeus looked over my work with begrudging approval, then nodded to a hooded figure, who pricked his finger with a knife and proceeded to chant, activating the ritual circle to add another layer of containment. What remained of Pestilence's army was butchered.

Following this, Thaddeus led me to a tent. It looked normal enough on the outside, but when I went in, I found a bedroom fit for a king, clearly larger than the tent that housed it. It contained an enormous bed, racks for armor and weapons, and, to my surprise, painting supplies. Half-finished or abandoned works were piled on the floor, a new canvas waiting on its stand. Indeed, the style was achingly familiar.

Salem was currently soaking in an enormous bathtub, his head thrown back in relaxation. It was only when I neared him that I realized a succubus was in the bath with him, her head bobbing up and down above his pelvic region.

"Women," he grunted disdainfully. "Treacherous, every single one. Wouldn't you agree... Caleb, was it?"

I lowered to my knees. I did not agree, but this was not a man to argue with. "It was an honor to fight for you, Lord Sotirios."

His eyes remained closed, not turning to look at me. "The men said you showed courage. Not many mortals would allow themselves to experience such pain, or risk losing their minds that way. Especially not for an army that hadn't even accepted them yet."

"I'm not most mortals," I said.

Salem let out another grunt, but this one sounded more like a chuckle. "You want to get back, is that it? Back to Earth?"

"Is that something you can offer?" I fought down the hope rising in my chest; by now, I knew better than to trust it.

"Perhaps. Whether I choose to is another matter." He finally met my eyes, a cruel little smirk on his face, still ignoring the succubus vigorously fellating him. "After all, now that we have the empress, we can make our way back to Elysium and I can finally leave this godforsaken place."

"The...empress?" I repeated, stunned.

"Didn't anyone tell you? That little bitch you caught is the emperor's wife. Why do you think Riven ordered Kaeru and I all the way down to this shithole of a realm?"

He pushed down on the succubus's head, forcing her to stay in place for a moment. Then he closed his eyes and groaned loudly. Her gulps echoed through the room before he finally released her, and she gasped for air as she rose up, wiping her face clean. As she stood to leave, Salem grabbed her arm and pulled her back down into the bath, so she began fellating him once more. I looked down to hide my discomfort.

"What did you do, when you were alive?" asked Salem, his voice huskier than before. "What life are you so desperate to get back to?"

"I was a violinist," I said, uncertain what else to say.

I'd expected him to laugh, but instead Salem looked at me with renewed appreciation. "Ah. A fellow artist." He adjusted his posture in the bath, causing the water to splash and the succubus to squirm. "I have work to do on Earth, Caleb. I'll need soldiers I can trust. You've helped me enormously with a mission I am very glad to put behind me, but I don't trust you quite yet. So I shall think about it as we make our way back. In the meantime, as a reward for your efforts, I have asked Thaddeus to gift you lilitu milk, specifically from the sanguinus bloodline. It is a rare, powerful variety, thought to be a link between vampirekind and lilitu like myself."

"You—you'll allow me to become a demon?" I asked, that desperate, hungry hope returning once more.

"Provided you don't continue to be this slow. Go." Salem returned his attention to the succubus. I rose to my feet and left the tent.

Outside, a celebration was afoot, the drumming and fire dancing continuing like before. The Blood Saints drank, smoked, and shot their rifles up into the air. "There he is!"

one shouted, and suddenly several of the fiends had taken hold of my shoulders, cheering excitedly. One dumped his mug onto my head, and my eyes stung from the salty alcohol-infused blood. Even as I rubbed them, the soldiers forced me to stumble onward until we reached the fire, where they pushed me down to my knees. Thaddeus watched from a wooden chair, a skull full of blood in his hand. He sipped gingerly before dunking it back into an open barrel.

"Are you ready, Caleb?"

I looked up to see one of the people touching me was Kaeru, pushing hard into my back, that Clara-like face split into a grin. Still weak from the battle, I felt barely able to breathe. But Kaeru didn't wait for my answer. She flew up into the darkness, then lowered between me and that enormous bonfire, now holding a circular basin. She slowly walked closer, hips swaying, before placing the basin onto the ground before me. It was filled with white and red liquid, like milk spiked with blood.

"Drink," she whispered.

The drumbeats thundered on, and the dancers swirled around the fire, and all around me, the fiends chanted, "Drink! Drink! Drink!" A horned, red-skinned priest was among them, reading from an enormous book bound in skin, his words drowned out by the soldiers. Even now, as they let me join their corrupted ranks, the fiends believed themselves holy. And who was I to deny a hand that offered me redemption?

I lifted the basin up to my face. It smelled like milk, but also coppery. Before I could second-guess myself, I tilted it down, bringing it to my lips.

God, it was good. It tasted like pure life: sweet, rich, and nurturing. I chugged it down, the milk compelling me to inhale it like oxygen. And when the basin was empty, I licked for what remained, wishing still for more. I wiped what had trickled down my chin and sucked it off my fingers, just to be sure I wasn't wasting a single drop.

The first thing I noticed was heat. I wiped a thick layer of sweat from my brow and even began to pant.

Then came the pain. My belly lurched, my bones cracked, and a repetitive painful throb rippled through me. I dropped the basin and fell to my side, seizing and clawing at myself. I could feel my intestines twisting, my muscles swelling. My entire body shook with overwhelming force. My chest strained, muscles vibrating until they grew strong. My teeth elongated into sharp, carnivorous fangs, piercing my tongue enough to fill my mouth with blood. The worst pain of all occurred in my back, which felt like it was being sliced apart by a thousand knives. But these knives were part of me, I learned, as bat-like wings ripped out.

"Wings!" I shouted, a sense of power surging through me. My newborn wings twitched, dripping rubies from membrane to spine. I continued to writhe, my body beyond my ability to control, and the sharp wings slashed open my scalp. Blood drenched my head, marking my hair with its permanent stain, turning it crimson. A crown of blood leaked down my face. Kaeru watched in fascination. The demons, my brothers, they roared.

My head and back still stung, but oddly were healing faster than they had when I was a mortal soul. None of the pain, nausea or weakness I'd felt from Pestilence's touch remained. I found the strength to stand, for I had *plenty* of strength now, and was briefly disoriented by how far away the ground looked. I was a foot taller than I'd been before. My arms now bulged with muscles. My chest felt hard as stone. Even my hands were stronger and larger than they'd ever been.

I'd become the version of myself I'd always dreamed of being: strong, masculine, powerful. But hunger clawed at my insides and itched inside my very loins. I wanted to fuck the world and drain it dry, tasting every cup it had to offer.

Kaeru dragged her fingers under my chin, lifting my face, and I realized with a start that I could smell her sweat: a sweet aroma that told me, with complete certainty, that she desired me. I smelled it as surely as I saw it in her eyes.

Part of me wanted to plow her until she forgot her name. The other part wanted to tear into her skin and drink her life. My throat was parched, but I also felt like I'd go absolutely toys in the attic *nuts* if my nethers didn't get some release soon. Indeed, while I wanted Kaeru, I felt half-inclined to accept whatever hand or mouth would have me. It was a baffling, shameful feeling, but I felt it anyway.

Kaeru took my hand and led me to a clearing just outside of camp, where she pushed me to the ground and lowered onto me. Her body seemed smaller than it had been, but pressing her chest against me was enough to bring me down to my back. My manhood was engorged like never before, but it slipped into her easily. She stretched, already soaked enough to accommodate me. Her shining, sweaty, desire-drenched body gyrated gleefully atop me, laughing and moaning, her hands rubbing down my chest, her breasts bouncing hypnotically. I was inside her, beautiful warmth spreading through me. She brought her wrist to my mouth, and I pierced it with my teeth, drinking in her sweet, salty blood. I couldn't help but shiver in delight. I licked her wound, but found that the two fresh piercings were already healing.

My new wings flapped madly with excitement, and the air sang as their spines slashed through it. They felt strong and sinuous, weapons in and of themselves. A mad thought manifested into my mind: I could *kill* someone with these things. And rather than shame, the thought brought only excitement.

"Why didn't you tell me," I breathed, "just how bloody good it feels to be a demon!?"

I grabbed Kaeru and whirled her beneath me, then thrust into her harder, harder, matching the rhythm of the drum, letting the pleasure build, and it felt so, so good. I pushed down to kiss her, and she squeaked in pleasure as her lips consumed mine, her fingers clawing through my hair, until I could feel her body quaking from a powerful, all-consuming climax. I couldn't help but imagine her as Clara, and the thought only made me thrust harder, grabbing the back of her neck to keep her in place beneath me, the pressure building, my rage and lust swirling around me in a maelstrom until, until, until—

Release. Sweet release. Relief like I'd never felt. It was like every awful, shameful thing I'd ever done had been expelled from my body, gushing into Kaeru with all the passion of life itself. She writhed beneath me, gasping gleefully, bucking her hips as if trying to squeeze out every drop with her hungry cunt. I panted with satisfaction, ready to collapse, but Kaeru kept on gyrating—first gently, then dramatically. I was still sensitive, and feared that it would hurt, but within seconds I was erect once more, and thrust into Kaeru until another orgasm took her.

My own second climax came swiftly. The next few, even more so, for Kaeru took me into her mouth, swallowing my seed over and over, until I was sure I had no more to spare. Then she mounted my face for a few turns of her own, her wing thumbs locking with my own as if we were holding hands. "That's it!" she cried. "Just like that!"

Kaeru was a passionate, messy lover, overly sweaty and prone to gushing. She was considerate enough to lick me clean each time she made a mess on me, and allowed me a refreshing helping of blood from her wrist. Even her scent was intoxicating: a sweet, minty aroma that seemed like it could have burned my nostrils if I inhaled too deeply.

After goodness knows how many climaxes, my rage and lust finally subsided, but I felt dizzy enough to faint. Kaeru exhaled with delight as she got off of me, before kissing her way down my chest.

"There now. Isn't that better?" she asked, sliding back up to wrap her arms around me.

It was. My body felt so peaceful. I closed my eyes and imagined Clara embracing me. Forgiving me. Accepting me, despite all my sins and all my weakness.

"Kaeru?" I whispered, my voice sounding almost as dry as it had been when I'd faced Pestilence.

"Yes, Caleb?"

"Are you her?" I was afraid to give voice to my question, in case the answer was no. But my need to know was almost as crippling as the need I'd felt to be inside her. "Are you... Clara?"

Kaeru raised her brow, as if perplexed.

Then a loud horn sounded through the camp.

Kaeru stood up. I did the same. Had we been attacked? Why else would another battle come so soon after the first?

We ran back to the others to find Thaddeus once again barking orders: "March! We march!"

"What happened?" I asked, but no one answered. I turned to Kaeru, but she spread her wings and darted up into the dark. I might have followed her, but I'd yet to learn how to fly, and it quickly became too crowded for me to feel like I could spread my wings.

I joined the other intoxicated, bleary-eyed soldiers in a line to grab weapons and armor. Heavy though it was, I had no difficulty wearing it with my new form. Then I joined the crowd marching from the camp.

"Which way are we headed?" I asked the demon to my right, a horned satyr.

"North," he barked.

A bristle of fear scratched up my spine.

"Why?"

"Not sure." He gave me a toothy grin, his chipped yellow teeth practically tusks. "We should find out soon enough. Welcome to the Saints, by the way. Lieutenant Gant, at your service."

He lifted an iron hand to shake my own. "Charmed," I said, trying to keep the fear from my voice. I told myself that we weren't headed for Byzantium. Hell was full of wretched things. Maybe a monster had attacked some scouts. Maybe we were going to pivot east or west. Maybe this was just the best way for us to reach another layer of Hell. There was no reason to assume we were marching for the city. No reason to panic.

"What's it like being a sanguinus lilitu?" asked Gant.

"I've only just become one," I said. Talking would fill the silence, distracting my thoughts from the fear of what might be waiting down the road.

"Some say it's a blessing to gain sustenance from either blood or sex. Others a curse, since you'll always want both." Gant chuckled.

"What do you eat, then?" I asked, eager to be distracted from my thoughts.

"Flesh." Gant's grin widened, strings of red meat wiggling between his oversized teeth.

Onward we marched. There were thousands of soldiers around me, even after the battle against Pestilence. It was more than enough to take a city, if it came to that—but no, I assured myself. That wasn't what this would be, no matter how familiar these surroundings looked.

"Just hope this one's worth it," Gant added after we'd been marching for a good hour. "Heard Pestilence just wanted a word with Lord Sotirios. Probably could have saved a lot of trouble if he'd just gone there himself, but that would have been beneath him."

"Probably didn't want to risk being infected and taken over," I said. I don't know why I was defending the fiend. Perhaps I just desperately wanted to believe that the group I'd joined wasn't all that bad, especially now, as we headed for what I feared might become a massacre.

"Aye, that's true," said Gant. "Sotirios isn't expendable like the rest of us. Nor Thaddeus. Both are ritualists, capable of incredible magic. Honestly, they can be terrifying sometimes. Thaddeus has this spell that turns him into a draconic form."

"Draconic?" I repeated.

An enormous shadow passed above us: a massive draconian creature with black scales and the horned head of a goat.

"Saints!" barked Brindle, riding atop a horse not far away. "Scouts witnessed what appears to be an enemy stronghold up ahead. Captain Thaddeus shall lay the first strike, then you lot will need to go in and clean up those left. Kill them and capture their bodies for when they rise again."

I told myself that it was another city. That I was just confused about where we marched. But deep down, I knew there was no denying it. With a dreadful weight in my gut, I stretched myself high to look over the shoulders of the others.

In the distance were Byzantium's gates. And flying straight toward it was Thaddeus's huge draconic form, moving at ten times our speed, with twenty times my size.

"Wait!" I shouted, pushing through the others in some fruitless attempt to get there first. I had no plan, no idea what I'd even do if I reached the city. But blind fear had overtaken me, the faces of those I'd left there flashing through my mind: Elias, Jeanne, Anika, so many others I'd never even learned the names of.

Then the goat-dragon spit out a burst of flame, and the city erupted in a great orange blaze. This was not like the fire from before. This was a great, all-consuming inferno, so staggeringly bright that I had to cover my eyes.

The demons around me cheered. "Fire in the hole!" one shouted, earning laughs from the others.

I pushed to the edge of the procession and spread my wings. It didn't matter that I'd never flown before and didn't know what I was doing; I had to get there. I had to save whoever I could. I flapped my wings, felt the wind beneath them, and finally kicked into the air. Higher and higher I rose, but I was flying with panic rather than joy, a terrified bat racing to protect his old colony. But Byzantium's walls were already charred husks, as were the warriors who had stood upon them. As I flew over them, the air around me became orange smoke. I coughed, and my flying became clumsier than ever, my suffocation making it harder to stay aloft.

The huge goat-dragon was still circling above the city, lower jaw dislocated to spit torrent after torrent of flame, each one accentuated with an ear-rupturing roar. Bodies were impaled on its massive teeth, their blood dripping out of its jowls like drool, their faces melting from the heat.

Screams pierced the air. Arrows, bullets and axes shot up into the sky. Many of them were aflame. Few found purchase. None of them seemed to damage Thaddeus at all.

I descended enough to see more mortal souls running on the ground or throwing utterly useless spears. Some aimed for me, their spears missing by inches. "Wait!" I shouted, lowering until my feet hit the ground.

More spears flew at me. Most of the faces were murky from all the smoke, but I realized Jeanne was among them, screaming, "Fight! Fight with all you have!"

Another massive wave of fire rained down from the sky, engulfing them all with a deafening blast.

"Jeanne!" I yelled, my eyes, nose, and throat all itching from the toxic air. As the initial plume of fire dissipated, I ran into the thick curtain of smoke it left behind. The bodies within were indistinguishable from one another, for all lay still on the ground, burning, charred red-black flesh bulging and popping. Any one of them could have been Jeanne. "Jeanne!" I tried shouting again, but my throat was so itchy and dry that it came out as a frail croak.

Everything we'd built was aflame. Elias's library. The barracks. The walls. The homes...

The great goat-dragon landed before me on two legs, its body shrinking until it was human-sized. Black scales shed from its body like hair, leaving bloody wounds behind. Thaddeus stood before me, naked and scowling. "Why did you leave formation, Saint?"

A hand appeared on my shoulder: Kaeru. "He was merely eager to join the hunt. Isn't that right, Caleb? You make a wonderful dragon as always, captain."

"Only cost me a lung this time." Thaddeus continued to leer at me, ignoring the flattery. I tried to make my face like stone, but even I knew it was a pitiful attempt. My hands trembled, my head hung, and no matter how much I tried to stop it, a warm river ran down my cheek, cutting through the smoke stains. I fell to my knees.

Thaddeus lowered himself before me, like a grandfather reassuring a child. "I bet you're wondering why we're here, boy. The truth is, we wouldn't be if it were not for you. You see, I still had my doubts about your claim that you came from the south, so I sent some scouts north, just to be sure. And lo and behold, they found a settlement." Then he broke into a grin, showing crooked yellow goat teeth. "Thank you, Caleb. Whether you intended to or not, you led us here."

I could not speak. I wanted to throw up. This was all my fault.

Thaddeus continued to grin as he rose back up to his full height. "Come, Kaeru. Let us make sure they are taken care of."

"Of course." Kaeru reached down to the burned husk of a man who was still conscious, his eyes filled with soot. She removed a black glove, then ducked down, touched his forehead, and whispered, "Shhh. There, there. You'll heal soon."

Her voice had become low, gravelly, and deeply masculine. Her body shifted, her muscles swelling, her hair shortening, her jaw becoming hard and thick, until I realized she wasn't a woman at all anymore, but rather an alarmingly handsome man. Bile rose in my throat, uncertain what it meant that I had lain with her.

Thaddeus stomped onto the burned man's head with his huge hoof. "I don't know why you always do this, Kaeru. Our job isn't to comfort them."

"They become numb without a little comfort. It keeps them alive enough that further torture hurts more." She—no, *they*—continued to walk, fingers caressing over the bodies of those still conscious. For each person they touched, their body changed, taking on form after form. Then they reached a woman's body—Jeanne, I realized with a start. Kaeru leaned down, put a hand on her cracked black cheek, and shifted once more. This time, the shape she took was that of a man with flaxen hair, blue eyes, and a thin body. It was how I'd looked only hours ago. My nausea worsened.

"She must really love you," said Kaeru with my voice. "I wonder if she still will, after this." They noticed me staring and offered a sad smile. "What? Would you prefer a more familiar form?"

They took my hand, and theirs shrank within my own, becoming smaller. Their chest swelled, and they smirked with full red lips, once again becoming the Clara-like succubus I'd made love to. I stumbled backwards, mortified, only for a frail hand to grasp my ankle. It was so weak, it left no pressure at all.

"Ceh-Caleb..." croaked one of the figures on the ground: Elias, his features barely intact, cooked until he was red and black. His lower half was gone, his intestines spilling out from the cut. With a twitching arm he reached for my leg, but he couldn't seem to control his fingers well enough to grasp it. As torn as he was, Elias's face still managed to twist into an expression of anger. "You...betrayed us..."

"I didn't mean to," I stammered. "I just..."

"Leave...us," he hissed. "You don't...deserve to be one of us." He let out a bloody cough and added, "We will...find you...after we heal. You will...pay...for this."

"But that's where you're wrong," boomed a low voice behind me, and I turned to see Thaddeus approaching. "Lord Sotirios has ordered these rebels be taken to Tartarus. They have special punishments for rebels there. Punishments that are said to be...transcendent."

"Captain!" came a shout from beyond a wall of smoke. Gant passed through it, pulling along a tiny shape: Anika. She was wounded, but intact. My heart leaped into my throat. "We found this one. Think we can fetch a high price for her?"

Thaddeus's eyes glimmered. "How good of you to bring her, lieutenant. Actually, I think I'd rather keep her for my own stable."

He grasped Anika's shoulder. She glared at him, then at me. It was the same glare I must have given Thomas: a glare that told me she would never, ever forgive me. That she would dream of killing me for the rest of her existence.

"Imagine killing a child over and over again." Thaddeus turned to show me his grin. "What a pleasure it will be."

Part of me wanted to charge at the bastard and break his neck. But another part wondered how I could have expected anything different. This was Hell. I'd chosen the stronger side.

And the stronger side was the cruelest force in the universe.

"Leave them, Caleb." Kaeru pressed against my back, their arms wrapping around my chest. They kissed my neck, and even with all the fire and smoke, I felt a tingle of pleasure from it. "Leave them," they repeated, their whisper cutting over the screams and the crackles of flame.

They pulled me back up to the hill, away from the fire. Then they pushed me onto my back and mounted me.

———◈———

Eventually, Byzantium became quiet, for not a single mouth was able to keep screaming. Kaeru, having ridden me until I was numb, put their gloves back on.

Below, the city was in ruins, but the fire had died down. The soldiers were dragging the remaining bodies in nets across the Patchwork Sea. Watching them, I could barely even breathe.

"They're not your responsibility, you know," said Kaeru. "This is Hell. There will always be suffering. That's why you made the choice you did."

I hugged my knees, exhaling, like enough breathing might send me back in time, so I could relive my entire life and do it all differently, even though deep down I feared I'd just make all the same mistakes all over again.

"What now?" I asked, my voice a strange, raspy sound.

"We return to camp," said Kaeru. "Lord Sotirios will wish for an update."

They spread their wings, and reluctantly, I spread mine. I had nowhere else to go, and nothing else to do but follow them into the cavernous sky.

CHAPTER THIRTEEN

ASHES IN THE WIND

I WISH I COULD say that I fought back. It was what I had probably always imagined I'd do in such circumstances. But to tell the truth, I didn't know what to do, other than return to the camp with Kaeru. Thaddeus assigned me a cot in a tent, then offered me a helping of bloodwine and all too human meat. That first night, I refused both.

Instead, I lay alone on a hard bedroll, trying to block out the sounds from outside: drinking, belching, singing, gunfire and clashing blades and despicable bloody laughter. It was more comfortable than the coffin house had been, but that was the most I could say for it. I had to lie on my side rather than my back, for my wings detested being crushed. Before, I'd only lay on my side in order to hold Jeanne as we passed into sleep. It was hard not to miss her, and even harder to not hate myself for what I'd done.

Eventually, a woman came into my tent and lay beside me. I was confused until they poked me, and their skin rippled into the familiar, Clara-like form. Kaeru stared at me with a concerned expression, head laying on their hands. I groaned and turned over, so that my back was to them.

"I'm sorry about your people," they said.

"No you're not," I grunted.

They were silent for a moment, but I could feel their stare boring into the back of my neck. "Are you upset with me?"

"Why do you even care what I think?" I said. "There's a whole army out there for you to feed on."

"And do you think I like everyone in that army? Has it never occurred to you that I might be selective with my meals?"

There was only the slightest hint of irritation in their voice. I turned to see them tilting their head, eyes wide, appearing not hurt so much as curious.

"You could have told me," I said. "You could have warned me that you weren't wearing your true face."

Kaeru shrugged. "It's as true a face as any."

"What do you mean?" I asked, scowling. "What even are you?"

Kaeru hesitated, as if worried how I might respond to their question. "Some lilitu bloodlines are more...unique than others. Sanguinus lilitu like yourself can derive sustenance from blood as well as sex. Then there are the Elysian lilitu, whose wings take unique shapes; Diabolos lilitu like Lord Sotirios, known for their strength and skill with rituals; Nerrings, who have tails and hoofs but no wings..."

"And what are you?"

"A Silkshaper." They met my eyes again, as if giving me the opportunity to interrupt if I'd already heard of them, but I had not. "When taking the milk, most lilitu attain the body they always wished they had. I am different. For every person I touch, I become the person they want me to be. If they want a redheaded man, I become a redheaded man. If they want a brunette woman, that is what I shall be."

"Then the woman you are now..." I began.

"Is the woman of your dreams," Kaeru finished. "But the moment I touch another, she will be gone." Their face hardened. "Sometimes, I'm repulsed by the things I become."

"But who are you underneath it all?" I asked. "Who were you when you were still mortal?"

Kaeru smiled, but their eyes softened into an oddly sad expression. "Unfortunately, I do not remember."

I frowned, confused. "Was it that long ago?" If Kaeru had been alive for many lifetimes, each one could be harder to remember than the last.

Their smile hadn't faded, but neither had the sadness in their eyes. "Every Silkshaper is required to drink from the River Lethe, the waters of which will wash your memories away. It is said that without this, a Silkshaper will go mad. It's better that I began with a clean slate, without a former identity to cling to."

"Don't you ever wonder?"

They shrugged. "It's the hand I've been dealt. There have only been a few proven Silkshapers in all of recorded history, for nearly all mortals perish from drinking our milk. I was a rare exception. I try to think of it as an honor."

But Kaeru didn't sound honored.

They let out a soft sigh before adding, "I'm sorry I didn't tell you what I am. I feared it would upset you. Besides, you needed someone to be your first feed, and why should it not be with the woman of your dreams?"

A hollow feeling settled in my chest. Even now, Kaeru's face gutted me with longing, but some part of me still yearned to make love to them once more.

"Is Tartarus as bad as they say?" I finally asked, even though I dreaded the answer.

Kaeru frowned. "Oh, Caleb. I don't think you should concern yourself with your old friends any longer."

"I just...want to know." My throat was tight, and my nails itched to tear open my skin. I would not admit this to Kaeru, but deep down, I wanted to find them and free them. It felt like it was the only thing that would free me from the prison of my shame. "And Thaddeus has Anika, doesn't he?"

"Thaddeus is your commanding officer. His spoils are none of your concern." Kaeru fixed me with a sorrowful gaze. "I need to know that you can move past this. You're lilitu now. A Blood Saint. And you must not let your mortal morality hold you back."

I turned my back to them again, nausea flooding my lungs. Kaeru waited for a moment, then stood up to leave.

It only took a few hours for the hunger to return. That itchy, pressure-filled sensation in my loins; the dryness in my throat...

Before I knew it, I was compulsively sitting up, bedeviled with a raging lust, the likes of which I'd never felt as a mortal. This was no mere hunger; it was *agony*. I felt like I might claw off my own skin to satisfy it.

I dressed myself and hurried out of the tent. There had to be other succubi here. Someone I could feed on who wasn't Kaeru. Maybe one of the dancers? My nails dug into my palms, and I found myself clenching my jaw, fangs dragging against my bottom teeth.

Through the camp I wandered. The demons around me continued their wanton celebrations, most of them already occupied with partners of their own, and ravenous though I was, I did not feel welcome butting into their affairs.

Without knowing where I was going, I stumbled into the area full of caged wagons. This was where we'd taken Pestilence, I realized. And indeed, despite the beating of the drum, I noticed distant voices echoing from within Pestilence's wagon—and one of them belonged to Salem.

"...I just don't understand why," he said, his voice a low, angry rumble.

This was probably not a conversation I was meant to hear. I moved away, but then I wondered whether the other wagons might contain my old friends, and took a deep breath, trying to push the awful hunger away. I could wait a moment, I told myself. A moment, that was all.

But as I passed by empty cage after empty cage, Pestilence's voice echoed after me, "I didn't think you'd be fighting me, my love. I thought we could run away together."

"Together, Valeria? Now, after all this time?"

Salem's voice was strained, like he was tempted against his better judgment. By now, I felt totally unable to move.

"What if I told you that we didn't need to fear Riven anymore?" Pestilence's voice was a hushed whisper, barely audible. "What if you could be the one sitting on that throne instead?"

Salem let out a humorless chuckle. "Is that why you stole the bridle? You should have known better, Valeria. I cannot betray the emperor."

"I betrayed him the moment I looked upon you. And you betrayed him the moment you came into my chamber. We betrayed him over and over, and what bliss it was, Salem!"

"If it was such bliss, then why did you tell me to stop when you did?" Any semblance of friendliness had left Sotirios's voice. He sounded very cold, and not all in love. "You cast me out. Would not speak to me. Would not hear from me. With no warning or explanation at all. Fifty years, Valeria. Fifty years, I hear nothing from you, and now—"

"I was a fool then, my love," Pestilence cooed. "I feared Riven discovering us. He would have killed you, had he caught you with his latest bride. But everything's different now."

"I'm sure it is. After all, why would he care if I touch this thing you've become?"

Pestilence let out a pitiful sob. "I know I no longer look as I did, but you must believe I spent all those years planning my escape, all in the hopes of reuniting with you. Stealing the bridle was the only way. I didn't know what it would do to me, only that it offered me the sole path to freedom. More than that, power. What if I knew a way to make you more powerful than Riven, my love? I've been experiment-ing, and—"

"Ridiculous. Riven cannot be harmed."

"What if he can? If you would just hear me out—"

"I will not," said Salem stiffly. "You speak of heresy, against your own husband."

"Don't you want to be emperor? I know you do. I know you harbor no love for him..."

"And I harbor no love for you either, *empress*." He spat the word. "Not anymore."

There was a pause. When Pestilence responded, her voice was cracked: "I know that's not true. I know it isn't. I can see it in your eyes. You love me. You have always loved me."

"That was half a century ago. More than enough time for me to realize the universe is full of women who can offer me what you did and more. What we shared happened before you took the mantle of Pestilence. Before half your skin rotted away. Before you fled from the palace, turned countless good soldiers into your ghouls, and caused so much trouble that I had to be pulled away from my duties to babysit you. Before you broke my heart and left me to stew in that pain for *fifty years*. And you expect me to throw away all I've worked so hard for now, after you've become *this?*"

Salem's voice was a bitter hiss, each word clawing through the air.

"It's too late, Valeria. My heart may have beat for you once, long ago...but in the years since we last spoke, it has grown cold. I imagined that when I finally saw you again, I would feel...so many things. Rage, lust, sorrow, perhaps even warmth. But now, as I look upon you, I feel nothing. No desire. No anger. Not even pity or disgust. I simply look forward to returning you to your husband's chains, so that I can return to Earth and resume my work. To me, what we shared was a dalliance. One of countless I've had in my life, appealing only because it was forbidden. You are and will always be nothing."

Sensing the finality in his voice, I hurried away before he caught me spying. My search had been fruitless anyway, and I needed to find someone to feed on. By now, my whole body seemed to rattle with need.

But I did not get far, and was still well within his eyesight when he emerged from the back of the wagon. Salem saw me immediately, a quiet anger still simmering in his eyes. He exhaled through his nose and said, "Join me, Caleb."

"Of course, Lord Sotirios." I followed him away from the wagons, hoping he didn't mean to punish me. "Where are we headed?"

"I need a meal," he said bluntly. "You look like you need one, too."

"You would...share a meal with me?" I asked, baffled. Was he suggesting that we feed on each other? My mouth watered at the thought, oddly intrigued, even though I'd never felt attracted to men before. Whether it was because of my new nature, my hunger, or Salem's unfathomable beauty, I knew not.

Salem strolled at a brisk pace, not even glancing at me now that we were walking together. "You helped us more than you could know by catching that awful woman. I think you have potential, and I want to see whether I can bring it out."

He led me back to his enormous tent. The succubus who had been feeding on him before was currently lounging on the bed, flipping through a book. As we entered, she immediately looked up and rose to her knees, something in her eye shifting, like a switch within her had been flicked, placing her in an entirely different frame of mind.

"Go find your sister and bring her here," said Salem.

"Of course, sir." The succubus kept her head low as she hurried from the tent.

"They weren't born sisters," Salem told me, sitting on the bed and unlacing his boots. "Fiona and Milena were just turned by the same woman."

"That is...good to know, sir." I stood there, still uncertain what to make of the fact that he'd summoned me, but I feared asking would make me look the fool. Salem either didn't notice how befuddled I was or simply didn't care. Likely the latter.

"You disapprove of Fiona's treatment?" he asked, tilting his head.

"Pardon, sir?"

"No need to lie. I noticed how you looked at us before. Like you were concerned for her." Salem's voice betrayed no disdain. He was perfectly content, perfectly in control. That was what frightened me. How the Hell was I supposed to know how to respond if I didn't know how he really felt?

"You were rather...rough with her, sir," I admitted. "I just wasn't used to it."

"At least you didn't deny it." Salem chuckled, removing his coat. "I can tolerate it when my underlings are shocked by me. It is dishonesty that I cannot stand. With that in mind, what would you say if I told you Fiona submitted to me, agreeing that I could use her however I pleased?"

Was it another test? I debated how to respond for a moment before deciding that I had no choice but to speak the truth. "I would wonder if she was under duress. If she truly had every choice before her. Or whether becoming a succubus, and your submissive at that, was something she was forced into."

"Honesty again. More points." Salem smirked. "This may surprise you, Caleb, but I'm not interested in forcing anyone to do anything. However, I do enjoy the process of convincing them that what I want is beneficial to us both. All this is to say, young Fiona always desired me. That required no adjusting on my part. However, she was initially anxious to give herself to me fully, as all inexperienced girls are. So, I took my time to train her, to show her that she did not need to fear this corruption—that it could offer us both pleasure beyond imagination. And over time, she began to understand. Little by little, she began to like whatever I did to her, simply because it pleased me."

He removed his remaining clothes as he spoke: his shirt, his pants...

"It's a question of nourishment," he went on, clearly loving the sound of his own voice, and honestly, who could blame him? "The theory is that the more pleasure your partner feels, the more sexual energy you derive from fucking them, and the more delicious the meal. It benefits Fiona to please me, just as it would benefit her sister to please you. And it's not like any of us still need to breathe."

Now his bulky form stood nigh naked before me, only his bulging crotch area covered by paltry black undergarments. By now, it was impossible to hide my uncomfortable attraction, but it did not seem to perturb him.

"Then Fiona and Milena are here by choice?" I asked.

"Quite so," said Salem, watching the entryway expectantly. "They may leave at any time, should they choose. But they won't."

"What makes you so sure?"

He smirked, thought for a moment, and lowered his voice. "With eternity to pursue their research, our scientists have discovered some remarkable insularities about how the brain works. Able to experiment on soul after soul without repercussions, we've learned much that the mortals of Earth have not. For one thing, it's quite interesting how the mind deals with fear."

"Fear?" I repeated, and damn if my own voice wasn't full of it.

"Indeed," said Salem. "When the human mind takes in information, the first part of the brain it goes to is its most primitive place: the threat center, determining the fight, flight, freeze, or appease response. Only after that does it reach the mammalian part of the brain, where it processes your emotional reaction. And only after *that* does it reach the area of your brain capable of critical thought. In other words, keeping people afraid keeps them primitive. Stupid. Unable to think clearly or form plans. So, if you want control over someone, all you need is to keep them afraid. Whether it's a girl you fancy...or an entire nation."

The tent's curtains parted as Fiona returned with another succubus beside her, and I froze, my throat closing. Like Fiona, Milena had tantalizing curves, leathery wings, and a smile too perfect to believe. But she also had golden cat-like eyes, sleek black hair, and a spade-tipped tail.

I knew her immediately. She was the succubus who had killed my father.

"My darlings," said Salem, kissing each of them. "You are hungry, yes? What do you make of him, Milena?"

Milena looked me over, pupils narrowing to slits. "I would be delighted to feed on him."

Just as with Kaeru, I could smell her desire. That was, perhaps, the worst part. She wanted me, and hungry as I was, that made me want her.

"What do you say, Caleb?" Salem asked. Something in his voice told me he'd be disappointed if I refused him.

My father had been inside this woman. She was his killer. And I was only here with these people in the hopes of returning to Earth, to be with Clara. How could I claim to love her, while taking advantage of other women alongside Lord Sotirios?

And yet gazing upon Milena's perfect form was more than enough to solidify my hunger. The quiet anger within me did nothing to quench this flame; indeed, it only made it burn brighter. I hardened as my fangs extended, my body already welcoming the thought of our unholy convergence.

"It would be a pleasure," I said, sinking my fangs into her throat.

Salem's bed was big enough for the four of us to share without difficulty, but this hardly alleviated my discomfort. Even as I forced myself to penetrate Milena, it was hard to not be distracted by Salem and Fiona going at it beside us. Fiona shrieked like he was killing her, and Salem growled and snarled as he held her face down against the bed. She'd raised her pelvis high to meet his distractingly huge cock, and plugged her own rectum with the tip of her tail.

I tried focusing on Milena, who I had in a missionary position beneath me, but the wretched knowledge of who she was made it difficult. Nor could I help but compare her moans to those of Fiona's. Even now, I felt inferior. I'd become nearly as strong and tall as Salem himself, but the bastard still made me feel like I was nothing. My gyrations slowed, my cock softened, and my thoughts became fuzzy with shame.

"What's wrong?" Salem asked, head snapping to my direction. "Why are you slowing down? Surely the poor girl is to your liking?"

Somehow, he hadn't slowed down in the least. I hated him more for it.

"Of course she is," I grunted. "It's just..."

Milena's moaning ceased so quickly that I knew it all to have been a lie. She stared uncertainly up at me, fear flashing in her eyes. It occurred to me that it would be very bad for her if Salem decided this was her fault.

Perhaps I should have welcomed the idea of her suffering. This woman had killed my father, after all. But Salem terrified me too. The only thing I could think to do was to thrust faster, forcing myself to perform and giving Milena the chance to do the same. Her moans resumed like nothing had happened.

"You should be using your entire body," said Salem, even as he continued drilling Fiona. "Your hands, your mouth. Not just your cock. Overwhelm her, boy!"

I groaned, not because he was wrong, but because it was humiliating to receive such criticism while inside a woman. I allowed my hands to wander, grabbing and squeezing Milena's breasts and rump, even as I kissed and bit into her throat. Milena's moans became more intense and genuine sounding, which encouraged me to keep at it.

"Hold her tighter," Salem added. "Like this."

He wrapped his enormous arms tight around Fiona, crushing her beneath him. I did the same with Milena. Salem grinned in approval.

"That's it. Compress her. Make her tiny. Remind her that she's powerless against you, yours to take as you please, and take you will. Not because she desires you, but because *you* desire *her*. Honor her with that desire. Your cock is not like the disappointing cocks of mortal men. No, yours is a cock that can change her. It is a privilege for it to be inside her, just as it's a privilege for Fiona to have mine. Isn't that right, my pet?"

"Yes, sir!" Fiona howled, the sound well-rehearsed.

And yet I wanted Milena to scream it to me, too. I didn't love her, didn't want her, and maybe even hated her, but right then, with her writhing beneath me, I wanted her to succumb to me with the same reckless abandon as Fiona to Salem. I stared into her eyes and brought my fist to her throat. It was sticky from the little scarlet rivers trickling down it.

"Don't push into her jugular, fool! Squeeze the sides." Salem grabbed the back of Fiona's neck, wrapping his huge fingers around its sides until she gasped for air. "It's like you have control over her whole body."

I compressed the sides of her throat, focusing on my anger, imagining the revenge I would inflict on her for stealing my father and my future. Milena's gyrations became more insistent. I raised my body higher so that my cock pushed down into her, deeper and deeper.

"That's it," hissed Salem. "She's nothing. Nothing! Only meat! Water crashing uselessly against your stone!"

I groaned again, my rage and lust swirling into some repulsive combination, squeezing so hard that her eyes bulged, her face a vulgar parody of pleasure that only aroused me more. I was not my father; I was not letting her control me. I was the one controlling *her*.

"You're fucking *mine!*" I snarled, the words coming out, unbidden.

"Yes, Sir!" Milena's voice was raspy, but it didn't matter. The words brought a tingling fire to my loins. The fog of pleasure clouded out any memory, any semblance of logic, any conscious thought. The entire world disappeared as Milena's moaning reached a crescendo, and her body convulsed as her womanhood gushed, coating my cock with her dew. I exploded into her in turn, so hard that the pressure caused my cock to slip out and spray onto her cunt and stomach.

And then there was nothing left but our panting, our exhaustion, and my endless self-loathing.

Salem snorted in laughter. "You covered her."

I backed away, sat on the edge of the bed and buried my face into my hands, crippled by the sudden clarity. I couldn't believe I'd fed on her. I couldn't believe I'd made love to my father's killer. Were it not for her, I might never have turned to that club; might never have been murdered by Thomas to begin with. I might still be alive up there on Earth. Yet when I risked a glance at her, she smiled, eyes caressing up and down my body like she was just as surprised. I'd given her what she'd wanted. For all my rage, all my desire to control, I'd only given her pleasure.

⸺⸺◆⸺⸺

Salem and Fiona finished shortly after. "Go bathe," he told them. "Clean yourself thoroughly. As for you..." He turned his gaze on me and grinned. "You've performed well tonight. I hope you won't be opposed to further lessons on the way to Elysium?"

How was I to answer? To say yes felt like agreeing to filling my mind with poison; letting this cruel man make me an ever-worse person. But if I said no, how did I know he wouldn't kill me for it?

So I nodded, even as acid filled my throat. I hid my agony, resisting my urge to hug my arms. And Salem must have believed me, for he smiled.

As the girls went to the bathtub, he loomed over my shoulder and whispered, "Just so we understand each other. While I am sharing this opportunity with you, Fiona and Milena are not yours, and you are not to speak with either of them when I'm not around. Will you respect this?"

Again, I nodded, not meeting his eyes. "Does the hunger always feel so...awful?" I asked, my voice a low croak.

"You learn to get used to it." Salem's voice was amused.

Just what had I become? Certainly, I'd known before that I would find sustenance through fornication, but I had not truly comprehended what that would mean. While I certainly had no intention of letting any hunger get the better of me, I doubted other incubi held such compunctions. Almost as horrifying was the unbridled pleasure I'd felt from making love to my father's killer; at choking her, controlling her, making her mine. Even now, as we watched them bathe, part of me yearned to be inside her once more.

"Where did you meet these girls?"

Salem raised a brow. "Years ago, at Elysium's Whore Pits. It's where some lilitu are taken after committing crimes. Far more humane than giving them the True Death, wouldn't you agree?"

My stomach twisted into knots. "Are these pits where lilitu come from when people summon them on Earth?"

"Why, of course." Salem watched the girls bathe with a fond smile. "Those who hide on Earth cannot always find other demons to feed on, and when the occasional mortal attempts the ritual, well, another fresh soul falls into the emperor's realm. In my younger days, I was quite the patron. Now, I no longer need to pay for such services, and Fiona and Milena are the perfect example. Earlier this year, they finished their sentences early for good behavior. They came to me by choice not long after." He chuckled. "They said I'd been their favorite patron."

It was all too much to take in at that moment. It had never occurred to me that my father's killer might not have come to him by choice. That she might have been serving a sentence, and been forced to go to Earth to claim the souls of those who summoned her.

"You see, now, why it behooves us to serve the emperor well," said Salem. "After all, if he wanted to, he could lock you or I away in the Whore Pits, too."

This was no less troubling a thought. I imagined how I might feel after years of being summoned to feed on people I detested. Of having to act like I desired them, maybe even loved them, all in the hopes of making it over faster. Would I, too, not have hatred in my eyes? Would I not relish in taking their lives, as Milena had done my father's?

"What of Kaeru?" I asked.

"Kaeru belongs to the emperor. I'm in no more position to lay claim on that one than you. They feed on who they please, and you should consider yourself very fortunate indeed if you gain a moment of their time."

I wondered if I'd been too hasty to dismiss them. Then again, I was still quite angry that they'd hid the truth from me. At that moment, with the hunger a quiet whisper, I didn't want to feed on anyone at all. But I knew in time it would once again become too loud to ignore.

"What happens if I have no partner? How will I feed?"

Salem's eye pinched, as if irritated he had to be the one to explain all this to me. "Incubus seed is a bit like rodent teeth. Just as a rat's teeth will grow and grow if unattended to, your seed will keep building and building up inside of you until it's unbearable. So you'll want to at the very least get it out, by your own hand if need be. That will stave off the hunger for a time. But keep in mind that if you're thinking about someone in particular when you do it, you may end up traveling into their dreams."

"We can enter people's dreams to feed on them?" I asked, immediately wondering how I might make use of this.

Could I contact Clara that way? Perhaps Jeanne, Elias, anyone I so desperately sought forgiveness from?

"It will sustain you for a while," Salem said, still watching the girls bathe. "It also will ensure that your partner survives, if they're mortal. We demons can feed on each other without consequence, but mortals... they do not survive in reality."

"It will *kill* them?" I asked, my manhood withering in horror. I'd thought my father had died from his wounds, but from the sound of things he would have been lost even without them. How the Hell was I going to be with Clara now? I shook my head. I would figure something out, assuming I was allowed to return to Earth in the first place.

Salem's eyes caressed the succubi, as though already he hungered to defile them again. "Dreams and self-stimulation are half-measures. To be at your strongest, you must feed in reality. There's no substitute for true shared sexual energy."

"But better than nothing?" I asked.

A low growl of a chuckle escaped his mouth. "Very well. Let's say an incubus is unable to release his seed. Perhaps he is captive, his hands bound, kept awake and unable to dream through magic or modern chemistry. Do you know what would happen, then?"

His tone was not threatening, and yet my throat became sore, as if stripped of a tender layer of flesh, some part of me wondering whether this was a punishment he'd save for me if I disappointed him enough. Pressure built up in my temples, as if his fingers were digging through my skull to penetrate my mind. I found myself unable to respond, unable to even breathe. All I could do was shake my head.

Salem's face split into a cruel grin. "It's a sight to behold. As I said, your seed will keep building and building within you, and if it isn't properly expelled... why, it finds all sorts of places to come out. There's also madness. Unimaginable pain. Hunger that will claw your brain away until there's nothing left. It is said to be one of the most agonizing deaths imaginable."

He finally turned to look at me, still grinning.

"Run along now, Caleb. I'd like the girls to myself for the rest of the night. And do remember what I told you."

<hr>

Back in my tent, I tried to enter Clara's dreams in the manner Salem had suggested. I did not wish to feed on her; merely speak to her. To see how she was doing, and assure her that I was coming to help her. However, no matter how hard I closed my eyes or how intensely I focused, I never managed to emerge into her dreams.

Next, I tried to contact Jeanne, but was no more successful than before. I tried Elias, uncomfortable though it was to think of him while caressing myself in such a way, but that didn't work either. Maybe they were all currently awake.

I sighed, frustrated by the defeat. What would I even tell my old allies if I managed to reach them? That I was sorry? That I wished I could help them?

There was no undoing what I'd done. Indeed, the more I thought about it, the less certain I was that I even wanted to see them. They certainly wouldn't want to see me. Besides, I already knew that I could not free them from Tartarus, especially not if I wanted to attain my vengeance. I'd have to live with this terrible sin.

If existing as a hollow shell can be called living at all.

CHAPTER FOURTEEN

DEATH GOSPELS

THE WORDS HERE MIGHT be blurry, the letters running into each other. This is because they took my eyelids today, and it's challenging to see with all the blood leaking down. I'm also running out of space. Already the walls around me are almost fully red, the words forming murals: the red canyons beyond these walls, the corpses I've left behind, the faces of everyone I've betrayed. No matter. It will be time to move up to the ceiling, soon.

It was a long journey to Elysium, taking us approximately five months, and as Salem and Thaddeus had clocks and calendars, I can say that for certain. That was one of the first things I learned in their company: my superiors and others like them broke or stole any clocks they found.

"We don't want mortals tracking time down here," Salem explained, pulling a circular watch from his waistcoat pocket. At the time we were riding side by side somewhere in the middle of the long line of soldiers, the tents long since packed up. The wilderness before us was a desert of ash grey sand, peppered with skeletal trees and enormous buzzards. Salem opened his watch, showing me the immaculate innards. Even the gears looked polished. "Mankind is here to suffer as punishment for its sins, and confusion adds to that suffering. Tracking the time would be a step toward understanding, which would go against the very purpose of this place. But *we* are on a schedule."

"And what is the date?" I asked him.

"July 6th."

"And the year?"

"1875."

He might as well have slapped me. I'd been in Hell for nearly three years.

"We were mortals once, too," I said. "Are we meant to suffer here as well?"

Salem smirked, slipping the watch back into his pocket. "We *have* suffered. And now we've been chosen by God to join the immortal ranks: to bring order to the underworld, and ensure its purpose is fulfilled. Who would punish sinners as God ordained, if not us?"

"But I've met children down here. Scholars. People who I can't imagine have sinned at all."

"All humans sin." Salem's eyes darkened. "Few will tell you what terrible things they've done, even here. Many will never recognize it themselves. And all humans carry the burden of original sin, don't forget."

I felt a twinge of surprise, even disgust. "Then you believe in the Bible's teachings? Even now that you've become a demon?"

"Not all of it. But we are in Hell, are we not? What else are we to make of this place?" Salem shrugged. "The emperor says there must be an Almighty, though he's yet to meet one, even after seizing the Ever-Burning Throne. Nor have we encountered any Lucifer, or Satan, even if many here worship them. Nor have I ever met a single soul who can prove the existence of Heaven."

"Then why uphold it all?" I gestured broadly. "Is this really what mankind deserves? And what makes it all right for us to keep sinning, if we punish mortals for doing the same?"

Salem chuckled and lowered his voice. "You are right to question, Caleb. Religion is, after all, merely a method to control the masses. You're too smart for it, just as I am. Still, the emperor believes that by upholding Hell, he will eventually find a way to contact the Almighty and attain enlightenment about the nature of our universe. For many, that is enough. For others... well, some of us fight for the emperor because he rewards those who serve him. Indeed, for those who serve him best, those rewards become quite compelling indeed. I, for one, am willing to do whatever it takes to live the way I want: free of punishment, in a Heaven of my own making, far away from this awful place. And we must not forget that Riven has been in this realm for longer than most. Who knows? Perhaps it really does bring balance to the universe, somehow."

The entire conversation left me baffled. I couldn't believe that even the demons in charge of Hell had no true understanding of our universe. Did God still expect us to have faith in him without proof, even here? Or was it just all a sham?

The question continued to churn in my mind for the entirety of our journey. During those months on the road, many of the Blood Saints would gather to listen to sermons from a satyr priest traveling with us. I remember the first night I listened to him read to a crowd of us from his skin-bound bible, his long grey beard blowing like a reed in the ashen wind.

"The Death Gospels are for we who are dead," he said, his voice a low croak. "They are not for the living, who still live in fear of what lies beyond the veil. They are for we who no longer fear what has already come to pass. We who have died and now live forever. We are immortals, part of the natural order. Here to remind people of what can be hiding in the dark corners of the earth, inspiring them to be better than we could."

The other demons around me nodded and murmured reverently.

The priest continued: "While mortals who perish are reborn in Hell again and again, we have but one life left. Some fear the True Death, but it is not a curse. It is a gift. An end to our suffering, and redemption for our souls."

Perhaps he was right. So what if I could die? That meant so could Thomas.

The Blood Saints all began to pray, hands pressed together to the God that had forsaken them, if he'd ever existed at all. I followed suit, but I felt like an island in that crowd, unable to fully abandon my mortal values.

At least until the music began. The succubus and incubus dancers came out, and began singing and frolicking as the drummer beat his enormous war drum. I realized that it was not merely entertainment, but rather a spiritual rite, bringing the soldiers together. Something stirred within me as I listened to those immaculate voices, and I realized abruptly just how hungry I was for music.

As the weeks passed, I began to recognize some of their songs, and found myself humming along, joining the other soldiers in a shared trance. It was hard to not feel like even more of a traitor for this, and the shame wasn't helped by my apparent inability to reach my old friends. Again and again, I tried to reach Clara, Jeanne, or my other former rebel friends through their dreams, but not once did I find success. I wondered if I was even doing it correctly, but I feared that asking Salem for additional details would only anger him. I had no idea where Tartarus was, and finding it would mean disobeying Salem.

The only Byzantian I had any indication might be traveling with us was Anika, but the wagon that contained Thaddeus's things was always guarded. I could not even see whether she was inside.

Meanwhile, my fellow demons instructed me on how to become a better warrior. Duncan had already taught me much, but the Blood Saints were more skilled than he'd ever been.

One night, Brindle had Gant stand against a wall with a skull on top of his head. "Shoot the skull," he said, handing me a rifle.

"Can't you just put it on a table or something?" asked Gant, his already bulbous eyes extra wide with anxiety.

"Indeed, what if I shoot off his face?" I asked.

"It's not like it's a silver bullet," Brindle scoffed. "Go ahead. Hold your breath, now."

I shrugged, aimed at the skull, and shot off Gant's ear.

"Oops," said Brindle as Gant wailed in pain.

I eventually became an experienced enough marksman that Brindle assigned me a Whitworth long-range precision rifle, which had been brought from Earth along with the horses. I'd never been a sharpshooter in life, but holding a rifle from England made me more homesick than ever.

It also led to me being assigned lookout shifts, flying above the long line of soldiers and warning them of any incoming attacks. It was astonishing how quickly this changed my outlook on it all. I was no longer a stranger to my fellow Saints; I was responsible for their lives. Even miles above, with the soldiers resembling a line of ants, the pressure of my task weighed on me. More than once, I spied hordes of mortal bandits charging to attack, and it was up to me to pull the trigger, stopping them in their tracks. The first time was difficult. The second time, far less so. The third time was easy.

Perhaps I'd grown numb to the violence. The endless carnage and gore, once so shocking, had become commonplace. What harm would it be to send a bullet through the skull of a mortal soul, who would only wake up again days later, completely repaired? It was merely another atrocity in a realm of ceaseless pain. But it troubled me how untroubled I was; how cold to it all I was becoming.

It likely didn't help that throughout it all, Salem was training me in the ways of domination. He had a wardrobe full of instruments made for the bedroom: black whips, rope, and sharper things. Milena and Fiona remained our willing submissives—or Salem's, anyway—with Milena allowing herself to be my training dummy as Salem instructed me on such fine arts as bondage and proper flogging. I was rubbish with knots at first, but Salem was a surprisingly patient tutor.

"Start with soft patting," he said, when both girls were bound in identical tortoise-shell patterns. He began repeatedly slapping Fiona's butt cheeks, causing them to jiggle. "Like warming up for exercise. This will increase blood flow."

It looked awfully silly, but I suppressed my urge to giggle. I didn't want to ruin the illusion that I was as strong and stoic as Salem, especially as he began smacking harder, harder, *harder*, until Fiona was wailing with pleasure-pain. I tried it on Milena, and yielded a similar reaction. I slipped the fingers of my free hand into the soft, moist folds of her womanhood, pleasuring her as I spanked her until she climaxed. I grinned, feeling a surge of strength course through me even though I had not climaxed myself. It also helped assuage some of the shame and discomfort I felt about using her this way. I was becoming accustomed to forgetting that she was my father's killer, as well as the manner of how she'd come to meet Salem in the first place. So it was that I was kept well fed for the duration of the journey.

One night, while searching, I found Milena standing just outside the camp we'd made for the night, smoking a cigarette that reeked of perfume. While Salem had forbidden me to speak with her alone, the weeks of ambivalence were getting to me. I wanted to see her without the mask she put on for Salem. I wanted to see who she really was.

I cleared my throat and raised my hand in an awkward wave. She brought the cigarette to her lips, exhaled purple smoke, and smiled, weariness in her cat-like eyes. "Good evening, Caleb."

"Evening." I kept my distance, lest she be alarmed. "I just felt I ought to say thank you. I know it takes a lot of trust—"

She laughed, cutting me off. "You really are a little pup, aren't you? Coming at me like you owe me some sort of apology. All this is still just an act to you, isn't it?"

I was baffled, uncertain how to respond. It was the first occasion in which I'd heard her speak more than a few words at a time, and they weren't what I had expected. "All what?" I asked.

She waved her cigarette around, spreading even more purple smoke. "All this. The fighting, the posturing. Control doesn't come to you naturally. You may have fooled him, but I can tell."

My jaw tightened. "I've found that I like control quite a bit, actually."

"I'm not surprised in the least." She laughed again, the sound musical and teasing. "Most men who are obsessed with power start off like you. Convinced of their own powerlessness, feeling like they have to apologize just for existing. It's where that hunger comes from. Go ahead and keep faking it, for now. It will become real in time. Now that you've had a taste, you'll always want to be on top. But there will always be someone stronger, won't there?"

"Like Salem?" I asked, my throat drying.

"Or the emperor." She let out one last puff, then dropped the cigarette onto the ground, not even stomping to put it out. Watching her, I was reminded of London's many painted ladies of the night, doing what they could to survive mankind's modern dark forest.

"I...just want to know whether you're here by choice," I said, the words stumbling out of me before I could think better of them.

"Oh, darling, of course I am." She waved her hand at me, shaking her head like I was a fool for even asking. "I yearned for Salem the moment I met him. He can be a cruel lover, but I've never been able to say no to him."

"Even if he asks you to feed on another man?"

"Certainly not in this case. You're a handsome devil, and you've learned well." She winked. "But you should run along now. As I said, men who desire control tend to be fragile sorts, and for all his armor, Sotirios is the most fragile of all. So do run along. For both our sakes."

I hurried away, but looked over my shoulder to find her checking the sky above. Weariness had finally creeped into her eyes, as if from the crow's feet that should have wrinkled their corners.

⸺⸻◆⸻⸺

One day, our scouts reported a rare lake with clear water not far from the path. Salem brought me along to investigate, and we discovered that the strange rumor was true: the water was indeed clear, rather than the usual bloody red. Salem looked down at it with a disgusted expression, and his face only contorted further when laughter echoed in the distance. In the middle of the lake, mortals were bathing, splashing each other. Free. They had not seen nor heard us, too caught in the throes of joy and relief.

We quietly hid behind some rocks, where Salem drew a circle of blood around himself. I watched him carefully, remembering my father's own ritual. After a moment of concentration and quiet chanting, Salem reached beyond the borders of the circle and poked his fingertip into the water.

Immediately, the surface of the water was engulfed with roaring flames. All the liquid burned away, transforming the lake into a pit of fire, and the mortals' laughter into screams of agony.

Salem chuckled as he watched them roast. I looked away, the reek of scorching flesh taking me back to Byzantium. Noticing my reaction, Salem only chuckled again.

"Why does it bother you? You are something more than them now."

I did not answer, for I did not know. Perhaps some part of me still seemed to think I was still mortal myself. But I could not voice this if I wished to remain in Salem's good graces.

"I forget that you are but a child," he said. "Your tender heart will harden in time. It's a beautiful thing, fire. Potent. Deadly even to vampires and demons like us, if there's enough of it."

He squeezed my shoulder, and as I looked down at his hand, I saw his fingertip had disappeared. Blood dripped freely from the stump; a rare reminder that, even though we were ostensibly the higher beings in Hell, we could be killed. It was all the more reason to fear Salem.

"Ah..." He withdrew, realizing he was staining my armor. "Spells take sacrifices. You lose a piece of yourself for every ritual you cast. Of course, for us demons, it will always regenerate. A loophole in the system."

"What becomes of this piece?" I asked.

Salem shrugged. "Not even I know that. Nor do I know the precise mechanics of why or how magic works the way it does. It is as elusive a truth as the origins of the universe itself."

The screams died down, but the reek of charred meat continued to infest my nostrils. I shuddered, my body betraying me, but Salem just ruffled my hair like I was a kitten.

I expected the memories of Jeanne, Elias, and the others to keep me awake that night, but I also found myself haunted by another thought. Salem had indicated that fire could harm us. So could silver. That meant there was more than one avenue through which I might attain my revenge.

And so, as shocked as I'd been, the following day I asked Salem if he could begin teaching me how to perform rituals.

He squinted as he rode beside me, visibly irritated. "This is no little thing you ask for, Caleb. Rituals are complicated, and each spell requires a different approach."

"What about just one or two specific spells?" I asked. "For example, the one you did yesterday. Turning water into fire."

Salem brushed me off at first, but I asked again a few days later, and once more after that. Finally, he acquiesced, and the next time we passed a river, we rode there for a private lesson. It was red, as usual. "The different chemistry may impact the success of the ritual," said Salem, crouching down before the river and inhaling its scent. "But it will have to do."

He instructed me to prick my finger with my fangs and draw a circle of my blood around myself. Next, I was to close my eyes and focus intently on my will. "It's a two-part spell," he explained. "First, you must imagine the water—or blood, in this case—becoming oil. Then, you must imagine that oil being set ablaze all at once, becoming a fire of such fury that it incinerates all who touch it. You must change its very chemical makeup with your will alone."

Salem further explained that this did not work for sentient beings, and that all manner of limitations and complications could emerge. But in the end, I simply had to meditate and focus my mind on my intention: manifesting the spell with my will alone.

"You should know that very few people succeed at this," he warned me. "Some waste decades attempting it."

And indeed, even after an hour on my first day, not even a drop of the blood became oil or fire. But the river was long and ran adjacent to our path, so each day I returned to it to draw a new circle around myself, close my eyes, and will that red water to turn bright orange.

Even after several weeks, my efforts yielded no results. I was amazed that Salem could accomplish such a complicated process in a manner of seconds. But then, he'd been a practicing ritualist for hundreds of years.

"Is it a gift only some possess?" I asked him as we rode together, after a frustrating two hours of fruitless meditation.

Salem's head waved back and forth as he considered the question. "Think of it like painting, or music. Everyone has the capacity to perform the basics, but some will have to work far harder to yield the desired results. It may be a few days before you successfully cast a spell. Or it may be centuries."

I scowled at him. Thomas had, I knew, delved into these arts. How else to explain the skelecrows? I refused to be that man's lesser in any realm, and if he'd figured this out, then I damn well would too. So I continued to practice, trying again and again to impose my feeble will on the fabric of the universe. It felt pointless, a waste of energy. But I forced myself to believe it was possible. More than that, inevitable. I *would* transform this bloody water into oil, and that oil into flame.

Finally, during one such meditation, I became aware of a piercing pain in my chest, as if a needle had been stabbed between my upper ribs. I opened my eyes, half convinced I'd been attacked, but I was alone. Then I noticed a small part of the river had changed in consistency, a rainbow sheen slithering across its surface. Excitement coursed through me, mingling with the sudden pain, and I continued focusing, trying to set that oil alight. But alas, that rainbow streak quickly flowed past me, disappearing into the stream.

In the weeks that followed, however, I was able to turn more and more of the river into oil. A few weeks after that, I manifested a single spark of flame on the river's surface. The satisfaction that coursed through me was potent enough to burn away every regret I'd ever had. *This* was power, I realized. The ability to transform the very fabric of the universe at will seemed more potent either than muscles or wealth. I doubled my efforts, spending more time than ever squatting beside the scarlet riverbank.

By my third month of practice, I was able to make that spark double in size. By my fourth, I could maintain it, preventing the water from quenching its heat until I released it, like opening a mental fist. Salem watched my progress with a look of surprised fascination.

But each time I was successful, that piercing pain returned to my chest, carving out more and more of what lay within. The ritual was not taking my fingers or eyes. It was taking pieces of my heart.

I traveled with the Blood Saints through forgotten warzones filled with trenches, endless fields of skulls, and fetid swamps full of inky black tendrils. We slayed hellbeasts. We shared stories over drinks, and laughed about our respective kills. And I continued attending the Death Gospels, taking in the priest's warm assurances and allowing myself to fall into the wondrous bliss of it all. When I felt at my lowest, the priest would be there to remind me that I had a place in the cosmos, and it was all I wanted to hear. Before I knew it, I saw the other Blood Saints as my brothers in arms.

Only then did I notice the absence of someone I'd been trying not to think about: Kaeru.

The realization came one night, after hours of traveling. I was drinking with other Saints around a fire, Gant rattling off beside me about past sexual conquests. "I've fucked just about everything there is," he gloated. "Anything with a cunt big enough for me, that is. She-vamps, maggotis, succubi of every bloodline there is."

None of us believed a word of it, but we laughed anyway.

"You fucked the Silkshaper?" asked an incubus sitting across from us, giving us a big toothy grin.

Gant's face wrinkled like a prune. "Kaeru? That ain't no real cunt. Imagine, fucking your dream girl, only to find out it's not a girl a'tall. Just a shapeshifter. A beast. Might as well be fucking an ox."

The men laughed at that. The incubus piped in, "I'd still do it, long as it kept the shape I want, anyways. But after, I'd kick that thing into the dirt."

"Hey! You hear that?!" shouted Gant, standing up to bellow into the dark. "You lurkin', Kaeru? I bet you are. Hidin' in the skin of somethin' beautiful, so no one will see what you really are!"

Again, the men laughed. Something rustled in the branches of a nearby tree, and when I looked up, I caught a glimpse of someone taking flight. Unbidden, the image of Kaeru in their Clara-like form intruded into my mind. I knew it wasn't their real face, and yet...

"Where ya goin'?" asked Gant, for I was already standing, spreading my wings. Drunk or not, I was seized by the compulsion to follow. I didn't answer Gant. I merely kicked off to pursue Kaeru.

I found them perched on another enormous dead tree, high above the camp. They'd taken the form of a blond incubus, and barely looked at me as I landed beside them. I hesitated, uncertain how to begin, but eventually barked out, "Don't listen to them."

Kaeru shrugged. Their expression wasn't one of sorrow, or even anger, but rather long-suffering acceptance. "It's nothing new. This is how people have always been. Happy to use me, happier to detest me."

My throat closed. I worried that listening to them would let them worm into my thoughts, or back into my bed. At the same time, I had to wonder if this was why they'd come to me to begin with: because I hadn't known what they were, and as such had not judged them.

"I'm sorry," I mustered out. "I didn't know what you deal with."

"I'm sorry too. I shouldn't have hidden what I was. I just find that people like me more, when they think I really am what they want." For the first time, they made no effort to touch me, to take the form I was used to, but they did turn to look at me. "Are we talking again, then? It's awfully awkward, trying to avoid you all the time."

To this, I was unsure how to respond. If I said yes, would they take it as an invitation into my tent? And deep down, did part of me want that? In life, I'd only ever yearned for women, and it was uncomfortable to know that I'd lain with someone who was not that. But had I not also yearned for Salem from the moment I met him? It was difficult to ignore my new desires, but I was far from ready to acknowledge them.

Before I could muster out any words, Kaeru sighed. "I suppose it doesn't matter. It's my final year, after all."

"Before what?" I asked.

It was Kaeru's turn to hesitate. "The emperor promised to return my memories to me if I served him one hundred years. It's year ninety-nine. Just another few months, and he'll give me a potion that will tell me who I am." The faintest smile formed on that unfamiliar face, something like hope swimming in their eyes.

It brought a piercing feeling to my chest. Surely Kaeru wasn't so foolish as to fall for such an obvious scam? I inched closer along the branch, frowning. "Kaeru... what makes you sure he didn't promise that already? How do you know he hasn't just been giving you more Lethe water every hundred years, wiping your memories over and over?"

Kaeru's half-smile told me that they'd considered this possibility as well. "There is no way to be sure, but it is the only hope I have." They paused, head tilting in thought. "The emperor tells me I died in the seventeen hundreds, but I do not believe him. There were no Silkshapers then. There haven't been Silkshapers for centuries, save for me. I always fantasized about finding another one, and seeing what they became around me, and what I became around them. I thought it could give me a sign of who I was. Show me a piece of who I desired, deep down. But I've never come across another, and any mortal I tried turning did not survive my milk. It appears that I was a happy accident.

There is no one else I can go to for answers. Riven is the only path I have."

There was a strain in Kaeru's voice. I wondered how many people they'd admitted this to, and why I was privileged enough to hear it. Perhaps I'd been among the few to ask.

I wondered if I would do any different in Kaeru's shoes. At that moment, riddled with guilt and weakness, the idea of losing my memories was almost appealing. To be freed from the burden of my shame and my aching desire for vengeance sounded almost as sweet as attaining it. Yet would I not then become obsessed with learning who I'd been, just like Kaeru? Would I not act in ways that I regretted, that didn't seem to fit me, simply because I didn't know who I was?

"What if you wanted to forget?" I asked. "What if you buried your memories on purpose?"

Kaeru's body became unnaturally still. "Even if I did forget on purpose, I want to know why. I want to know who I was, even if that person isn't who I am anymore." They breathed, chest swelling. "I know my name is Kaeru. I believe this name originates from Asia, so perhaps I did as well. I can only speculate as to my original sex, but I do not think Riven would trust an agent who was born a woman. This is, perhaps, the most confusing part. I don't know what I am. Man, woman...or something else entirely."

"Maybe you don't need to be one thing or the other. Maybe you just are what you are." I met their eyes, finally understanding that they were in at least as much pain as myself, no matter how well they'd hidden it. "There's nothing wrong with being unique."

"But I want to know who I am for me, rather than just what others want me to be." Their response was immediate. They'd clearly been frustrated about this for some time, and no doubt felt unable to express it.

"Then I hope the emperor is true to his word, because I don't think you'll find that while working for him."

Kaeru nodded, but the hope had not left their eyes. Naive or not, they needed to believe that it had all been for something. And how could I blame them, believing as I did that my own sins would lead to me returning to Earth, to bring justice to the Immortalist Club and Thomas most of all?

"Thank you, Caleb," they said finally.

"For what?"

They looked down, shrugging again. "Everyone wants me to be the person I become for them. They don't care who I am inside, or how I feel. You're one of the few who's ever asked."

Again, I felt a pang in my chest. I hugged them, and even as they changed into that familiar Clara-like form, I found myself relieved that I'd listened to them after all. I would need friends in the days to come—especially if we were going to the city home to the Emperor of Hell.

Chapter Fifteen

The Silver City

A s the Blood Saints and I neared Elysium, the wasteland gave way to a land of gnarled black trees and shrubbery, with a thick road plowing through it all. The road led us to the gate of an enormous black wall, its battlements guarded by an army of demons, all clad in the uniform black iron armor of the Blood Saints. The gates opened for us incredibly slowly, forcing us to stand still.

"Almost like we're mortals again, lined up like this," scoffed Gant. "It's torturous, it is. I want to rest my hooves in a whorehouse tub already..."

I breathed in and out. This was it: the place that would offer me a way back. If ever I would find a path back to Earth, it would be here in the heart of Hell.

When we were finally allowed through, the city on the other side was so vast, sprawling, and opulent that I almost thought we'd left Hell already. The city was both impressive and terrifying, with countless towering structures, labyrinthine roads, spires and bridges made out of bone, great spined archways, and crimson canals that ran through the city like veins. There was a divine splendor to the place that I wouldn't have thought possible here in the underworld.

The streets had crowds of demon aristocrats and more armored Blood Saints. Some watched us from a higher balcony-like street. I did spot a few mortals in the crowd as well, but they all wore metal collars, each with a chain held by a demon master. Some were blindfolded or covered with scars. My guts twisted, guilt stabbing into me. I averted my eyes, but it was no use. To our right was a rail overlooking a lower part of the city full of red pits, canals with Reaper ferrymen, and bleak gutters. Indeed, Reapers were hiding behind every corner, performing all manner of labor to keep the city pristine.

On a high hill overlooking the entire city was an enormous palace of silver and black. It was surrounded by immaculate gardens with fountains and statues, and its central tower stabbed up into the sky like a blade. Swarms of lilitu circled it, their pleasant voices a soft, soothing echo even from the city gates. The emperor had a bloody choir.

"Oy!" Captain Thaddeus rode up beside me, fixing me with a jealous glare. "Sotirios wants you up front."

"Aye, sir." I lashed my horse's reins and navigated him to the side of the line, hurrying along to the front. I passed the wagons, which were now covered to shield those inside, but this did nothing to hide Pestilence's stink.

I joined Salem up front to find that he'd put on a red ceremonial robe and hat, the garb of a Vatican Cardinal. Kaeru was with him, still in the form of the blond incubus from the night before.

"We shall present Pestilence to the emperor," Salem told me. "As you were the one who captured her, I want you to join me there."

"You—want me to see the emperor with you?" I asked. The thought was blindsiding.

"Of course." He gave me a queer look. "Is this not what you wanted? To rise through the ranks?"

My nod was hurried, cold sweat suddenly coating my back.

As we neared the palace, Thaddeus led many of the other Blood Saints to a large square building I presumed to be their barracks. Pestilence's wagon was taken around the back of the palace, where a loading dock no doubt awaited, while Salem, Kaeru, and I climbed an exhausting staircase up to the palace itself. Guards checked us at the entrance, taking our weapons before letting us in.

The entrance hall was in and of itself jaw-dropping, with white marble floors so shiny you could see your face in them and a vaulted ceiling that looked a mile high. Little red imps with messenger bags flew overhead carrying papers. Pillars topped with ghoulish horse statues bordered our path, and when another hallway cut across our own, I saw that one side led to an enormous church nave full of pews, many already occupied, and paintings taller than some peoples' houses. The opposing side led to a gigantic pool, where winged, horned nuns clad in white robes lowered people into the water, whispering prayers.

"The ballroom is twice that size," said Salem, his scarlet robes swishing as he walked. "And the bloodwine cellar is even larger, containing stock from every era and ethnicity in recorded history. It's even said to contain the blood of Jesus Christ, though I'm sure the emperor himself started that rumor." He laughed before lowering his voice and adding, "I would advise you not to call this place Hell around the emperor. He is, after all, the founder of the Church of Black Heaven."

Everywhere I looked, I saw sculptures and paintings of Christ hanging from the cross. Yet this version of Christ had fangs, and his crown of thorns had been replaced by a circle of horns. This demonic Christ watched from every wall with eyes of paint or black marble, silently judging. The priests and nuns formed crosses across their chests as they passed. Salem did not bother doing the same, but Kaeru did.

At the end of the hallway were two enormous doors, currently closed and heavily guarded. "That way leads to the Ever-Burning Throne," Kaeru whispered reverently. "Very few are allowed to even see it."

Instead, we turned right. Guards led us through massive doors, up a colossal staircase, and through yet more doors until we at last reached a chamber that, for all its elevation, resembled a dungeon more than anything else. It was dark and cavernous, its walls decorated by silver chains that hung in arcs, just like my guts had on the day I'd died.

Groans of pain echoed through the room, cutting over the choir. I found the source as we passed a large cage with a huge, heavily scarred horse lying inside, red eyes practically bulging with hatred. It had to be twenty-five hands tall, far larger than a normal horse. A silver and crimson saddle was fixed to its back, kept in place with bolts that drove into the horse's flesh. Draconian wings were folded at its sides, silver spines jutting up from their edges like they'd been stabbed in. A unicorn-like silver horn protruded from its forehead, looking no more a part of its natural body than the saddle.

My throat closed at the sight of the poor beast. If silver wounds didn't heal, then how long had it been in such pain? I went to the bars, thinking I might reach through, though I did not know what help I might offer.

"Don't," Kaeru hissed.

"But it's in pain," I said, just as the horse jolted toward me, the horn stabbing out between the bars. It missed me by no more than an inch.

The horse's lips peeled back to reveal a grin that might have seemed human were its teeth not all long, sharp canines.

Guards hurried over and began hitting it with the hilts of their swords, making the beast retreat to the center of its cage. Still, it continued grinning at me, laughter gurgling out from its throat.

"Back away, Abaddon," said Salem, pulling me away. "You should not have let it look you in the eye," he added to me in a hiss. "The emperor is very fond of his horse, and Abaddon delights in carnage. Even more than I do."

A low-pitched whinny echoed behind us as we proceeded into an enormous and lavish bedroom with a silver marble floor, a luxurious red rug beneath the bed. Floating candles offered dim light, their red flames reflecting in the water of a large bath carved into the floor. The suitably huge bed was cloaked by thick veils, giving me only the briefest glimpses of Riven's form. Low, shuddering breaths echoed out, mingling with the distant choir and the clinking of unseen chains.

"Your Grace." Salem lowered to his knee. Kaeru and I followed suit.

"Why are you wearing that face, Kaeru?" The emperor's voice was a low, regal rumble, powerful enough to split a mountain. "Wear my favorite instead."

"Yes, Your Grace." Kaeru reached into their pocket and procured what at first looked like a key ring. But it didn't hold keys. Instead, a series of dried-up severed fingers hung from its ring. One of the fingers was kept in a small glass vial. The finger was blackened, gnarled, and looked centuries old. Kaeru seemed extra careful to avoid it, as if even through the vial it might pose a risk to them.

Instead, Kaeru grabbed a finger that was masculine, long, and pale as alabaster, while possessing none of the polished smoothness. It was gnarled, even grotesque. One of Riven's fingers, perhaps?

This close, I heard their transformation more clearly: the cracking of their cheekbones as they jutted out into a more prominent shape, the shifting of their blood as they became smaller. I could even smell Kaeru's change, their scent becoming a pungent perfume that made my nose wrinkle in protest. Their wings shriveled and retracted until only stumps remained, and their body thinned to the point of looking sickly. Long straight black hair bordered beautiful features that reminded me of Pestilence's own, without any of her deformities.

"Ahhh... so good to see that old face. Before it was ruined." Riven's hiss filled the entire room. "I understand that you have brought my sweet empress back to me. Isn't that right, Salem?"

"Indeed, Your Grace." He turned back to the entry door and barked, "Send her in."

The door opened, and men dragged in a cage with wheels on its sides. Pestilence sat within, a red circle drawn around her on the cage floor. This time, I was struck less by her rotting face and more by her expression. She looked like she was trying to hold back tears; like she desperately wanted to seem defiant, but inside, felt utterly broken. She pointedly did not look at Salem, nor at myself.

"Empress Valeria is once again yours," said Salem, bowing. Then he swept his hand out to gesture to me. "This young Blood Saint fearlessly worked to apprehend her. His name is Caleb Schwartzenfeld, Your Grace, and I feel he holds great promise."

I risked raising my head just enough to stare at that enormous bed.

Another low, ragged breath filled the room. "Where is her horse, Salem?"

"Her...horse, Your Grace?"

"Without the horse, Pestilence is not truly captured." Riven let out another crooked groan of a breath. "But at least Valeria cannot do any more harm. Thank you, Salem. And you as well...Caleb."

He spoke my name as though he was intimately familiar with it. So chilled was I that all my breath instantly left my body. I had to hold myself back from gasping.

"Is something wrong, Your Grace?" asked Salem.

The entire room seemed to throb as Riven breathed in and out, chains clinking all the while. "Please take Valeria to the dungeons," he said. Once the empress was gone, he asked, "Are you aware, Salem, that Mr. Schwartzenfeld was part of a rebellion until very recently?"

I froze. There was amusement in Riven's voice, and it was just as sinister as his horse's. Salem shot me a glare that demanded answers.

"I abandoned that rebellion to join the Blood Saints," I said. It was impertinent, but I'd come too far to not at least speak on my own behalf.

"He even participated in the apprehending of this same rebellion," added Kaeru, stretching the truth in a way I desperately wished to protest. I'd done nothing but fly in there in a panic, overcome by the shame of my betrayal. But at that moment, all I could do was bury my shame and lower my head in agreement. This was another stage, that was all, and I had to play my part, submitting to whatever the emperor said, no matter how dreadful. It was the only way I'd get back to Earth. The only way I'd have my revenge.

I risked meeting Salem's eyes, expecting them to be filled with rage. Instead, he smirked. I wondered if he was imagining all the wretched things he'd do to me.

Riven's crooked laughter echoed through the room. "It is fortunate for you that Lady Weaver was not a friend of mine. She was the sort of woman who would punish as she saw fit for her own amusement, rather than to fit the sins committed in life. Indeed, I considered sending Kaeru to assassinate her once Valeria was returned. So you have done me two favors, Caleb Schwartzenfeld. Whether you intended to or not."

I exhaled in relief. Even Salem's smile widened. But Riven was not done. Several haggard breaths later, he said, "The problem is, Caleb, I believe that rebel is still inside you. You may be working for us now, as it suits you... but that does not make you loyal. And so I would like to give you a demonstration to ensure that your loyalty does not waver. By joining my Blood Saints, you've given me your soul. And that means you are *mine*, Caleb Schwartzenfeld. Mine, to do with as I please."

The door behind us opened again. Guards dragged a man into the room, then threw him forward onto that silver marble floor. The man coughed, his nose broken, his beard caked with blood, messy hair covering his eyes. All the same, I recognized him immediately.

Duncan looked up at me through the cracks in his bangs, his body quaking with fear. "C-Caleb?" he coughed out uncertainly, already in so much pain.

I heard the tussle of shifting bedsheets behind me, and another ice-cold chill trickled up my spine. I could all but feel Riven standing behind me, a dreadful shadow over my back, but I could not possibly turn to face him. My body was frozen.

"People always ask me how I tamed Abaddon." Riven's voice was definitely closer now, just behind my ear. "Truthfully, it was simple. I gave him a choice: the carrot or the stick?"

It was as if Death itself was threatening to put its hand on my shoulder. Fear's icy grip was so tight that I could do nothing but stare down at poor, doomed Duncan. My body seemed to have decided, without even seeing him, that Riven was something *wrong*—something unnatural, uncanny, too awful to exist. Salem watched me with excitement blazing in his eyes. Kaeru's gaze remained fixed to the floor, a statue like me.

"This same principle applies to society," Riven went on. "To the ideas of Heaven and Hell. Do as the world and as your faith asks, and you will be rewarded. Go against the law, and you will be beaten. Now, a horse is stronger than its rider, could kill him if only it dared. But a horse's spirit breaks when he understands the ultimate futility of his efforts. He may throw his rider off the first time, but his rider will get back up and punish him for it. He may kill this rider, but then another will come and punish him harder. And should he keep killing them, they will put him down. The horse comes to understand that its efforts are fruitless, and so it obeys...and is rewarded with a delicious carrot. He obeys again, and gets another carrot. And so, his mind adapts.

"Over time, the horse begins to crave not power, but rather that next delicious carrot...and by extension, the approval of the Master who has tamed him. Soon, he is fond of his Master. He wants only to please him. Just as we come to crave the approval of our own betters, sometimes even for its own sake. And so, you please God. Please your king. Your boss. Your husband. You will please them all, for the alternative is the stick."

Chains clinked, sharp fingers curled around my shoulder, and the chill that spread through me pierced into my very bones. Duncan paled as he looked past my shoulder. Then he let out a horrified howl and stumbled backwards, trying to flee, but the guards grabbed him and pushed down on his shoulders until he was once again on the floor.

"So what will it be, Caleb? The carrot...or the stick?"

Nausea soiled my throat, rising all the way up until sour spit filled my mouth. My body began quaking, almost as intensely as the cowering man at my feet. Then came a violating, bone-crunching pain, far worse than that of my first metamorphosis.

I found myself unable to stand, and fell to all fours. My mouth felt too small for my teeth, which ached and closed in on my tongue, even as my jaw cracked and extended out. My hands curled up into gnarled fists, fingers fused together, the lines between them disappearing. A single thick nail stretched out from where those lines had once been. No, not a nail—a *hoof.*

Chains hooked into me, and a great weight pushed down against my back, threatening to shatter it. I tried to scream but all that came out was a distorted neigh. My vision shifted as my eyes began pushing further and further apart, until they were separated entirely, on different sides of my head. My skull crunched painfully inside my head, jolting as it extended, longer and longer until the skin snapped, a long bone nuzzle was before me, and my human cheeks hung from its sides like tattered rags. My hooves were still growing, tearing through more of my flesh.

Silver hooks dug into my sides. Again I tried to scream, and again there was only a neigh. My rider laughed. He was so heavy that I felt sure my spine would snap any moment. I jerked my body back and forth, trying to throw him off, but no matter how severely I moved, he remained. It only made the hooks on my sides hurt more.

Then I smelled something *good*. Something so good that even the scent was enough to distract me from the pain. A long orange shape hovered just before my nose, dangled by a hand with long fingers that curled into sharp silver needle-tips. A carrot! Oh, God, I felt I'd die for a taste. I sniffed the air desperately, and even though the air reeked of blood, that delicious carrot smell stood out. I stretched out my tongue, but the carrot shifted just out of reach. That only made me want it more. It would be a relief from the pain. It would be freedom. If I just could get it in my mouth, all would be right in the world.

"Ah-ah-ah. First you must earn it." My rider laughed. Laughing was good, right? It meant that Master was pleased, that Master would feed me. "Punish the man before you, Caleb."

The pitiful thing before me cried out in terror. I didn't want to hurt it, but I also didn't want Master to hurt me. Even the single moment of hesitation was enough to earn a lashing. I cried out in pain, for it felt like my sides were splitting open.

"Punish him, Caleb!" Master repeated, anger creeping into his voice.

I neighed my acquiescence. What did it matter? The whimpering thing before me was a lesser being, and needed to learn its place in the world. I was stronger than it, bigger than it, and besides, Master liked me, which spoke well of my character. If Master wanted the lesser being dead, it would happen!

I pummeled the lesser being with my hooves, neighing in the sheer joy of my superiority as its face scrunched smaller and smaller. I would get that carrot now, oh yes! The lesser being screamed, bones cracking from the force of my hooves, red lines appearing in its meat as it split open for me. Master laughed again, and that meant I would get that carrot, and all would be right, all would be well. The blood was sweet on my tongue, and the lesser being stopped screaming, unable to make any sound other than *crunch crunch crunch crunch crunch CRUNCH!*

I snapped, dizzy, an incubus once more. It was like I'd woken from an awful dream: my trembling hands dark with blood, a scarlet pool on that silver marble floor, leaking out from the pulpy mess I'd made of Duncan. He was no longer moving. Pieces were missing from his flesh, and something chewy was between my teeth. I spit it out, shaking, trying not to look at it.

I was no longer a horse, but nor was I the person I had been when I'd died. My wings, which had seemed so freeing when I'd first turned, were now a reminder that I wasn't human. I felt the weight of Duncan's suffering press down on the back of my neck, broil in my belly, swell in my throat. For all the strength of my new body, I felt weaker than ever.

Icicle-cold fingers coiled around my shoulder again. "You were right, Salem. He does have potential. Deep down, he is a vicious thing." His winter-bleak breath tickled my cheek as he spoke.

I kept my gaze low, afraid to show Riven how horrified I was by what I'd done. Still, my panting surely gave it away. Had he really changed my body, or had it just been a vision? The patterns on the lump of flesh before me struck me as more likely to have come from fists rather than hooves, but some part of me felt certain it had been more. The air behind me rippled from movement, my body tensing up once more.

"Go now," Riven said. "Join the celebration in the Blood Hall and forget your worries. For tomorrow, Salem, you shall return to Earth to show it to whom it belongs."

Salem rose to his feet. Kaeru took my quivering hand, helped me up as well before pulling me from the room.

The moments that followed were a blur, for I remained dizzy and delirious, still not entirely sure of my body's boundaries. Kaeru led me through hallway after hallway, but I just kept looking down at my hands to check that they hadn't become hooves again. I think at some point I must have thrown up, but I do not recall where.

"Did that really...?" I stammered, breath reeking from the discharge. I still didn't trust Kaeru, not really, but right then, they were there, and I felt strangely embarrassed at the thought of them seeing me that way. It was humiliating enough to be seen so broken; for them to see my new body, which had seemed so strong at first, prove absolutely powerless against Riven's magic.

"Worry not," said Kaeru. "I think we could both use a night to be rid of our thoughts."

They were not entirely wrong. Troubled though I was, I was eager to put it behind me. I followed them downstairs to an enormous mead hall, where tens of thousands of demons had gathered, many of them drinking mugs full of bloodwine. I recognized Gant, Thaddeus, and Brindle among those in attendance.

The Blood Hall was far more chaotic than any festivities we'd enjoyed on the road. Lilitu flew above with mugs in their hands, spilling on those beneath, sometimes fornicating upon the tables or against the huge stone pillars thirty feet above. Little flying imps carried long trays holding unconscious mortals with apples in their mouths, ready for vampires and satyrs to feast on. Other mortals hung from hooks on the walls, wailing in pain. Succubi danced inside huge bird cages hanging from the wall. There were all manner of ladder climbers: vicious dandies wearing frilled collars, horned beings whose faces were covered by black veils, satyr priests eager to grope all in their path, even maggotis demons whose enormous white abdomens bounced as they pranced about.

No matter where we went, people bumped into us. Kaeru kept hold of my hand, but their skin rippled again and again as more drunk people collided with them, always threatening to bring another shift. They grinned, excited by the lustful energy around us.

We passed a strong female satyr, who split open a mortal's skull with her bare hands to devour his brains. Another satyr fucked a succubus against a pillar, the table beside them rumbling, its bloodwine keg spilling everywhere. An incubus whose tail was tipped with a knotted cock swayed it before him like a fisherman's lure.

It was all too much, so I did what I was learning to always do at such parties: I drank to numb away the terror.

Soon the room was spinning, and I yanked Kaeru about in an absurd dance, giggling stupidly until we ran into Salem, enmeshed in a cluster of naked succubi. Milena and Fiona were not among them.

"Yes!" said Salem, his eyes dizzy with intoxicants. "Enjoy yourself, Caleb. Loosen thy mind!"

Hands touched my shoulders on either side as Salem's succubi pulled me and Kaeru to him. The room continued spinning as Salem's chiseled jaw came closer and closer, his eyes like daggers stabbing into me, both scintillating and terrifying. His hand grabbed my own, a firm and powerful squeeze.

"You two," he said. "Join us."

Even with the succubi squishing against his arms and waist, his free hand wandered to Kaeru's face, thumb pushing into their mouth, and they changed, their breasts swelling, their hair becoming long and flowing, their face a perfect porcelain doll. Yet again I was reminded of the empress; healthier though this version of her seemed, the features were not dissimilar. But this new Kaeru was so lovely, so exquisitely feminine, that I almost wondered if my version of them would change just from seeing it. Salem pulled their lips to his own.

Then he pulled mine in as well. I submitted to the kiss out of a nauseating mixture of fear and unwilling attraction. He reeked of desire for me, and it only worsened my lust for him. I felt desperate, famished for his flesh, eager for his attention.

And when he led the lot of us to his room, what else was there to do but follow? Salem's bedroom was nearly as vast and lavish as Riven's own, and while the bed was not large enough to house us all, there were chairs and divans and an enormous mirror that took up almost the entire wall. The succubi were well-practiced, immediately pairing up at the chairs to eat each other out, becoming dolls for atmosphere, adding a few extra moans to the chorus for Salem's pleasure. Perhaps excess was the entire point. After all, I was there, was I not?

Salem invited me into the bed, then took Kaeru into his arms and rutted into them beside me. Even though Kaeru's form was not the form they took for me, I felt a strange flash of jealousy. This persisted even as another succubus, an utter stranger to me, climbed onto my lap and began to ride me, while another thrust her breasts into my face. Salem rarely looked Kaeru in the eye; he seemed more focused on the mirror, on watching his reflection fuck them.

Once he was spent, Salem abruptly threw Kaeru off of him, then reached over to grab the hips of the succubus who was atop me and pulled her onto his lap instead. I groaned in frustration, having been only moments away from my own climax, but a wide-eyed Kaeru crawled atop me in her place, changing as they always did. I was still drunk, dizzy, and felt more than a little sick. I knew the moisture within Kaeru, the moisture coating my cock, had been left behind by Salem. And even as Kaeru rode me, Salem seemed to inch closer and closer, until he was right beside me. He stared at me like a hungry jackal as he climaxed inside the girl, then threw her off as he had Kaeru.

And I knew then that I could no longer deny him without incurring his wrath.

Yet another part of me welcomed the stare. Maybe it was the alcohol, or maybe my desire to be like him, but I hungered for him. My lips parted, mouth watering, certain that I was tough enough to endure whatever came.

"Enough of this dance," he groaned into my ear. Then he grabbed the back of my neck and forced my head down.

<hr>

When Lord Sotirios was done with me, he pushed me away as he did the others and barked for the girls on the chairs to attend to him.

I shambled away from the bed and collapsed onto a divan, trembling, confused and ashamed. My incubus hunger was sated; there had been pleasure, and the satisfaction that came with it. But I also felt damn near paralyzed by the aching pain in my jaw, rump and back. My throat felt clogged. My skin was sticky and bruised, actually *bruised*. I wanted to wash out my every hole, and yet I also felt like I'd never be clean again.

I didn't understand. I'd wanted it, hadn't I? Even longed for it. It was impossible to put my finger on when exactly that had changed. Even now, as the women moaned in pleasure behind me, part of me envied them, still yearning for Salem's attention. But another part of me wanted to never lay eyes on him again.

Most confounding of all was the sense of overwhelming, crippling shame. I should have been honored that Salem gave me a moment of his time. That he chose me, even if in a moment of intoxication. But I didn't feel honored at all. I just felt like throwing up.

Even when the others finished hours later and were all asleep in one big pile of skin, I found myself unable to do anything but sit there. It was not the fact that Salem was a man that upset me. It was more the vicious intensity with which he'd used me. I hadn't cried out, hadn't begged him to stop, but he'd surely smelled it when my desire turned to suffering. He'd known, but he'd kept going anyway...only to discard me without a word when he'd finally had enough. Like I'd been nothing. Another worthless accessory for his cock. Just another pet, unique only because I was the rare man to be allowed into his bed.

I detested myself for submitting. *I* wanted to be the one at the center. *I* wanted to be the one who was yearned for, who could control others with a single glance. But while Salem had taught me much, he had never taught me that. He'd never wanted me as an equal, just as no father ever truly wants to be surpassed by his son.

At the same time, it repulsed me that I should envy him. I had done all this to return to Earth, get revenge on Thomas, and return to Clara. But I wondered for the first time what she might think about the person I was becoming.

Breathless and lethargic, I got up, wrapped a spare blanket around myself, and went through a door that led out to a balcony. It was dim outside, as always, but the balcony offered a grand and strangely beautiful view of the city. Elysium gleamed like Hell's own jewel, as vast and ornate as any great city on Earth.

"You're a fairly young soul, aren't you, Caleb?"

I jumped. Salem had followed me out. He remained naked, letting the entire city see his perfect form. Irritatingly, he was no less impressive while flaccid. My skin crawled, but I forced a nod, unwilling to show weakness.

"Died only years ago, I think?" he said, his voice languid.

Again I nodded, the hairs on the back of my neck standing on end, fresh echoes of pain throbbing through my throat and rump. I was inexplicably certain that Salem was displeased with me, and the fear of punishment was all-consuming.

"Then you must have memories of who you were in life."

"Some of them all too fresh." My voice came out as a ragged croak.

"How strange that must be." He shook his head, bemused. "I was down here for centuries before I was allowed to change. Like most souls, I forgot everything about who I was in life. My name. My sins. Even the country of my birth."

"Aren't you curious who you were?"

"Why should I be?" Salem's tone was not offended so much as genuinely confused. "All I remember about being a mortal is weakness. How easily my mind was broken by the centuries of suffering. How easily I was reduced to nothing more than bestial hunger, rage, lust. It...embarrasses me now."

Where was this going? Surely Salem wouldn't be telling me all this without purpose. And yet I had the feeling that this conversation would be circuitous, with him slowly guiding me around the crux of the matter like a predator trapping its prey. "Then where did your name come from?" I asked, curious despite my fear.

He chuckled. "My centuries as a mortal were spent in a city called Salem. A pitiful attempt at creating Hell's own Jerusalem, I'm sure. One day, some of my fellow mortals rebelled, killing the demon who ruled them. Afterwards, I was contacted by lilitu who wished to regain control of the city. They offered me a choice: tell them where it was and become its new demonic ruler, or suffer with everyone else when they inevitably found us. Of course, I accepted their bargain. Why should I live up to mortal standards of morality? This was Hell, and whoever I'd been in life, in death I could become someone new.

"And so, as Salem burned, I took its name. I was rewarded with immortality and a throne. All I had to do was ensure the mortals I'd once suffered alongside were punished each and every day. I tortured them far harder than my predecessor, shattering their spirits and any chance of revolt. Under me, they understood that hope was a cruel promise that fate would always break. I embraced my new identity. Allowed the past to burn away along with what more foolish men would call my soul. In so doing, I found my salvation—a word which translates, in the language we spoke in that town, to Sotirios. And as I rose through the ranks of the Church of Black Heaven, I realized that my purpose was to bring that salvation to not just the city I'd known, but to all of Hell. And even to the land of the living."

He put his hand on my shoulder, startling me.

"That's why I like you, Caleb. You remind me of myself. You're willing to do whatever it takes to get what you want."

I swallowed, shaken. It was hard to not fear that I might become something like Salem if I continued down this bloody path, and yet part of me welcomed the idea of being so above reproach. Some awful, ravenous, weak part of me that sought only pleasure and retribution.

"Where are they now?" I asked, my voice hollow. "The mortals you once knew?"

Salem blinked, caught off-guard. "That was...centuries ago, Caleb. I honestly haven't thought of them in years. I imagine most are still suffering in the city of my name-sake. Perhaps one or two realized the pointlessness of it all and ascended like me, but I've yet to hear of any rising far. Then again, I can't say I still recall any of their names." He paused before adding, "I take it what's really on your mind is what has become of the mortals *you* knew."

I hesitated, then nodded. What use was there in deny-ing it?

Salem chuckled. "Suffice to say, they will receive an eternal reminder of what happens to those who fly too close to the sun. You will forget about them, in time." He slowly turned to meet my gaze with that all too pene-trative stare, his smile fading. "But it behooves me to tell you that if someone attempted to tamper with that fate, such a person would experience suffering far worse than anything they could imagine. Now, I certainly wouldn't accuse such a thought of crossing your mind, Caleb. But I would invite you, too, to heed the story of Icarus. After all, even you could fly too close to the sun if you're not careful."

I bristled. This was a man for whom nothing was ever enough. Who was he to caution me against flying too close to the sun?

Salem smirked at me. "You should get some sleep. To-morrow we go to England, a far, far greener country than this." He patted my shoulder, and I flinched, freezing in terror once more. It was a mercy that he took no notice as he returned to his room.

I was so rattled that I almost didn't notice he'd confirmed what I'd been waiting months to hear. He was taking me back to Earth, and England at that. I should have been overjoyed. Instead, my body trembled, jaw so tight that my fangs dragged against my lower canines. Why? Had I not wanted to join Salem in his bed? And was he not rewarding me with the very thing I'd fought so hard to attain? Perhaps the bloodwine had addled my thoughts, making me unable to see these gifts for what they were. It was *my* fault I hadn't enjoyed our time together, not Salem's. So many of my other struggles had been my doing in one way or another. Why not this, too?

I exhaled and stared down at the opulent city, with its seemingly endless sprawl of scarlet and silver, and spotted a hooded woman leaving the palace doors. She turned to look up at the balcony, golden cat-like eyes gleaming in the dark. Milena... she was fleeing. I had the sense she was checking whether Salem was still out here.

With a start, I realized that I might never see her again, especially if I was indeed returning to Earth tomorrow. A cool anger coursed through me. If Milena was fleeing, that meant she was no longer under Salem's protection. I was unlikely to ever find my father in Hell, but that didn't mean I couldn't avenge him.

I hurried back inside. Salem was already asleep again in his bed, lost in a tangle of limbs. No one seemed to notice as I dragged on my clothes, grabbed my silver knife, returned to the balcony, and kicked off into the air.

The wind tasted of sulfur and blood as I flew, searching for Milena. I quickly spotted her on the central thorough-fare. She was not running, but nor was her gait languid. It was all too easy to catch up and land beside her.

"Milena…" I said, breath catching in my throat. The silver knife was holstered in the rear of my belt. All I had to do was get close, unsheathe it, and slash her.

She stopped, and turned to look over my shoulder at the palace before meeting my gaze. "Yes, Caleb?" Her expression was blank, giving me nothing.

I stood there, the anger in me building as I debated whether to kill her then and there. Part of me wanted to tell her everything first: how my father's death had sent me down this path; how she was to blame; how that first night, even as I'd fed on her, I'd harbored a wish to see her dead.

"You're leaving," I said, stepping closer. "Without even saying goodbye?"

"My time here has passed. It has been stimulating, but it's time to move on."

"Why?"

She again looked at the palace, her tail twitching nervously. "This place changes you. It's a place where only the cruel thrive. For a time, I wanted to thrive here. But I think it is time I tried thriving somewhere else."

Then she turned and walked away.

"Wait," I stammered, following. I might have cracked her neck, or stabbed her from behind, but…no. This could not be quick. I needed answers. Needed to confront her with the truth of what she'd done. But how to get there? The words left my throat in a mad fumble: "Your time in the pits…the people you fed on…was it by choice?"

Milena let out a soft sigh and gave me one last glance, still too distant for my knife. Her eyes held no affection for me, no reverence for the times we'd shared. But nor was there hatred.

"Is it your choice when Lord Sotirios orders you to kill?" she asked.

Then she turned again and went her way. My hand reached around, fingers curling around the hilt of the knife. I could throw it. End her here and now.

But at the same time, I couldn't. I let her disappear into the shadows of the city, in pursuit of some corner of the underworld where hope might glimmer like starlight.

Her awful question haunted me long after she had gone. Did one ever truly have a choice when refusal would lead to death or worse? And yet I could not deny that even had I not joined Salem in his bed, I had been giving him my body from the moment I met him. I fought at his command. I let him order me to kill. Who was I to judge Milena for ruining my life, when I might do the same to countless more?

I thought of the bargain of Faust. He had chosen the darkness in a single moment of weakness, while I was actively and repeatedly putting hours and effort into my journey down a darker path. And yet, like Faust, I was certain it was the right and only thing to do. Even now, no alternative made sense to me. After all, Thomas deserved to perish, and Clara to be freed from his reign. It was too late to save Jeanne, Elias, or any of my other fellow rebels.

Except one, I realized with a start. Anika. Thaddeus had Anika.

And I knew where Thaddeus would be staying. Even from the thoroughfare, I could see it: the huge, block-like building that made up the Blood Saints' barracks. Yes, that was where she would be, and it would be far easier to search than the camp had been. Better yet, it would be unguarded and empty, as all the men were celebrating in the palace's Blood Hall.

I entered the barracks through a window to find them virtually empty. They looked like a dark crypt, the black stone walls bare of decoration. Much of it was a long hallway, its many doors open to show row after row of bunk beds. Further on were the private rooms of the higher ranked officers. I quickly found the one with Thaddeus's name, locked of course. I heard nothing on the other side, so I broke it down.

Inside was a bleak and surprisingly modest room with only a bed and a chest. I broke the chest's lock with my bare hands and forced it open. If I had to thank Thaddeus for anything, it would be for being painfully predictable, for there Anika was, tied up and gagged, red wounds slashing across her body. She was conscious enough to point her bloodshot eyes at me, absolute rage broiling within them.

I hoisted the girl up out of the chest, cut her bonds, and pulled free her gag. The first words from her mouth were, "I will fucking kill you!"

She tried to wrestle the knife free from my hands, but she was small and weak, and the attempt was pitiful. "Stop that," I said, fearing I'd accidentally cut her. "I'm getting you out of here."

"Horseshit. I saw you at Byzantium." Those eyes remained with rage. "I saw you marching with them. And I see what you are now."

I squashed my desire to argue. She had every right to be angry with me. "Just let me help you out of here," I said, but she tried grabbing the knife again, quick as a mouse. I jerked my hand backwards so it wouldn't cut her—just as the door burst open behind me.

"Who the fuck is in my room?" Thaddeus bleated as he charged in, his booze-slurred voice sounding more goat-like than ever. His eyes widened at the sight of us, hesitating only because he was too drunk to immediately react.

I took advantage of the moment by striking him in the throat with my silver knife once, twice, thrice, before slitting across for good measure. Thaddeus bleated wordlessly, blood sputtering out from his hairy jugular before he collapsed face-forward to the floor. I stabbed his head a few more times just to be sure, then gave Anika what I hoped would be a reassuring grin. She only stared at me in horror.

"They've made you a damn killing machine!"

"Shush before someone else hears you," I said. "Now, we need to hurry. More soldiers could come back anytime." I offered my hand.

She scowled at me, but took it. I hoisted her up and fled from the room, careful not to step in Thaddeus's growing pile of blood.

Once beyond the barracks, I kicked into the air and carried little Anika beyond the walls of the city, and then further still. "They may hunt you," I warned. "It looked like you killed him."

"What makes you think I won't tell them you did it?" she growled.

"My hope is that they don't capture you in the first place," I said. Investigators would likely conclude that the killer was experienced with a knife, but who was to say Anika couldn't be? She'd been in Hell far longer than me.

When the city was a speck in our sights, she writhed in my arms like she meant to fall. "Set me down. I won't see you a moment longer."

"Fine," I said, slowly descending to the ashen ground. I'd hoped to bring her somewhere safer, but then again, where in Hell was safe? I'd betrayed and condemned the last place that had been. Even I had to admit Anika was right to hate me for that.

Free from my grasp, she brushed herself off and shot me one last scowl. "Don't you dare think this makes us even. I will never forgive you, Caleb. It sickens me that you still draw breath. You might think you're a good man for this, but you're not. And nothing you do will ever make you such after all that you've done."

Then she turned and ran. Something lodged in my throat, but I swallowed it down. She was probably right. Killing Thomas and saving Clara would not undo my sins, but would it not still count for something? I had to believe that it would.

In the end, there was nothing left to do but fly back to Salem's balcony and try to get some sleep. Tomorrow, I would return to Earth, one step closer to my sweet revenge.

SCRIBBLED ON THE CEILING

CHAPTER SIXTEEN

THROUGH THE GATEWAY

APOLOGIES IF YOU'RE CRANING your neck. I've run out of wall space, so it's time to write on the ceiling. When I first came here, I was bothered by the fact that the ceiling was so low, but I now realize it was all so that I could write on it. If it's any consolation, my neck hurts, too.

The crying has resumed: that all-too-familiar voice echoing from every wall. It helps, perhaps, that I don't need to bite my fingers this time. The visitors took off my nails during their last visit to my cell. The pain is louder than the weeping, so here I am, smearing the words above my head in a weak attempt to block the sobs out.

The visitors come inconsistently and without warning. Sometimes, it is one right after another. Other times, long stretches of time will pass before a new one enters my cell. They do not speak. They do not ask me questions. They merely hurt me, over and over. A torrent of pain, ceasing only so my wounds may heal just enough to be opened again.

Sometimes, I long for company so deeply that I welcome the visitors. Part of me wonders if I only imagine them. For what would I do to myself, if I found myself trapped in a box, and could inflict whatever punishment I wished?

Do not misunderstand; I take no pleasure in this suffering. Even now, I am no masochist. But to tear myself apart for what I've done? That, I would take great pleasure in indeed.

Perhaps that's what I'm doing by reliving all these wretched memories: tearing myself apart, piece by piece. Not for penance, nor for the benefit of anyone who may read this, but to stoke the boundless flames of my self-loathing. Deep down, my reasons for chronicling my story are as selfish as anything else I've done.

—◆—

The morning before our passage to Earth, I awoke on a divan in Salem's bedroom, restless and despondent. Salem, Kaeru, and about a dozen succubi were all asleep in the bed in one big puddle, and I found myself oddly afraid of waking them. I couldn't shake the prior night's events from my mind: Anika's hateful words, the vision Riven had given me of my own awful transformation, Salem making use of my every hole... the salty taste of his cock lingered on my tongue like a stain, and the soreness in my rectum had not abated either. I wondered if he'd want more when he woke, and could not decide whether I welcomed the thought.

I decided to shake the thoughts away the only way I knew how: with a nice, mind-numbing climax. I considered nudging Kaeru awake, but I'd lost track of which person they were in the pile, and even though some of the succubi had been happy to lay with me last night, that didn't mean they wanted to be woken up for more. I was, after all, a total stranger.

So I stumbled to the lavatory, lifted the toilet seat and furiously tugged myself. Strangely, it was difficult to become properly excited, for my thoughts kept returning to the night before, to Salem making me feel like a thing. The memories were vague, no more than flashes, but I struggled to keep them away. I tried biting my lip to sate my bloodlust, but it did not help. I was hungry, but the feeling spreading through me was one of helplessness, of pain, of being nothing.

The door creaked open behind me. "Caleb?" a gentle voice asked—Kaeru, surely.

"Don't bloody look at me," I snarled, embarrassed. I covered myself with my wings so they wouldn't see, but the wet slapping sound was unmistakable.

"You could have woken me." Kaeru entered, closing the door, before pressing against my back and shifting. Then they turned me around and lowered to their knees.

I stood there, afraid the sound might wake Salem, but Kaeru made sure I didn't take long. They worked me expertly, giving me such blinding pleasure that it was like they'd been born for it. And when at last there was release, the thoughts of Salem faded—for a moment, at least.

"There, now. Isn't that better?" Kaeru wiped their mouth with the back of their hand, then stood up to embrace me. I shuddered in their arms and breathed deep, finally able to think clearly in the wake of my climax.

"Is he always so rough?" I asked weakly.

"Every time." Kaeru smiled, still glowing. "It is how I like it, but it is not for everyone. Was it too much for you?"

I did not answer. It seemed too shameful to show such frailty.

Kaeru and I took a bath. As we finished, I took a deep breath, preparing myself for the fact that Salem was right there in the next room, and I could not show fear to him. It would be all right, I told myself. We were going to England, and everything would be fine. Kaeru watched me carefully, no doubt sensing my unease, but they said nothing.

We returned to the bedroom to find Salem sitting cross legged on the floor, his eyes closed in meditation, the girls dismissed. A red circle had been drawn around him, and one of his fingers looked to have been cut away. His wings folded onto his back, shrinking and pressing against him until they took up no space at all. Finally, he opened his eyes and smiled in relief. "There."

Aristocratic suits were waiting for us on a table by the door. Kaeru took one and handed me the other, while Salem procured a fine suit from his sizable wardrobe. We all got dressed beside each other in front of an enormous mirror, though I knew not how to put on the shirt, coat or tie with my new wings. "Just leave those off now," said Salem, buttoning up a silk white shirt of his own. "You'll understand soon. There should be money in the trouser pocket, an advance for the work we'll be doing together. Oh, how wonderful it will be to return to Earth and get back to my real mission."

I checked the pocket to find a huge wad of pounds. I was so startled I damn near dropped it all. After living on pennies, it was an obscene amount of money. My body felt so jittery I could barely get my boots on. "And what is this mission exactly?" I asked.

Salem's grin sliced up into his cheek. "We're calling it the Nightfall."

The Nightfall? I buckled my belt, the leather oddly sharp against my hands.

"Sunlight is fatal to our kind. You didn't know that, did you?" Salem looked at me from the corner of his eye. "I suppose it doesn't matter down here, but it matters a great deal in the world above. It has ensured that we immortals must hide in the shadows while on Earth." He took a deep breath. "I don't know about you, but I tire of this underworld. The stench. The ash in the air. The endless stream of mortal souls, infesting every last corner like a plague. So too do I tire of pretending to be one while trying to enjoy the luxury of returning to the world above. And I am not alone in this sentiment. The Nightfall will change all that, Caleb. It will allow us to take control: blackening the sky, toppling Earth's governments, and ensuring that mortals everywhere serve us, as nature intended."

Frankly, it sounded utterly absurd. But Salem's smile was confident and reassuring, like this was a good thing for us all, not some mad scheme with no hope of success.

"England is an especially important location to the Nightfall," Salem continued, adjusting his tie. "We believe the Iron City of Mekra is near it, perhaps even within its borders. Our mission will be to destroy it after we gain control over England."

"And what is this Iron City?" I asked.

"A group of mortals who know about us, and seek to hunt us to extinction. Riven believes they have agents in England, trying to influence its government. Which is all the more reason why I will need your help." He lowered his voice and added, "One more thing. Last night did not occur. Is that understood?"

My body froze. "Perfectly."

Salem moved as if to pat my shoulder, but stopped short of contact.

Once we were all cleaned up, Salem led Kaeru and I to a heavily guarded room in the lower levels of the palace. To the left was a small indentation in the wall with a stone floor and a drain. Straight ahead were black iron bars from floor to ceiling, a single gate offering passage through. On the other side of the bars was a staircase leading up to a wall taken up by what looked to be a huge circular mirror, only this mirror's glass was bright red.

I gasped. "Is that...?"

"The gateway," said a voice behind me.

I turned to see a smiling vampire with dark brown skin, faded gold eyes, and hair cut into a black fringe. He wore circular spectacles and a three-piece suit to rival Salem's own. He also had an enormous broadsword at his belt.

"Luciano," said Salem. "I trust you've been briefed?"

"I have, sir. This lad needs orienting." Luciano shot me another fanged grin.

"Excellent." Salem flashed me a grin of his own. "I'll see you there, Caleb."

He entered the gate, and from there, the crimson portal itself.

It was only then that it truly hit me. This was really happening. I was returning to Earth.

Luciano presented me with a scroll and a quill. "You'll find the details there. Please sign there at the bottom."

I hurriedly looked the scroll over. It was my promise to follow orders while keeping my true nature and mission secret, and my acknowledgment of the consequences of my failure. It was difficult to take in more than that; now that we were on the precipice, I found myself eager to get on with it and leave this wretched place behind. The words blurred, my excitement making them swim. I knew there was a chance I might somehow be swindled, but that refusing to sign would likely result in them killing me then and there.

So I signed. My soul was already theirs. What more could they take?

"Excellent," said Luciano, snatching the scroll away. "Now, as discussed in section five, you'll need to cut off your wings."

I froze, my wings retracting with phantom pain. "I've barely even had the chance to use these puppies."

Luciano waved a hand. "Don't be so dramatic. It's standard procedure. Besides, they'll grow back." He looked left and right, then lowered his voice. "I'll do it for you this time, but you'll have to get used to doing it yourself a few times a week. Just like shaving. Only until the Nightfall."

He spoke as if he was putting his own head on the line to offer me a great kindness. No wonder Salem had made his wings invisible. The bastard could have done it for me, too.

"Can't I just hide them under my suit?" I asked.

Luciano laughed. "Even if they fit, which they won't, you'd look like a bloody hunchback. You'll just have to cut them off like everyone else, Mr. Schwartzenfeld. Now, please remove your clothes and assume the position." He gestured to the area with the drain.

Something jumped up into my throat. "Right here?"

Luciano nodded, unsheathing his broadsword.

I crouched down over the drain, crossing my arms out of fear. My wings had felt so strong until now, but under the shadow of a sword, they seemed so weak and frail, and so did the rest of me. Why hadn't I become something even stronger?

The air sang a single note, and I screamed, pain lancing through me like steel lightning. I felt the water of my life spray out from the fresh wounds in my back. So little of me had been left after my change, but now it seemed even more of myself was draining away. I trembled with agony, jaw clenched, nails digging into my palms.

My wings lay on the floor behind me, black islands in the red pond. I reached into the red and cradled them: pieces of me, stripped away, sticky and reeking of copper. Part of me wanted to stab Luciano with their spines. I'd do it in the face, I decided. Right through the cheek.

Luciano snapped his fingers, and attendants came forward from behind him: one with bandages and towels for me, the other with a cloth for Luciano's sword. Kaeru lowered to the floor beside me and wrapped the bandages around my chest and back. "It will heal soon," they promised.

The red pond at my feet shrunk as more and more of it spiraled down the drain. Some, however, clung to the grout between the tiles, burgundy stains that could never be washed away.

As Luciano wiped his blade clean, Kaeru helped me to my feet. I was still trembling, barely able to stand, much less clean myself off. But Kaeru was patient, whispering that it would be fine. "Here," they said, bringing their wrist to my mouth.

I pierced it, drinking some of their life. It was hard to not keep gulping and gulping until there was nothing left, but after a moment they pulled away, leaving me to exhale in both frustration and relief. I did feel stronger now; better able to stand. But it was only because I had taken what Kaeru had offered.

I put my clothes back on, overwhelmed by the conflicting emotions swirling within me: my mourning for my wings, my shame over what I'd become, and my excitement over what was to follow. The crimson mirror awaited, just as inviting as Kaeru's wrist had been, and I knew that I would become just as lost in what was waiting on the other side.

Eager to put Luciano's condescending smile behind me, I followed Kaeru through the gate in the bars and proceeded up the stairs to the crimson mirror. A throbbing hum emitted from it, louder the closer I reached, and for some reason the sound filled me with overwhelming nausea. Of course, this was a Hellgate; its very existence was unholy. But could the same not be said about me?

I pressed my hand to the glass, and it rippled, ice cold. I shivered, instinct telling me to pull away, but the crimson creeped out like liquid, consuming more of my hand and inviting me through. I closed my eyes, thinking of Clara's bruised face and Thomas's fanged smile. I'd come this far, had I not?

So I walked into the cold red glass. The freezing sensation lasted only a moment, and then, quite suddenly, I was in a dark room.

Two men stood here, both in suit and tie, firearms at their belts. They grinned, showing their fangs, and I showed mine in turn. Behind me, the wall was taken up by another crimson mirror. Kaeru walked through, the red glass rippling as they emerged. "He's with me," they assured the guards.

"And you would be, miss...?" one asked.

Kaeru reached into their pocket to procure their key ring, again pointedly avoiding the vial with the black finger. They touched a feminine finger and shifted into a large, bearded man. The guard lowered his head in understanding.

"Forgive me, sir. Didn't recognize you."

"Take me for a mortal?" scoffed Kaeru, now speaking in a gruff Scottish brogue. "They can't cross the gates, and you know it. Come, Caleb."

They led me out the only door ahead, and then through a labyrinth of hallways, many with paintings of dark creatures. I still felt cold, even with three layers on, but perhaps I'd become accustomed to the warmth of Hell.

"What's with that black finger, anyway?" I asked as we went. "Is it dangerous?"

"Quite," said Kaeru. "It belonged to someone with particularly unusual tastes. It's a powerful form, but not one that's wise to assume in most cases. Especially as it impacts my mind, not just my body."

"Do your other forms impact your mind as well?" I asked.

Kaeru didn't answer, their expression just shy of reproachful.

We came into a large room, and I froze, throat closing. The stage, the balcony, the satyr painting... I knew it all immediately.

This was the room in which I'd died. I half-expected to see Thomas or masked figures in the balcony even now, but no. We were alone. I stared at the wall where I'd been sacrificed, under the satyr's portrait. There were no marks. No bloodstains. It was like I'd never died there at all, or even existed in the first place.

"We're working with the Immortalist Club?" I asked quietly.

Kaeru looked at me like they were surprised I hadn't figured it out yet. "Caleb, we *are* the Immortalist Club. The entire effort is Riven's creation, and it is our mission to ensure its success here in London."

A quiet anger curdled within me. I should have known. Even now, as I looked at the satyr painting, I realized why I'd recognized Salem's style. It was here that I had encountered his work, here where his awful renditions of Hell were being displayed. In retrospect, I don't know why I didn't draw the connection sooner. Why wouldn't Salem's forces and the Immortalists be one and the same?

But how was I supposed to take revenge upon Thomas Rife if we were to be allies?

Kaeru led me out into the London night, and all my ennui faded into the fog. The city's many smells came at me with full force: the smog, the rot, the shit. It might have all been awful once, but compared to the deathly reek of Hell, it was practically paradise.

Still, the city of my birth was not how I remembered it. Enormous airships floated overhead. I'd read of such machines before my death but had been unsure whether to believe them. Now, there was no denying it, with at least a few becoming fixtures of London's skies.

Additionally, with my new eyes I could see better in the darkness than my mortal form would have ever dreamed. I'd never before noticed just how beautiful the night was: the glimmering stars, the swirling cosmic patterns, the silver gleam of the moon. I could also make out the twisted, hungry things lurking in alley after alley, waiting in anticipation of their next victims.

It was like stepping into a new world, not returning to the familiar comfort of home, and I could not help but feel pangs of longing and even grief for the world I'd thought I'd understood. I'd never been a religious man, but perhaps the Bible was right about one thing: knowledge was a curse. Knowing the truth about the universe had changed me, all but destroying my ability to feel comfort or peace. My naive ignorance had left me vulnerable, but it had also been a blessing. Now, all I wanted was to forget everything I knew, by crawling into a bottle if necessary.

Still, at its core, London hadn't changed at all. It remained a festering black pit where men were reduced to animals, squabbling over whatever scraps of humanity they could find. That much was clear from the Thames alone. The festering river snaked through the city like an enormous open sewer, its brown water full of fly-swarmed lumps, its ever-present stench telling all who neared what manner of city this was. My dead, damned self would fit right in.

As we passed the shopkeepers and vagrants and ladies of the night, all of them immediately looked upon me with a mix of attraction and fear. It all felt so strange. While I'd never been hideous, I was not used to being lusted after either. But then, I'd never strolled through London in a three-piece suit before. I was a gentleman now. A man with money. A man who was still glowing from recently getting his cock wet. A man who'd signed his soul away for wealth and power, and was enviable for it.

In short, I'd become precisely the sort of man my old self had always wanted to punch out of sheer envy. Moping felt like a waste of my efforts, so I forced myself to grin as I strolled the familiar streets. Let the world see me as happy, and maybe eventually I might be so.

"You look like a madman with that grin," said Kaeru.

"Perhaps I am one." I stretched my smile even further, letting the madness creep into my eyes. I leered at those who watched me, choosing to delight in my new form. No, I decided; I would not feel ashamed of the choices I'd made. It had all been to come back here. Duncan would regenerate soon, as all souls did. As Jeanne and Elias and the others would. It was Hell. It was only natural for there to be suffering.

What mattered was that I'd gotten out. For the first time in my life, I could hold my head high and face the air before me rather than the ground beneath me. I was finally going to get what I wanted.

CHAPTER SEVENTEEN

THE DEAD MINISTRY

KAERU AND I STAYED at a demon-only bordello called *Le Boudoir des Ténèbres*, its black towers equipped with red stained windows. As with the Hellgate, its guards required us to show them our teeth. Inside, the other guests all wore masks, but it was clear that everyone here was a demon. I could smell the difference even when they lacked wings or other telltale signs. The only ones who weren't masked were the succubi one could hire for an hour or three. Judging by their often-decorated wings, I wondered if they were ever allowed to leave the premises.

The *Boudoir*, I learned, was something of a haven for London's immortal community, one of the few places where they could be open about what they were. The decor was decadent, with plush cushioned seats, chandeliers, and very tall wooden archways. There was a bar with what looked to be a blood sommelier offering patrons fancy-looking bottles, as well as a stage for succubus burlesque dancers who covered their naughty bits with their wings.

Kaeru and I had conjoined rooms already booked and waiting on the fifth floor, with a door allowing easy access between them. It was mercifully quiet inside, with the walls fully muffling the music and moaning from down below. I had a smoke and cracked open a paper I'd procured during our walk, trying to catch up on all that I'd missed.

Before long, Salem came to collect us. "I have called an urgent meeting with the Dead Ministry," he said. "They are the highest members of the Immortalist Club. Think of them as the secret government of London's undead elite. I'd like you both to come along."

A coach was waiting for us outside, large enough for the three of us and then some. A hooded woman sat within, looking down, giving me only the barest glimpse of her pale face. Her smell told me that she was mortal, a fact that was as baffling as it was alarming. Why was a mortal sharing this coach with us? Before I could ask, Salem knocked on the roof and we were whisked off into the night.

"I want you to see who these people are," he said, "because I may need you to assist me with those who pose a problem. Not all will agree with what we're doing, you see. Some may need to be removed."

Of course, I knew what he meant by that. He was telling me that I might have to kill them for a cause I didn't even believe in. Once, I would have balked. Just then, however, I felt so utterly minuscule that I thirsted for any morsel of power; anything that might give me a feeling of strength, even if it was an illusion. I wanted so desperately to believe that all my suffering, all my trials, all the sacrifices I'd made had been for something. I'd already unwittingly caused the defeat of people I cared for. What was pulling the trigger on a stranger after that?

The woman beside Salem made a quiet squeak, and it struck me again how odd it was for her to be here, listening to us. "Are... are you sure you want me to come, Salem?"

Her voice was so high pitched I wondered how old she was. Was she even a woman at all?

Salem shot her a cruel smirk. "Of course, darling. The ministers must see you."

Darling? What bloody game was Salem playing? I kept my lips tight, wondering what this girl would think if she found out about Fiona, Milena, and however many others had been in Salem's bed the past week. For that matter, what would she think if she knew Salem had lain with me? My guts tightened, the memory sending ripples of discomfort through me.

"Will I be...safe?" the girl asked. "They won't be able to enter my dreams if they see my face?"

"I told you. The Morpheus Pentacle will protect your dreams. No one will be able to enter them but me."

Did Clara have one as well, I wondered? Was that why I couldn't reach her?

"You're safe. I'll make sure of it." Salem wrapped an arm around the girl, and let her lean onto his chest. But in his eyes, there was something akin to impatience, possibly even annoyance.

— ◆ —

Deep within the Immortalist Club's headquarters was a council chamber: a dim circular room with multiple rows of cushioned seats. I sat beside Salem, Kaeru, and the hooded woman, trying desperately to look like I belonged as I sized up the dozens of other men present. It was like some secret parliament full of pale gentlemen, many of them already muttering to each other from their seats. Sitting upon the highest seat was a hairless man who wore spectacles and a top hat, his unusually round head at odds with his twig-thin body. And to his right...

My blood froze.

There, sitting across from me, was Thomas Rife. His gaze was currently fixed on Salem, a smug half-smile on his face. If he recognized me, would he expose me? Would anyone care if he did? Clearly, while I'd been dead the bastard had risen to the highest echelon of the club. My fear gave way to anger, and I had to grip my fist to stop it from trembling. I wanted to throw a knife into the bastard's face.

"Sitting up there is Warren Cillian," Kaeru whispered to me, jerking their chin at the man in the high seat. "A necromancer who studied under General Mordra herself. He's the High Speaker of the Dead Ministry and head of the Immortalist Club. Beside him is his apprentice Thomas Rife, who has recently become a minister in both the Dead Ministry and the mortal parliament."

A *minister?* The ice in my veins had well and truly boiled now. Rife leaned over to whisper something into Cillian's ear before returning his gaze to Salem, face splitting into a wicked smile.

"Ahem," tutted Cillian, his voice unusually nasal. He thumped his cane against the floor, and the room became silent. "As you have all noticed, Cardinal Salem Sotirios has arrived. Lord Sotirios, I believe you had something you wished to express?"

"Yes, Warren." Salem stood up, his huge wings stretching out above us. "This past year, Cardinals like myself have been preparing throughout Europe for what we call the Nightfall: a new era, where we immortals will no longer need to hide in the shadows. The time has come to take what is ours. We shall reign above men as God and nature intended."

The room was silent for a moment, and in truth, I was not surprised. The whole thing still sounded so absurd that I had trouble believing it myself.

"Yes," Mr. Cillian drawled. "We have questions about that, Lord Sotirios. Some of us have lived here for hundreds, even thousands of years without oversight, and to be frank, we rather like it that way. The change you are proposing strikes many of us as a shift not just for England's mortals, but also its long-standing immortal community. Why should we submit to the whims of Black Heaven?"

Salem's lips quirked up into a smile. "Believe me when I say it would be in your best interests to ensure the Nightfall's success. Consider the current industrial revolution. Mortals are developing technology beyond anything we could have expected in recent years. Soon, they will create weapons that can kill us. Consider Mekra, the Iron City, which remains dedicated to hunting us to extinction. One day, they may acquire proof of our existence...and then all the world will hunt us."

Cillian frowned, apparently unable to disagree on that point. "And you believe coming out of the shadows to take control would thwart this? We've discussed the possibility of coming out of the grand old coffin many times before, and we've always concluded it to be an unfathomably bad idea."

"Because it is," a new voice piped in: a young-looking man with shoulder-length dark brown hair, a pointed beard, and perfect circle spectacles. "We don't have the numbers for it, and our sensitivity to the sunlight would put us at a profound disadvantage. Our best option remains manipulating the world in secret, from the shadows, rather than exposing ourselves."

Salem's smile did not fade, but his eyes flashed with a quiet anger. "You are Alkin Beauxdera, correct?"

"I am, sir." The young-looking man lifted his chin, defiant, even though Salem would have dwarfed him.

"Tell me, Mr. Beauxdera. Do you enjoy pretending to be something little better than a cow?"

"I beg your pardon?"

"You wish us to blend in with mortals. Obeying their rules, or at least wasting an enormous amount of time and energy pretending to. But they are our livestock. Beings who nature and the divine have decreed are beneath us. All this time, we have been wearing their spotted hide to live among them, letting them control us...why? Is that not an offense to the universe itself?" Salem lifted his enormous arms to gesture to the world around us. "You say that this is the best option, but I can't help but think you are all just too cowardly to consider another. All we need for this to work is a stronger grip. More bodies committed to our cause."

Cillian's face twisted in disgust. "Are you suggesting we let commoners join our ranks?"

Thomas mirrored his expression, clearly repulsed by the idea.

"Nothing of the sort," said Salem. "We can keep the bloodlines pure. We'll invite England's noble families to join us, promising them immortality. And if they refuse, they will be made examples of. They, and anyone else who resists, can join your Reaper army. That's right, Warren. You'll be our general, granted with the authority to execute whomever you like and resurrect them as your soldiers."

Cillian's eyes glazed over as he envisioned it, clearly tempted, but not yet convinced. "Even with the threat of death, I find myself doubting that England's nobles will simply sign up. They are Christians, after all." He made a sour face.

"Then we shall be as well. We shall tell them that we have the blood of angels. Immortals, chosen by God. After all, who's to say we aren't?" Salem grinned, eyes glimmering like they reflected some distant starlight. He gestured to the room around us, chin held high, indomitable. "Even after all this time, no so-called Heaven has shown itself. No angels. No God. Only us. And if we are the closest this world has to gods or angels, then it behooves us to claim what is ours. To make Earth into the paradise that we've been denied. We, the Church of Black Heaven, shall be shepherds for these new undead souls. How can they deny eternal life and strength beyond measure if it comes from the holiest source of all?"

Many of the ministers had begun whispering excitedly to one another. They were actually starting to believe in this mad idea. But Cillian's face remained sour, his will as indomitable as Salem's own. "What of the sun?" he asked. "How can we possibly reign if we are vulnerable during the day?"

Salem grinned. "What would you say if I told you that with the help of Black Heaven, we could conquer even that?"

A cold, bristly silence filled the room. I stared at Salem, jaw damn near dropping.

"Impossible," said Cillian. "Ritualists have been trying for centuries."

"And Black Heaven has found the solution." There was not even a hint of doubt in Salem's voice.

"No, no, this is absurd." Cillian shook his head. "And even if you really do have a way, even with thousands more of us, even with an army of Reapers, for any of this to work, the commoners would need to *submit*. And how can we be sure they would?"

"The Church of Black Heaven will be happy to help every last Englishman understand why things must be this way," said Salem. "The people won't merely submit to the new system, Warren. They will *embrace* it. They will fight to protect it. They will see us as gods, gods they want nothing more than to be like, because they understand the rewards we offer are nothing less than magical. Besides, if there are difficulties, the other nations will help. This will happen all over Europe, all at once, once the Vatican falls."

The sheer scale of it all was astounding. Baffling. There were so many facets that seemed doomed to fail. And yet a sense of dreamlike fascination had settled within the chamber as, one by one, more ministers were convinced. Murmurs echoed. Gazes softened. Thomas had an expression of awe.

But Cillian's hairless white brow remained wrinkled. "And what of the royal family? Do you intend on usurping them, and crowning yourself king?"

Salem chuckled. "Why would I want to be king of a little island like this? No, Warren. I've arranged for the crown to fall to a proper royal figurehead. One the people will trust."

He turned to the cloaked woman, who finally lowered her hood, revealing a girl of eighteen or nineteen, her raven hair in a tight bun, her gaze cold, her features a mix of stern and immature. Her black diamond earrings and tiara looked more expensive than this entire room.

Hushed gasps echoed, and several ministers bowed their heads. "That's the princess," someone whispered. "Princess Isabelle…"

"Soon to be Queen Isabelle," said Salem. "She has agreed to become a succubus. A new ruler for a new age."

The girl's eyes pinched. She struck me as uncomfortable, frightened and repulsed all at once. Then she looked up at Salem, and her expression softened into one that was vulnerable and besotted. This girl was nowhere near ready for the stress of rulership. But that only meant she would turn to more experienced advisers for support. People like Salem.

Cillian's pale lips finally twisted into a smile, his cheeks wrinkling like pinched taffy. "By Jove, this might actually work…"

"Excuse me," Mr. Beauxdera interjected. "Thus far, this conversation has focused only on whether we *can* rule mortalkind. Why are we not instead debating whether we *should*? Isn't anyone going to consider the question of whether this course of action is just?"

Chuckles echoed through the room. Cillian rolled his eyes. "Enough, Mr. Beauxdera. We're all well aware of your sympathies."

"We're talking about enslaving humanity," said Mr. Beauxdera. "Is no one disturbed by this? This revolution will open doorways for all manner of cruelty."

A new figure cleared his throat and stood up: an incubus with a curling goatee, his blond hair sculpted to match his horns. "I, for one, feel that mankind would greatly benefit from greater external control. We've all seen how the poor squander their lives. We could dissuade men from indulging in their base impulses, elevating the species to greater heights. It's a win for us all."

"Thank you, Mr. Winscroft," said Cillian, as much of the room rumbled in agreement. Mr. Beauxdera looked mortified.

Sotirios lifted his chin. "Why don't we put it to a vote, Warren?"

"Fine," said Cillian. "All in favor?"

He raised his hand, as did the vast majority of hands in the room.

"All opposed?"

Mr. Beauxdera and several others lifted their hands into the air. It was not enough. I committed each dissenting face to memory.

Mr. Cillian broke into a grin to match Salem's own. "Well then, gentlemen, it appears we may be on the verge of a great change."

I stood there, still unable to believe it as the ministers left their seats and began to mingle and murmur, as if they'd all experienced the same exciting vision of the future. Salem went to share a few words with Cillian and—my fists clenched—with Thomas. All three of them sported fat grins.

Meanwhile, Mr. Beauxdera put his face into his hands and left the room.

I exchanged a look with Kaeru. "Do you really believe this... Nightfall could happen?" I whispered.

"It doesn't matter whether I believe it can," they replied. "Only that we must make every effort to ensure it does. Those are our orders."

I stared, unable to understand how they could be so unwilling to think for themselves. But then, how could one think for oneself when one knew not who they were? I could only presume Kaeru did not trust their own conclusions, their own mind, their own opinions, if they always just fell back on their orders. But then, even their body was subject to the demands of others.

Sotirios returned to us, still beaming. "It's good that things went the way they did," he said. "Had the Dead Ministry refused, Riven would have had them all slaughtered. Now, I shall be joining Mr. Cillian and Mr. Rife for a little soiree. They always do this after these meetings. Kaeru, would you like to join us? I'm sure they'd be delighted to see what you can do."

"Of course," said Kaeru, instantly matching his smile and rising from their seat. I stood up as well, but was ignored.

"May I come, too?" I blurted out.

Salem glanced at me, brow furrowed. "I'm afraid these gatherings are strictly for the highest echelon of London's immortal community."

Then he, Kaeru, Thomas, Cillian, and a few others made their way to the exit. A cold sweat broke out on my temples. Even after all I'd done, they still made me feel like nothing. Worse, a soiree was the perfect occasion to kill Thomas. I could even find out what had become of Clara, whether she still lived, whether she was still mortal. I'd waited for so long...

To hell with it, I decided. I would follow them, sneak in, and find a way.

I went outside to find many coaches waiting. And when Salem, Kaeru, Cillian and Thomas all went into one together, I got into one behind them. "Follow from a distance," I told the cabbie. "And be discrete."

❧

I should have known the soiree would be at Rife Manor.

I almost didn't recognize it at first. The field around it remained barren, but the place was not as I remembered. There was a new, towering iron fence, far more guards than I remembered, even a bloody watchtower. It looked almost like a fortress. Or a prison.

Dozens of other coaches were already parked outside. Only the highest echelon. Right.

"Stop here," I said, before we got too close. Then I snuck out and climbed up the fence. My new demonic body made it easy to surmount. I just had to hope the guards couldn't see in the dark like I could. Once inside the grounds, I kept to the shadows and remained in the back to avoid the watchtower, all the while wishing I still had my wings.

Still, I found myself able to climb, lizard-like, up the outer walls. Maybe I could sneak in through a window, I thought.

The incoherent barks from not-too-distant guards made it necessary to be careful. If I was discovered, I doubted Salem would vouch for me. Indeed, he would no doubt punish me. The memory of his bedroom in Hell clawed in my mind, and my bones rattled so violently I nearly fell to the dirt.

Then I reached a bedroom window and froze.

Clara. Lying on her side on the bed, curled up into herself, the very picture of pain. Her wispy white nightgown tangled with the bedsheets like she'd tossed and turned all night. She still looked mortal, as far as I could tell, but there was a bandage on her neck, stained red.

My fingers dug into the windowpane. The bastard was feeding on her. Using her as a blood doll. And I somehow doubted she'd accepted such a fate by choice. I imagined how sweet her blood must be, calling to him each and every night. My own fangs extended at the thought, and I recoiled, horrified by my body's reaction. My throat was dry, and the hunger was building, urging me to creep into her room and drink from that open wound. What would Clara think upon seeing my powerful new form? Would she recognize me? Would she love me, as I loved her? Would she let me drink from her, more willingly than she let her husband? My music had made her cry, after all. Part of me fancied that would be enough.

But another part of me wondered whether in my new form, I was as much a danger to Clara as Thomas was. It was a fleeting thought, easily chased by the wolves of denial. I wanted to save her, didn't I? I'd never hurt her the way he did. All would be well when I killed him and reunited with her.

A distant caw broke me from my reverie, and I looked up to see Thomas's wretched skeleton crows circling above. I knew he'd be able to see through their eyes. And if he saw me...

Fury coursed through me. I was so close. *So close.* My vengeance was practically within my grasp. But even if I managed to kill Thomas tonight, I knew I would not fare against Salem, Cillian, and all the guards. I tried to exhale out my rage and reminded myself to think clearly. If I was too hasty, I'd never see him dead. If I wanted to be victorious, I had to get out of here before I was seen.

With a great push I leaped from the window and across the fence, dropping to the ground with a loud, painful crunch. I winced, clutching my ankles, but the wounds were minimal. I could still move just fine.

The crows cawed in alarm. They'd seen someone, even if they hadn't seen me clearly. A guard barked something, and more converged around my side of the manor. I crouched low into the dead fields and moved away as quickly as possible. If I just reached the coach…

A loud sniffing sound quaked from nearby. The dead grass around me rustled. The reek of death filled my nostrils. I glimpsed huge white shapes in the cracks between the grass: huge, misshapen amalgamations of bone. Each one had a human skull for a head, with other creatures' body parts grafted on: huge jaws, long horns, and head spines that might have once been fingers. Goat-like, they were, but as tall as elk. The skelegoats skulked down on all fours with the finger bones that looked all-too-human as well, at least up to the long, clawed tips. It seemed Thomas was getting creative with his minions.

I considered fighting the beasts, but if I engaged, Thomas would see me clearly for sure. They would fall when Thomas did, but I did not know where precisely Thomas was, nor how many beasts he had under his command. Fleeing seemed a better option for now. The beasts had likely only seen a vague figure in the darkness, and I intended to keep it that way.

I snuck around the side of the manor and dashed away, staying low. The skeletal beasts growled and skulked around, but I managed to elude them, putting distance between Rife Manor and myself—only to collide with some-one who still had their flesh.

"*What are you doing here?*" hissed a familiar voice: Kaeru, morphing into the form they always took from touching me.

I froze, terror spreading through me. Whose side would Kaeru be on? Would they report me?

They lunged for my throat, squeezing a fistful of my cravat. For a moment I thought they meant to wallop me, but they merely yanked me further away from the house. "How could you be so foolish?" they whispered, pulling me on. "Salem told you to stay behind. Do you have any idea what they'll do if they find you?"

"I was just getting some practice in," I huffed, following as quickly as I could while keeping low. "Salem said he wants us to remove problems. Why not get acquainted with the art of sneaking around?"

"These men are ritualists. They have spells to see if some-one came in. If you want in, you'll have to work your way here." Now that we were further away from the manor, Kaeru stopped and turned to fix me with a piercing gaze. "You have an in with Sotirios. Don't throw it away. If you want to come here, then do as he says until he invites you."

I stiffened. Thomas and Clara were right there, and yet beyond my grasp. How many people would I have to kill to reach them?

"Do not come back here without me," said Kaeru, fear in their voice. "I'm telling you this for your own good. We do as the Emperor and Cardinal Sotirios instruct, and no more. Do you understand?"

⸻ ✦ ⸻

It was difficult to not feel morose as I rode the coach back to the city. Indeed, by the time I returned to the *Boudoir* I had a truly bad case of the morbs, unable to shake my frustration and feelings of inadequacy. Why was it that even now, I felt powerless? Was I so weak as to not have proper control over myself?

If Kaeru was right, then killing Thomas and saving Clara meant doing whatever Salem told me: killing, maiming, and barking at his command. It was a path forward, but I feared that it would only plunge me deeper into the darkness. I'd envied Sir Thomas for his strength and wealth, but now that I had strength and wealth of my own, would I become something just as vile? No, I told myself; it would never happen.

It all churned in my mind as I climbed the steps to my room in the *Boudoir*. I had money now. More than I could have ever dreamed of in life, with probably more to come if I did as Salem asked. I had tallness of stature, strength, handsomeness, and access to the body of someone who could take the shape of the woman of my dreams: changing into a form my mind thought of as more desirable than any real single person I'd met.

Yet I felt no happiness. No satisfaction. No sense of triumph or growth. Merely a hollow lack of whatever had once filled me. I'd sacrificed everything to be here. Betrayed those who had cared for me rather than suffering alongside them. Should I not have felt something, anything?

And there was no way back.

It startled me, how hard the realization hit. There was no way back; not to the mortal I'd been in life, nor to the mortal I'd been in Hell, nor the world as I had seen it before my death. I could not unlearn the terrible truths I'd learned about this world, nor undo the terrible things I'd done to navigate it.

I clenched my teeth. Fine, I decided. What was a little blood work after everything else I'd done?

Chapter Eighteen

Blood Work

"**A**RE YOU SURE YOU'RE ready for this?" Kaeru asked. They were sitting across from me in a coach in the form they always took with me, minus the usual wings.

A night had passed, and we were on our way to kill our first target. Kaeru had been given all the details at Rife's gala.

I forced a nod, wondering if they were going to bring up what had happened. So far, neither of us had broached the subject, as if not talking about it would magically render it undone. Just like how I never spoke of Byzantium.

Kaeru had already taken me to a weapons dealer, an oily-fingered vampiress named Mrs. Smith, who'd gleefully sold us magically silenced revolvers, silver bullets, and knives: everything portable, pocketable, and easy to hide from the authorities.

I was trying to think of it as an opportunity to sharpen my skills. I was no slouch after my training under Duncan and my time with the Blood Saints, but Thomas would be a formidable target. I needed whatever practice I could get.

Still, a sick feeling had settled in my gut as our coach trundled closer and closer to the train station. Again, Kaeru must have sensed this, for they whispered, "If you're having doubts, I'd rather you stay behind. I care for you, Caleb, I do, but this is my job. My one chance at finding out who I am. I won't be held back."

I restrained my urge to remind Kaeru that there was no guarantee Riven would fulfill his end of the bargain. "I won't hold you back. I'm committed. What's the plan?"

Kaeru handed me a murky tintype of an old man with white mutton chops. "This is our target."

I immediately recognized him from the papers, for I'd been trying to read as much as possible to catch up with everything I'd missed. It was William Ewart Gladstone, the former Prime Minister and the leader of Parliament's Liberal Party. "Why not go after Disraeli?" I asked.

"Disraeli is on our side. Indeed, he was with us last night. But I would remind you that it isn't our place to question our orders. Only to execute them."

"I know, I know," I scoffed, but I doubted I'd ever get used to such an arrangement. I'd grown up a musician, not a soldier. I lived to freely express my thoughts, and it vexed me greatly to suppress them.

Kaeru's eyes narrowed. "The target is taking the train north to Scotland. He will have a private compartment. Our plan is to find him and execute him quietly, then remove ourselves from the train before we are seen. Understand?"

I forced a nod.

"Then repeat the plan."

I exhaled, trying not to be insulted. "Get on the train, kill Gladstone—"

"Execute the target," Kaeru corrected.

"What difference does it make?"

"I already told you to stop questioning." Kaeru scowled. "Final chance. Repeat the plan as directed."

If I screwed this up, I might lose my standing with Salem. For all I knew, he might just send me back down to Hell. I buried my anger into my chest and recited, "Get on the train, execute the target quietly, and get off without being detected."

Kaeru's lips thinned. I gathered that they still didn't quite believe me. "Look outside, Caleb. Look at how these people live. Most of them have twenty years at most. Little more than rats. I know this cause may be hard to swallow, but it's worth fighting for. Mortal governments have had their chance and failed again and again and again. We have magic. We can be better. But we won't get there if we're not afraid to make sacrifices."

Unfortunately, my nausea was only growing. Killing fellow demons in Hell had been one thing. But executing mortals on Earth in service of a cause I didn't even believe in? If I succeeded in this mission, it would bring me closer to my goal, but it would also bring the unholy dream of the Nightfall closer to reality.

The train was waiting as we reached the station. Gladstone—no, the *target*, I reminded myself—was likely already on board. Kaeru put on their gloves and whipped the tickets from their purse. But the further across the platform we walked, the worse my nausea became.

"All aboard!" shouted the conductor as we neared. There was no time to waste. The train would depart at any moment. And yet...

I thrust my hand out before Kaeru. "Wait."

They shot me an irritated look. "What now? Are we had?"

I steered them to a nearby pillar and lowered my voice. "What if someone does spot us?"

"Then we'll remove the problem," said Kaeru simply.

"If things go awry, that whole train could find out about us," I said. "And then we'd have to remove *all* of them."

The train doors shut, and its horn blew, and before we knew it, it was leaving the platform. Kaeru shot me a look of absolute fury. "Damnit, Caleb, I should leave you behind!"

They bolted toward the station exit. "Wait!" I said, scrambling in pursuit.

Outside the station, Kaeru ran to the nearest cabbie and said, "How much for your horse?"

"Er, what?" asked the cabbie, blinking, visibly distracted by Kaeru's beauty.

"How much?!" Kaeru demanded.

"Er, fifty pounds?" the cabbie guessed uncertainly.

Kaeru handed him the money and detached the horse from his coach, wasting no time before getting on its back. I got on behind them.

"Wait, no, a hundred!" the cabbie barked as Kaeru lashed the horse's reins, launching us ahead. "Two hundred!"

We rode through the streets until we could ride beside the tracks themselves, slowly catching up to the train as it chugged on into the countryside. I wished I had my wings, and the wounds on my back itched as I remembered them.

"Should throw you off," Kaeru snapped. "I might miss this chance because of you, and then they'll have both our heads."

"Let me make it up to you," I grunted, hanging on to Kaeru for dear life. "We'll do this right. We just need to catch up..."

Soon we were riding through the country alongside the train. When we were close enough, and there were no prying eyes, Kaeru leaped across the gap to grab hold of the caboose. I followed. As the horse continued galloping beside the train, Kaeru and I entered through the back. "See?" I whispered. "We're fine."

"We almost weren't," Kaeru whispered back.

We moved through the train, car by car. When we inevitably encountered the ticket inspector, Kaeru presented our tickets, and we passed on without incident. They kept throwing me unkind looks as we moved on, their hair frazzled from stress.

It didn't take us long to reach a sleeper car full of private compartments. One had a guard standing before the door. "Think that's the one?" I whispered.

Kaeru nodded and jerked their head at a lavatory right next to us. "Hide in there. Wait for my signal."

I nodded and went in. The train made a great racket, but I could still make out Kaeru's voice from the other side as they went to the guard. "Oh, excuse me, sir! I know you must be busy, but I could use your help ever so much." I could practically hear them batting their lashes.

"Oh—er—I'm actually supposed to stay here," the guard stammered, just as beguiled as the cabbie had been.

"It will only take a moment. You see, sir, I saw a most suspicious gentleman entering the lavatory. I'm sure a big strong man like you would have no trouble apprehending him. After all, who knows what he might do? I would be ever so grateful if you just had a look..."

Footsteps followed, and then the lavatory door slid open to reveal the blushing guard. I was about to strike him, but Kaeru was already behind him, a hand on either side of his head. They rotated it with a snap, breaking the guard's neck in one swift motion. I moved out of the way as the guard collapsed onto the lavatory floor.

"Hurry," Kaeru hissed, and we awkwardly kicked the guard's legs into the lavatory fully and shut the door.

Then we turned around to see a woman in a fur coat staring at us, mouth hanging open.

Before Kaeru could reach her, the woman had already screamed. The compartment doors opened and guards came rushing out, weapons drawn.

"Abort?" I whispered to Kaeru, but they had already drawn their revolver.

Kaeru shot the woman in the chest. She fell backward onto a guard who had just come out, blocking his gun, giving Kaeru enough time to shoot him in the head.

"Great Scott!" bellowed another guard, just before Kaeru shot him in the head, too.

Kaeru and I took cover behind a half-wall as more gunfire rattled, bullets missing us by inches. "Help me, you fool!" Kaeru hissed, poking out to shoot the men, but my hands rattled as I tried to draw my gun. This was precisely what I'd wanted to avoid: another damn slaughter. Byzantium all over again.

While I waffled, the door to the previous car tore open and the ticket inspector emerged with a foot-long billy club, which he immediately tried to strike my head with. I dodged, drew my knife and jammed it into the man's jugular. A geyser of blood spurted out in an impressive arc as the man stumbled, wide eyed, clutching the wound, only for a stray bullet from the corridor to send him to the floor.

More screams echoed from every direction as the guards closed in on us. I yanked my knife free from the ticket inspector's corpse and lashed it at the first guard to reach me, while Kaeru shot another, and another after that. A bullet barely missed my head. Blood was splattering everywhere, the entire fight becoming a confused mess. Rage took hold of me. I wanted this to stop. Wanted to end it however I could. Even if that meant killing the people who were shooting at us.

I stabbed and slashed and shot, cutting out eyes, knifing crotches. If I was going to kill them anyway, why be sporting about it? I was not here with anything to prove, merely to accomplish what I had to in order to get what I wanted. As one dead man fell onto me, I used his corpse as a shield and inched closer to a gunman, who I took out by shooting in the face point-blank.

It was then that I noticed the door to the target's compartment was open, and the other guards were all at the end of the car fighting Kaeru. My hands shook as I entered the compartment.

William Ewart Gladstone—no, I told myself again, *the target*—huddled in the corner, terror filling his eyes. I aimed my gun at him, but my grip remained unsteady, the blood on my hands sticky and uncomfortable.

"P-please," the target whispered, eyes wide.

I trembled so hard that my teeth chattered. The target must have known, because before I could find it in me to pull the trigger, he threw himself past me, far faster than I'd have expected from a man his age. He bolted up the train car opposite of Kaeru. I tried shooting him but missed.

"Kaeru!" I shouted as the target made it to the next car. I followed, only to find the car full of people in seats. Many stood up and shrieked as I came in. The target kept on running in the slim space between the seats, fleeing like a rabbit. I fired, missed, and made a hole in a woman's head. More screams echoed. A baby was letting out an ear-splitting wail. Gentlemen came rushing at me, raising canes or fists, but I shot one after another, and when my chamber was empty I swung my knife to slice off a man's nose, and stuck my fangs into another man's throat, refusing to let them hurt me. It didn't matter that these were mortals. It didn't matter that they probably couldn't do any real damage to a demon like me. What mattered was that they were in my way, and I'd already cocked this up, and if I cocked it up even more I might get sent back to Hell, and would never attain my vengeance.

The target was already scrambling into the next car. I trampled over the corpses I'd made to catch up, trying to ignore the shame, the screams, the baby's ceaseless cries. Behind me, Kaeru launched through the door and began firing at the people I'd missed, one by one, until even the baby abruptly stopped crying. I stopped in my tracks, a freezing sense of horror passing through me. "A baby, Kaeru?" I hissed, whirling around.

"He's getting away!" said Kaeru.

"A *baby?!*"

For just a moment, something flickered in Kaeru's eyes: a flash of discomfort, perhaps shame. But immediately their expression hardened, and they pushed past me, tearing open the door to the next train car, no less occupied than this one. With a groan, I followed.

This time, most people were huddling behind their seats. The target had only made it several paces, for he was slow, limping, his old age catching up to him. Kaeru and I aimed our guns.

Then the train screeched to a sudden stop, and we were launched forward. I landed on the floor, almost cracking my head in the process. More screams pierced the air, but then everyone began getting up, racing to the exit doors now that the train had stopped. Someone must have told the conductor that the train was being attacked.

I scrambled to my feet, Kaeru beside me. Through the window I saw that outside was wilderness, with a large body of water directly beside us. Everyone was jumping down into it, fleeing for their lives. I dashed to the exit and leaped into the water myself, Kaeru already opening fire at my side. "We can't let any of them escape!" they said, their words barely registering in my ringing ears. "They've seen us! They've bloody seen us!"

Body after body fell into the water until it turned red from all the blood. The target was still running, the most distant of them all. I aimed my revolver and fired, missed, and fired again. I would need to get closer. I waded into the bloody water until it was up to my ankles, then my knees, then my waist. All the while, more mortals fell to my left and right, turning the water redder by the second, until I could have sworn that it was just a lake of blood. I was back in Hell: the sky above full of black clouds, the lake stained red, bodies falling all around me.

Further and further into the blood I waded, until I was too far to turn back. But why should I? Why not go deeper into the darkness, if it was the only way to find light?

But as I waded on, the blood up to my chest, I began to wonder if there really was any light to be found this way, or if I'd only convinced myself of such out of a desperate need to justify my actions. I banished this thought as soon as it came; if I allowed myself to turn back, I would never go anywhere at all. Especially as I was finally closing in on the target.

"Shoot him, Caleb!" Kaeru hissed from behind me.

This time, I had no awareness of pulling the trigger, or even lifting the gun, but red mist sprayed from the target's head, and he fell into the water. The smoking gun was in my hand.

The ringing in my ears had only worsened, even though no more bullets were flying, even though no one was left to scream, even though around me there were naught but corpses floating in a scarlet lake. Kaeru waded to me, beaming with relief. They said something, but the ringing was still too loud for me to make out what. They took my face in their tender hands and kissed me. Then they pulled away, smile wider than ever, confronting me with this strange facade of Clara drenched in blood.

How could I explain the twinge in my chest, like a screwdriver digging into my heart and twisting around? I looked at all the dead around us, afraid to even count them. How many new souls would be falling into Hell at this very moment because of me? How much more time on this Earth might they each have had?

But I could not frown; could not let Kaeru see how awful I felt. So, I tried to force a smile as they pulled me into another bloody kiss.

I'd expected Mr. Cillian to be upset when he arrived, given what a mess we'd made. Instead, he clapped his white-gloved hands together excitedly, beaming at the derelict train. "Delightful. Just delightful! This exceeds all my expectations. Look at all these fresh bodies! A hundred new Reapers for my army. Quite impressive, my good fellows. Quite impressive indeed."

He practically danced through the train, absolutely gleeful at the carnage we'd left behind. I was puzzled. "Won't all these deaths raise questions?" I asked. "Won't people wonder why this train stopped?"

"Indeed." Cillian grinned. "The papers will be aghast. The public will be mortified and desperate for answers, and their faith in the crown will fracture. Let them find this derelict train, and despair."

He drew a circle of blood and performed a ritual to raise the dead. The bodies ruptured, their muscles becoming bone, and as one they rose up under the crescent moon: Reaper warriors, crimson water dripping down their bone musculature. A hundred new puppets for Cillian to play with.

Perhaps I should have given up on it then. How could I possibly think that what I was doing was just after this?

But what else was there to do but stay the course? I'd turned my back on everything else. After all, I was filthy with blood. My clothes, skin and hair were drenched with it. I reeked of it. And repulsed though I was, I was compelled to answer the blood's call. I lifted my hand to my mouth and licked it, sucking each finger for good measure. I relished in the sweet, coppery taste, even as I hated myself for giving in.

<hr>

"Well done, boy. Well done." Salem slapped my back at the *Boudoir*'s bar, beaming with pride. Kaeru had told him the whole blow-by-blow, and he'd been just as excited by the higher-than-expected body count as Cillian. I chugged the bloodwine Salem had bought me, desperate to addle my brain to oblivion.

"You're a natural," Salem went on. "Human shields? Diabolical. This is what you're made for. I knew I saw something in you. I *knew* it. Here. You've earned this."

He grinned at me, face so close that I thought he might kiss me again, a thought I strangely welcomed.

Instead, he stuffed a fat envelope into my hand. It was full of cash, even more than before. It was more money than I'd ever even seen. I was rich. Filthy rich. And all it had taken was slaughtering a train's worth of innocent souls.

I looked back up to find Salem had returned his attention to others, and I was once again left with a vague feeling of being discarded. I'd been a dalliance to him; a toy, perhaps an experiment. It wasn't that I'd hoped he might let me back into his bed; indeed, the idea filled me with dread. But I still yearned for his affection and approval.

I ended up buying myself a bottle of premium bloodwine and taking it up to my room to drink alone. My back itched as I stripped my clothes, and I checked the mirror to see that my wings were beginning to grow back: little black nubs on my shoulder blades, itching as they tasted the air.

I lay in those satin sheets for hours, never quite finding my way to sleep. The room was dark and quiet, but my mind was too troubled to let me relax. I lay on my side, for my back was sore where the wings had pushed out. The faces of the dead haunted me, passing through my mind over and over. When I closed my eyes, I heard their screams, and above it all, the crying of the infant, abruptly cut short. Just as I at last began to fade, the clinking of chains echoed through the air, and I froze, paralyzed with fear.

"Things are going well for you, aren't they, Caleb?"

Riven's voice sliced into the room. My body felt like it wanted to quiver, but it remained frozen, stiff to the point of pain. I did not see him, but I did not need to. The very air bent for him.

"I hear you did excellent work tonight." That voice, so deep and sharp, seemed to pierce my ears like needles. "You are more skilled in this blood game than we could have hoped. And I reward those who serve me well. Tell me, Caleb. What do you want?"

Chains clinked all around me, dragging against the walls and floor in the dark.

"You can take whatever you want from this world. Women. Wealth. A castle to call your own. So long as you remain loyal and useful to us, the world is yours. Whomsoever you covet is a possession to acquire. All you must do is reach out and grasp them."

I clenched my jaw to keep my teeth from rattling. I wondered if I should ask for Thomas's head, or Clara's hand, but I knew I would attain neither. Riven could not offer me anything but fleeting distractions from my pain.

But when the alternative was endless suffering, were those distractions not something to treasure?

"Of course, it is also possible that you are having second thoughts about this arrangement," Riven went on. "And if that is the case, young Caleb, then I would remind you that whatever pain you think you feel now, it is nothing compared to what can follow. So seek the carrot, Caleb. You will be happier for it."

Pressure built up in my temples, as if his fingers were digging through my skull to penetrate my mind. I found myself unable to respond, unable to even breathe.

"I see potential in you, Caleb. A thirst for power. And while that may feel wasted now, just imagine how far you can climb in the wake of that glorious pain."

Suddenly, my body inhaled on its own, twitching to life. The sound of the chains was gone, but the hairs on the back of my neck were still stubbornly erect. Riven seemed to remain, hidden just behind me no matter which direction I turned, reminding me always of the unthinkable punishments I would face if I disobeyed him. The entire room felt unsafe; tainted; a place I should not sleep.

How was it that even now I could feel so powerless? Memories of every time I felt weak crashed upon me like great waves: the street boys who'd call me queer and beat me bloody; returning home to my father, who'd beat me further for not defending myself better; watching him stick out his barrel chest and bark, "*This English air has infested you and turned you into a runt. My son, the runt!*"

There was no way to be strong enough for this world. I imagined my father was somewhere down there in Hell, even now, suffering over and over as I had. And who in the world was strong enough for that?

I wondered if I might be, if only I got what I wanted. I'd endured endless suffering to have my revenge, and now it felt close enough to taste. Yes, I'd waded too far into these bloody waters to turn back now.

So I opened the bottle and sipped the bloodwine. Then sipped a little more. It was sweeter than I expected, but the rich flavor and ensuing intoxication helped me feel something at least. A burning in my throat. A fuzziness in my head. A feeling of all being right in the universe. Before I knew it, I'd downed the whole thing.

I felt hollow, but maybe if I was hollow, it meant I had to fill myself up with someone new. Maybe the old Caleb was dead, giving me an opportunity to birth a new self entirely. Not Caleb the weak, mournful violinist, but Caleb the powerful incubus assassin, who had slain demons, bedded Silkshapers, and even earned an audience with the Emperor of Hell. That Caleb sounded like someone who would be having the time of his life right now.

After all, if Salem could use and discard people as he saw fit, why not I? Why should I be the one to have my will denied? It was an ugly thought, and I knew it, but it came so naturally that it was challenging to deny. Hell had changed me, or perhaps just brought forth the vicious hungers that had always lurked in the back of my mind, the all-consuming need for *more*. More love, more sex, more alcohol, more decadence, more of my unholy existence spent on my own terms. For giving up on my own needs and desires seemed like succumbing to the death of the soul, rendering me into not a man, but a husk, who had forgotten how to want or how to speak or even my own name. How could I not pursue my desires after witnessing such eternal desolation?

Why not become an ever-worse person, just for one fleeting moment of pleasure? It was what everyone else was doing.

So I brought a brothel girl up to my room, and as we fed, I told myself that I was happy. After she'd left, I lay there alone in the seed-stained bed, and forced another mad grin. Maybe if I slept with it, it would stick, and I would wake up without any worries at all.

CHAPTER NINETEEN

BLOODY CALEB

T HERE ARE A FEW best practices when it comes to dismantling a group in power.

The first is to understand that a ruling class remains in power only because the people they rule allow it. Therefore, the ruling class must convince the people that without a force of authority to keep everyone in check, there will be chaos. They're not entirely wrong about that, but you must make the people view chaos as the more desirable alternative.

Successful revolution requires numbers. You only need a small number of people to light the match, but it should be a fire that most people are happy to spread. There must be a common struggle, such as widespread hunger. But many struggles apply to some but not all, and it benefits the powers that be to divide us as much as possible.

If your intention is to dismantle the ruling class, then your goal must be to transform the problems of some into the problems of the many. There can be no division, or when violence breaks out, it will be too easy to quell.

Finally, you must communicate a dream. Everyone must share the same vision for what could be after the years of struggle, and must believe that dream to be both possible and worth giving their lives for. It should be an ideal: something simple to grasp, even if it's unattainable.

Revolution is not possible without disruption, and a falling empire will have many vulnerabilities in its infrastructure. Your job is to identify and exploit those weaknesses. Water. Air. Food. Electricity. Sewage. Jobs. The press. The military. These establishments must fall, one by one, and when they do, you will blame their failure on the very government responsible for providing them. After all, they tax the people for this very purpose.

It helps, of course, if you have powers that the ruling class doesn't. Better technology, for example. Or magic.

This was what I learned while killing people alongside Kaeru week after week.

A simple look at the papers of those days would give you evidence of my work. An explosion that went off at the Metropolitan Water Board. A bag full of plague-carrying rats that just happened to find its way into a food mill. Various churches burning to the ground, creating a vacuum for a new religion to exploit.

The heads of several important papers mysteriously vanished, only for these papers to all be purchased shortly after by a man named Rupert Walters. Such notable figures as John Bright and Robert Gascoyne-Cecil disappeared as well. Meanwhile, other public figures became scandalously nocturnal as they joined our cause. One such example jowas Wilkie Collins, whose crippling opium addiction had ruined his health, or Cecil John Rhodes, who was all too eager to spread the Nightfall's purported new regime to the colonies in Africa.

I could practically smell the instability in London's air. Whenever I went out into the streets, everyone seemed worse off than before, with more and more people succumbing to poverty, hunger, and death. Fights broke out with increasing frequency as man turned on man, all looking for someone to blame.

"We're right on track," Salem told me one night in his Mayfair mansion, its every wall made a mural from his paintings. He stared out the window at the city below, the teeth of his grin glowing in the light of the crescent moon. "Riven wants it all to happen at once, so every nation will be overtaken as one. That way none have any warning, or go to each other's aid."

Again and again, Salem promised me untold riches once the Nightfall proved successful. I could be a baron, a viscount, perhaps even a duke. So long as I didn't cross him, so long as I was his dog, he would give me whatever I wanted.

But there was no happiness to be found as Salem's dog. Only emptiness. A soul crushing certainty that I had forgotten who I was. I'd forgotten my mother's face, and all the wealth and sexual partners Salem rewarded me with only served as fleeing distractions from this fact. The voice telling me this was my conscience, but I did not recognize it as such. It was a dreadful voice, a voice I was loath to listen to. Salem offered me a more comforting voice: one that promised everything I wanted was within my grasp, so long as I obeyed him. That all the death and horror I was unleashing upon England was for the greater good. That the Nightfall would purge the city's evil and bring about a new, noble era.

And if that was a lie, well, at least it was getting me closer to killing Thomas and freeing Clara from him. Surely that made it all worth it.

Still, many nights I was unable to sleep; unable to close my eyes without feeling haunted by the faces of those I'd wronged. Jeanne. Elias. Anika. Duncan. Gladstone. The woman in the fur coat. The infant, whose crying had been silenced by Kaeru's bullet. The countless strangers whose names I would never even know.

And that list was growing by the night.

After the train, it became a familiar rhythm. Salem would give us a mission, and Kaeru and I would accomplish it. Then I'd return to the *Boudoir*, shave off my wing nubs, and douse myself with alcohol to forget whatever atrocity I'd performed that night.

Kaeru and I were good at our job. Exceedingly good. So good that the missions became both more frequent and more difficult.

And after every mission, we were paid handsomely.

I used my ill-gotten gains to buy new suits, top hats for every occasion, a collection of ornate silver knives, blood-wine bottles to drink the morbs away, girls from the bordello down below, and extra towels for the constant vomiting I was doing in my room's little lavatory. But my most treasured new possession was a beautiful violin. Playing it from the comfort of my room, sometimes with a pretty succubus or two in my bed and fine bloodwine in my throat, it was easy to forget the hollowness gnawing within me.

I tried to assuage this hollowness with more fruitless attempts to reach Clara through her dreams. I longed to speak with her, to ask after her, to comfort her without Thomas's knowledge. But no matter how often I tried, I was unable to reach her. I grew all but certain she, too, had her dreams concealed by a Morpheus Pentacle. By now, I'd also given up hope of reaching Jeanne, Elias, and the others. Or perhaps... in all honesty, perhaps I was no longer trying to.

Remy was another figure I considered contacting, but the thought frustrated me. What if my old friend really had been involved in my murder? Even if he hadn't, he'd brought me to that club in the first place, unintentionally leading me to my death. Would I have to add him to my list as well? It was a question I was not yet ready to process, not with everything else going on.

I was always around people, and yet I was always lonely, for I had no one to speak the truth to. No one to turn to for true comfort. All I had were the lies I told my fellow demons and the lies I told myself. Lies that, I feared, were beginning to eclipse the truth.

The only time I truly felt myself was when I was continuing to practice the art of rituals. Salem was too occupied to direct my tutelage, but I was continuing my education without him. My room was outfitted with a bathtub, which was more than enough for what I had in mind. Whenever I had a spare hour or two, I filled it up a few inches, drew a circle around myself, and practiced. Soon, I became able to turn some of the water into oil in mere moments. But as before, it took far longer to transform it all, let alone set it ablaze in a fire potent enough to turn someone to ash.

I made many mistakes. I would often accidentally boil the water, or in my excitement try to turn it directly into fire right away, only for the flames to be immediately quenched. I additionally tried to set the oil ablaze with a match, but found the fire too slow and weak for my purposes. I needed a blaze that consumed flesh with all the power of the sun.

In the end, rituals are about bending the rules of the world to your will. As such, to be successful you must have a will of steel. I learned, over time, to focus on my hunger for vengeance; to let it fuel my will. As the weeks passed, it became easier and easier to turn those still waters into roaring flames. I grinned as they licked the porcelain walls of the tub, my brow sweating from the heat.

At first, I put the fire out using the faucet, but the fact that I could do so only showed how weak the flames I'd conjured were. I began purchasing slabs of meat to place in the tub, and focused my efforts on improving the spell: making it faster, more potent, until the meat was not merely roasted but immediately reduced to ash. Of course, a full-sized vampire would be far more durable than a mere slab of pork, but satisfaction still flowed through me as I watched that meat disintegrate.

Each time I turned the water to flame, I felt that same piercing pain in my chest: my undead heart screaming as more and more of it was sliced away.

⸺⸺◆⸺⸺

Amidst this, of course, I had to stay fed. I became better acquainted with my sense of smell, following my nose to distinguish who lusted for me, who found me merely adequate, and who had no interest at all. I quickly learned that no matter a woman's beauty, I was utterly uninterested in feeding on her if I did not smell her yearning for me. The *Boudoir* succubi were excellent liars, with convincing smiles and moans they'd honed to perfection after decades or even centuries of practice, but most could only pretend to want me at best. I had to respect them for how professional they were, for how hard they worked to transform the act of feeding into an art form. Most vampires were unable to smell as I did, while most incubi simply didn't care. They would take the lie. I could not.

I did not want to be merely tolerated by a lover. I wanted to be *desired*. I wanted to make her tremble, for her to feel intoxicated by my presence, for her to close her eyes and think of me when other lovers were inside her. What joy was there in petting a cat that did not purr?

So I found the girls who wanted me. I'd pass them at the bar or in the hallways down below, catch a whiff of their scent, and turn to meet their gaze. Most were in the bordello's employ, but every so often, it would be a masked woman: a married vampiress in search of a distraction, perhaps, or a newly turned succubus keen to experiment. Sometimes, I'd bring someone up to my room only to discover they were Kaeru all along, and they'd laugh as they straddled me, delighting in the game.

But none of these women were Clara. Sooner or later, I would always end up lying awake in bed, nauseated and bitter, bedeviled by that same hollow feeling.

Soon, I began experimenting with men as well. I'd never considered myself a mandrake as a mortal, but after my time with Salem, I'd found myself curious what it would be like with other men. Besides, I wouldn't compare men to Clara like I did the women I brought to my bed.

In the end, I found that it mattered not the gender of my feeding partner; only that they succumbed, giving me control, allowing me to drive them wild and out of their mind with pleasure. *This* was the feeling that energized me with a sense of power. No fantasy was more appealing than that of being more than an ant in a universe that would squash me without a second thought.

Many nights, there was no one who truly wanted me. I'd search for a means to sate my hunger, but those who had lusted for me so intensely before were otherwise occupied or not in the mood after a long day of serving other customers. Certainly, they would smile and wink and make it clear that my coin could buy them for the night, but that didn't mean the desire was truly there.

I'd always imagined that being stronger, taller, and more conventionally handsome would yield me endless options, but that was not the case. Mine was a world of beautiful immortals, and in it, the standards were higher than ever. Even now, I soon found myself wishing I had become just a *little* taller, or just a *little* stronger. I wished that I was richer, even though I had more money than I'd ever known. It was never enough, somehow. Nothing ever could be.

The people who fed on me saw me as a fleeting distraction, not one to fall for. Granted, I didn't want them to fall for me. I wanted Clara. And yet part of me wished that, just once, one might view me as worthy of such. A few women expressed that I was a bit too pretty for their tastes, and bloody hell, I had no idea what that was supposed to mean.

"Your problem is that you look like you're trying too hard," Salem told me one night, whilst we drank together at the *Boudoir's* bar. "Most women are put off by the appearance of desperation, so you have to look good without making it seem like you're even trying. If you wear makeup, it must be invisible. And you cannot act as if your life depends on them reciprocating your affections."

The comment rankled me greatly. "I don't—" I began, but he steamrolled over me anyway.

"It is better to hint at desire. A gentle suggestion, ambiguous enough to make them wonder, to let their imagination run wild. Tease them with a feather, to make them wonder about what the entire cock might be like. But for them to come to you, they must be uncertain. Held in suspense, as if reading a penny dreadful. There must be some little voice in their head telling them that they aren't good enough." A cruel grin spread across his face. "If you can make someone feel that way with a single look, then you can enslave the world."

"Indeed?" I asked, feeling not inspired so much as chilled.

"Oh, yes." Salem took a swig of bloodwine and chuckled. "People will bend over backwards for you if they want to fuck you enough."

The conversation haunted me for weeks. I wondered whether my attraction to Salem made me more inclined to obey him; whether I was only proving him right by killing at his command. I also could not help but feel disgusted at the dishonest manipulation of it all; the implication that it was acceptable, even encouraged, to put women through such emotional tumult to have my way with them. Sober and clear-headed, I thought there was no way I would adopt such behavior.

And yet, when I was hungry and intoxicated, I began following Salem's advice anyway. It became easy to justify, once I had the will to. Whispering sweet words to succubi to tempt them into my bed seemed harmless when I was too broken to care. Feeding benefited us both, did it not? And if they struggled with confusing or painful feelings as a result, what fault of that was mine? After all, I had my own pain to attend to.

More than once I broke down and wept during feeding, throttled by thoughts of Clara or Jeanne. I accepted invitations from partners I did not desire, convincing myself that I would enjoy it once it began; that it behooved me, as both an incubus and as a man, to gladly accept what was offered to me. I buried the pain as much as I could, locking myself in the haze of drunken lust. What else could I do? How else was I to endure the self-loathing I felt when I was sober? The endless, ever-larger mountain of regrets?

London's underworld of demonic elite proved a difficult world to navigate for other reasons as well. Everyone detested each other. Simply talking to one man might lead to another glowering at you from across the room, making enemies without even knowing it. Centuries of life meant centuries of drama, with many of my peers still holding grudges from events that had occurred hundreds of years ago. My fellow members of the demonic elite were often incredibly childish, trapped in states of perpetual adolescence from the way they spoke to and of one another: vicious rumors, unkind assumptions, and endless curiosity about who was shagging who.

One night, while drinking at the *Boudoir* bar, I saw Thomas stroll in surrounded by a gauntlet of gentlemen, lighting his cigars and jeering at the girls they passed and jabbering on and on. Thomas was no longer a mere gentleman; he was bloody royalty. Even now that I was a demon like him, he passed me by without even a single glance. I was mere furniture to him, just as before.

Salem emerged from the other end of the room and penetrated through the throng of Thomas's sycophants to pat his back. Looking over Thomas's shoulder, he caught my eye and waved me over. My jaw tightened. I did not wish to get any closer to Sir Thomas, at least not until I had a chance to slit his throat. But I could not refuse Salem's beckon.

"I'm envious," said the incubus sitting beside me, his fancy, faded clothes stinking like they hadn't been washed in decades. "Imagine, an audience with Lord Sotirios and Sir Thomas Rife."

I trembled with rage, but pried my jaws apart long enough to ask, "You know Sir Rife?"

"Why, of course. Thomas Rife is a provider. A good man to get good with. You've got the cash, he and his mates can get you whatever you want." He grinned, showing his fangs.

Salem waved again, so I went over, my fists clenching and unclenching. I wondered what Rife would say when he realized who I was. Would anything flicker in his eyes as he realized I was back? Even if the game would be up, part of me yearned for that flicker. Part of me even felt it all might have been worth it just to see such terror flash in the bastard's eyes.

"Mr. Rife," said Salem as I approached. "May I introduce my good friend Mr. Caleb Schwartzenfeld?"

Rife turned to face me, smiling with glazed eyes, like I was a stranger he doubted was worth his attention. He didn't recognize me, I realized with a start. Not even after hearing my name. When I closed my eyes at night, I remembered every bloody face on that train, every soul in Byzantium. But Thomas didn't remember killing me at all.

I don't know why I'd expected any different.

"An honor, Mr. Rife." I forced a smile, and hoped he failed to notice the cool hatred in my eyes.

Rife let out a bark of laughter. "Oh, I like this one, Salem. Look at that gaze. Soulless as can be. No wonder you get along." He leaned in close and added, "You must be full of sick fantasies if you're anything like Salem. So, what can I do for you?"

Die, I wanted to say, but of course I couldn't. Before I could think of an answer, Rife laughed again, his cigar smoke blasting into my face as he patted my shoulder.

"No need to be modest, Mr. Schwartzenfeld. What's your pleasure? Top quality opium? Live mortals to feed on? Dates with girls much younger than the ones at this piffling establishment?"

I shook my head, forcing out the words. "I need nothing from you at this time, Mr. Rife." I sounded more aggressive than I'd meant to, but Rife didn't notice. He was already prattling on.

"Oh, but surely you can't be so prudish as to deny the charms of a very young girl? What are you, a nun?"

The men around us all laughed, as if on command.

My guts twisted in disgust. "Such girls are but children. No more appealing to my loins than mice."

"He really is a nun!" laughed one of the men.

Rife grinned. "It says much about you, Mr. Schwartzenfeld, that you would deny the tastiest, most forbidden fruit when it is within your grasp. Ours is an age of ambition. An age where great men shall prove themselves, and make Britain greater in turn. Men like Cecil John Rhodes, whose plans for Africa are awe-inspiring. Men like Cardinal Sotirios. All men of ambition seek forbidden fruit. Perhaps your ambition is lacking. And England has no need of men who lack ambition."

He turned away again, bringing his cigar back to his lips. The others roared with laughter. I wanted to throw up. I wanted to tell him that he was a monster, that his "forbidden fruit" repulsed me, and that if he knew of my ambitions he would quake in fear.

But I held my tongue. If I upset him, I would never make it into his manor. Never find him when he was alone and squeeze whatever pathetic excuse for life still remained within him. Did Clara know that Thomas was out there, getting rooms with girls young enough to be his daughter? It boiled my blood to think about what the bastard was getting away with.

Salem cleared his throat. "Not to be contrary, Mr. Rife, but I find that taste among our kind is anything but uniform. Why, I myself have sometimes been surprised by the sheer variety of my palette. Perhaps you will also discover this about yourself, should you live another few hundred years. You certainly will about other great men."

That shut Rife up. Salem's eyes met mine for just a flash, silently communicating that he remembered our rendezvous, even if he never spoke of it. As though he thought of it as a beautiful secret. The memory howled in my mind, my skin crawling with agony, and even as my head jerked down to avoid his gaze, I could feel it on me, transporting me back to his bedroom in Hell. Phantom pain throbbed in my throat and pelvis, along with an all-consuming terror that Salem might one day summon me to his bed once again—a request that I would be unable to refuse, both because I could not risk upsetting him, and because even now part of me yearned for his affection. I had tethered myself to this man, and could not run from him. Not if I wanted to kill Thomas. Not if I wanted to save Clara.

I told myself that I should have been thankful Salem had humiliated Thomas on my account, just as I should have been thankful to have shared his bed.

———◦———

Later that week, Salem invited me to an important gathering at the Immortalist Club.

I arrived alone and masked, but the strange doorman bowed deeply as he let me in, recognizing me for what I was without me needing to flash my fangs. I was not quite sure where Salem was, so I wandered through those familiar halls until I found myself in the gathering room where I'd met the Rifes that very first night. It was even more crowded than before, full of jabbering initiates. This time, I did not see Clara or Thomas, but there was one scent I recognized immediately: that of a young man drinking alone in a corner, a dourness to his demeanor that likely put off the ladder-climbers. The mask covering his eyes did nothing to hide the golden tumbles of his hair.

Remy Halligan.

I went over to him, blood throbbing in my veins. "I can't believe you're still here, old boy."

Remy looked up, puzzled. I raised my mask, letting him peak at the face beneath. His jaw dropped.

"It can't be... *Caleb?!*"

Before I could respond he was embracing me like a brother, letting out the most morose laugh I'd ever heard. Smelling him, I realized with a start that he was still mortal. Somehow, after all this time, Remy had not been promoted as Thomas had.

"Good God, Caleb. Where the hell have you been?" He pulled away to gape up at me. "And when did you get so damn tall?"

"You really have no idea what happened to me?" I asked.

"What happened?" Remy repeated, stunned. "I should be asking you! I bring you in, you shack up with those Rifes, and the next thing I know you're nowhere to be found. I figured you'd just become too busy for the likes of me. *Blimey*, you've gotten tall. How the hell did you get so tall?"

I heard no deception in his voice, only confusion. He still had no idea what this cult truly was. A numb ache filled my chest. "It's a long story," I said. "One I'm not at liberty to tell just yet. Suffice to say I've...risen through these ranks. I'm surprised you didn't as well."

"Yeah, well, I'm surprised too," Remy grumbled. "Must have stepped on the wrong toes. To be perfectly honest, Caleb, my life has been one failure after another for the past few years. I joined this club hoping it might offer me a change, but it's been just as rubbish as anything else. Growing up, I always imagined I would become someone else, something else. But I should have known from the start that it was impossible."

"Someone important," I said, nodding. "I understand."

"Not that." Remy winced. "Look, I... I don't know how to talk about it. And anyway, look at me, getting all weepy on you when we finally reunite. Tell you what, let's talk about you. You seem to have done well for yourself!"

The face of the woman in the fur coat flashed through my head: the light leaving her eyes as Kaeru's bullet entered her.

"Quite well," I said.

Remy beamed. "Got any tips?"

I'd wondered before whether I should kill Remy for his role in my death, but now that I was here with him, I felt no malice. No desire for revenge. Indeed, I was worried for him. I debated telling him to run; flee from not just this club, but the country, from Europe as a whole, from the whole bloody world. But where would it be safe for him? For anyone, at that? If the Nightfall really happened, and Remy was left behind...

"I could put in a good word for you," I said. "If you wanted. It might help you ascend to the next level."

My guts squirmed as I said it. I didn't want Remy to be trapped in this dark world as I was. But I feared he would be no matter what I did. The only difference was whether he would be predator or prey. And whatever pain he'd unintentionally caused by bringing me here, I did not want my old friend to be prey.

His face lit up. "Mate, it would mean the world to me."

I nodded, still uncertain whether it was for the best. But I wanted to do something good. Something right, even if it wouldn't undo my sins.

"There you are, Caleb." I turned to find Salem standing beside me, as masked as the rest of us. "Come with me. It's almost time."

"I'll see you soon, Remy," I promised, before following Lord Sotirios out of the room, up a staircase and through snaking hallways.

"Rubbing shoulders with mortals?" asked Salem, a note of surprise in his voice, even disapproval.

"An old friend," I said. "One who deserves to be promoted, I feel. Remigius Halligan."

"Indeed? The Halligan family has a long history, and we do need notable noble names to join our cause. Tonight is

Isabelle's ascension. Perhaps this Mr. Halligan may follow her."

"Isabelle's ascension?" I repeated, taken aback. The Nightfall had to be close. "She seemed quite fond of you. Are you planning on wedding her?"

Salem flinched, vulnerability flashing in his eyes. "I won't lie. Seducing the princess had its charms, at first. But she remains a princess, and it turns out such creatures are obnoxious indeed. I will, of course, continue to attend to her to make this work, especially after tonight. But there's been someone else I've been rather fixed on recently. Someone whose dreams I can't seem to stay out of."

"Who?"

"You'd laugh."

"Let me laugh, then."

He hesitated. "A mortal girl. She...shot me the other night, you see." He chuckled and flipped up his mask, showing me the scar on his nose.

I was baffled. "Why would you fall for someone who shot you?"

Salem shivered in pleasure. "Can you imagine the courage? The spirit? Oh, how I long to break her..." He sounded delirious, like the very thought of her made him drunk, even after all the women he'd been with.

"Is she so beautiful as that?" I asked.

Salem's grin was sheepish, even boyish. "Ahh, she...does not look as you might expect. Her flesh is imperfect. Too abundant, one might say. But there are few things more delightful than watching a mortal girl of humble endowments transform. They long for beauty more than anything, so their transformations can be dramatic. It is said that when a mortal becomes lilitu, they become their ideal self, attaining the body they most long for. I can't wait to see what she becomes."

Then he let out a surprised chuckle, shaking his head.

"What?" I asked.

"Just a memory. Oddly, it involves that spell you've been practicing. Once, back when I was in Hell, I used it to burn a mortal soul to ash. Then I turned her ashes into a diamond. Just to see if she would still regenerate."

"And did she?"

"You know... I can't say that I remember. But there's something fascinating, isn't there, about turning filth into beauty?"

I wondered how he could compare a woman he admired to filth. I would certainly never think that way about Clara, or indeed anyone I yearned for, save perhaps Salem himself.

"I didn't know you could make a diamond from human ashes," I admitted.

"Indeed," said Salem. "It's even possible without magic, just far faster with it. When you think about it, even the very worst of us could become something perfect, pure, and beautiful. All our sins and regrets carved away. You could almost envy them, if their existence wasn't destined to be bound to someone's finger."

He grew silent as we reached a pair of guarded doors. The guards took one look at Salem and opened up, allowing us into a dark chamber. Most of the figures were hooded as well as masked, but the shadows shrouded Salem and I well enough. Ritualistic droning echoed through the chamber. In the center of the room burned a circle of candles, the sole area that was illuminated. Sotirios whispered to a hooded figure beside us, who then disappeared out the door.

Another hooded figure approached the circle of candles. Just before entering, she shed her cloak to reveal her naked form, her black hair up in a tight bun: Isabelle, I realized with a start. She crossed into the circle and lowered to her knees, expression reverent.

Across from her, a familiar nun approached the circle's border, carrying a basin, naked save for her habit, black gloves, and stockings. She sported huge bat-like wings now, but my fists clenched as I recognized her. It was Pursha, who had danced and fucked as my blood rained down upon her.

Pursha placed the basin on the floor at the edge of the candles and lowered herself above it, before cupping her pendulous breasts and squeezing them until milk squirted out into the basin. Pursha's eyes closed in pleasure, lips opening slightly, until the basin was full. Then she placed it into the circle, and Isabelle lowered to drink.

"How does that work?" I whispered to Salem.

"Only succubi can produce the milk," he answered. "And only when they choose to."

A wail of agony echoed through the chamber, cutting through the droning. Isabelle was writhing on the floor, her limbs and waist twisting in pain. Blood trickled down her forehead as long curving horns stabbed out, and raven wings ruptured from her back. I winced, remembering my own painful transformation.

It took a few moments for Isabelle's body to settle. She breathed in and out, her hair messy, the bun undone. Finally, she sat up, a severe, regal, porcelain beauty. "Why didn't anyone tell me how much that would hurt?" she growled.

A masked, hooded figure reached out to take her hand, leading her away from the circle. Then, behind Isabelle, a man shed his robe, entered the circle, and drank from the milk basin to begin his own transformation into an incubus. A line had formed, I realized. And at the end of it...

Remy looked bewildered, even with his mask. His body language alone told me how terrified he was. Salem must have asked that hooded figure to bring him up, but I doubted Remy had been told what he was witnessing, or what he was about to endure.

Don't worry Remy, I wanted to tell him. *The milk will make you strong. It will make you have the body you always dreamed of.* But he was all the way on the other side of the room, and I didn't dare interrupt the ritual.

After the other initiates endured their own agonizing transformations, it was finally Remy's turn. Even if he didn't understand, he had the good sense to do as the others had done. He awkwardly stripped, entered the circle, and lowered himself down to lap the milk. Then, as with the others, Remy changed...but not in the way that I'd expected.

The agonized screams weren't anything surprising. What was surprising was how they shifted; how their pitch became higher. Discontented murmurs rippled through the crowd, loud enough that I heard them even over the monotonous chanting and Remy's piercing screams. His body was changing in unexpected ways, as well: in addition to the wings, horns, and spade-tipped tail ripping out from his flesh, his waist was shrinking, and his chest and hips bulging, his lines becoming curves. I pushed through the crowd, trying to get closer, to see better. Remy's hair was elongating, brightening, becoming a frizzy golden-orange mess.

I jumped at the hand gripping my shoulder: Salem, right behind me. "Tell me, Caleb," he hissed into my ear. "Precisely who did you ask me to vouch for?"

Remy's body had settled: tall and slender, with a long, pale neck. He slowly reared up to look at the crowd with beautiful green eyes, his tail twitching left and right, his breasts as pendulous as Pursha's own.

"Abomination," a gentleman murmured. It was the nasal voice of Mr. Cillian. Ice shot through me as the rest of the room murmured in agreement.

Remy slowly got up to his—no, *her*—feet. She looked around, body quaking in fear as she sensed the danger in the air. I couldn't imagine how confounding it all must have been. I knew first-hand how overwhelming it was to become lilitu at the best of times, but in her case...

Salem's grip into my shoulder became painfully tight. "Do you have *any* idea how embarrassing this is?" he whispered, voice trembling in barely contained rage.

I was stunned, utterly confused, but also afraid. "But—Kaeru—"

"Kaeru is a special agent with a unique and *useful* ability. What just happened with your friend undermines our entire establishment." He let out a furious, uncomfortable breath. "Look, you don't need to understand. Just get rid of it. Take that thing out of here and do what you do best."

I nodded hastily and pushed through the crowd, then into the circle, and removed my coat to cover Remy up. She was hunched over, awkwardly trying to cover her breasts with her arms. "Caleb, what... what's happening?"

Remy had always had soft, pretty features, with a weak chin, but that wasn't uncommon for aristocrats. If I squinted, ignoring her body from the neck down, she still had my old friend's eyes.

"Stay close to me," I whispered, leading her out of the circle. The crowd parted for us, as though she were carrying some disease.

"Abomination!" repeated Cillian, louder this time. Thomas parroted him, repeating the awful word, but he sounded amused rather than angry. I restrained my urge to reel on them, to shout back. It would only get us killed.

"What's happened to me?" Remy repeated, panic in her voice.

I led her downstairs, through hallway after hallway, trying to find the fastest way out, my blood racing in my veins.

I took Remy to a deserted corner of the docklands under a bridge. "You took me here to kill me, didn't you?" she asked, looking across the water with a despondent expression.

I stood there, hand gripping the gun in my holster, but somehow unable to draw it. "I haven't decided yet."

"So, what, you want me to convince you not to?" Remy shot me a scowl. "You want me to beg for my life? Bargain with this new body?"

"No. Just." I exhaled. "Would you just give me a moment?"

If Salem got wind that I was disobeying a direct order, it would be the end of me. But killing Remy didn't sit right with me any more than massacring that train had. And right now, I didn't have Kaeru around to ensure I follow orders.

I was tired of compromising myself; tired of seeing ghosts every time I closed my eyes.

Remy crouched down to grab a small stone and skipped it across the water. "Jesus, Mary, and Joseph, Caleb. This whole time, this is what the club was really about?"

"I'm afraid so."

"And you kill people for them?"

I didn't answer.

She shot me another glare. "Why?"

Hadn't I asked Kaeru the same, not so long ago? And yet it felt like an eternity now. After the train. The sabotage. All the awful things we'd done together.

"It's complicated," was all I could say.

Remy tossed another rock. "This doesn't usually happen, then? When people drink that milk?"

I let go of the gun fully and sighed. "I'm quite new to this world myself. But the way they spoke, it seemed less like it was something they'd never encountered before, and more like something they feared."

Remy looked down. "Maybe it happens more than you think. Maybe they just don't want anyone knowing about it when it does."

It wouldn't have surprised me. Old memories resurfaced: all the little signs that Remy wasn't comfortable in her own skin. I, too, had struggled with my body growing up, obsessed with the idea that I wasn't becoming who I wanted to be, but it had never crossed my mind that I was anything but a man, even if I felt like a failure of one. I wondered, had I come to a different internal conclusion, whether the milk might have turned me into a succubus as well. What did it say about me, that I'd fixated so strongly on my failures of manhood? That even now, I was fighting to be the person

I'd thought I'd wanted to be, and was finding not happiness, but pain? What did it say, that after all that, I still felt like a puppet, a tool, used by men I detested and felt inferior to?

I'd thought I had to be this way. That I'd *had* to be as masculine as possible, because the world would accept nothing else. But now, after Remy's transformation, and after learning Kaeru existed outside the black-and-white world of men and women... I wondered whether I ought to simply turn my back on the whole thing. Was part of me not trying to save Clara because I thought it was my duty as a man who loved her? Was part of me not still bitter at Thomas because I envied how comfortably and naturally he embodied the masculine ideal?

...Ah. I may be getting ahead of myself. I was likely not ready to consider such thoughts at that time. Perhaps I even rejected them, if they even occurred to me at all. But now, as I write this in my cell, I look back on that night as the one that I truly began to realize how lost I was. It was not just my indefensible actions, but the very foundation on which my sense of self had built.

If only I'd realized sooner. If only that night had been enough, truly enough. If only I'd known then what I know now.

I sat down beside Remy, crossing my arms. "Lilitu milk... it's supposed to transform you into the person you always wanted to be. Give you the body you always wanted, deep down. That's why I became taller, stronger. Perhaps... you wanted something else."

Remy watched the moonlight rippling across the black water, eyes softening. It was a long moment before she responded. "I never wanted to admit it. Not even to myself.

Part of me still wants to deny it now." She exhaled. Then, slowly, a smile creeped onto her face. "Is it odd that part of me feels relieved?"

I was utterly surprised. "Remy, you're in danger. You'll have to go into hiding."

"Wasn't I hiding already, though?" She faced me, breaking out into a breathless grin. "And honestly, I'd rather hide from others than from myself. Don't get me wrong, this is all a *lot* to take in, and I really could have used a bloody warning. But I don't know if I ever would have allowed myself to admit it, if I'd known. I don't know if I'd have ever stopped hiding, no matter how unhappy I was."

A lump formed in my throat. No, I wasn't going to kill Remy. I simply couldn't.

Nor could I share her sense of relief, not with the danger I'd unwittingly put her in. I tossed a rock of my own, but it didn't skip. It merely crashed awkwardly into the water, as clumsy as anything else I did.

"Remy, I just need you to know that I asked them to bring you up because I was scared you'd be in danger. That club has plans that could change England forever. I was trying to save you, not put you in these dire circumstances."

"Maybe you did save me, though. I always felt like there was this...weight within me, one that was killing me from the inside. And it's gone now." She let out a panic-stricken laugh and added, "Of course, now I have the weight of being hunted, but..."

"I'll tell them you're dead," I said. "A change of clothes, hair, makeup... you'll be any other succubus to them."

Remy groaned. "You're right. Only then, instead of trying to kill me, they'll be trying to get into my bed. Honestly, fuck that whole club."

I tried to think of where she could hide. I couldn't take her to the *Boudoir*; they'd just expect her to work as one of the girls. Besides, the Immortalists loved going there.

Then I had an idea that I was not sure I liked.

"Do you know a gentleman named Alkin Beauxdera?" I asked. I had not seen him tonight and had the sense he was laying low. Likely because Salem would send me to kill him if he became a problem.

Remy tilted her head. "One of the higher ups in the club? He's been friendlier to us lower ranks than most."

It was a profound risk. Beauxdera had no reason to trust us, and Salem would be aghast if he learned we were planning to meet with him. But damnit, Alkin Beauxdera had been the one person in the club to voice any conscience at all, and I could think of no other avenues. "Any idea where we could find him?"

Remy nodded. "I do, actually. He has an airship parked at St. Katharine Docks. I visited a few months ago, just to see it up close. It's an impressive contraption."

"Then let's head there." I stood, brushing off my clothes. "One more thing. You're going to need a new identity. A new name."

She thought for a moment, another smile forming on her lips. "Roxanne," she decided, as if the name had always been within her, waiting for her to look for it.

I smiled back. "Roxanne it is."

Alkin Beauxdera's airship waited at St. Katharine Docks, currently resting on a landing pad at the end of a pier. I'd yet to be aboard such a vessel, and my body trembled with trepidation as I stepped onto the pier. I had been diligently cutting off my wing stubs for the past few months, and the idea of falling into the black water below was quite unappealing.

The airship might have looked like a galleon, were it not for the propeller-bearing wings, the enormous engine pipes, and the dome-like roof covering it. *The Snickering Bovine* was painted along the side, matching the cow-headed mermaid carved beneath the prow.

I knocked on the vessel's door several times before a slit opened to reveal a sooty-faced man, his expression sour. Roxanne, who still wore only my jacket, tried to hide her wings within it. It had been challenging enough sneaking her through the city. Now, with the light from the airship's interior spilling out, it seemed impossible to hide what she was. The crewman peered at her wings but did not remark on them. Perhaps, given Mr. Beauxdera's own immortal nature, his crew had been warned.

"We are hoping to speak to Mr. Beauxdera," I said. "It is of the utmost importance."

The crewman's eyes narrowed, but he closed the slit, and the door opened downward into a staircase, allowing us inside. Once in the orange glow of the gas lamps within, the crewman closed the stairs behind us and patted us down. One by one, my weapons were removed and put onto the table: guns, daggers, even the knife in my boot. I hated it, but I could hardly blame them.

The crewman led Roxanne and I through a grand hallway full of pipes until we reached a door labeled *Captain's Quarters*. He knocked, earning a bark of, "Enter."

Inside, Mr. Beauxdera was sitting behind a desk, pouring over schematics I found too challenging to make sense of. He tore his gaze away to look us over, surprise burning in his pupils. "Wait outside, Ezekiel," he said.

The door shut behind us. Beauxdera put the schematics down and stared at me. "You were at the Dead Ministry. Next to Lord Sotirios." His tone was hardly affable.

"I am not here on his behalf," I said quickly. "Nor do I mean you harm. I understand if my word means very little, but..." I trailed off. This was already off to a wretched start. I glanced at Roxanne, encouraging her to step forward. "Mr. Beauxdera, at that meeting, you struck me as a good-hearted man. I have no right to ask for your help. But this woman is a friend of mine, and... I don't know where else to turn."

Beauxdera stood up from his desk and looked Roxanne over. "A new succubus, are you? Unwilling to work at the *Boudoir*? Or perhaps on the run?"

Roxanne looked down, nodding slowly. Beauxdera frowned, eyes softening in sympathy.

"I may know a place for you. But I want your word that you aren't still loyal to the Immortalists."

"Absolutely not," said Roxanne, her voice firm.

"I sincerely hope you're telling the truth," said Beauxdera. "If this is some attempt at subterfuge, my contact will find out. She's powerful, and is no friend to Sotirios. But she cares a great deal for women in need."

"What do you say?" I asked Roxanne.

She nodded immediately. "I would be glad to join her."

Beauxdera smiled, but his gaze became skeptical as he turned to me. "And just who might you be, sir?"

I hesitated. "Caleb Schwartzenfeld."

"And do you support the Nightfall, Mr. Schwartzenfeld?"

I looked down, uncertain what to tell him. Be it yes or no, any answer seemed a lie.

Beauxdera watched me carefully, latching onto my hesitation. "Perhaps I should put it this way. Do you support progress in society's norms? Opportunities for the poor to ascend above their caste, the curing of diseases, the abolition of unjust laws? Or would you prefer regression to a darker time, where progress was merely a dream of the naive?"

"I would prefer progression, of course," I said. An easy thing to say, if impossible to live.

"Then we cannot allow the future to be one where our rulers live forever." Beauxdera's stare was firm, taking in my every twitch. "Rulers are always obsessed with immortality. But how could anyone possibly make the world better, when they fear anything different from what they were taught as children? Only through death can the world change. Without it, the cycle is broken. Without it, the world is ruled by corpses. So tell me, Mr. Schwartzenfeld. Are you really Sotirios's man? Or have you just told yourself that you have no other choice?"

Part of me wanted to say yes. Yes, I was his man, for he had made me stronger, and had been the one to ascend me from the depths of Hell. Yes, I was his man, if it meant I would survive the coming Nightfall, eliminate Thomas, and finally free Clara. Yes, I was his man, not because I wanted to be but because it truly was the only way. Beauxdera could lie to himself if he wanted to, but I would do no such thing.

And yet I was here, disobeying Salem, risking his wrath, simply because it was right.

In the end, I said nothing. I merely forced a smile and hoped that Alkin Beauxdera was as good a man as he seemed, if only because someone had to be.

⸺◆⸺

"It is done, then?" asked Salem, the candlelight reflecting in his eyes.

We stood in the entrance hall of his mansion in Mayfair. Every wall was painted with enormous murals, and the tiny flames of the candles transformed the figures on the walls into shadowy beasts.

"Remigius Halligan is no more," I confirmed.

Salem smiled, a hint of relief in his eyes; not because I'd been successful, I wagered, but because now he didn't have to kill or dispose of me. "It couldn't have been easy. He was a friend of yours, was he not?"

"Indeed. But one must always make sacrifices to achieve their ends." It disgusted me to play along this way; to act as though my friend was some aberrant monster. But Salem beamed with pride, slapping his huge hand onto my shoulder.

"That's what we need, Caleb. Loyalty to the cause, no matter how much blood you shed. *Bloody* Caleb, that's what you are! My blood drenched dog of death. That's what we shall call you from now on. And that's why I think you're ready to join the upper echelon of the Immortalist Club."

Something fluttered in my chest. Could it be? I bowed my head. "My lord, I would be honored."

"It's only right. After all, it's thanks to your efforts that the Nightfall is finally almost upon us." Salem's eyes burned with excitement. "Riven has confirmed that it's all in place. In two nights, the sky shall be scarred by the darkness. And tomorrow, there shall be a celebration at Thomas Rife's manor. Please, join us."

I had to restrain myself from letting out a mad laugh. Perhaps it should have mattered to me that in two nights, the world would fall into darkness. But right then, there was but one thought that concerned me: at last, at bloody last, vengeance would be mine.

CHAPTER TWENTY

THE LAST GALA OF THOMAS RIFE

THOMAS RIFE'S NIGHT-BEFORE-NIGHTFALL GALA was so luxurious, so impressively decadent and so well-attended that it only made me want to kill him more.

I almost couldn't believe it when I followed Salem and his version of Kaeru in through those iron gates, past the guards, into the crowded manor itself. The entrance hall had been transformed into an enormous ballroom, with enchanted paintings of winking women, tables full of glasses of bloodwine, and circus performers spitting fire and swinging above on bone trapezes. The gas lamps had been enchanted to be deep violet, and glamorous succubi danced burlesque on a makeshift stage, their glitter-drenched eyes shining. It was no doubt all to distract from the prison-like exterior, but even I was taken aback by how little it resembled the dour place it had been only a few years prior.

There were mortal servants in attendance, many of them with terrified eyes, but I recognized not one of them. No Croft, no Henrietta. I wouldn't have been surprised if Thomas had already drained them all.

Virtually every room offered a new example of excessive, repulsive splendor. In one, a sad-eyed chimpanzee was being forced to juggle for a chortling audience, while an overseer lashed him with a whip. In the next room, a gaggle of guests admired Thomas Rife's enormous taxidermy collection, which featured quails, monkeys, a tiger, a rhinoceros, and even a stuffed nude woman with terrified glass eyes. "Rife hunted all these himself, so they say," barked one of the gentlemen, scratching his brown fangs with a toothpick.

We found the man of the hour in a room where a mummy was being unwrapped. Already, a bespeckled man had removed its hand and was pounding it into black dust with a mortar and pestle. "Mr. Jones is a professional mummy unwrapper," Thomas gloated to the rotund vampire standing to his right. And to his left...

My heart almost leaped into my throat. Clara, her posture tight, eyes flashing madly from side to side, trying to keep track of every monster around her. She wore a small iron amulet with a pentagram drawn onto it in blood. This must have been what Salem had called the Morpheus Pentacle, protecting her dreams from intrusion. I wondered if Thomas made her wear it to ensure no incubi invaded her sleep.

It did nothing to hide the pinpricks on her neck. She was still mortal—I could smell it. Thomas's arm was snaked around her waist, keeping her in place, but her shoulders betrayed how uncomfortable she was. Somehow, no one seemed to care.

As Salem and Kaeru moved on, I remained, leaning against the wall in what I hoped was a casual sort of way. Right now, Thomas and Clara were protected, but sooner or later at least one of them would leave. All I had to do was wait.

Pursha, still dressed as a nun despite her demon wings, was guiding a frightened-looking young mortal man wearing a white tunic. I met her eyes, wondering if she recognized me, but it seemed she'd lost all interest in me now that I was a demon. The feeling was mutual; this close, she reeked of overripe fruit.

"Are you sure it's safe for me to be here, ma'am?" asked her young mortal companion.

"Hush, Charleston. Have some mummy dust." She shoved his face into the plate, compelling him to snort up a line of the black powder. The young mortal's eyes went dizzy as the high took him. Pursha moved her face right up to his and tilted her head like a curious snake, before licking his cheek, grabbing hold of his throat and dragging him from the room with an excited chuckle.

"There's been talk of trying to appeal to the Irish," Thomas was saying to the large vampire standing to his right. "Perhaps even Scottish separatists. Anyone who takes umbrage with Parliament, really."

"Rather beastly people, aren't they?" tutted the gentleman. "Can we really trust them on our side?" He lifted a toothpick to his mouth, lifting his lip just enough to show the hint of a red-stained fang.

"We can always betray them after," said Thomas, voice cold. "We can string them along with promises of immortality, but when it comes down to it, it is we who decide who receives the dark gift. We just need to get them drunk enough. And since they're always drunk anyway, that won't be hard at all."

As his companion chortled, someone brought Thomas the plate of mummy dust, and he snorted up a line. His eyes spun. "Jolly fucking *good!*"

I had to figure out a way to get him alone. Somewhere unguarded. My fists rattled in my pockets. As always, so close and yet so far.

Clara put her hand on Thomas's shoulder and whispered something, but he ignored her. She broke away, walking past me and through a door that led out into the hallway. A prickling sensation spread through my body. Thomas would have to wait, but this could be my chance to speak with Clara.

I followed her through the hallway, and then up a staircase that led away from the gala to the highest floor, until it was quiet enough that I could hear her sniffling. The sound brought a twinge of pain to my chest, and it only worsened as she pressed her back against the wall and slid all the way down to her feet, sobbing all the while.

This time, I felt no hunger. Merely an overwhelming longing to make her happier, just as I'd felt the day I'd first played her *Ashen Threnody*. I remained in the shadows, keeping my distance, afraid to show myself. I didn't even know if she would remember me. But maybe there was a way I could ensure she did.

I whistled *Ashen Threnody*. She looked up, eyes wide and wet, blind in the darkness.

"You better not try anything," she said, voice shaking with fear. "I'm claimed. My husband will kill you if you lay a hand on me."

I kept on whistling, keeping my distance. I did not wish to threaten her. She breathed in and out, eyes pinching, like she almost recognized the tune, but was not sure. It hurt that she did not immediately remember me, but in retrospect I'm not sure how I could have expected any different. She had known me for only a week, and that had been years ago. I let the sorrow creep into my lips, letting it impact the song's shape, so she would feel as I felt.

Beads of moisture trickled down from the corners of her eyes. "Why are you whistling that song? How can you know that song?"

I whistled on, the tune answer enough. Clara's lips trembled, her chest heaving as she considered the possibilities. Perhaps she wondered if it was Thomas, playing a trick on her, but he hadn't been in the room at the time. No, there could only be one answer, mad though it was.

"It's you, isn't it?" she whispered. "Caleb..."

I said nothing. I was strangely afraid to come out of the shadows and confirm it, for I still did not know what she would think when she learned what I'd become. I could only hope that she wouldn't detest or fear me.

"He said you were dead." Her voice echoed gently through the dark hall, still strained with tears. "Are you a ghost? After all I've seen these past years, a ghost could be as real as anything else..."

I remained frozen at the threshold, so tempted to show myself, but afraid of what would happen if I did. I was too far away to smell her, but oh, how I wanted to step closer.

"Whatever you are, you must go, or he will kill you all over again. Go, before he realizes you're here!"

She turned and ran further into the dark. This time, I did not follow. I felt frozen, unable to pursue her, no matter how much I wanted to. I could do nothing until Thomas was dead.

"So that's it," a voice hissed from behind me, and I turned to find Kaeru, still in the pale empress-like form they took for Salem. "That's why you've been trying to come here. That's why I take on a face similar to hers when I touch you. You love her. You love her, and want to steal her away."

My body froze. "Kaeru..."

They kept one hand in their pocket. If they were certain they wanted to kill me, they would have already done so, but that didn't mean they weren't strongly considering it. I debated pulling my knife out, but if I drew my weapon, so would they. I didn't fancy my chances. While I'd become a prolific killer, Kaeru had decades more experience than I. Besides, I didn't want to kill them after all we'd been through together.

But I would, if it came down to it.

"One night, Kaeru," I said. "That's all I ask. Turn a blind eye for one single night."

"Why? What do you have planned?"

"Only what is right." My voice became strained, a soft whisper in the dark hallway. "Only what I have been owed all this time."

"You are owed nothing," said Kaeru. "You should consider yourself lucky to be privileged enough to be here, among the elite. Is that not enough?"

"Rife and this cult murdered me, Kaeru." A mistake to admit, surely, but it filled me with relief to finally tell the truth.

Kaeru's face was impassive. "Then perhaps even your death contributed to the cause. It brought you to Salem and I."

I kept one eye on the hand in their pocket, preparing to react the moment it came out. "You say that the Nightfall will be better for mortals, and yet not even a mortal wife is safe from her vampire husband. He will kill her someday. I know it." I gestured to the darkness where Clara had stood only moments ago, which was now as empty as if she'd already passed away. "The world will not miss him, Kaeru. Indeed, it will be a brighter place without him."

Kaeru stared at me, silent, impossible to read. I wondered whether this form made them as heartless as they had wished. I stepped closer, fists trembling. I'd admitted some of the truth. Why not the rest?

"I did all this to get here, Kaeru. Every life I took, it was to bring myself to this moment. A million terrible sins, all to do one right thing. Please, Kaeru. Let those terrible acts all have been worth it. Let them all have meant something."

I offered them my hand; the chance to touch me, change, and feel that compassion Salem would have them bury. But their gaze remained on my face, piercing, almost venomous in its steadfastness.

"I ought to report you."

"Report me, then."

"I ought to kill you."

"Then kill me."

"Maybe I will."

"Then try it. After all, you already killed a baby."

Kaeru glowered. "Who are you to judge? You were part of that, too."

"A *baby*, Kaeru."

"We've fed since then, so you can't be that repulsed by my actions."

They were right. And I'd continued to work for Salem after that, hadn't I? But with a growing sense of nausea, I wondered if I still could after tonight. I realized that my free hand had moved on its own into my pocket, fingers coiled around the hilt of my knife. I tried to prepare myself for the possibility of killing Kaeru. But no matter what they'd done, the thought made me sick, just as the thought of killing Roxanne had.

I fished my hand out from my pocket, no knife within it. I offered Kaeru both open, empty palms.

"Don't tell me you're proud of everything they've made us do. We can justify our sins by claiming we had to, by telling ourselves it was the only way to seek our dreams, but we both know they'll never give us what we truly need. They will never let you find out who you are. They will never let you be free to become who you want to be. They will never let you live on your own terms."

Something shifted in Kaeru's eyes, the words piercing them as surely as a dagger to the heart. "You don't know that."

"I do," I said. "Because you have a power they cannot replicate. A power that terrifies them. How could they not control you with lies and memory manipulation and promises they have no intention of keeping?"

I stepped closer, but Kaeru stepped away. "No. Don't touch me."

"Why not?"

"Because you were right, when you said it's not just my body that changes." Their voice sounded clogged, now, like a frog was lodged inside their throat. "And when I'm in the form I take with you, I feel remorse in a way that I don't from the others. Like you want me to be someone kind. But I'm not kind, you hear me? I can't afford to be. If I let myself fall into that pit, I'll never come back out." Their expression hardened. "I can only find out who I am by being who the emperor needs me to be. And right now, he needs me to be heartless."

"You speak as if you are a puppet," I said. "A marionette, like Cillian's Reapers, so it's never *really* your fault when you kill someone. But you're smarter than that, Kaeru."

"Am I?" They scowled. "How could you know? Not even I know. Perhaps I used to be even more awful than I am now. Perhaps I was someone so evil that I lost the right to be my own person, and my penance is to become whatever others want me to be. For all I know, it could be better for me to never find out."

Their voice was fractured, as if this was a thought they'd been afraid to voice for some time now. Deep down, they were scared to learn the truth they so desperately sought. My chest tightened as I realized part of me would have loved to forget everything and live without the pain of knowing what I'd done to Jeanne, Elias, Duncan, Anika, and all the others I'd betrayed. To not feel this undying rage at and envy of men like Thomas and Salem. To not feel burdened by my thirst for vengeance, or my obsessive longing to be by Clara's side.

Would it not be a relief to not have to be my own person? To forget everything that made me who I was? To become nothing more than a tool, free to follow orders without remorse?

And yet even if I lacked any sense of self, I had the sense that I'd still feel shame for what I'd done. After all, the fact that I was following orders did nothing to alleviate my shame now.

No matter what I did, I felt like a failure as a man. When I obeyed my superiors, I was subservient. When I pursued my own interests, I was a traitor. I feigned confidence at all times, lest anyone discover how powerless I felt. But in the end, the person I most sought to fool was always myself.

No, I decided. I would rather remember who I was, and what I'd done, no matter how awful. Anything else was cowardice. In Kaeru's shoes, I would feel just as much of a constant, burning itch to discover my past self as they did.

"Kaeru..." I began. "What if the person you were matters less than who you choose to become now? What if your identity is yours to shape from this point on?"

Their eyes shone, glistening in the beautiful darkness, reflecting the gleaming stars. "I don't know if I want that, Caleb. Because if that's the case, I don't know that I like who I've become."

"Then perhaps it's time you began to decide that for yourself," I said.

Kaeru hesitated, then at last removed their hand from their pocket. Then they clasped that hand around my own, our fingers lacing together as they took on that Clara-like form. I squeezed their palms and exhaled in relief.

"You ask a great deal of me," they said. "To turn a blind eye to treason is treason in and of itself. But you are right that they may not keep their promise to me. I have seen what Mr. Rife does to his wife, and I do not envy her. Nor do I feel I, nor the world at large, would miss him in his absence. But... no matter what form I take, I fear that I would miss you in yours. If your heart is truly set on this plan, I hope you understand how dangerous it is."

"I do," I said.

They sniffed, then broke away and fled into the darkness, opposite from where Clara had gone, either frightened or embarrassed by their admission. I closed my eyes and breathed, preparing myself for what was to come. I knew it was selfish to expect Kaeru to lie for me, but in a way it wasn't. They were as much a prisoner as I was, and maybe lying to Salem was the first step to stop lying to themselves.

Once it was safe, I made my way outside, and then to the bathhouse, which I was pleased to see remained intact. It was larger than I remembered, having grown labyrinthine from a multitude of added passageways. The air was so clogged with white steam that I struggled to see, even with my enhanced vision. The walls and floors were light gray, making it hard to discern where steam ended and stone began. It was also so hot I half thought I'd walked directly into the sunlight. Perhaps that was why no other guests had wandered in.

Eventually, I reached the great pool of water, which was just as I remembered it. I grinned. It was perfect.

⸺◆⸺

I found Thomas in the yard, laughing with his cronies as he sipped bloodwine. A naked old mortal was tied to a tree, mouth gagged with cloth to muffle his screams. A demon wearing an executioner's hood tossed hatchets, first just barely missing the old man, then hitting one of his arms. Thomas guffawed with the others.

It was as good a time as any. I cut through the crowd with an air of purpose and whispered into his ear, "Mr. Rife. Lord Sotirios wishes to speak with you. Alone."

He looked over his shoulder and rubbed under his nose, still high off the mummy dust. "Where?" His scowl told me that he wanted to berate me, but even he knew better than to question Salem.

"The bathhouse, sir. I will take you to him."

"What in God's name does he want this time?" groused Rife, waving off his friends with a plastered-on smile before following me. Behind us, a hatchet landed in the elderly mortal's skull, and the crowd of demons roared with delight. Rife groaned. "You made me miss it, boy!"

I led him into the bath house's warm, maze-like halls, the opaque steam blinding us both. The knife holster inside my coat felt heavier than ever. Three long silver knives were already loaded into it, all aching to stab him. Soon, now. So soon.

"Where is he, then?" asked Thomas.

"Just up ahead, sir." I led him closer and closer to the pool, walking slowly, relishing in the moment. The scent of murder was in the air, and it was a most glorious scent indeed. It was as if Riven himself had his hooks in my mouth, tugging their corners up into my maddest smile yet.

"Then why are you walking so damn slowly?" He marched past me, his face glistening with sweat, blue veins bulging, likely just as uncomfortable with the sweltering humidity as I was. "This better be bloody important."

"Oh, yes," I said, barely able to contain my delight as I reached into my coat pocket. "Very bloody important."

I jabbed the first knife into the small of his back.

Thomas didn't yelp like I'd hoped. He merely grunted and whirled around, prying the knife free and letting the blood trickle out. "Silver?" His face contorted into an expression of rage. "I really cunting hate silver."

He slashed at me with my own blade. I swerved away, another knife already in my hand, but his own sliced open my shirt and waistcoat, barely missing my chest. The bastard kept slashing, faster than I'd expected, rapid and relentless.

He utterly ignored the wound in his back, showing not a bit of weakness or clumsiness.

I dodged and slashed, cutting ribbons off his clothes, but largely missing his skin. I wanted to circle him to get a better strike, but the hallway was too cramped, and I soon found myself darting backward with Thomas in pursuit. By now, I'd shredded his waistcoat and shirt, but he took no notice of this. I narrowly avoided his blow and struck his arm, hitting an artery this time, painting the wall and his bare chest with a scarlet spray.

As he recoiled, I drew my final knife, went after him with both blades at once, and pinned him to the wall by his shoulder and stomach. At last, Thomas let out a real groan of pain. He dropped his knife, unable to keep his grip. My blood surged with delight.

"You know what *I* hate?" I asked, leaning in as I stabbed deeper. "When you try to bring a brute to justice and get murdered for it. Or should I say sacrificed by his shitty little cult?"

Thomas met my eyes, truly met my eyes, perhaps for the first time. He coughed out a torrent of blood, which trickled down his chin. "Sacrificed?" he repeated in confusion. Then some vague glimmer of recognition came to his eyes. "It can't be...that violinist?"

"You might have seen this coming if you'd bothered to remember my name." I dragged the knife in his stomach upwards, slicing a keen line that yielded his loudest yelp yet. I pulled it out and shoved it into his other shoulder. Red chasms covered his chest, but the bastard managed to choke out an awful, taunting laugh.

"Do you know what it means to sacrifice, boy? It means to make sacred. We made you into something sacred. Allowed you to contribute to our power. You should thank us!"

He headbutted me, harder than I could have anticipated. I found myself stumbling backward, the room spinning, and that brief moment of confusion was all he needed to elude me, the pitter-patter of his footsteps disappearing down one of the other halls. I couldn't tell which way he'd gone; the steam was too thick. I'd managed to retain hold of one knife, but the other had remained embedded into Thomas's flesh. I listened for more footsteps, but heard nothing. Had he run for help? I doubted Thomas would embarrass himself that way, but it was possible if I'd wounded him enough.

The air behind my ear sang, and I just barely ducked in time as the knife sliced over my head. One of my hairs drifted above me like a tiny thread, cut away as Thomas passed me by like a ghost. He must have pulled it from his shoulder.

I recovered and whirled around, looking for him again, but he'd again disappeared into the fog. I squinted to the floor, seeing if I could maybe follow his trail of blood, only to duck again from another sudden strike. He was the hunter, now. I was all but blind in this steam, against an enemy I myself had armed.

"You're still after Clara, aren't you?"

Thomas's voice echoed from somewhere around me, but again I could not tell where. This bathhouse was a labyrinth, and Thomas my minotaur.

"There will be no one to protect her if you kill me, you know."

The voice came from just behind me. I whirled just in time to see Thomas slashing at me again, this time in a low strike. His posture was strong despite the waterfalls of blood drenching his entire torso.

"I'll protect her!" I snarled as I dodged, my anger getting the better of me. I tried to counter-attack, but Thomas danced into my peripheral vision before disappearing entirely. He was here, somewhere in the white fog, but where?

Choked-sounding laughter haunted me from every direction at once. "From whom? The Immortalists…or yourself? You have the same hunger as I." The voice sounded ragged. He was wounded, but stronger than I'd hoped, and confident enough to stay and fight rather than get help. I couldn't believe the bastard was still standing. Maybe the wounds I'd given him hadn't been as deep as I'd hoped. But he had to be low on blood. I just had to keep at it long enough for him to pass out.

I dashed back to the intersection, down another path, and there he was, coming out from behind a wall. His blade just barely missed my eye, shaving through my lashes before he eluded me yet again.

"Do you truly think yourself my better? I've heard tell of your sins, Caleb. All those murders, all that carnage. If what they say is true, then you've killed far more people than I have."

The voice was a cruel echo, and in this fog, I was as blind as a mortal on a starless night. For a moment, I could not help but wonder if he was right. What if I really was just as dangerous to Clara as he was, if not more so? I shook my head to clear the thoughts away. I couldn't succumb to his manipulation. He deserved the True Death, not I.

The air shuddered from the sound of flapping wings and the thunder of hooves against the floor. A white shape emerged, barely visible in the steam: one of Thomas's hulking skelegoats. Steam gushed from the nose hole of its human skull face, its enormous animal jaws opening wide to reveal canines. The tips of its long horns pointed right at me. Skelecrows flew above it, cawing incessantly.

Somewhere close by, Thomas snickered. He'd been the one buying time, and I'd been foolish enough to give it to him.

"I've never had the pleasure of getting to murder someone twice. Shall I let my birds feast on your guts a second time?"

I whirled around to find him standing behind me, slightly hunched over—the first sign of weakness. More enormous skelegoats were behind him, stepping closer. I was pinned down from all sides.

"Good," I said, forcing a grin. "I was wondering what I'd do about everyone seeing your puppets fall. But you've got them all gathered here with me, don't you?"

For the first time, uncertainty flickered in Thomas's gaze. I'd guessed correctly. Dazed from the mummy dust and panicking from the silver, Thomas had summoned every last one of his creations. Certainly, he could have made his bone beasts try to lead others here to help him, but then they would have seen his open wounds. They would have known he'd been foolish enough to be taken by surprise. That he'd been weak enough to ask for help. Rife was far too arrogant to suffer such humiliation.

Before he could skirt away, I grabbed his arm and slashed across his jugular. Blood sprayed onto my face, but I spit it back out into his eyes. Thomas gasped for air as the scarlet waterfall gushed down his chest, his eyes bulging in pain and rage and then—finally—sweet, delicious despair.

He pulled away and bolted, the skelegoats parting for him and swarming toward me. I was surrounded, the damn things coming after me at once: horns, beaks, teeth, and claws all slashed open parts of my flesh while Thomas got away. I shouted in rage, flailing at the beasts, but as lethal as a silver knife might be to a vampire, it barely even chipped the skelegoats.

Thomas reached the enormous bath and ran alongside it. I threw my knife, hoping it might make him slip into the water, as mad as the idea was. The knife sailed above the skelegoats and landed in the back of his knee. He stumbled, but kept moving, and I cursed as his monsters dragged me further away from him. A skelegoat sliced my own ankle with its horn, and a skelecrow pecked at my face, aiming for my eyes. I screamed in pain and swatted it away. I was covered with cuts, sharp pain erupting all over my body. Thomas would get away, and these damn things would tear me to pieces. It would be a pitiful end, after all I'd endured to get here.

Then Thomas's silhouette froze, just beside the ledge that led into the bath. A figure emerged before him in the steam, walking slowly toward him.

"Clara?" Thomas gasped, confused. He was likely half-blind, just as I was.

But it wasn't Clara.

Kaeru reached into their pocket and pulled out the key ring of fingers.

"Out of my way," Thomas growled. "I'll tear you to shreds!"

Some of the skelegoats were already moving off of me to charge at Kaeru instead. But Kaeru met my gaze, a mad gleam in their eye. They lifted the key ring, reached for the vial holding the black gnarled finger, and squeezed so tight that the glass shattered.

Immediately, Kaeru began to grow.

Thomas stepped back in horror. All of his skelegoats tore away from me and instead ran toward Kaeru—or rather, whatever Kaeru was becoming. The Silkshaper swelled and swelled until they were as tall as an elephant, bulging with muscles, their clothes tearing to rags, skin darkening to pitch black. Enormous dragon-like wings ripped from their back, and gnarled horns protruded violently from their skull. Their face was that of a mad woman, cackling with glee. Their eyes blazed with fire, their arms looked big enough to lift a train, and they had to hunch over to avoid hitting the ceiling. The key ring clattered to the floor, only to be smashed by a cloven hoof. A skelegoat came charging, but Kaeru stomped on its head, shattering its skull to pieces.

Another skelegoat approached, but Kaeru crushed it in their enormous fist, before whipping their thick, sinuous tail in a wide arc to smash another. Dozens of the beasts converged on Kaeru, biting and pecking and tearing the Silkshaper as they had me.

With the skelegoats distracted, I seized my chance, rushing toward Thomas and pushing him into the bath. Excitement surged through me, overcoming any pain from my wounds. This was what I'd been waiting for. What I'd been planning for. Thomas thrashed in the bath, his blood pooling around him. I crouched down and dipped my finger into one of my wounds before smearing a quick circle around myself.

Kaeru continued smashing the skelegoats with hooves and fists alike, but they were quickly becoming covered in wounds. There were still dozens of the bone creatures assaulting them all at once. One of the beasts gored Kaeru's stomach open with its horn, and Kaeru cried in pain, movements slowing, the blood loss overcoming them. My time was running out. Fortunately, I'd practiced, and now all I needed was a moment. Just one moment. I closed my eyes and willed that great pool of water to become oil.

Then I willed that oil to burn.

The fire roared to life. Thomas screamed as his body burst into flames, his skin charring, his gaze wide with terror as he realized he was going to die. The sight of it filled me with joy. For just then, everything at last felt worth it. Every wound, every sin, every sleepless night, all of it in exchange for this one moment of perfect bliss. No matter what came next, I felt sure I would treasure this memory for the rest of my nights: the sight of my enemy realizing he was dead at my hands.

Thomas reached out toward me with a blackened skeleton hand, his head reduced to an equally blackened skull. Its jaws were open in a silent scream, eye sockets blazing with fire. The charred fingers groped the air pointlessly before crumbling to ash. At that same moment, pain carved through my chest. It was like that black hand had managed to reach through and tear out my motionless heart.

And as the fire began to fade, my chest was filled with a terrible, aching emptiness. My heart was gone. The spell had claimed it in full, and who knew how long it would be before it returned, if it ever returned at all.

At that moment, drunk on rage, I judged the pain worth it. Rife's skull collapsed into itself, and the skelegoats around me clattered to the floor: lifeless piles of bones, as dead as their master.

I breathed in deep, drinking in the scent of his disintegration. I was covered in wounds, my body felt dry with blood loss, and the hollowness in my chest was spreading everywhere else, but none of that mattered. I exhaled in relief, in bliss, in endless emptiness. Thomas Rife was dead. Fantastically dead. Exquisitely dead.

And in death he would have more use than ever.

For an idea had occurred to me, as I watched him burn. An idea that would resolve the whole Clara problem in one fell swoop. I knew, suddenly, how I would save her while also ensuring that I posed her no threat. I chortled as I realized just how obvious it was. What a delight this vengeance was becoming!

Something huge touched my back: Kaeru's hand. Their body shrank beside me, but even in this Clara-like form, their skin was a tapestry of wounds.

"Are you all right?" My voice came out a dry croak.

Kaeru nodded, standing on their own. "It takes more than that to kill a Silkshaper. But we ought to get out of here before someone notices he's gone, or how messy we look."

I stared at that clump of ash in the pool, fascinated. "Later. There's something I have to do first."

Kaeru listened with glassy eyes as I explained to them what I had planned. Even then, we both knew that we were on the precipice of a great shift, and feared that what was coming might tear us apart. But Kaeru also understood that my mind was set, that I could not be swayed, and that the nights before us were as uncertain as the wind. And so they held back, recovering from their wounds, while I crouched down to begin the next part of the spell.

CHAPTER TWENTY-ONE

THE ASH DIAMOND

WHOMSOEVER TELLS YOU THAT revenge won't bring you peace is lying. For just a moment, I felt more peaceful than I had in years. Ours is not a fair, orderly world, but at that moment, I felt as though all was right with it.

I must admit, however, that the feeling did fade. And faster than I would have imagined.

Throughout Rife Manor, the gala raged on. Most everyone in attendance was drunk on bloodwine and addled from mummy dust, so nobody noticed their host's mysterious disappearance, let alone my wounds. Indeed, quite a few guests had passed out on the furniture or even the floor, giving me plenty of opportunities to prepare for the next stage of my plan.

I did not walk so much as limp, the aching emptiness in my chest becoming a sharp sting. Soon, I felt it in my throat, so dry it was like someone had slashed it. I quickly procured a bottle of bloodwine and chugged it to expedite my healing. It helped with the dryness, but the place where my heart had once been only stung worse.

Empty bottle in hand, I went looking for Pursha. No one took any notice of my bloody clothes. Indeed, many other guests were covered in red stains themselves, having feasted on their mortal companions.

Eventually, I noticed the stench of spoiled fruit leaking out through the crack of a nearly closed door. Muffled moans emanated from within. I pushed the door open just enough to see Pursha on the bed, naked save for her habit. She was riding the corpse of her young mortal companion, his lifeless eyes staring up at the ceiling as she moaned atop him.

I snuck inside, shut the door quietly behind me, then creeped up behind Pursha and rotated her head so quickly that it cracked her neck. Pursha fell, eyes devoid of life, as still as the boy beneath her.

Confused, I poked her forehead, then her throat. No reaction. There was no way it had killed her, but I decided to finish the job after getting what I needed. After all, killing her might ruin what I was here to procure. I opened the empty bottle and hurriedly performed my task.

That's when the knock came. I jumped, corking the now-full bottle.

"Mother Pursha?" called a voice from outside. "Are you in there? Something has happened…"

A guard's voice. Panicked. Had they realized Thomas was dead? If so, all the guards in the manor likely knew already. Worse, I realized with a start that I hadn't locked the door.

"Pursha?" the guard repeated, knocking again. There was no time to finish Pursha off, but I seriously doubted she'd spotted me. No, better to sneak out through the window. I already had what I needed, after all.

I opened the window as quietly as I could and slithered out, before crawling lizard-like to a higher window and into a vacant guestroom. From here, I emerged into a mercifully empty hallway and hurried toward Clara's room. Even now, I was not positive I hadn't been spotted, and my body rattled with fear, cold sweat drenching me. I just had to get Clara out, and then all would be fine.

As soon as I reached Clara's door, I rapped upon it, then rapped a second time before her answer finally came.

"Come in." Her voice was full of fear, so I tried to open the door slowly. She was standing by the window, her white nightgown made blue by the pale moonlight. Her eyes widened in shock as she saw me. For a moment, I feared she might scream. But she merely stared, taking my new form in.

Clara looked much older than she had before, her eyes bordered with crow's feet. Her back was ever so slightly hunched.

"Is this why you were in the shadows before?" she said finally. "You didn't want me to see that you became one of them?"

I looked down in shame. "I'm here to help you, Clara. To help you escape. But we need to hurry. They may already be on their way." My voice remained hoarse, a monstrous parody of what it had once been. Speaking only reminded me of the stinging in my chest.

She stared at me, ignoring the urgency in my voice. "Then it was you? You were the one to kill him?"

"You know?"

"He always has a crow here to watch me. It crumbled." She briefly looked beside the bed, where a bird cage now held only a pile of bones. Her face betrayed nothing; no sign of approval, relief, or anger. A bilious bubble formed in my throat. I'd not expected her to be so distant; so slow to respond.

"Please, my lady. We must hurry."

But still she remained where she was. "How do I know I can trust you? How do I know you're not just here to drink away my life?"

"I would never hurt you, Lady Clara." Yet even now my guts twisted, wondering if this was a lie. No, I assured myself. What I had planned wouldn't hurt her. Indeed, it was the only thing that would save her. I stepped closer and offered her my hands. "I mean it. I killed him to save you, but you won't be safe while you remain here. They already know he's gone, and they will be coming to find you any moment."

She hesitated. Then she clutched my hands and stared up at me, eyes filling with desperate hope. "Can you really get me out of here?"

"I can. I promise." I squeezed her hands. "Do you have a hood? Something to hide under?"

She nodded and procured a hooked cloak from her wardrobe.

I led her downstairs through the crowds, over the unconscious bodies. Clara kept her hood up, and her hand squeezed mine as we stepped over the ravaged corpses of slain mortals. She moved slowly, no doubt weakened from a lack of blood. I kept my eyes peeled for Salem, guards, and any other prying eyes.

Then I spotted a figure lumbering awkwardly through the crowd, her neck bent sideways: Pursha, still wearing only her habit. A chill licked up my spine. Some of the other guests pointed at her tilted head and laughed, but her gaze was fierce, constantly turning in search of...me, perhaps?

"Hurry," I whispered to Clara, rushing her along. There was no way Pursha had seen me, but I could take no risks at this juncture.

At the gates, Clara kept her head low, and I flashed my fangs at the guards. Mercifully, they knew better than to question a demon on a night like tonight. Still, my pulse raced. At any moment, Pursha might spot me and scream for my death.

We managed to reach one of the waiting coaches. I told the cabbie to take us North, opposite of London, far from here. There was an inn I was sure we could reach before sunrise. Once our coach got moving, I exhaled in relief. It would be fine. Everything would be fine.

"What will we do?" asked Clara, her voice sounding choked. "Their plan will continue even without Thomas, won't it?"

"Shh," I said, trying to soothe her, and wishing an embrace would comfort her. But I knew better than to get too close just yet.

Hours later, the cabbie dropped us off at a ramshackle roadside inn. It was the only building around as far as I could see, and I feared that sunrise would come before we reached the next. It was hardly a comfortable establishment, but it would serve our needs for now. As far as I could tell, we were the only patrons. I rang the bell and got us a room.

The room was dusty, cold and grim. Even in her cloak, Clara shivered. "Are you sure it's safe here?" she asked, staring out the window at the rolling countryside. "What about tomorrow?"

"One night at a time," I said, hand in my pocket, fiddling with what lay within. I was eager to present my plan, but the time did not feel right. Not yet.

She shook her head, eyes squeezed shut, not even looking at me. "You aren't even supposed to be alive. Will he come back, too?"

"He is gone. I made sure of it." I longed to reassure her with my touch, not just my words. To hold her, and bring warmth to her trembling form. "Clara..."

Slowly, I reached for her hands. Her honey eyes were glistening as they met mine, but she allowed me to take them.

"You would not believe what I've been through to come back to you," I said. "I confronted him about what he did to you, and he killed me for it. I fought through Hell itself to free you from him. If his friends come for you, I will protect you from them, too. If I have to kill them as I did him, so be it."

"How can you promise that?" she whispered. "They say this darkness will enshroud the entire world."

"I will protect you from whatever comes," I said, squeezing her soft palms. And then I smelled it: *desire*. The aroma bloomed out from her and swirled through me, electrifying all it touched like the purest drug. Her lower lip hung open, trembling—waiting, perhaps, for a kiss. But a kiss, I knew, would lead to far more.

My hunger clawed inside my chest, itchy and painful. I reminded myself that I could not feed on a mortal in reality. If I succumbed, then everything I'd fought so hard for would have been in vain. I had so many regrets as it was. *Why not one more?* the hunger seemed to ask. *Why not claim her soul, here and now?*

No, this moment had to be perfect. I pulled away, then lowered to one knee, and removed the box from my pocket.

She inhaled sharply. "Is that...?"

"Yes." I opened it to reveal the diamond ring, leaving out the fact that I'd created it from Thomas's ashes. I had to stifle a giggle just from thinking about it, and I'd probably have a laughing fit from saying it out loud. No, that would have to be revealed at a later time. She could wear it proudly, ignorant of the fact that it was her dead husband on her finger.

My lip must have curled unwittingly to reveal a fang, or perhaps the primal hunger glowed in my eyes, for Clara's gaze became tinged with fear.

"How can I accept this?" Her voice was just as sharp as her breath. "It's been hours since he died, Caleb. Hours!"

"Hours since you were rid of that monster. Hours since you were set free." I tried not to frown, but I was becoming worried. "Clara... you cannot even imagine what horrors await beyond the veil. You already know of the darkness taking hold of England. I won't tell you that this is your only option, but I promise that if you'll accept me, I will protect you. I will love you. You will be free with me, Clara. Free, and safe. For I have brought not just this ring, but also a bottle of succubus milk—milk that will make you a fellow immortal. No one will be able to harm you ever again."

I pulled the bottle from my coat pocket. Again, I had to restrain the sheer glee from creeping into my voice. Clara as a succubus was almost too lovely to imagine. She was already so beautiful. What would she look like with wings?

"I...can't," she said, backing away.

I froze, confused. Why was she so afraid? A performance, perhaps, to ensure I didn't think less of her. It would be unbecoming to be too eager.

"It's all right," I said, standing to step closer. "I promise everything will be fine."

"I can't!" she repeated, before bolting to the door.

I was taken aback. My enhanced reflexes might have allowed me to block her, but I was too shocked by her sudden departure. "Clara!" I said, but she was already rushing out and down the stairs. Before I knew it, she'd fled from the inn, not once looking back.

Panic surged through me as I pursued her out into those rolling hills, the cold night swallowing us up. She couldn't see in the dark like I could, and the ground was full of stones and brambles.

"Wait, Clara!" I shouted. "It's dark!"

"Leave me alone!" she screamed, voice hoarse. "All of you wretched things!"

It was like being stabbed in the heart. It had never even occurred to me that a moment that I'd imagined as romantic could be something else entirely for her. I'd so long believed that we were star crossed lovers, separated by the planes but destined to come back together. And Clara *had* desired me, if only for a moment. I'd smelled it!

But you can desire someone even when you fear them. You can desire them even when you hate them. You can desire them while knowing you should stay far away from them. More than anything, I wish I had understood this then.

"I'm not like them!" I shouted. "I won't hurt you, I swear! I just want you to be safe!"

I'd come all this way. I'd fought to reunite with her for years. I'd killed Thomas for her. I was offering her a way to survive what was to come. Why was she acting with such vicious hostility? Clearly, I just had to get through to her. If she only listened, she would see sense.

But Clara only continued to run. Further and further away from the inn we went, until its dim lights were too far to provide any illumination at all. There was only the pitch-black countryside.

"Clara!" I shouted.

She whirled to face me without slowing down—and tripped. I surged forward, pushing everything I could into a single mad vault, desperately trying to catch her before...

Her head hit the dirt. No, not dirt. Stone. The wet sound made that clear enough.

"Clara," I whimpered, finally reaching her. Her eyes twitched madly in their sockets, quiet grunts escaping her limp mouth. I lifted her head up, and my hand was immediately drenched in the blood leaking out. She'd bashed her head completely open. My jugular tightened, moisture formed in my eyes, and the piercing pain in my chest only worsened.

"Hang on," I choked. "Hang on, Clara...please..."

She twitched in my arms. More and more blood leaked between my fingers and onto the jagged stone below. She was dying... and it was my fault. She'd been running from me. She would fall into Hell and be tortured as I was, because of me.

How long did she have left? Minutes? Seconds? I tried to meet her eyes to ask for her forgiveness, for her understanding, but she would not look at me. Whether it was because of her injury or because she detested me, I could not say. I only knew that her life was in my hands, and there was but one way to make this right.

I had no time to delay; no time to contemplate the consequences of my actions. But I didn't need time. I already knew what I had to do. It was the only way to fix this mess. I opened the bottle and brought it to her lips. "Drink," I whispered. "Drink…"

Her head fell sideways, the milk dribbling out from her lips, but I tilted her head so the rest would find its way in. "It will save your life," I said. I didn't know if she could hear me. Her eyes were no longer dancing in their sockets, but merely staring ahead, the lids half-closed as she swallowed the milk.

When the bottle was empty, her body remained motionless. "Clara," I sobbed, wrapping both arms around her. "Please come back. I'm begging you to come back."

Had I been too late? The body in my arms was limp, silent, lost.

Then it began to tremble.

Hope bloomed within me as Clara's body convulsed, harder and harder, until she broke free from my arms. She fell onto her side and vomited onto the ground. Then she reared up, her body contorting under her nightgown, bones crunching, wings ripping from her back, flesh becoming smooth. I exhaled in relief. She was alive. Alive!

When her transformation was complete, her skin was flawless to the point that it had lost many of the imperfections that made her so beautiful. Indeed, she looked much like Kaeru did after touching me: a version of herself that seemed unreal, almost uncanny with its beauty.

She tried to push up to her feet, but even now, she was quaking so hard that she struggled to stand. "What did you do to me?" she choked out, her voice furious.

I stood there, stunned. "I saved your life," I said. "I... you were going to die, Clara."

Still shaking, Clara looked down at the puddle of blood left by her head. The moonlight had turned it black, but with her new eyes, she could still see her reflection. She looked down at her hands, reached up to feel her face. Her expression was absolute disgust. "You fed me that unholy milk? You turned me into this thing?"

"You're not a thing," I said, reaching for her, but she batted my hand away.

Her eyes trailed down to her new wings, twitching in the corners of her vision. Then she hurriedly looked away, as though they were not beautiful appendages but rather leprous disfigurements. "You should have let me die!" she choked out, brow narrowing into a scowl.

"How could I? I just wanted to help—"

She ran, stumbled, and it was just like before: her fleeing, me chasing her, feeling helpless to do anything else. But this time, she had wings. "You killed me!" she screamed as they began to flap. "You killed me to turn me into a monster!"

Her feet left the ground, carrying her higher than I could reach. Having severed my own wings night after night, I had no way of pursuing her, and before long she was so far away that even my enhanced eyes could no longer see her. The night swallowed her up.

I froze, breathing frantically. "Clara!" I called. "Clara!"

She did not answer. I was alone.

I broke into a run, heading in the vague direction she'd went, but I became less certain with every passing second whether I was going the right way.

For hours, I searched through those cold, barren hills. Again and again, I called for her, but there was never any response. Where had she gone? What if someone saw her and decided to shoot? Worse, sunrise was near. It was possible that she knew sunlight would kill her, if she'd noticed Thomas's own sensitivity after his rebirth, but there was no way to be sure.

When the first rays of pale light began creeping across the field, I still had not found her. If I did not find shelter, I would burn.

With nowhere else to go, I returned to the inn, drew the window's drapes, and sat on the hard bed. I raked my hands across my skull, going over the night's events again and again, confused, ashamed, imagining a thousand variations of what might have been.

My reverie was broken by the creaking of the window and the rustling of its drapes. Clara had opened it and was crawling through, still trembling. Her body was covered in wounds, to the point that her nightgown was stained red. Many looked to be closing, her body regenerating already.

"Clara..." I whispered, a pit forming inside me. "Did someone do that to you?"

She bared her teeth. "Why won't they stay?"

Behind her, the sun rays were becoming increasingly bright. Within seconds, it would burn her. Panic surged through me.

"Get away from the window!" I hissed. "The sun...!"

Something like triumph formed in her eyes, and that's when I realized that the wounds must have been self-inflicted. She wanted to die. The True Death. And I'd just told her how to do it.

Smoking cracks spread across on Clara's skin like craters in the earth. But even as tears of pain filled her eyes, her lips pulled back into a relieved smile.

I ran to her, tried to close the drapes, even as the fire appeared on my own hands, but I was too late. Clara leaped out into the sunlight, wings stretching, arms spreading, head thrown back in spiritual bliss as the sunlight consumed her.

She became a burning angel, her entire body engulfed in flames. I wish I could say that I'd jumped out to reach her, to hold her in mid-air and let the flames take us both, but I was a coward, and despite everything, I found myself darting back into the shadows, just beyond the sun's deadly rays. It was not that I feared death; it was more that I knew she did not want my embrace. Even if she wanted to die, and perhaps wanted me dead as well, she did not want me to die *with* her.

There was nothing for me to do but watch as Clara became nothing but ash.

Chapter Twenty-Two

The Nightfall

IT'S ASTONISHING HOW THE mind can flatly refuse to accept truths it finds too threatening. As I stood there, I told myself that perhaps Clara fell into Hell. I merely had to find her. But then I remembered I'd turned her into a demon, and demons didn't get reborn when they died. If I hadn't given her the succubus milk, she might still—no. I couldn't think that just now.

Well, maybe they were wrong about sunlight. Maybe it was possible for a demon to regenerate after being scorched. Maybe Clara was a rare exception!

Or maybe she'd flown back in through a window on the first floor! Maybe I just hadn't been able to see it because the sun was so bright, and the fire that had seemed to engulf her had been a trick of the light too. Or maybe... maybe there was a spell that could bring her back, oh yes! My fellow hellspawn performed rituals left and right. Surely they must have cracked the problem of True Death?

Again and again, my mind tried to manufacture some way, any way, to deny the simple truth that Clara was gone. Gone forever, and it was all my fault.

No, not my fault, my mind raged. It was easier to blame Riven, for starting the Nightfall; Salem, for bringing me here; Thomas, for killing me! I was a victim, just as innocent as Clara!

But...no. It felt like impaling my own skull to admit, but no one had made me do anything. I'd been the one to commit my sins, because I'd felt justified, and because I'd felt that I had to, and most of all, because I'd *wanted* to. I'd made my bed and shit in it all by myself.

I wanted to throw up.

The pain where my heart had once been was unendurable. I was tempted to walk out into the sun, but I found myself paralyzed, and instead continued to replay the evening's events, trying to pinpoint the exact moment it had all gone wrong. Should I have waited until after the Nightfall began, giving her more time to come around? Or had I used the wrong words during the proposal? Surely, a better speech would have convinced her!

And yet each and every one of these suppositions disintegrated in the wake of one simple truth: she had feared me. She had probably barely remembered me, rather than dreaming of me for years as I had her. There was nothing I could have done to win her heart. Not killing her husband, not saving her from demonic enslavement, not even capturing her heart in my songs. Why, then, did I still tremble with such longing and rage? Had I not done all this to save her?

What a sick joke it was. I'd fought all this time to avenge myself against the Immortalist Club, but now I was high in their ranks, helping them doom the world to darkness. I had told myself that I'd been fighting to protect Clara from

Hell, but in reality, I had only condemned the whole bloody world to it.

Perhaps it was inevitable, given the men I'd envied and learned from: Salem, Riven, even Thomas. They were the worst, men no one should ever want to be like, and yet how could I not when the world gave them whatever they wanted? It would be easy to lay blame on Salem for poisoning my thoughts on sex and my role in society, but truth be told, it had started long before him. It was the entire world I'd grown up in, and its constant prioritization of wealth and power over goodness.

These realizations did not all come to me at that moment. In truth, my thoughts were a confused blur; my body aching with hunger, pain, and the crippling weight of my self-loathing.

Even after sunset, I found myself too morose to leave the bed. My wing stumps were itchy, for I'd neglected to shave them. I fantasized about letting them grow back and flying far away, to a place where no one knew me. I could become someone new. Someone untainted by the past. Maybe I could even find water from the River Lethe and forget everything I'd done.

But that was not what I deserved, and it was not what fate had in mind, either.

My reverie was eventually broken by a rapping at the door. A pit formed in my stomach, and at first, I merely remained. Let them think me dead. Let them be spared from my cancer. But the knocking continued until I had no choice but to rise and open the door.

On the other side stood Kaeru, still in the form they took for me, their face so close to Clara's that I could barely look at them. Kaeru's eyes were still glassy, hopeful. Then they realized I was the only one in the room, and their face fell.

"Caleb...?" they whispered.

I squeezed my eyes shut to block out the tears, then felt their arms around me. "No," I choked out. "Take some other form. Any other form. Anything but this."

Kaeru squeezed me. "What happened?"

"I can't talk about it. I won't." Each word was harder to push out than the last.

"Did she leave you?" Kaeru sounded heartbroken. "Even after all you did to save her?"

My eyes became moist, my entire face warming until I had no choice but to choke out the awful truth. "I didn't do it for her. I didn't do it for her at all."

It was the only conclusion I could come to as I sobbed into Kaeru's neck. Whatever my delusions or intentions, I had become a monster, no better than Salem or Riven. Every dreadful sin I'd committed to get here had only been for myself.

I'd risen up Hell's ranks abnormally, even absurdly quickly. I'd have realized that, had my mind not been so addled with rage. What did it say about me, that I'd been so successful rising through such a twisted regime? In retrospect, I had not even truly earned these victories. I'd merely purchased them by stealing the lives of others, convinced that I deserved happiness more than they did. I had been given everything, but earned not a jot of it. I was rancid. More carcass than man. A beautiful corpse, desperately convincing itself that it knew what was right for the living.

"I have a cab waiting," said Kaeru, taking my hands in theirs. "Let us leave this place. Leave England, perhaps Europe entirely. We can both find out who we want to be, what we want to live for, how we want to live our lives."

The lump in my throat was so thick I thought my neck might burst open. I hardly deserved such a kind fate, but it seemed the only way I might move on and become someone better. So I nodded and followed Kaeru outside. I even allowed myself a meager feeling of hope as I saw that there was indeed a coach waiting at the road.

Its driver, however, lay dead on the ground. Kaeru froze. Their eyes traveled up into the air.

A figure floated high above us, his arms crossed, wings flapping to keep aloft: Salem Sotirios. He must have followed Kaeru without them knowing.

"You tried to kill Pursha." Salem's eyes were fixed on me, his voice perfectly audible despite his distance. "People saw you leaving with Clara as well. Have you nothing to say in your defense?"

I glowered up at him, anger burning in my chest. Why had I ever idolized this man? Why had I let him change me? Only now could I see clearly. Only now did I recognize what it was that he'd done to me in Hell, in his bedroom, while I'd been drunk out of my mind on bloodwine. Clara's death had been my fault. Byzantium had been my fault. But what Salem had done to me in Hell had been his actions alone, no matter what I'd told myself to justify remaining by his side. My hands balled into fists, nails digging into my palms, wishing he'd lower to the ground so I could tear him limb from limb.

"What of you, Kaeru?" asked Salem. "You don't seem to be here to apprehend him."

"I'm here to free him and myself both." Kaeru didn't hesitate. They didn't even sound remorseful. Indeed, they smiled, fire blazing in their eyes. Kaeru looked alive in a way they never had, finally determined to live on their own terms.

Salem's lips curled into a pitiless smile. "In a matter of hours, the Nightfall will begin. Everything we've worked so hard to create will at last manifest. And you would flee without witnessing the fruits of your labor?" His voice became bitter and husky. "I thought I could count on you."

In a flash, he was right before us, his fist launching toward me with the force of a locomotive. I prepared myself, but suddenly Kaeru's body was in front of mine, shielding me from the blow. "Wait!" I shouted, but it was too late. Salem's bloody fist punched out through Kaeru's back, the air quaking with the sound of shattering bones. Kaeru choked out a thick wad of blood, changing into empress.

Salem's eyes were electric with rage, his teeth bared: a flicker-quick change from his normal demeanor. He pulled his fist back out through the hole he'd made in Kaeru's chest, and my friend fell onto me, skin twisting until it was like watching Clara die all over again.

"Why?" I choked out, fresh tears forming.

Kaeru's breath was rapid, their voice strained. "To save the only person who ever asked me to be who I wanted, rather than who they wanted." Kaeru reached up, hand pressing against my cheek. "What better way to live on my own terms, than by protecting those I care for?"

Salem let out an amused tut, head tilted, lips peeling back to reveal teeth speckled with Kaeru's blood. "Something went wrong with you this cycle, didn't it? Well, that'll be easy enough to fix. Riven will give you a nice, clean new mind, unburdened by all these complicated thoughts."

Horror flashed in Kaeru's eyes. "No, please don't take this away from me!"

"Don't you dare," I hissed, clenching my fist.

But Salem's own was already flying into my skull.

⸺◆⸺

I faded in and out of consciousness in the back of the coach, the floor rumbling beneath me. My head, or what was left of it, pounded with wave after wave of pain. Salem had only needed to hit me once to black me out. Kaeru lay beside me, coughing, the wound in their chest still bleeding profusely. They reached out to clutch my hand and I squeezed it, knowing fully well that we would be torn apart and the Kaeru I'd known would be wiped away, just like Clara had.

Eventually, we reached London. Salem was no doubt taking us back to the crimson mirror, back to Hell. I managed to reach for the doorknob, but it was locked. All I could do was stare out the window as the city passed, taking us closer and closer to the gateway from which we would never return.

In the distance, I spotted the Palace of Westminster, standing tall, its windows bright in the night.

And then it exploded, endless pieces of it flying as it was utterly consumed by an unfathomably great swell of fire. Blindingly bright it was, and with a sickening toxic stench that even penetrated into the coach. Black smoke rose up into the sky like a pillar, enshrouding the stars and moon. Tendrils of darkness spread across the sky like oil filling an impossibly large pan.

In the distance, more smoke was spreading—from the south, I believe. The dark clouds converged and crawled further and further across the sky, blotting out star after star, until there was nothing left. Gone was the night's texture, that endless swirl of seemingly limitless possibility. There was now only oppressive, inky darkness, the night's beauty destroyed.

The air was filled with the sound of low, soulless groans. Bone-muscle silhouettes rose up in Westminster's smokey ruins, each one moving like a marionette. Dozens of Reapers, emerging from Parliament's ashes.

"It's begun," I choked out, my voice so hoarse I didn't even recognize it. "The Nightfall..."

But once more, exhaustion took hold of me, and my eyes fluttered closed.

When I came to, we had stopped before the building in which I'd died. The coach doors opened and Reapers pulled us out, their bone fingers sharp against my skin. I saw now that our driver was a Reaper as well, its skull face utterly devoid of empathy.

I tried to break free as the Reapers dragged us through the dark hallways, but to no avail. Soon, we beheld that great crimson mirror, the gateway through which all manner of terrible things would emerge.

Kaeru choked something out as the Reapers pulled them into the crimson glass, but I couldn't make out their words. I struggled, trying to break free, but a Reaper punched me and I blacked out once more.

⸻⸺◆⸺⸻

When I opened my eyes, it was to pain.

I was in a dark room, chained to the floor. Dark silhouettes stood on a high circular platform above me, standing behind a long, curved desk, barely illuminated by the candles of the ceiling's chandelier. Something was sticking painfully into my arm, and I turned just in time to see the Reaper beside me withdraw a spear, its wet red tip shining in the firelight.

"Caleb Schwartzenfeld," a deep voice rumbled. "You have been charged with committing acts of treason against the Church of Black Heaven. How do you plead?"

The voice was both unfamiliar and emotionless—that of a judge who saw not reasons, but only rules, and whether they had been broken.

My body was wrecked, exhausted, covered in wounds. But I felt only rage as I bared my teeth at those shadowy figures. "Damn right I did."

Pain exploded at the back of my head as the Reaper clocked me with the end of its spear. Weak as I was, this was enough to send me to the floor. I spit blood, first by accident, and then on purpose, just to give these bastards more to clean up.

"You are hereby sentenced to Tartarus indefinitely," said the deep-voiced judge. "There, you will be punished for your unspeakable crimes."

Tartarus... the place where my fellow rebels had ended up. Where they were no doubt enduring unimaginable pain, far worse than anything they'd known before. Now, I was to share their fate.

"There is nothing more you can do to me," I said, baring my teeth. "Nothing you can threaten me with. You have already taken it all. And that means I have nothing to fear."

Laughter crackled through the room, and despite my words, an ice-cold feeling caressed my back. It was Riven's laughter. He was somewhere in the shadows of this room, watching me.

"That's where you're wrong, Caleb." That crooked voice slithered out from the darkness all around me like a sea of tendrils. "There is always more to take. And there is one more thing I want from you before your penance begins."

Long chains shot out of the dark, each ending with a silver blade. And they landed in...

"Your *wings!*"

They had not fully grown back; indeed, they were barely more than nubs. But there was enough to hook into. Enough for it to hurt.

The pain was the least awful part. When I'd lost my wings before, it had not been to silver. It had been easier, knowing they would at least return someday. Now, the pain was tinged with a sense of unspeakable loss. After Riven had slashed them to ribbons and torn their stumps free from my back, I found myself cradling their ruptured forms in my quivering arms, surprised by how much they'd meant to me. It was like he'd slain two friends I'd barely even gotten the chance to know.

Riven cackled in pleasure, the vicious sound echoing all around me. "You pledged yourself to me. Promised to serve me as my dog. And that is what you shall be, always and forever. You shall understand that, in time. So don't worry, little dog. Ask us a thousand years from now, and we may consider giving them back."

But he had sliced them with silver, and that meant they were gone forever. I was done believing their false promises.

And I was done giving them the satisfaction of watching me suffer.

I looked up into the darkness and forced out a crazed laugh, as loud as I could muster, even though it came out hoarse, even though I didn't sound amused in the least.

"You want to break me, is that it?" I asked, letting the madness creep into my eyes. I didn't care who stood in this absurd courtroom. I wished to scare them. To make them feel, just once, like they were not in control.

The Reaper hit me again, and I spit up more blood, but I pulled my lips back anyway to give everyone in that room a real shit eater of a grin, letting them all see my sharp, stained fangs.

"You never fucking will. I'll never be yours to command again, no matter how long you make me suffer. You won't break me, because there's nothing left to break. I have lost everything. Every piece of myself has been burned away. And I will not let you sculpt these ashes into your monster. Not anymore."

And I continued to laugh, sounding madder than I ever had as they pulled me deeper and deeper into the darkness, until there was only my own distorted echo for company.

⸻◦⸻

Thinking of it now, I wish I could laugh all over again, except this time it's because I can't believe how naive I was. I thought I was above it all. That I could endure things no one else could. That I would keep my mind in a place where no one else did. I still hadn't learned the lesson my entire life had been trying to teach me. Now, I know the truth: no matter who you are, Tartarus will break you.

When was it that I truly gave up hope? Was it when I was dragged into Tartarus's impossibly vast halls? Was it during my first punishment session? Or was it when they dragged me to this solitary box and confronted me with the awful weeping?

I hear it even now, as I write these words: Clara's voice, sobbing and sobbing as if she's right beside me. I heard it the moment I arrived and immediately knew the voice for what it was. Thomas made her cry this same way, but now, it was because of me. Because of what I did. What I made her become. I fell to my knees, overcome by my guilt, and it is on my knees that I have remained.

Sometimes, when I'm at my most desperate, I even want to believe that Clara is here in Tartarus with me; reborn in Hell rather than granted the True Death. But that is madness and I know it. They must have yanked Clara's cries straight from my head, knowing that these would torment me more than anything else. Sadly, painting the walls with my blood has done nothing to muffle her.

It is in this box that I have remained, alone save for the weeping, the wordless screams from the adjacent cells, and the visitors who come to punish me. I have tried speaking through the walls, but my neighbors have gone as mad as the husks I encountered when I first landed here. I have tried escaping with blood magic countless times, but to no avail. It should be no surprise; I imagine Tartarus houses far greater ritualists than I. Its walls must be warded to prevent any magic from proving successful.

I believe it has been years since I was first taken here, but I am not sure how many. Four? Ten? Fifty? I've long since given up trying to track the days. I never know which living nightmare will come, nor what new tool they will wield. Clippers for my privates? Needles for beneath my fingernails? It is never enough to kill me, but they always ensure that it hurts.

Sometimes, I wonder what became of the world above. If it fell to Riven's forces, are things any better up there than they are down here? Is there any point in trying to escape if Earth has been remade in the underworld's image?

My mind is not what it was after being in this place. I expect no mind could be. I write these words hoping that they reflect the truth; hoping that I will be able to use them to remember who I am. That in fifty, one hundred, one thousand years' time, I will still have the capacity to read. But I know in my heart that the longer I remain here, the more doomed I am to become a husk, unable to remember the meaning of a single word. Perhaps that is what I deserve. For what am I if not a walking corpse, clinging to the elusive dream of life?

Most of the time, I feel more dead than alive. Perhaps it is my malnourishment, but it feels as though parts of my body no longer work, even when my wounds are minimal. My muscles, once so strong, have atrophied. My cheeks sting when I try to smile or laugh, uncomfortable with the now foreign movement. When I curl up on the floor and try to sleep, my legs are restless, screaming to fidget. My entire body aches, each new wound stinging relentlessly. When I finish myself off, it is dry, without discharge, maddeningly unsatisfying. The Morpheus Pentacle they made me swallow ensures I can enter no one's dreams, either.

What is there left for me to do, now that I've told my story? Month after month, year after year... throughout it all I remain, bored and afraid and utterly lonesome, wondering always if and when this room's single door will open. When will they release me from this misery? When will they kill me, or provide me with the means to do it myself? When will Clara stop crying? When will my sentence at last be over?

It won't. That is the fear that haunts me.

Yes, I detest myself. Yes, I deserve to suffer. But must I really do so...forever?

There is but one corner of the ceiling left, and I shall fill it now.

Earlier today, the door opened for the first time in a good long while. I tensed at the creaky sound, preparing my body for pain. But instead of one of my usual tormentors, guards poured in, bound my wrists, and pulled me into the hallway. I inhaled, taking in the damp, fetid air, my throat itching, my lips dry as sand.

The halls of Tartarus are utterly devoid of hope. But simply leaving my box was enough to make me remember that there was, in fact, a world beyond, and I was filled with a renewed thirst for it all. Just as a little water to moisten your cracked throat can bring newfound thirst, so too did my very bones scream for the chance to be free once more. To stretch my legs with a walk through the woods. To make love to someone beautiful. To play or even *hear* a song.

The guards led me to a room with a table and sat me down. A lanky man sat across from me. He was clean shaven, his short, wavy brown hair swallowing up his ears but framing his forehead like a mushroom. A scarlet sash cut diagonally across his tight black uniform, and his spade-tipped tail swished from side to side like that of an irritable cat. I immediately knew this man for who he was: Warden Leopold, ruler of this prison. By now, the very sight of him was enough to make my body tense.

"Caleb Schwartzenfeld," said Leopold, smiling with pale, thin lips.

I'd not heard my name spoken in so long that I almost didn't recognize it. Certainly, I have written it again and again on these walls, but to hear it aloud felt like listening to another language.

Leopold must have sensed my confusion, for he chuckled. "I'd say you're halfway to husk, my good man. Unless, of course, you were to enjoy an early release."

I perked up, electricity surging through me. I ought to have known by then to never trust a hope, but Tartarus's cruelty was such that I was desperate for one. I would take it, even if it was a lie.

Leopold tapped the table with black gloved hands, each finger long and clean, even here. "Tell me, Caleb. What would you do for freedom?"

I tried to swallow, but my throat was dry. "Anything." My voice was not as I remembered it; strange, harsh and uncomfortable to my ears, the word coming out slurred. Like a drunkard or a child still learning to speak. Even that one word was enough to make my sand-dry throat tickle and sting.

Leopold watched me carefully. "We need someone with your skills. Someone who can be a ruthless killer. What if we asked you to become Bloody Caleb once again?"

My body became so still that it ached. I knew that I ought to refuse; that a deal with Riven or his subordinates would only dig me deeper into the darkness. My cell was where I belonged. It was a place where I could cause no more harm, if I was to live at all. But I hungered, practically salivated, at the thought of freedom. And even though part of me knew I deserved my sentence, I could not bear the thought of returning to that dreadful box. Even this tiny taste of life beyond its walls made me want to say yes to whatever Leopold proposed.

The warden slid a tintype photo across the table to me. It showed a beautiful young woman with long, flowing hair, and wings that looked to be part bat and part butterfly. I'd not seen a woman with my own eyes in so long. Only in memories tinged with pain. What did she smell like? What did she look like in color? Oh, but she was beautiful, even in this sepia. So beautiful...

"We are willing to grant you your freedom if you bring her to us. What do you say, Caleb?"

"Who is she?" I managed to croak out. I ached for the name of the woman who I yearned for; she who I would hunt; she who I would bring here to take my place.

The warden steepled his long, gloved fingers together in satisfaction. He knew, as Riven no doubt did, that all my bravado had been a show, a desperate bid to convince myself that there was still good in me. "She is Maraina Blackwood, the most dangerous succubus in London. Do you accept, Caleb?"

Maraina Blackwood. I ran my fingertips down the smooth tintype. How wonderful would it be, to have the strength of character to refuse? I wish I could say that I accepted eternity in a cell, that my spirit was stronger than ever, that I had finally learned my lesson.

But after years of endless torment, all I could think about was how much I wanted to leave; to see this beautiful woman with my own eyes; for a taste, just a *taste*, of clean air. What else could I do but wade deeper into that endless bloody sea, embracing the eradication of my soul?

I laughed, tears forming in my eyes, and barked like the dog I was.

Afterword & Acknowledgments

I N March 2020, *LILITU: The Memoirs of a Succubus* finally hit shelves, just as American bookstores (and everything else) closed due to the COVID-19 pandemic. My debut novel's launch plans? Nuked. My UK trip to advertise the book at StokerCon? Nuked. My mental health? You can guess.

I'd always intended to write more *Lilitu* books, but after that experience, I needed a break from the series, and spent the next few years working on an unrelated novel. However, I never quite forgot about Maraina Blackwood and her friends. I'd structured the first *Lilitu* book to end in a satisfying enough fashion for the short term, but the loose ends continued to gnaw at me years later.

By mid-2023, I decided that enough time had passed that it was probably "now or never," and reached out to Joe Mynhardt at Crystal Lake Publishing to ask if he was still down to publish more *Lilitu* books. Joe was kind enough to green light my pitch for the series, and ever since then my life has been *Lilitu* all day, every day.

Bloody Caleb was originally supposed to be a novella: an optional spin-off/prequel to tide readers over before the "real" sequel, while also acting as an alternate jumping-on point for new readers. I envisioned it as *The Count Of Monty Cristo* by way of *Dante's Inferno—Edmond Dantès' Inferno*, if you will—following a murdered man who wanted to get revenge, but could only escape from Hell by becoming a demon himself. It would act as a backstory for a major character in the sequel, which I knew even then would be too long to have time for that.

After completing and workshopping the first draft, it became clear that *Caleb* had to be a novel. The characters, themes, and world building all needed more room to develop. This would also allow it to better mirror the first book: while *Memoirs Of A Succubus* explored the horrors of misogyny, *Bloody Caleb* was to explore the horrors of toxic masculinity.

I fretted quite a bit about the content ("Is this problematic? Is this too fucked up? Does this go too far?"), and I'm sure some readers will say "yes" to all three, while others will feel it doesn't go far enough. But in the end, I felt the book had to be what it had to be, and let the characters do what felt true to them. The book was, after all, set in a Victorian-era Hell, and the *Lilitu* series has always been about exploring difficult themes. I can only hope that readers will exercise media literacy, and recognize that Caleb's actions are not intended to be celebrated or emulated.

Since I'd promised Joe an optional *Lilitu* novella, I ended up writing one through his Author's Journey program (which I highly recommend) in 2024. This became *Saintkiller: A Lilitu Novella*, which at 45K words is just shy of novel length on its own because I have a *problem*. And so *Bloody Caleb* became *Lilitu*'s second volume, paving the way for characters from both books (and *Saintkiller*) to converge in Volume III. Predictably, Volume III has also gotten so long that I anticipate it will be split into two books. I'd planned on three *Lilitu* books, and somehow seem to have ended up with five.

With that in mind, some very fine people are owed their acknowledgments.

First, all the thanks to Joe and everyone else at Crystal Lake Publishing for believing in this series and sticking with me throughout its development. Couldn't ask for a kinder or more understanding publisher.

Additional thanks are owed to this book's beta readers, including the Soft Shoe Writing Workshop and my good friend Amanda. Thank you as well to Emz and everyone else at HorrorAddicts.net for helping me through the door to begin with.

Finally, thank you to everyone kind enough to read these books. You've been very patient with me as I've taken my time to continue this series, but this time the pizzas really *are* coming. I hope you'll find them worth the wait.

ABOUT THE AUTHOR

JONATHAN **FORTIN** IS A neurodivergent author and voice actor from Oakland, California, whose dark fiction has been published by such presses as Crystal Lake Publishing, Dark Recesses Press, Mocha Memoirs Press, and *Sirens Call*. In 2017 he won the Next Great Horror Writer competition from HorrorAddicts.net. He is an affiliate member of the Horror Writers Association, a graduate of the Clarion Writing Workshop, and a *summa cum laude* graduate of San Francisco State University's creative writing program. When not writing, Jonathan enjoys wearing Victorian gothic attire, growling along to black metal, and exploring all things odd and macabre in the San Francisco Bay area. You can follow him online at jonathanfortin.com.

THE END?

Not if you want to dive into more of Crystal Lake Publishing's Tales from the Darkest Depths!

Check out our amazing website and online store or download our latest catalog here.
https://geni.us/CLPCatalog

We always have great new projects and content on the website to dive into, as well as a newsletter, behind the scenes options, social media platforms, our own dark fiction shared-world series and our very own webstore. Our webstore even has categories specifically for KU books, non-fiction, anthologies, and of course more novels and novellas.

Readers...

Thank you for reading *Lilitu: Bloody Caleb*. We hope you enjoyed this novel. If you have a moment, please review *Lilitu: Bloody Caleb* at the store where you bought it.

Help other readers by telling them why you enjoyed this book. No need to write an in-depth discussion. Even a single sentence will be greatly appreciated. Reviews go a long way to helping a book sell, and is great for an author's career. It'll also help us to continue publishing quality books.

Thank you again for taking the time to journey with Crystal Lake Publishing.

You will find links to all our social media platforms on our Linktree page.
https://linktr.ee/CrystalLakePublishing

Follow us on Amazon:

MISSION STATEMENT

S INCE ITS FOUNDING IN August 2012, Crystal Lake has quickly become one of the world's leading publishers of Dark Fiction and Horror books. In 2023, Crystal Lake officially transitioned into an entertainment company, joining several other divisions, genres, and imprints, including Torrid Waters, Crystal Lake Comics, Crystal Lake Games, Crystal Lake Kids, and many more.

While we strive to present only the highest quality fiction and entertainment, we also endeavour to support authors along their writing journey. We offer our time and experience in non-fiction projects, as well as author mentoring and services, at competitive prices.

With several Bram Stoker Award wins and many other wins and nominations (including the HWA's Specialty Press Award), Crystal Lake Publishing puts integrity, honor, and respect at the forefront of our publishing operations.

We strive for each book and outreach program we spearhead to not only entertain and touch or comment on issues that affect our readers, but also to strengthen and support the Dark Fiction field and its authors.

Not only do we find and publish authors we believe are destined for greatness, but we strive to work with men and women who endeavour to be decent human beings who care more for others than themselves, while still being hard working, driven, and passionate artists and storytellers.

Crystal Lake Publishing is and will always be a beacon of what passion and dedication, combined with overwhelming teamwork and respect, can accomplish. We endeavour to know each and every one of our readers, while building personal relationships with our authors, reviewers, bloggers, podcasters, bookstores, and libraries.

We will be as trustworthy, forthright, and transparent as any business can be, while also keeping most of the headaches away from our authors, since it's our job to solve the problems so they can stay in a creative mind. Which of course also means paying our authors.

We do not just publish books, we present to you worlds within your world, doors within your mind, from talented authors who sacrifice so much for a moment of your time.

There are some amazing small presses out there, and through collaboration and open forums we will continue to support other presses in the goal of helping authors and showing the world what quality small presses are capable of accomplishing. No one wins when a small press goes down, so we will always be there to support hardworking, legitimate presses and their authors. We don't see Crystal Lake as the best press out there, but we will always strive to be the best, strive to be the most interactive and grateful, and even blessed press around. No matter what happens over time, we will also take our mission very seriously while appreciating where we are and enjoying the journey.

What do we offer our authors that they can't do for themselves through self-publishing?

We are big supporters of self-publishing (especially hybrid publishing), if done with care, patience, and planning. However, not every author has the time or inclination to do market research, advertise, and set up book launch strategies. Although a lot of authors are successful in doing it all, strong small presses will always be there for the authors who just want to do what they do best: write.

What we offer is experience, industry knowledge, contacts and trust built up over years. And due to our strong brand and trusting fanbase, every Crystal Lake Publishing book comes with weight of respect. In time our fans begin to trust our judgment and will try a new author purely based on our support of said author.

With each launch we strive to fine-tune our approach, learn from our mistakes, and increase our reach. We continue to assure our authors that we're here for them and that we'll carry the weight of the launch and dealing with third parties while they focus on their strengths—be it writing, interviews, blogs, signings, etc.

We also offer several mentoring packages to authors that include knowledge and skills they can use in both traditional and self-publishing endeavours.

We look forward to launching many new careers.

This is what we believe in. What we stand for. This will be our legacy.

Welcome to Crystal Lake Publishing—Where Stories Come Alive!

www.ingramcontent.com/pod-product-compliance
Lightning Source LLC
Chambersburg PA
CBHW021406310726
48971CB00005B/1223